ANGELINA J. STEFFORT

THE HOUR MAGE

ANGELINA J. STEFFORT

THE
HOUR
MAGE

THE HOUR MAGE

First published 2023

Ebook: ASIN B0B6WPC998
Print: ISBN 9783903357624

MK

www.ajsteffort.com
www.thequartermage.com

ONE

I picked up the bowl for what felt like the thirteenth time, hiding my gagging at the stench of infestation behind the cloth wrapped over my mouth and nose.

Dust swirled in the shafts of sunlight creeping in through the half-shaded windows where the heat of Jezuinian summer was making my job difficult.

Tristan hadn't checked in this morning, occupied with finding herbs in this landscape so different from what he was used to in the lush fairylands of Askarea. And I hadn't found a minute to wonder when he'd return, my hands busy with cleaning wounds and preparing potions.

Following the dim corridor to the small backyard where I could dump the dirty contents of my bowl before I fetched some fresh, boiled water from the kitchens, my chest constricted more with every step into the half-light.

Not too long ago, I had gone into the dungeons beneath the fairy palace to find Tristan. And not too long ago, I'd been caught in the process—not to mention that my cousin Dimar had been captured because of me as well. They all had. My Aunt Zelia, who'd been the Master Mage of Aceleau before she'd gotten on bad terms with the fairy king and lost her Mage Stone.

Again, because of me.

I paused, leaning my back against the cracked wall, and closed my eyes, heaving a breath.

They were free, I reminded myself. We all were. And we were as safe as was possible, given I'd destroyed their Mage Stones.

Instinctively, my fingers curled around the edge of the bowl as if trying to grasp one of those little crystals storing magic for human Mages to wield.

"There you are, San," Zelia's voice sounded from the end of the corridor, and I pushed away from the wall, eager to hide my moment of weakness. "We need fresh water."

I nodded, rushing on to the back door, pushing down the handle with my elbow before I dumped the contents of the bowl in the sewers. "I'll be there in a moment."

Zelia caught up with me as I crossed the yard to get to the kitchens, her plain linen robes so different from the colorful attire she'd worn in Aceleau. Where all shades of purple had adorned her from head to toe, sands and browns now defined all our clothes. Peasants. That was what we'd become.

"By Eroth, San. You're shaking." Zelia caught me by the arm as I turned into the abandoned hallway at the other side of the building where we'd taken up residence.

"It's just the smell." I gestured at the bowl before I discarded it in the large pot on the stove to boil it. "I don't think I'll ever get used to it." She could read from my eyes; what I had the real trouble getting used to was Tristan's absence, the risks he was taking when he went out there to gather supplies—past the city gates to where the Guardians knew who would spy him. And Dimar—

My cousin had returned to the Jezuinian palace to *keep an eye on things*, as he'd called it. Since Cyrill had never learned about Dimar's involvement in my escape, didn't even know I was still alive, he'd decided to return to my husband's court—*my* stolen court—where he hoped to gather information without raising suspicion.

I gulped down a breath, reaching for a fresh bowl and filling it with water, eyes on the Master Mage whose magic I had on my conscience.

"How many are waiting?" I jerked my chin in the direction we'd come from.

We'd helped over fifteen people already today, and it wasn't even noon. When, in the beginning, we'd snuck into the city, disguised in the traditional southern Cezuxian linen shawls drawn up to our noses, nobody had cared for yet another group of peasants trying their luck in the capital. But with every new week, word had gotten around in the outermost ring of Jezuin that the herbs and teas we provided worked better than those the healers in the inner rings charged horrendous sums for. So it hadn't surprised me when, at the end of the second month, a line of sick had formed in front of our dwelling by the time we opened the doors.

"Ten, maybe more. No emergencies so far, and the rest must wait until we've taken care of the ones who are staying with us." Zelia collected a stack of cloth from the cupboard while she waited for me to cross the room. At the door, she followed me, her gaze lingering on my shoulders like a crawling animal.

Of the three Mages, Zelia was the only one with residual magic, and that was only because of the way my lignified hand had absorbed it from the Mage Stones and channeled it into my aunt at a touch of our palms.

I glanced at my now human hand and wondered if the fairy prince had known that my injury would aid me in the end. His golden eyes flashed before me, and I could hear his words in my mind as if it had been yesterday.

Because everything will be easier when you hate me again.

I glowered at the bowl between my fingers, breathing evenly as I trailed the corridor, this time with my thoughts occupied by what Recienne had shared with me.

Killing the male who sold out his lands wouldn't make me a hero. It would make me a fool.

Shaking my head at anything and everything that connected me to Prince Recienne Olivier Gustine Univér Emestradassus de Pauvre the Second, I followed the humid half-light back to where I was needed and where I could truly make a change, no matter how small.

Zelia ventured to the front door, assessing through a crack in the boards how many were waiting in line—so fragile, humans without magic, so easily destroyed. In Askarea, where magic was plentiful, it would have cost Zelia a moment to heal all of them, but the human lands had run dry on magic, the borders keeping it in by some ancient power so the fairies couldn't leave their own realm without consequences. That alone should have allowed me to breathe more easily when, late at night, my throat closed up as if the prince was locking in those words I hadn't dared speak to anyone: He'd helped me. Even if he'd let me suffer through all those trials, in the end, he'd aided me to end his father.

What that made him, I wasn't sure. I couldn't even think of him without that sense of my throat-tightening returning, so I didn't. He'd told me to forget. And I was doing my best—for my own sanity.

Setting down the bowl by the cot of the woman I'd treated earlier brought my mind back to the task at hand—as did the foul odor of her festering wound.

"Your eyes, girl, look familiar," she croaked as I reached for a piece of cloth from the nightstand and dipped it into the water before I brushed it over her forearm.

"We all have similar eyes in this region of Cezux," I deflected, grateful for my scarf around the lower half of my face. I couldn't ever take it off, or I'd risk exposure. And if word of my presence in Jezuin traveled to the palace, I'd be dead faster than I could pack my things and run back to the fairylands—not that I needed another taste of horror. Escaping the fairy court once was enough. When I'd been merely coveted for being human, now they'd hunt me for having killed their king.

I swallowed and forced a smile onto my lips, even when the woman wouldn't see it, and continued my work.

Here, I could do something for my people. Whereas, on my throne, my husband was ruling with all the cruelty I expected.

Entering the city had been a shock—even with the fleeing families we'd met on our path through Cezux, who'd left their homes in Jezuin to escape the reach of the tyrant on the throne.

And when I eyed the woman before me—

"The wound will heal easily once the infection is gone," Zelia said from beside me, noticing that I'd frozen in my thoughts. "Apply this, and she should be much better by tomorrow."

She pushed a vial into my hands, taking the bowl from me to set it on the floor by the nightstand.

The familiar scent of Leeneae crept into my nose, driving out all other smells, and for a moment, I could breathe. For a flash, I could see Tristan's face, his smile when he woke next to me in our little bedroom, his steady presence by my side when we prepared the healing potions, even without the final touch of magic.

Soaking the edge of a new cloth, I leaned over the woman's arm and dabbed the tincture onto her wound, cautious with the jagged edges where the knife had drilled into her like a screw into a piece of wood.

"If my daughter hadn't brought me to you, I'd be dead," she said between gasps, and I flinched at the sound of her panting, eager to relieve her of her illness but lacking the right tools, the magic to do so. So all I did was nod.

She wasn't the first one who'd never been able to afford a healer other than us. When they came, desperate for our aid, they didn't ask questions about who we were and where we'd come from. All they asked for was to save them. And when they left, patched up by the makeshift healing potions that were less than what I'd seen both Zelia and Tristan and even Dimar produce in Askarea, but still a lot more than what the best healers in Cezux could produce, they didn't ask again because we didn't ask for their money.

"You'd be facing the Guardians with every last stain on your mortal soul," Zelia said over my shoulder.

I hadn't realized she was still standing there, watching my progress even now when she could no longer teach me magic.

The woman didn't object, but a silent anger entered her tired eyes as she glanced at her wound. "He did that. The king."

Goosebumps spread over my back at the thought of the new King of Cezux, the signature my father had left on the marriage contract. Bound by Cezuxian law, I was his. And if he ever got his claws on me, there was little I could do—especially now that he had ascended the throne.

The official coronation ceremony would be held in a few weeks. Whether I'd find a way to eliminate him from this realm by then was written in the stars. All I could do was wait. Wait for Dimar to return from the palace with information on where and how to strike. Not that I had any weapons in my arsenal. But I'd figure it out. Together with Zelia, Dimar, and Tristan, I'd brought down the fairy king of Askarea; I'd find a way to get rid of a human one.

I suppressed a shudder at the proof of Cyrill's violence—even executed through his guards and sentinels, the imprint of his terror lingered on the woman's flesh.

"What happened?" We didn't usually ask the same way we didn't want to be asked. But this time, now that she'd brought him up, I couldn't help it, despite Zelia's warning look.

"I gifted a loaf of bread to a hungry child rather than sell it to one of the king's procurers."

The way she shook at the thought of it... It brought back memories of my own, when I had resorted to stealing bread from a fairy's market stand and ... how Tristan had found me, pulled me off the streets and into the safety of the Mages' House.

"You are baking for the palace?" Zelia asked nonchalantly, her tone so at odds with the stern Master Mage I'd gotten to know in Aceleau. How she'd learned to take on these roles as needed never ceased to amaze me—or scare me, even when I'd come to fully trust her the moment she'd revealed that we shared blood. And if not then, the moment she'd tried to save me at the fairy palace, when the fairy king had tricked me into giving up my freedom, all doubts would have been erased.

I shoved the thoughts of those days away, my hand already going numb with the phantom effect of the magic that had turned it to wood—and the tingle when Prince Recienne's power had stopped the lignification.

"They buy our bread occasionally. Not nearly often enough to make a living from it," the woman replied, tearing me from my thoughts, reminding me the only direction I could allow myself to peer was forward. The past had been a bloodbath, and if I spent one more moment there, I might break.

So I screwed the lid back on the flask. "Who bakes while you're indisposed?"

"My daughter," the woman said, eyelids drooping as the Leeneae potion took effect.

Zelia met my gaze when she noticed it too, the power of the residual magic she'd channeled into the healing draught.

It had been fading from that day in the fairy palace and was now a bare flicker of the ungodly force that had driven a shadow-spear through the king's head.

My stomach churned at the memory, and I had to remind myself to look ahead.

"How much longer will I need to stay here?" The woman tried to sit up, but the wound had taken its toll on her body, and her age didn't help much either.

"A few days," Zelia predicted before she told her to rest and ushered me away to the next cot.

Head heavy and fogged from the smells and the heat, I sat by the next patient's side, wondering if perhaps helping those people who otherwise wouldn't be able to afford such care was the best way to spend my future.

Then my eyes fell on the cut on the man's side where he'd been stabbed in a fight, and the sight alone pushed me right back into the temple where Cyrill had killed what should have become my court.

It was then that I knew I wouldn't be able to settle until I'd taken back my throne.

ANGELINA J. STEFFORT

TWO

"Hand me the powder."

Tristan glanced at me over the narrow table, face grim as he was stirring too little of the Leeneae extract we needed to make proper healing potions.

I quietly picked up the morsel containing a crushed type of stone that he'd procured I didn't know where—the way he got most of our ingredients from secret sources.

How he'd managed to build a network of suppliers, I couldn't tell. All I knew was that, every time he left the house, my gut knotted with a sense that it might be the last time he kissed me goodbye. And judging by the look on his face, he was about to announce he'd need to head out soon and collect more herbs.

"Zelia could go," I suggested, without even expecting a reaction. We'd had this discussion about a hundred times. "At least, she has a drop of magic to defend herself."

Zelia couldn't go, he'd say, because she needed to do the actual healing at our secret little sick house. Dimar couldn't go because he needed to keep his cover at the palace. And I could most definitely not go because I was too recognizable. That left him. I didn't even try to point out that he was recognizable with a comparatively pale complexion. Even if the intense sun of Cezux had tanned his face, his skin tone was nothing compared to Zelia's, Dimar's, or mine.

"I'll leave soon for more." He took the bowl from my hands, his lips quirking into a half-adorable smile that I assumed attempted to be apologetic. "If we want to make sure your patients are taken care of, someone has to go."

"*My* patients walk out with both their arms because of all of our efforts, thank you very much." I stared at the half-pained, half-frustrated expression on his features before I sighed and stepped around the table, leaning my hips against the edge. "I know it's hard to get used to not having magic at your disposal, Tris. But we're doing something good here. We're *helping* people." While we were waiting to learn everything we needed to bring down Cyrill. He knew as well as I did that it was the only reason we'd chosen Jezuin as a base, to begin with. Otherwise, Brolli or a remote village in the north of Cezux would have been the smarter option.

He sighed, and I smoothed his hair back from his forehead as he set down the bowl, fully facing me. "I'll be back in a day or two."

He always took longer than that, but I didn't confront him.

"We need the ingredients, and I'm learning a lot about what's going on in the city by talking to the right merchants."

The ones who travelled to Askarea. He didn't need to add that.

"And what *is* going on?" I tilted my head, reading from his face what little he gave away.

Instead of a response, he leaned in and kissed me.

He'd done it the other day when he'd returned from his latest trip, bag only half full with Leeneae and pockets full of those little rocks now sitting in jars on the shelves. I'd forgotten to ask him about them when he'd sealed my lips with a kiss and made all thoughts vanish from my mind—similar to the way he was doing now, actually.

I stifled the moan that would inevitably come when he nipped at my lower lip, trying to focus instead.

But Tristan's fingers were already grazing the nape of my neck, the sensation evoking in my mind a replay of the way his hands had trailed over my naked body soon after his return.

"We need to finish the potion," I told him, my lips eager to taste him rather than talk to him, my fingers hungry to feel the hard muscles of his arms and chest instead of returning to the tasks laid out on the table behind me.

Leaning his head back and eyes directed at the cracked ceiling, Tristan groaned. "Right now, I wish I had magic, just so I could finish all of this up and bed you right here on the table," he gestured at the collection of vials and tubes and the fat candle heating one of the fluids.

That put a smile on my face. "I don't think Zelia would appreciate it if we used her dining table for—"

"This is no longer Zelia's house," he reminded me with more authority than I cared for. "It belongs to all of us."

Well, that technically wasn't true since we'd found the house abandoned and simply occupied it. The reason no one had objected might have had something to do with the way people had been fleeing from this part of the city. With Cyrill raising taxes and coming after everyone who couldn't pay, the poorest of Jezuin were forced to seek refuge in villages far away where the cruel king's fist wouldn't reach them as easily.

The baker's wound flashed in my mind. How much longer would she be able to stay in the city? Would Cyrill's need for power and control, for wealth and recognition, eventually drive away even his own suppliers?

The irony of it grinned at my face. The true seeker of power had been the fairy king, who'd installed Cyrill on this throne through a ploy that had demanded my father's blood—and mine.

With a sigh, I rested my forehead on Tristan's chest. "Let's get back to work."

I could feel his nod against the crown of my head. "We've got a lot of work to do if we want to prepare enough for the time I'll be gone."

His words ached between my ribs, but before I could say anything, he pulled away, tilting my head up with two fingers, and placed a kiss on my mouth. "We can finish *this*"— he amended another kiss—"later." When the city had fallen dark, and the oil lamp on the crooked nightstand in our little room would be our only companion.

As for now, the boiling fluid was evaporating into a glass tube, and that demanded urgent attention.

So I turned back to the ingredients while Tristan collected the ready vial and opened it for a spoonful of the ground stone in the morsel, that heat in his gaze turning into full focus—on his work rather than on my lips, as before.

Another time, we'd find that moment of peace to simply be together. Another time, we'd share breath and warmth and our racing hearts. Another time—that was my new credo.

By the time the sun sank, we were done. The potions sat ready in a row on the table, waiting for Zelia to apply the final touch. Tristan had left to tend to the sick and wounded while I remained in the kitchen to clean up the mess we'd made with our makeshift equipment. Since we'd left most of our things at the Mages' House in Aceleau, Tristan had acquired our new tools little by little, and it took us longer than usual to get anything done.

By the time I rinsed it in the sink, the rag in my fingers was soaked with a combination of fluids that I'd better keep away from open fire lest I risk an explosion in our humble kitchen. The scent of herbs still magically lingered in the air, despite the open door to the little yard, and the humid heat felt surprisingly hotter as the scent of orchids drifted in on a breeze.

True to the ranks in our little group of no-longer Mages, as the apprentice, I got to do the dirty work, mopping the floor after a hard day's work and cleaning the bowls and utensils needed to treat our patients and brewing our potions—*potions* was probably no longer accurate. Since the magic involved had become marginal, we might as well have called it a simple tincture or medicine. But it would take time for that habit to die. As it would take time for Tristan not to reach into his pocket for the Mage Stone that was no longer there.

I didn't complain about the tedious work of cleaning when Zelia was the only one who could still apply some droplets of magic and when Tristan and Dimar were both risking their lives each in their own way on their missions.

My stomach did that nervous jolt that always came with the thought of what either of them could encounter out there—in what used to be my city. Where I was now a stranger who had reached high with her hopes for happiness on her way to learning the only thing that might have helped to defeat Cyrill. And that was no longer available.

No more hopes of becoming a full Mage. I'd stay a Quarter Mage forever. Not even that. I'd become a dead princess on the run once more. And I'd chosen to hide in plain sight.

"Tristan told me you were done." Zelia entered the room, her face drawn from the strain of the day.

I inclined my head, unable to get my royal demeanor entirely wiped.

Zelia circled the table until she stood beside me by the sink. "It's getting less and less each time he returns," she noted, eyes on the flasks containing Leeneae essence. "Almost as if Askarean flora is no longer inclined to provide us with what we need now that we left." *Now that we're no longer Mages.* She didn't need to add the words. They were clearly written in the mild lines on her forehead. "If we want to continue our little sick house, there will be a point where we'll need to return to the borderlands to harvest Leeneae ourselves."

Something in my stomach tightened at the thought of returning to the dangers of the fairylands, to the borderlands, where I had first traded a syllable of my name in exchange for transport by the fairy prince. As if in response to the thought of him, my throat went dry, unwilling to speak.

I cleared it, eyes on the greenish essence in the vial Zelia was holding up. "When?"

With a wave of her hand in the direction of the corridor leading to where Tristan was finishing treating our patients for the day, she gave me a long, tired look. "I fret for them whenever they leave the house. Dimar hasn't returned from the palace in weeks, and I'm reluctant to send Tristan into the fairylands sooner than absolutely necessary. Without their powers, they are both vulnerable."

Like me. The hair stood at the back of my neck at the mere thought of Tristan crossing the border by himself. If he got caught—I couldn't even think of it. And if he ran into the bandit? Well, having helped me or not, Prince Recienne might put Tristan right back in a cage to avenge his mother some more.

A shudder walked up my spine as the image of flared pupils set in golden orbs flashed before me.

I'd escaped, I reminded myself. We all had escaped.

"You look tired, San," Zelia noted with more concern in her voice than I was used to. "Why don't you go rest? I can finish this up alone."

A dim flicker of light sizzled between her fingers through the vial holding the Leeneae extract.

Zelia noticed my stare and gave a mild smile. "It's getting weaker every day."

Her magic.

"What if you ration more? Only allow a few drops every day. Not all of our patients need actual magic for their healing."

By the way she looked at me, I already knew my suggestion would not be of any use.

"It doesn't matter how little I use. If I don't use it, it disappears anyway. You can imagine it like a glass of water exposed to the sun. Either drink it, or watch it slowly evaporate."

Zelia rarely spoke about that ounce of power remaining in her tissues, the thought of losing her magic forever probably too painful. With a sigh, I took the vial from her hand and placed the next one there instead. "Then let's drink it."

Zelia's smile was laden with worry as she read my face. "We'll keep up our work here for as long as we can, San. We still have some rare potions we brought from the Mages' House, and with that droplet of magic I have left, I will aid our people for as long as I can." She closed her hand around the vial, letting magic dribble into the purple liquid. "We'll find other ways to fight him when the day comes."

Cyrill—she'd fight him and everyone who'd laid a hand on our family. Including the prince who would sit on the Askarean throne by now. Even if it was with her bare hands, she'd fight. For the sister she'd lost in Jezuin, for the magic taken from her, for her son and her niece and the man she'd adopted into her little family.

Picking the next vial from the table, I took a steadying breath.

"And until that day, we'll keep our cover, learn as much as we can about the situation in Cezux, and rely on Tristan for supplies and on Dimar for information."

And do nothing but wait. That feeling in my stomach came to life once more as I thought of all the ways I'd failed them. With Zelia and Dimar descending from the line of original Mages and the magic saving Tristan from certain death on the streets, even when I'd freed them, I'd taken from them what defined them—their magic, their power, their status in the fairy city of Aceleau. And their home.

"I'm here to help in whatever way I can," I let her know, taking the ready vial from her and replacing it with the new one. Even if I'd be cleaning the floors until we had our plan figured out, I'd happily do it. It was the least I could do for everything I'd taken from them.

Tristan wasn't in our bedroom when I retired at sunset, sweaty and tired. I managed to wash up in the small bathing room before crawling into bed, not bothering to dig up my nightgown and opting for one of Tristan's shirts instead. The humidity had never bothered me before I'd left Cezux to find refuge in the fairylands, but ever since we'd returned, I barely found sleep in the stifling heat of the city.

Perhaps it was because I wasn't residing in the cool marble and sandstone halls of the palace. Perhaps because the memories of dancing in a too-tight dress for hours on bleeding feet spun me whenever I closed my eyes. That sense of no longer being in control of my own body—

"I'm back." Tristan's murmur floated into the room alongside the odor of healing herbs.

He stopped to drop a quick kiss onto my forehead before he headed for the bathing room, shucking his tunic on the way in.

I marveled at the strong column of his spine, the rippling muscles on either side as he grabbed the waistband of his pants and pulled them off.

The Sanja of a few months ago might have been nervous about staring at his glorious body, but this Sanja, the one who'd already lost everything and fought to get it back—this Sanja let her gaze linger on his long, powerful legs, on his backside, his hips, and, when he turned—

Tristan disappeared from view, and I rolled out of bed, tugging my shirt in place before I stepped to the open window and watched the darkness settle over my city.

"Can't sleep?" His arms folded around me, pulling me against his chest.

In response, I merely shook my head. It wouldn't help either of us if I repeated all the many reasons drifting into my dreams wasn't a good idea. It didn't change the way I still felt my hand turn into wood, how I smelled the treacherous scent of violets that would now always remind me of the flesh-eating plant in the fairy king's maze. And the moment his control had fought for my body against Prince Recienne's—

It wouldn't change the way I saw my failure to save his magic whenever I looked at Tristan.

I shoved the thought aside, focusing on the moment as his fingers curled into my shirt above my hip, but another thought flashed to the front of my mind instead. "How long are you staying this time?"

It was always too short. And those few days were filled with the bittersweet taste of how short our reunion would be—of how we'd have never had to run in the first place if it hadn't been for me.

Tristan, of course, would never speak those words, but I'd overheard his quiet conversations with Zelia in the hallway when he'd thought I was already asleep. He missed being a Mage, missed the power he'd once carried in his pocket. And, most of all, how he hated to be so helpless again.

He shook his head, grazing the side of my face, my neck, with his lips, and burrowing into the hollow of my throat. "Let's not talk about that now while I'm very much invested in making us both forget that I have to leave again at all."

Of course not. That would require actually facing that he'd need to pack his things, not too far from tonight, and be gone again to danger and duty—while I remained here where all I could do was wait and regret and burn with remorse for what I'd done. For what I'd sacrificed so we could be free. And even when his touch ignited a fire in me, made me burn and burn, I wondered if what I was able to give him would ever compensate for what he'd lost.

"There are more interesting things we can do." His soft laugh danced along my shoulder as he pulled the shirt aside with efficient fingers. I didn't object. Any measure of distraction was welcome—especially the sensuous sort that Tristan brought into our bedroom.

"I love you," he whispered as he turned me around in his arms until our gazes locked and we fully faced each other.

The troubled oceans that were his eyes lingered on mine for a moment—long enough for me to have to scramble for the words I should have been speaking. That I was sorry for all I'd taken away from him.

But he was faster, lips finding mine in a gentle, explorative kiss that made me painfully aware he hadn't bothered to dress after he'd washed. I leaned into him, rising to my toes to meet his kiss. It was better this way—ignoring the pain, the guilt of taking what had been such an innate part of him by destroying his magic. And as long as he could ignore it, too, perhaps this could work. Perhaps he'd continue to love me as desperately as I loved him.

Tristan's tongue nudged against my lips just as I opened for him. He tasted like the cinnamon tea we often had with Zelia after a long day, and of the devastation of having been so forcefully parted in the fairy palace. But there was more. As his tongue swept through my mouth, I wondered if the way he poured all his focus into that single movement was only one more sign of how he was searching for a new purpose now that he could never return to what he used to be.

My tongue met his in a dance, eliciting a groan from him that ran through my entire body, shaking away the heaviness, the thought of finally confronting him about it. About what I'd overheard—

But as his hands found my hips, clasping them and pulling me close enough to feel his heat through the thin linen separating us, I stopped thinking at all. And, in that moment, every last part of me, so anxious during the days, shook awake, relishing his presence, needing his presence.

"I love you," I whispered, voice trembling from his fingertips tracing my curves on one side, the other hand remaining firm on my hip.

All worries evaporated in the heat between us, and I could simply be Sanja and him, Tristan. Nothing else mattered but the way his fingers slid between my legs, straight through my core, and the wetness pooling there.

He groaned against my throat, lips sliding all the way to my collarbones, down the front of my chest, finding my breast through the shirt that felt suddenly like too much.

So did he. I made a small noise of protest when he paused the slow pumping of his finger to peel me out of my shirt.

It dropped to the floor soundlessly, and Tristan palmed my breast with one hand while the other tracked its path back to that bundle of nerves at the apex of my thighs. I arched into his touch, fingers digging into his biceps while the other hand reached between us, to the proof that he wanted more—needed more—as well.

But Tristan merely wound his arm around my waist, guiding me back toward the bed, his fingers never once stilling between my legs, and laid me down on the hard mattress.

Pleasure raked through my body as his thumb circled that spot while he nudged my legs apart with his knee, moving over me. This—I wanted this. Wanted his heat to fill me, to drive out the guilt. I could believe he'd forgiven me in these months. I could believe he loved me as much as he had when he had anxiously watched me from his cage while the fairy prince had pushed me across the dance floor.

"You're thinking," Tristan murmured onto my skin, his mouth inches from my nipple, and his tickling breath made me arch into him so his lips brushed the tip of my peaked flesh.

I shook my head, fingers catching his hair and digging into the silky texture. "Of how much I need this," was all I said as I wrapped one leg around him, reaching down with my other hand to guide him inside of me until all thoughts left my head.

Then Tristan was moving, hips rolling in slow, powerful thrusts while his arms carried his weight above me. I felt the world fade, the fire he induced in my flesh the only thing that mattered now. And each thrust pushed me closer to the edge where I'd shatter into a million pieces for a blissful moment or two.

THREE

Tristan met me at breakfast the next morning, carrying a cup of herbal tea in one hand and a slice of bread in the other, eyebrows already knitted together by whatever news he'd received before the day had even started. True to our routines in Aceleau, we still rose at dawn and were ready for the day before the sun even kissed the seam of clouds in the east.

"Zelia said we'll need more Leeneae soon," he said by way of good morning as I squeezed past him to grab a plate from the cupboard.

He caught me around the waist with one arm, his lips finding mine before I could object that I hadn't even properly woken. But his scent, the feel of his embrace—I was back in our bedroom in the hours we hadn't slept the night before when he'd silenced my doubts, my mind.

Perhaps, in a few more months, he'd adjust to his new situation. Perhaps I would, too. And I'd forgive myself for what I'd done to him—to all of them. But for now ... this physical connection, touching him, feeling him, maybe it was what we both needed to get over our nightmares and move on.

Leaning into him, I abandoned all thoughts of food or otherwise, allowing my fingers to curl into his shirt instead of reaching for the nourishment my body should have demanded.

He leaned down, brushing a kiss to the corner of my lips, continuing along my jaw. "I'm leaving today."

His words were a bucket of ice water.

Stepping back, I noticed his travel garbs only now—the dirt-colored pants, the boots that were much too hot for a casual walk in the city, the shirt of sand-colored linen.

"Now?" I looked him over, wondering how long he'd be gone this time, how far from Jezuin he'd need to travel to procure all we needed.

"After breakfast." His brows pinched, and he rolled his shoulders as if to shrug off a burden.

I realized then that he must have known the night before, and instead of telling me, he'd indulged me and given me what I'd been craving.

"And you didn't think to tell me when you came to me last night?" I hated the accusation in my words. It wasn't his choice when he went and what he bought. That was still Zelia's decision. But he could have told me.

"I'd rather enjoy what little time I have here with you than see you sad about my pending absence."

The way he said it—I turned and grabbed the plate before I cut a slice of bread for myself, trying not to focus on how he thought he knew what was best for me.

"What makes you think I'm *sad* about your *pending absence?*" I threw over my shoulder as I picked up the teapot and poured myself a cup. The scent of herbs spread under my nose, reminding me with painful accuracy of the many times they'd kept me in the dark in Aceleau—for my own good.

I ground my teeth and sat at the small table by the wall so as not to disturb the new set of vials and flasks, of tubes and bowls set up for the day, on the large table at the center of the room. There, I'd worked all day and worried about Tristan while he didn't even bother to tell me he was leaving a night in advance.

He sat across from me, eyes the same troubled blue that had spellbound me the night before, and placed his cup and plate in front of him, reaching for my hand.

"Have you thought for a moment how hard it is for me to be away from you for any period of time?" He held my reluctant gaze, which would have preferred to stare down the bread before me or the vase holding a dried rose in the corner of the table. "Especially when I know Jezuin is not safe for you?"

My breath was deep as I steadied myself. He had been scared for me before—since the moment he'd found me stealing bread from the fairy market. And everything he'd kept from me had been to protect me. Zelia had done the same; so had Dimar, who'd even pierced my flesh with a dagger to save me from my husband. Oh, what a mess—

With a sigh, I set down the bread and rested my forehead in the palm of my hand, bracing my elbow on the scratched wood.

"I know." And I did. I truly did. As hard as it was for me to see him leave. I glanced up at him, marking the details of his face: the soft curve of his lips when he smiled, the dark lashes, the sharp-cut cheekbones. Handsome in a way even the finest of courtiers could have never been. "Just promise me you'll return safely."

His lips quirked in a grin that didn't touch his eyes. "I always do."

My chest tightened the way it always did when he left, and I swallowed my anger for now. I could endure this for a while longer—until we knew how to best ambush Cyrill.

Tristan's hand cradled mine between his fingers as he studied me with more concern than I liked seeing on his face. The half-hearted smile he gave me did little to conceal it. "Just promise me you won't go to your husband while I'm gone."

There—There it was. Like a monumental whale sitting on the table between us.

"Do you remember what *my husband* did?" Breathing was difficult when the memories of blood and screams filled my head.

"He's the reason you left Cezux." The reason we'd met, he didn't need to add that.

"And he's a tyrant as much as the fairy king was. As much as his wretched son—"

"Is he?" Tristan interrupted me, eyes inquisitive.

"Who?"

"The prince."

A knot formed in my throat at the thought of the fairy prince, at how his power had controlled me, head to toe in the fairy palace.

Maybe the time had come to finally tell him that Prince Recienne had played a role in my victory over the fairy king. Maybe I should have admitted that I lay awake some nights, fearing his powers would reach me even here in the human realm.

My mouth remained shut until I was able to push those images away.

"He played his games at the fairy palace with the king the only one keeping him in check. Who knows what he will aspire to now that the monarch is gone?" Tristan's words rang true.

Yet, a part of me wondered if the prince had been afraid of his father or of someone else.

Before I could make up my mind, Tristan leaned over the table to kiss me. "We'll confront Cyrill together when the time comes. Dimar should be back soon, and if Zelia is right, he'll have more information on Cyrill's routines and his vulnerabilities. Guard rotations and staff should all be noted by now. We won't be stuck here forever, San. Soon, we'll break free of the chains this human realm has put on us."

Chains—

All budding anger died inside my chest at the realization of how much he suffered from the absence of his magic. And *I* was the reason for those chains. He'd been captured because of me, had been caged because of me, had lost his status and his magic because of me. Yet... Yet, he looked at me like I was something more than the reason for his losses. Yet, love shone in every word he spoke, even the ones filled with frustration—and I didn't deserve it.

Linen scarf covering my mouth and nose, I entered the main room of our sick house, legs dragging and body heavy from another night of little sleep. The baker with the injured arm had left the night before, refusing to accept a flask of tincture after everything she'd already received from us. "I'll bring you a cake for the next holiday," she'd promised instead—payment of sorts for our service. It was how most of our patients decided to pay even when we didn't demand it of them. Some brought fruit and vegetables, others, grains or fabrics to sow something from.

If only I knew how to do that, I'd have made myself a new skirt. But the brown linen clothes we wore were less suspicious than the colorful garments we'd been gifted. And again, Princess Sanja of Cezux died a little bit in my chest at how far Cyrill's terror truly reached. I couldn't even choose what to wear for fear we'd be exposed.

Zelia was already at work, bandaging a hand and mumbling behind her scarf. I didn't need to see all of her face to know she was trying to apply magic.

"Ah, good, you're here," she said to me, pointing at a pair of scissors on the shelf in the corner. "Hand me those."

Collecting them in passing, I handed them to Zelia and made my rounds through the few filled cots.

"There are more waiting outside," she told me as if I'd asked. There were always more.

Tristan had been gone for five whole days, and the only thing keeping me from falling sick with worry was that I could help the people who couldn't otherwise afford it. In a sense, it was the first time I could truly help them—not just a copper here or there but true help.

Handing out cups of tea and whatever tinctures and potions Zelia had prescribed, I wandered through the room, inquiring about my patients' well-being and needs. Most of them were recovering just fine, and some of them would return to their homes today.

A knock on the door announced the arrival of new patients. Setting down my tray, I scrambled to the door and glanced through the cracks. A young man was waiting, hand braced beside the door as if he was having trouble standing straight. A cut split his bushy eyebrow, and his eyes appeared unfocused.

"Help," he rasped, swaying on his feet despite the support of the wall.

I opened the door to let him in, barely catching his weight as he stumbled over the threshold where he collapsed, sliding from my arms.

Zelia was at my side in a heartbeat, hands reaching under his shoulders and dragging him inside. "Close the door." She didn't wait to see if I followed her order but rolled the man over on his back. "Can you hear me?" She snapped her fingers before his crossed eyes.

The man uttered something unintelligible, followed by a groan.

I saw it then; the wound cleaving on his side where his dark brown tunic had hidden the blood at first.

"Is this from a knife?" The phantom pain of my own injury throbbed in my side at the sight of where the man had been stabbed.

"Arrow," Zelia corrected, unceremoniously ripping his tunic apart where a thin cut in the fabric had given away the injury. "Someone already removed it. He's bleeding out." She pressed her palm on the wound as if to quench the bleeding. "Get me tourniquets and bandages."

I hurtled back to the shelf, almost falling over my own feet as I avoided colliding with the foot of a bed, and returned with my arms full of utensils. Kneeling at the man's other side, I handed Zelia what she'd asked for before cutting the shirt open farther until the man's chest lay bare and I could clean the spilled blood off his skin to check for further injuries.

At the pressure of the tourniquet, the man winced, eyes fluttering and locking on mine as if on an anchor while he gritted his teeth against the pain.

"What happened?" I placed my hand on his shoulder, both to comfort him and to pin him down as Zelia worked her no longer literal magic on his wound.

"Guards," the man rasped and sucked in a sharp breath when Zelia pressed the tourniquet deeper into his wound. "They followed ... me." His breathing was uneven but strong, a good sign when it came to the function of his vital organs; I'd learned over the past weeks helping Zelia. But if we weren't quick, he'd fade from blood loss.

Zelia's gaze met mine over our bloodied patient, and my stomach churned as I realized what the man had said. *Guards.*

"Did you lose them?" A flicker of concern was all Zelia let slip onto her features.

If the man had led them straight to this place—

I hadn't finished with my thought when the door burst open, banging against the wall and wobbling on its hinges. The bright light outside cut the outline of three broad shapes on the threshold, burning around them like a corona of menace. Their faces were impossible to make out against the sun, but the weapons in their hands told me everything I needed to know.

I'd spent a major part of my life near those blades under the scrutiny of my father's sentries. Now, the sharp end pointed toward Zelia and me as Cyrill's guards entered the room, one after the other, and demanded for us to step away from the thief.

Lowering my head and grateful for my scarf, I angled myself to hide what was visible of my face even better.

Zelia didn't take her hand off the wound even when, above the scarf covering her mouth and nose, her eyes widened with what I could've sworn to be fear.

"I said, step away from the thief," the guard hissed. He didn't need to add a threat—that was obvious in his tone. Eyes that were so much darker than my mother's that she wouldn't easily be recognized, while I—

"My patient will die if I do," Zelia responded, her voice measured, composed, ever the dignified Master Mage with the same authority she'd wielded in the fairylands. Only, here, she was no one, nothing. Just like me.

"That's the whole point." The man at the front nudged the shoulder of the man on the ground, whose breathing had turned shallow and even beneath our palms. For a moment, I wondered if it was the Guardian's mercy letting him pass out so he wouldn't see his death coming or if it was Eroth's punishment for the crime he'd committed that he'd be unable to defend himself, unable to run—the way I had run from the fairy market. Bile rose in my throat as the panic from not only my first hours in Aceleau flooded me, but the fear of being discovered drowned any other thought.

One step closer, and the man might get a good view of my eyes. While they weren't unique in Cezux, I was sure one of the palace guards would recognize them anyway. Too many days had they spent watching my every step—in a different life that now belonged in history books where the Princess of Cezux had ceased of a fatal illness alongside her father. What a shame.

I swallowed and forced my hands not to shake.

"Your *patient*," the man drawled, "will be dead either way when he stands before the king for his crimes."

"You say he's a thief?" Zelia conversed, unnervingly calm at the tip of a sword. Then, she'd lived among fairies for decades before she'd left her home for me. What were three trained, armed men compared to the constant danger of walking between fairies? "What did he steal that demands his blood?" Her hand never left the wound.

Whether she was attempting to apply magic to heal him... By Eroth, I hoped not. If the guards noticed, they'd have her head for it—and mine, too, just for living under the same roof. The entire sick-house would be executed, be it us or our patients, who had gone still as death on their cots as they waited for us to handle the situation.

And for the first time since he'd left that morning, I was glad Tristan wasn't here.

"His crimes are none of your concern, woman." The guard gestured at the other two, who stepped around him, close enough for me to feel a leg belonging to one of the men beside my shoulder.

If I was quick, I could knock him off balance while his weapon wasn't pointing at me.

Noticing the direction of my gaze, she shook her head the tiniest bit. *It's too big a risk*, her eyes seemed to say even when her body was tense and ready to fight.

"Let me treat him until he's stable. Let him heal before he stands trial." Zelia's words weren't the plea any normal peasant of Jezuin would have on their tongues but a cool demand, an attempt at bargaining, at buying time for the man whose crimes we didn't know, whose right to live or die we didn't know.

In Askarea, I'd have lost my life for stealing had Tristan not found me, perhaps. Perhaps something much worse would have been my punishment.

But these were humans. They didn't bargain the way fairies did, didn't delight in the game of promises the way the magical creatures of Askarea did. They were Cyrill's men. And they demanded the man's death for a crime potentially committed from hunger and desperation.

"Please." The word spilled from my lips before I could think better.

I didn't lift my gaze at the men who could never learn who I was but whom I so foolishly had offered my voice.

"He'll be better in a day or two. At least, he'll be lucid enough to look his executor in the eye," Zelia cut me off before I could draw more attention to myself.

"And who are you to demand a criminal's healing for a trial he'll never stand?" The leader of the three said, bending low enough for me to see his harsh features. I'd seen that face before, had walked past that man every day on my way to see my father. But the bloodlust in his eyes? That was new.

Not so different from the fairies, I thought as I prayed to Eroth that he wouldn't direct his gaze at me, read from that sliver of my face visible that he knew me just as well—better, perhaps, with his only task watching and guarding while I'd simply noted him in passing.

"The king doesn't care for trials," he whispered as if sharing a secret.

A moment later, he angled his sword and plunged it into the man's heart.

The gasp in my throat got stuck as the man twitched beneath my hand, his breath gurgling from him.

On instinct, I reached for the wound the moment the guard pulled his sword from the man's chest—and felt the blade at my neck instead.

"Don't bother. He'll be dead before we walk out that door." A shiver of ice ran down my spine alongside the meaning of his words.

The other guards hauled the dying man off the floor, his boots scraping over the uneven wood flooring as they dragged him out the door.

Shaking, I didn't dare turn under the sword to watch them disappear. I was about to glance at Zelia for help when I was kicked in the back, the weight of the guard's boot sending me face-first into the puddle of blood before me.

"You can consider yourselves lucky that we were here with a single task in mind today, or I'd take the time to browse through your facility and figure out what exactly it is that you are up to."

Even when his footsteps crossed the threshold, his laugh lingered like a presence of cruel cold.

FOUR

I was still scrubbing at the enormous crimson stain by the front door when Zelia returned from her round with the patients.

We'd spent the rest of the day calming them, reassuring them they were safe as long as they weren't on the run from Cyrill's men. Now that they'd been made aware of our sick house, they might know where to look for escapees.

Luck—it had been sheer luck they hadn't taken a closer look at us. Next time, we might not get away so easily. Even when the price being the man's life couldn't be considered easy.

Sitting back on my haunches, I wiped the sweat from my brow with my sleeve, the pungent odor of iron and salt climbing into my nose from my bloodied fingers.

Zelia took the rag from my hands, gesturing for me to take a break. So I did.

With legs like lead, I made my way to the bathing room where I stared at my reflection in the cracked mirror as I peeled the scarf away.

Where eyes of amber fire had once glinted, a flat stare was all that I could return to myself. No light shone in my irises; my cheeks, once flushed with the expectations of life, now sallow. Even my hair, once bouncing in waves around my head, was now neatly braided and coiled into a bun at my nape so it wouldn't get in the way with my new work.

My figure, swallowed up by the peasant garbs that were now my attire, disappeared beneath baggy layers.

With a sigh, I washed my hands in the basin, using the soap Zelia had cooked from sage and grease, the origin of which I'd chosen not to learn.

I was placing the soap back on the rim of the basin when a brief knock sent me whirling for the blade on my hip, hidden beneath my long, slitted tunic.

"It's just me," Zelia's voice sounded through the wood of the door.

"Come in." I dipped my hands back into the water, scraping off the crimson half-moons beneath my fingernails.

Zelia had removed her scarf, her mouth bracketed by tension now visible, and her eyes hard the way they'd been on the first day in Askarea.

"We need to consider leaving." She sat on the stool under the small window, wiping her hands over her face, and sighed. "Even if they didn't figure out who we are today, they will be back sooner or later. And when they are—"

She didn't need to finish her thought for me to understand. "We'll fight." It was all I had to say.

Zelia shook her head. "If we want to stand a chance at defeating Cyrill, we'll need to avoid discovery at all costs. If he finds out you're here, he won't even demand for me to stand back before he drives a blade into your heart."

No. Cyrill wouldn't waste a moment before he killed me—and everyone who knew I was alive.

My heart did a painful thud for Zelia and Dimar—and Tristan. More than ever, I yearned for his presence, if only so I could feel that Cyrill hadn't gotten hold of him.

I studied Zelia through the mirror as she reached into her pocket, face more exhausted than I'd ever seen her, and pulled out a small item on a leather string. "I want you to have this," she said as she held it in her palm, waiting for me to face her.

With shaking hands, I reached for a towel, drying off my fingers before I took a look at what she was offering to me—and swallowed the lump in my throat at the sight of a tiny crystal.

"Is that a—"

"A Mage Stone," she finished when I couldn't bring myself to speak the words.

"How—" I kneeled in front of her, examining the tiny structure, not daring to touch it. "How do you have a Mage Stone?"

I'd destroyed them during my trials—all three of them—and now... Now I was staring at one. Not bigger than a fingernail, the crystal not as bright and brilliant as the others were. But this was unmistakably a Mage Stone.

It took all my willpower to calm my breathing and actually listen when Zelia picked up the leather string and dangled the crystal in front of me. "You remember how I told you the magic is going away whether I use it or not?" I nodded. "So I decided to use what was left to give you a chance at defending yourself by funneling the remains of it into the Mage Stone I'd started preparing for you in Aceleau. Not a shard, like what you used at Ret Relah, but a real Mage Stone."

Her words floated into my mind, settling, even when comprehension lagged. Only full Mages got a Mage Stone. I wasn't even a Half Mage. Not even a Quarter Mage anymore without a Mage to teach me the use of magic—without magic to begin with. A shard had been all I'd used in self-defense so far.

"Why?" It was all I could think to ask. For this choice—it would leave her defenseless when she'd been the only one with some power in our circle. And now—

"Because you are a symbol of freedom, Sanja. You being here, drawing breath after what Cyrill has done, what the fairy king and the prince have done to you—it gives me hope. And hope cannot die."

I gaped, eyes following the dim play of light in the narrow facets of the stone held to the leather by a sling of simple brass.

"I started working on it the day you passed my test with the Crow Fairies."

A tear slid from my eye. Surprise and gratitude and guilt. Lowering my gaze, I tried to escape the spellbinding colors swirling in the crystal. "I can't take it." Because I was undeserving of such a gift when her magic had been taken because of me. "You should use it."

Zelia's free hand found my shoulder, squeezing lightly.

"I told you that a Mage can only have one Mage Stone in their existence. Once that is destroyed, there is no way for them to use magic."

Yet, she had used the magic channeled through my body, had stored somehow inside her tissues, had used it—to help others, to help me. To defend her family.

"Maybe"—I swallowed—"I can learn how to use it to channel magic into you, like with the rogue power from the stones I destroyed." It was a long shot, but—"If we want to stand a true chance against Cyrill, we'll need every edge we can get. If I can find a way to give you magic—"

"That won't work." Zelia didn't even let me finish. When, after a long moment of silence, I lifted my gaze to meet hers, her eyes were full of an emotion I couldn't read. "I was able to use the magic because part of it was from my Mage Stone. But this one is yours." She lifted my hand with hers and placed the crystal there with a reverent gentleness that reminded me of a prayer to the Guardians. "It might be tiny and not be able to store the same amounts of magic as what a regular Mage Stone stores, but it will work. Whatever magic you'll store in there will answer only to you."

My breath caught at the cool feel of the stone in my palm, half expecting a magical explosion the way it had felt when the magic had surged into me in the fairy palace—or out of me.

But it just sat there, a minuscule weight that was supposed to change my fate—all of our fates.

Before I could ask her what I was supposed to do with it, a tingle crept through my skin, spreading from the point where the tip of the Mage Stone lingered in my palm.

"Wait and see," Zelia whispered, eyes on the stone as the light inside it started swirling in all colors of a muddy rainbow. Beautiful. So very beautiful that my heart stuttered a beat before it picked up pace, fear mingling with the excitement of holding actual magic in my hand.

"What is happening?" My voice was breathless, a near whisper. And I couldn't look away. Couldn't bring myself to lower my hand and let the crystal roll back into Zelia's palm as she held it out for me to drop the stone if I so wished. Spellbound, I watched as the glow expanded just enough to encompass my fingers, subdued and so weak. But it was a Mage Stone, and I was no longer helpless. The realization rang through me like a bell, reverberating in every last cranny of my body. Magic.

I was still staring in awe when Zelia cleared her throat. The light dimmed, and the tingling left my skin as the crystal returned to that simple, tiny thing she'd dangled before my face.

With a smile, Zelia closed my hand with hers, gesturing for me to pocket the Mage Stone. "It will take some time to get used to the stone, Sanja. But you'll learn fast, just like you've mastered everything else."

My mind was full of questions, but none of them as pronounced as the one regarding what would happen if I accidentally used it.

Eyebrows knitting together, Zelia tilted her head and watched me pocket the Mage Stone. "Magic doesn't act without being summoned—at least, not for humans. If you want to use the Mage Stone, you'll need to properly summon and channel the magic stored in it. And before you ask, there isn't much stored at all. If you want to use it, you'll need to recharge it soon, or it will be as useless as the glass charms people in Aceleau hang in their windows to ward off the Crow Fairies."

"They do that?" My mind wandered to that day when Tristan had pulled me against him in the middle of the street, when he'd first kissed me to show the hunting Crow that I wasn't available as a bride. A shudder raked down my spine, not only because of the thought of what could have happened had I not followed Tristan's plan and played along. The thought of his front against mine, his arms around me, his lips on mine—it sent me right back into the ache to lose myself in his embrace for an hour or two.

"People do all sorts of wondrous things when they have little to pitch against their nightmares but hope," she said, eyeing me carefully. "Especially the less educated population of Aceleau. They believe glass made by humans works because the Crow Fairies can't cross the border to the human realms."

"The way all fairies can't cross?" I inquired, my mind drifting to the day she'd explained how fairies no longer roamed the human lands because they lost their powers when remaining in those realms too long. They slowly wasted away the way any human would.

Yet—the fairy king had found a way to strike a bargain with Cyrill and made him a tool to warm the Cezuxian throne until he could claim it. And now, the prince was probably waiting to do just that.

I closed my eyes, my fingers still curled around the Mage Stone in my pocket in affirmation of its presence.

"Trading glass might be just what we need to charge the stone," Zelia mused. "Perhaps, if we manage to get some pretty glass shards, we can make charms to sell in the fairylands. We don't need to get anywhere near Aceleau in order to find interested fairies. Some will buy them merely because it's human glass and won't worry one bit about its effectiveness against the Crow Fairies."

Everything in my body tightened at the mere thought of returning to a land where I was hunted for my species alone.

"Whatever happens, Sanja. I'll be there to teach you how to use it." She stroked a hand over my hair, a motherly smile lingering on her lips, and I could see the resemblance to my mother. Something painful stirred inside my chest. Another secret my family had kept hidden from me—that my mother had been not only Queen of Cezux but also a Mage. A spy willing to marry a king in order to find a way to reverse the Mages' exile from Cezux.

"We'll figure it out, Sanja. Even when it gobbled up every last ounce of my residual magic, I'm still here to help you."

I wasn't alone. I had a new family now. One I didn't deserve.

As if in response, the crystal painfully pushed into my palm, taunting me with what should have been Zelia's—should have been *theirs*—and was now mine.

Dimar arrived that night as Zelia had predicted. Instead of sneaking into our new home under the cover of night, he knocked on the door, greeting us with a grim face and a glance of warning before he pushed his way over our threshold, his golden strand of hair hidden beneath his mass of black waves but his golden freckles glimmering in the candlelight.

I'd been lying awake in bed, fully dressed and not even half calm enough to process what had happened that day. Now, I was shivering at the sight of two more sentries in Cyrill's coat of arms following Dimar inside.

Zelia was standing by the edge of a patient's bed, scarf slung around her head and covering the lower half of her face while I was still fumbling with the linen in front of my face. So fast, my head nearly spun, I turned away and fastened the garment so I wouldn't be as easily recognized. Thank the Guardians, the candlelight disguised my distinct eyes.

While Dimar stood right of the door and the second sentry left, the third stopped in front of it, a smirk on his features as he assessed our humble facilities.

"I've heard rumors that this place is in use again." He let his gaze drift as far as the light reached, hand on the hilt of his sword, and took a step forward. "What do you say, Dimar? Is this the place Erald described?"

My eyes flicked to my cousin, who seemed to have frozen at the question, conflict twisting his features before he slammed down a mask of indifference and shrugged. "One never knows with Erald. He likes to blow things out of proportion just for a bit of attention."

"He was quite thorough with the thief, though?" the third sentry put into consideration, and my eyes involuntarily found the spot where I'd been scrubbing the murdered man's blood away mere hours ago.

The sentry noticed. Of course, he did. He was skilled, experienced, and deadly like all sentries trained in my father's regiment. And Dimar had brought them here. Brought them or had come along to prevent the worst from happening. The expression on his face when Zelia had opened the door was enough to make my stomach turn, as was the tense stance he'd taken, ready to leap between us and a blade should the sentries decide to end us then and there.

I swallowed the lump in my throat, praying to the Guardians that they would protect Zelia and our patients.

"You." The sentry pointed at Zelia, finger curling inward to summon her. "Come here and remove that ridiculous cloth from your face so I can see you."

Fear shook through me as Zelia took a slow step toward the man, completely ignoring Dimar, who did his best to appear unbothered as his mother halted a good two strides away from the sentry and folded her scarf back from her face.

"There," she huffed, disguising her fear with a lot of disdain. "Now you know what an old woman looks like. Satisfied?"

The way she wrinkled her nose, I could have sworn she was about to spit in the sentry's face.

The man merely grinned, assessing her like a pretty flower about to be broken. "I'll let His Majesty decide if he's satisfied. As for you—" He raked his gaze over Zelia's unbound, grizzled hair, her proud face, before he turned to me, leaving her standing in the doorway. "You can pull off your scarf as well."

No. If I pulled it down, there was a good chance he'd recognize me—even when, at a second look, his face wasn't familiar, as was that of the man left of the door, who had raised his sword a Zelia. Cyrill's men, then. Trained with his cruelty in mind.

My throat tightened, but I cleared it, my pending panic searching for a way to incapacitate me. I didn't let it.

"We are healers, My Lord," I said in my best humble tone. "We don't mean any harm."

The sentry stopped, cocking his head as if trying to remember where he'd heard my voice before.

I blew out a breath, hands fisted at my sides to keep them from reaching for my scarf—or my knife. Not yet.

"Of course, you don't. Doesn't mean you didn't harm, anyway." The sentry pulled himself up to his full height before he sauntered a step closer.

From the corner of my eye, I noticed Dimar grabbing for his sword.

"We heal those in need. We don't ask questions concerning how our patients get injured," I explained, a weak attempt at reasoning with a man who had already made up his mind long before he'd walked in the door.

"You harbor criminals, offenders to the crown. You know what the punishment for that is in Cezux?" He didn't need to speak the words for me to read them from his eyes.

Death. Shivers of ice crawled up my back and neck.

"Down with the scarf, pretty eyes," he growled.

Dimar shook his head infinitesimally as he prowled closer. "I think the two of them are scared enough." He stopped beside the man, lips pressed into a tight line as if keeping himself from speaking.

A barked laugh from the sentry by the door was all the response he got.

"I said down with the scarf," the sentry repeated and took another step closer until he towered over me.

For a moment, I debated running, but he'd have me captured within two strides, and I'd face worse than his scrutiny.

I heaved a breath, pondering my options while the sentry became growingly impatient.

"If your eyes are that pretty, I want to know what the rest of your face looks like," he whispered, leaning in an inch, making everything recoil inside of me.

My hand found my knife on instinct, holding onto the slender hilt with all my strength. One step closer, and I'd plunge it into the man's stomach. As would Dimar, judging by the barely hidden fury in his eyes.

It must have taken him all his self-control as he said in a bored tone, "Peasants are filthy from hard work, Lisc. Let's find something clean to play with in the third ring."

The more questionable quarters of Jezuin, where some sold their bodies for money, lay in the third ring of the city. Not the poorest areas, so even the noblemen wouldn't attract attention when they visited one of said facilities. I'd given them a wide berth on my little trips to the market in my days of remote freedom before Cyrill had entered my life—and ended it.

Eroth bless Dimar for his efforts. But the sentry had his mind set on finding out if the rest of my face matched my eyes before he'd decide what to do with us.

One of the patients whimpered as the man's fingers surged up and took hold of the linen. Humid night air brushed my mouth, and my knife found its path into the sentry's arm where his leather armor wasn't protecting him right under his biceps.

The man stared at me, anger boiling behind the black of his eyes. A fist hit my jaw, sending me staggering back into a cupboard where I grasped for support. Stars danced in my vision, a glimpse of Dimar's blade flashing behind the man's back the last image before I blacked out.

FIVE

I woke to the sound of hushed voices and the scent of Leeneae.

"It's the princess," one of them said.

"The princess is dead," another one corrected.

The first voice insisted, "But it's her. Look at her. I will remember that face long beyond Eroth's veil."

Feet shuffled around me, tuning out the whispers as I was lifted by shoulders and legs and carried to what had to be a bed. A groan of pain slipped from my lips. When I listened hard, the whispers had disappeared completely.

"Hand me the tincture," Zelia ordered in their stead.

I was still wondering what had happened when the smell of Leeneae wafted past my nose so strong it made me wince. As I did when something warm and soft was pressed onto the throbbing side of my face where the source of my difficulties made it nearly impossible to focus.

"We'll pack our things and leave," Zelia said to me, or to someone standing beside her—I couldn't tell. My eyes wouldn't open. "Tonight. We can't stay here after what happened. Others will come looking."

"I'm sorry," Dimar said, tone grave. "I was trying to talk them out of coming tonight. I thought I'd have a few hours to warn you. But they insisted. So I chose to go with them rather than leave it up to the Guardians what they'd do to you."

"We killed a man, Dimar." Zelia's hands wandered over my face, probing for more injuries and finding none.

But the pressure on the bruised spot finally drove my eyes to open. I found myself staring at the slanted ceiling of my bedroom, Zelia leaning over me with a horrid expression on her face.

"Thank the Guardians." Dimar sank to his knees beside my bed, his hand grasping my shoulder. "For a moment there, I thought he'd snapped your neck."

It didn't take more than that for me to recall what had happened, and I jackknifed, almost hitting my head on Zelia's chin. Dimar's sword—

"Did you kill him?" I'd injured him, yes, angered him through my defiance. But he'd seen my face. As had the other. "Both of them?"

I hated how that was truly the only solution. Two lives to protect my secret. Whether I was worth it or not, only the Guardians could decide.

"The second one escaped," Dimar admitted as if it was a great failure. "I went after him, but taking down Lisc slowed me, and by the time I made it out of the house, he was gone." He wiped his brow with a still-gloved hand, the crimson stains on the leather dried enough to not leave a bloody trail across his skin. "I combed the streets nearby and the main road toward the palace. But he's well trained. Smarter than to take a route I'd anticipate. By now, he's probably reached the palace and informed Cyrill about what happened here."

I wasn't certain what shocked me more—that I was relieved the first sentry was dead or that I regretted the second one wasn't. "Did he—" I cleared my throat. "Did he recognize me?"

Dimar shook his head, golden strands uncovering at the shift. "I don't know. They were Cyrill's men, but your portrait hangs in the throne room where Cyrill likes to make sad moony eyes at it when he holds audiences. Ever the suffering widower."

Nausea racked my stomach, making me heave before I could turn to the side, and I spilled the contents of my dinner over my clothes and pillow.

Zelia cursed and pulled the sheets up to clean off my face and the mess on my shoulder and sleeve.

"It doesn't matter if he recognized you. We'll be hunted for murdering a royal sentry. All three of us. We need to get you into fresh clothes and pack our things. Then, we sneak out before they come back."

Running—again. I merely braced my hands beside my hips and pushed myself up.

Dimar's arm was around my waist in an instant, keeping me from stumbling.

"What about Tristan?" He didn't know we'd be leaving, and we couldn't leave him a message. Anything indicating where we would be going was a risk we couldn't take.

"He is a grown man whose face nobody knows in Cezux. He won't be in any danger unless seen with us." Zelia's response wasn't nearly enough to soothe my nerves.

"How will he find us?"

Zelia was carefully pulling off my tunic and wiped the rest of my vomit with the Leeneae-wetted rag in her hand while Dimar kept stabilizing me.

"By Eroth's mercy and guidance if we're all lucky," she said, and I could have sworn there were tears in her eyes as she dropped the rag and picked two brown tunics from the cupboard—one she slid over my head, the other she put on a stack of clothes already gathered by the door beside a pack.

Silent tears trickled down my cheek as Dimar helped me down the stairs, the pack Zelia had prepared slung over his shoulder. But all I could see was the bloodbath that my wedding had been, how closely they'd escaped—and how, now, there was nowhere safe for them in Jezuin. They'd be running again, and my body was truly in no condition for a hike through Cezuxian summer—or any other place or season.

As my sluggish legs stumbled along beside Dimar's, Zelia led the way with her own pack weighing on her narrow frame. She'd gathered a few bottles and some provisions from the kitchen, but I had no idea what or how long they would last when we'd be on the run, on foot.

We'd sold the horses upon arrival in Jezuin to gather some funds to build our supplies—those were lost now, left behind alongside those few patients who had sworn to Zelia they'd tell Tristan what had happened but hold their tongues when the royal sentries returned.

In truth, it didn't matter what they told the guards. The sentry would long have alerted Cyrill to the fact that my heart was very much beating. Believing anything else was wishful thinking, a hope I could no longer afford.

I pulled my scarf more tightly around my face, ignoring how my silent tears soaked it, and kept pace even when every step hurt—not only the physical pain that pierced through me, head to toe, but the guilt. That Eroth-damned guilt that wouldn't leave my stomach, driving me to near pause with every breath, every thought, every heartbeat.

It wouldn't be the first time I was fleeing Jezuin with nothing but the garbs on my back and the minimum to survive a day. Only, this time, I wasn't running from a wedding—I was running for my life, as were my aunt and my cousin. And the man I loved—he'd need to find a way to us with Eroth's help. The thought was a stab to my heart and Dimar tightened his arm around me as he guided me into the moonlit streets.

"We'll take the street behind the market," Zelia murmured as we turned a corner away from the sick house. "And from there we'll go right to Askarea."

"Askarea—" I mouthed but couldn't get my voice to function.

"Once we make it to the borderlands, we'll travel the seam of the mountain range on the Askarean side all the way to the Hollow Mountains." The way she said it—as if she was expecting for us to ever make it that far.

"We might as well walk straight back into Aceleau," Dimar remarked with a scoff that reminded me of how much of his life he'd spent in danger of being found out. All those years of spying in the Jezuinian court. And Askarea.

"In the Hollow Mountains, no one will know or care that we killed their king." Zelia's tone was even darker than Dimar's.

I was about to ask why we hadn't fled there, to begin with, after the massacre at the fairy palace, when my mind wandered to Cyrill and his guards, who'd be hunting me for the rest of my life. *He* was the reason I would return to Cezux over and over again, no matter the danger. Because I wanted my throne back—needed my kingdom to be free. But not before we had a plan—a real one this time.

Dimar tugged me to a halt, fingers digging into my sore shoulder where I'd hit the cupboard, his other hand pressing a finger to his lips. In front of us, Zelia had already crossed the street, her outline disappearing into the shadows of a narrow alley, when I heard the footsteps. Slow and deliberate.

Guards. It struck me a moment before I spotted their forms passing by a smashed window of the house across the street. A gasp escaped me before I froze, Dimar's hand flapping over my mouth to keep me from making any more noise.

But the heads of five guards had already whipped in our direction, their hands lunging for their blades and one for a bow.

Shit—*shit-shit-shit.*

"Over there!" one of them called, running in our direction.

Across the street, Zelia pressed against a wall, her head shaking in denial of what was about to happen—or silent plea to the Guardians to spare us.

There was no sparing us. Just as the heat never really left Jezuin, the guards wouldn't miss us in the darkness even if we bolted and ran for our lives. I was still too wobbly on my feet to even attempt to, especially now that they'd noticed something hiding in the alley.

With a nod, I tried to signal Zelia that I understood, that I was about to do what I could to save at least them if they couldn't save me. Without her magic, Zelia was no match for even one of the guards, and Dimar... He would hold his own for a few minutes if I managed to balance my weight against the men, but eventually, he'd fall in this battle.

Praying to Eroth that the guards hadn't been able to see how many of us were standing in the shadows, I slammed my elbow into Dimar's side and shoved him behind the corner where small bushes were gracing a rare back garden in the first ring of Jezuin. If he was smart, he'd stay hidden until the streets were clear once more and then flee to the Hollow Mountains or wherever they could find a new life.

I didn't take that reassuring glance over my shoulder before I ran into the street, my head throbbing, every step painful, and ready to meet my fate.

Tempted to close my eyes and cower on the ground, I kept running as I braced for the impact of an arrow or the tip of a blade slicing my flesh.

It was neither an arrow nor a blade that brought me down but the soft command of a familiar voice calling my name on a dark breeze. Like vines holding together a crumbling wall, my body was locked in by the power that had tormented me in Aceleau, had saved me.

I hit the street face first and fainted to the sound of my body's limp thud.

SIX

Violets and sugar. I hadn't smelled that scent since my childhood.

Not true—I had. As I tried to clear the haze in my mind, the new meaning of my once favorite scent swept through me, shaking me awake with terror.

Maze. Flesh-eating plant.

I shot to my feet just to tumble back onto the soft mattress that didn't give me nearly enough stability to keep my wrecked body upright. I tipped sideways onto a heap of silk-encased pillows and soft sheets, my neck and my shoulder not the only parts throbbing with the aftermath of the guards' assault at the sick house.

My gaze searched the spacious room before me, the carved bed frame, the marble floor, the tall windows with a view on the tower of the palace.

The palace—

I scrambled to my feet, hitting the nightstand and pushing over a vase holding freshly cut violets. Gagging, I staggered a few steps before catching myself on the wall right beside a portrait of my father and, with a gasp, shrank away from his stern gaze; even if it was only an oil painting, the way he looked at me—as if I'd failed him. Again.

"About time you woke up," a whisper hushed from the corner of the room.

I whirled around, my father's immortalized eyes now lingering on my back as I found myself staring into a pair of cold, dark ones framed in an untypically pale face for Cezuxian standards. A perfectly groomed line of beard framed his jaw and his lips, giving him the appearance of the cultivated man he wanted to be seen as.

My stomach turned to lead, my legs and arms to stone, as I stared at Cyrill Tenikos sitting with his legs crossed and hands folded in his lap, dressed in white finery that reminded me too much of our wedding. There was nothing pretty in those handsome features as he leaned forward an inch, bracing his hands on the armrests of his cushioned chair, ready to stand, but not making the effort—yet.

"I've been wondering for a while if the rumors were true or if the poor of Jezuin were just praying to a phantom in the hope their princess would come and save them." He cocked his head, his short dark hair catching the sunlight creeping in along the seam of the window. "A phantom or a very much alive princess who has somehow come back from the dead," he mused as he looked me over, head to toe, disgust, malice, and bold interest mingling into a fearsome grimace on his face. "Tell me, Sanja Zetareh Lazar—how did you survive a stab to the heart?" The knowing glint in his eye almost made me blurt a question of where Dimar was, if they'd caught him, too—and Zelia.

But my voice was an animal in a trap, straining for a scream.

"Did the gods show you mercy? Then maybe I should let you live, Sanja." He raised his brows, two black arches above those dark pits that were his eyes. "Maybe I should make something better of you than my wife." Slowly, he rose to his feet, boots clicking across the marble as he decreased the distance between us.

My heart pounded in my chest while I marked each potential exit—the carved door, the window. It didn't matter which direction I'd run, Cyrill would always catch me. With my wobbly legs, I was no match for him. I couldn't even feign death. That had worked once—but had it ended any better than what I'd hoped for that day in the temple when I'd seen death coming? Me back in Cyrill's hands, alive, was probably an even worse fate.

He lifted one of them toward me, and I noticed a jeweled band around his ring finger—a wedding band.

"Saint Sanja."

I inched to the side with every step he took toward me, aiming to make it to the door even when I'd never make it far through the palace.

Stall—it was the only thing I could do. Keep him busy so he wouldn't attack, wouldn't make up his mind and kill me instead of—"What do you mean: *saint*?" His words registered.

Amusement flickered in his eyes, a black fire that promised nothing good. "The people of Cezux loved their princess. They still do. Even when they believe you dead— most of them. If they learn you've risen from the dead, they will no longer care about what loyalty they have for the Tenikos line. They'll offer their hearts on silver platters for their queen." His grin stretched wide, teeth flashing in what felt more like a threat than an opportunity to keep a beating heart.

As I was rifling through my still-hazy mind for anything to barter with, my legs carrying me too slowly toward the door, Cyrill closed the gap between us, fingers gripping my chin and locking me in place. I gritted my teeth against the pressure, the pain around the bruise where the other guard had struck me, and where I'd hit the street when that familiar power had bound my gait and made me faceplant into the dirt.

"They will offer their coin as well, Saint Sanja. They will offer anything you ask them for." His breath was a gust of mint and something bitter as he leaned in another inch. "And you... You will ask them for anything I tell you."

I prepared my words, ready to plead for him to let me go, to let me run and disappear to somewhere quiet, where I could heal and live out my days as someone who wasn't a threat to his claim of my throne. But if I gave in to my fears, who would stand up to the tyrant before me? Who would stand up for *my people* if not their princess? Once I gathered my strength enough to fight back, I would. But, for now, with my mind still catching up, all I could do was watch for every weakness I might be able to exploit. Gritting my teeth, I rallied my defiance.

But Cyrill let go of my chin, lightly patting my cheek instead, the touch eliciting an avalanche of soreness radiating through my face, my skull, all the way down my neck, and back pressed against the wall as I shrank as far from him as I could.

"Don't touch me," I barely managed, my hand batting his away in a too-slow movement to have any true effect.

He merely laughed as he stepped away.

"Saints aren't for touching, Sanja. They are for show to the devout." He wiped his fingers over his sleeve, leaving a trail of crimson, and it hit me that a bruise wasn't all I'd come away with from my encounter with the rocks on the street. "They are a means to appease the uneducated mob that has set their mind on denying my claim to the throne."

Somehow, his words scared me even more than the thought of him touching me. After everything I'd gone through—and survived—in Askarea, this man was ready to break me. Not by torture the way the fairy king and his beloved son had tried but by making me a tool against the very same people I was trying to save. My stomach felt suddenly full of sharp rocks.

If there were rumors... Maybe not everything was lost if my people were ready to fight alongside me.

However the rumors had come to life, I couldn't tell, and I wasn't going to dignify Cyrill by begging him to tell me. If there was anything I could do, it was to pull up that facade of Sanja, the princess, who'd show no fear, no emotion—and silently crumble behind it until my mind was clear again to make a plan for my escape.

Cyrill crinkled his nose at the stain on his jacket before he turned and stalked to the door. With a knock, the lock clicked, and a pair of guards became visible when the door opened.

"Don't even think about running, Sanja." Cyrill glanced over his shoulder. "The window is too high up for you to climb, and the door will open only at my command. So you can spare your energy for praying to the Guardians the way good saints do." He was about to cross the threshold but paused once more, revealing a smirk on his features as he looked me over, head to toe. "I'll send someone to clean you up and clothe you in something worthy of your new status. Now you look like nothing more than a queen of the poor, and we don't want to induce any wrong impressions, Sanja, do we? You are *my* queen now and mine to wield. I believe I don't even need to mention that speaking to anyone about how you *died* and were *resurrected* will lead to a particularly painful punishment—for you and whomever you share the truth with."

The bolt of the lock shot into place the moment the door closed, and I slid down the wall, slumping to the floor, my body trembling.

I couldn't tell how long I'd been hovering there, only that the sun hadn't moved past the edge of the window to allow the sunset shadows to penetrate the hues of beige and creme that were the room, when the door opened once more, and in swept a pair of light feet, shuffling toward me.

"By the Guardians—Sanja." Leahnie wrapped her arms around me in a painfully tight embrace and released me the instant I flinched to assess me with a mixture of awe and concern. "When Cyrill came to me, at first, I didn't believe it."

She grasped my hand to pull me to my feet. "Can you stand?"

I gritted my teeth and tried.

With her help, I made it to the bed where she settled beside me on the edge of the mattress, arm around my shoulders once more. Her tear-stricken eyes studied me from the side as I breathed through my own tears, my words bound in a knot inside my throat. *Cyrill had me killed, Leahnie.* My tongue wanted to form the words, but his threat—

I'd treated enough victims of his wrath in the sick house to take it seriously. A puncture wound to the arm would be harmless compared to what he'd do to both Leahnie and me if he found out I'd shared the truth.

"You were dead," she said, shaking her head. "I attended your funeral."

I considered lying. But this was my friend, and if I couldn't tell her the truth, I'd rather tell her nothing.

"I'm back." It was all I could say as I focused on her lovely face, the warmth in her eyes as my hoarse voice sounded through the pompous space. "And I think I'm here to stay." I was paraphrasing a lot, but at least it wasn't a lie. By now, it was safe to believe that Cyrill didn't intend to kill me right away. I was a much more powerful tool to him alive. A saint. By the Guardians. There weren't many in Cezux—especially no living ones.

Whoever had recognized me and sold me out—be it the sentries who'd escaped from the sick house or one of the patients who might have recognized my eyes—I was here now, and any hope of escape had dwindled the moment I'd shoved Dimar around the corner. He'd helped me at the sick house, and if the punishment for a simple thief was death, as a disloyal sentry, his punishment would be at least the same—probably combined with a degree of torture I wouldn't wish upon anyone.

So I bit my tongue and inhaled a steadying breath. "It's good to see you."

"Is it true what he said?" Leahnie pushed, her lips tightening for a moment as her mind obviously wandered to the lord posing as a king. "Did the Guardians send you back to us from the realm of the dead?" A reverence swept over her face that had me pulling back an inch. This was still my friend, but Cyrill had been quick to plant the idea of my *resurrection* in her head. Leahnie had always been a firm believer in Eroth and the Guardians. She'd question his claim less than a lot of the nobles would, who believed in coin and jewels more than the Eherean deities.

"In a way, they did." Again, I stuck to a half-truth. They might not have brought me back from the dead, but they hadn't let me die in Askarea either. I bit my lower lip, keeping the words in that were building in my chest. *He killed me, Leahnie. He killed Father and Eduin and the entire wedding party.*

She let her arm glide off my shoulder, sliding a few inches away from me to sweep her gaze over me once more, and this time, she noticed the bruises and scrapes on my face.

"He said they found you in the streets of Jezuin, dressed in"—she gestured at my peasant garments—"this. The Queen of Cezux walking among the commoners like a servant."

I winced at how Cyrill had already used the truth to spin his lie, making it easy for me to play along. "They did," I confirmed, guilt already pooling in my stomach like a puddle of molten lead. If Tristan could see me now—a trapped liar unable to ask even her friend for aid for fear of subjecting her to Cyrill's cruelty. A glance at her wrist confirmed that she had already made the acquaintance of said cruelty in one way or the other. I recognized the bruise there that I'd witnessed on Cyrill's servants during the visits in his home before my father had sold me to him.

"So that's how you got injured? In the streets?"

I nodded, letting her make her own assumptions to spare myself another lie.

"He also said that you'd been aiding the sick like a healer..." Leahnie's eyes wandered over the cheek Cyrill had patted. "Is that what the Guardians sent you back to do? To heal?"

I shook my head. "I don't know." Because I didn't. I could no longer tell why—if the Guardians had anything to do with it—they had let me escape Cyrill's claws just to thrust me right back into them.

"How long have you been back?" *From the dead.* The unspoken amendment hovered in the air between us as Leahnie slowly folded her hands before her and slid off the bed to kneel.

Scrambling for a response that wouldn't give away the truth but also not be a lie, I collected my wits and slid to kneel as well. "Don't, Leahnie. Don't kneel. I'm still me. I'm still Sanja. Still your friend."

She lowered her eyes, the distance between us settling despite the proximity. "He called you a saint, Sanja," she whispered, that reverence returning to her voice that had me stunned into isolation. "They have been whispering it all over the palace ever since King Cyrill carried you inside in his own arms."

In his own arms... Bile rose in my throat at the mere thought of Cyrill's arms. "I don't remember any of it."

So Cyrill had achieved his goal to convince the palace of his tale.

"He said that, too. That you had gaps in your memory of what happened since your death. He warned us not to push you with questions. It's inappropriate to question a saint."

I couldn't tell what stung more—the way she seemed to believe every word Cyrill claimed to be true or the fact that, no matter how much I wanted to, I had to admit that he was a mastermind in setting up his lies for success. He'd managed to trick my father. But then, all the fool had yearned for was the wealth the alliance with Cyrill had promised.

With a shaky hand, I took hers, extracting it from the pose of prayer that made everything I'd gone through a mockery of this new truth Cyrill wanted the world to believe. And no matter how much I wanted to tell her what had really happened, I couldn't damn her to the consequences. At least, not until I had a plan.

So I steeled myself for her reaction and squeezed her hand. "I don't know what plan the Guardians have for me by bringing me back here, but I know that I can't fulfill it bloodied and in dirty clothes." I attempted to smile, but my face throbbed, and it turned into a grimace.

"Of course." Leahnie leaped to her feet, curtseying. She reached under my arm to help me up and guided me to the bathtub in the corner where she placed me on a stool and turned on the hot water. Despite her smile and her dutiful aid, despite having my friend back, with Cyrill's lie, everything had changed between us. We were no longer two girls growing into different roles within a power structure, but I'd become untouchable, and it was evident in every glance she slid my way, in every touch with too careful fingers, that this was a rift that would make the truth even more difficult to believe. For, with Zelia, Dimar, and Tristan all gone from my life, I wouldn't be able to confide in anyone.

ANGELINA J. STEFFORT

SEVEN

When Cyrill said he was going to make me a saint, he hadn't exaggerated. After bathing me and helping me into a simple nightgown, Leahnie had left me to a night of rest, which I had spent stumbling through the room on the search for one of the secret passageways the Jezuinian palace was known for. But there was none. This room was a fortress to protect the *saint* Cyrill claimed I was—when, in reality, I was nothing more than a prisoner. I'd pulled my Mage Stone from the pocket of my bloodied clothes when Leahnie had been busy with the bath water and slid it into a corner behind a statue of a Cezuxian horse. When she'd left, I'd retrieved it once more, combing my memory for anything useful that would make it ignite and *do* something, ending up at the one magical word I'd learned in Aceleau—*Yetheruh*.

But all it had done was make tears of disappointment spill from my eyes when nothing happened. Only when the first light of dawn assaulted my eyes had I hidden the Mage Stone in a pillowcase on the settee and collapsed into a fitful sleep on the rug before the bed, too exhausted to even climb into it.

Now, the sun was standing high, and the room was buzzing with activity. Cyrill himself had come to wake me with a cruel whisper to my ear. *Up with you, little saint,* he'd said. *Or do you want them to observe another resurrection?* The threat in his words was still ringing through me, numbing every tug and pull as one of the older handmaidens worked through my hair, neatly braiding it into ropes that she wound around my head and pinned into place with shaky fingers. Whether it was from fear of Cyrill, who hadn't left the room even when I'd been changed into a pure-white dress, which reminded me painfully of my wedding dress, behind a screen. He'd merely gone on about how blessed all of them should feel to be assigned to *Saint Sanja, Guardian-blessed.*

My head had stopped throbbing halfway through the procedure, and I'd tuned him out, pretending to not notice how they all fell over their own feet to tend to me—or to avoid his displeasure if they didn't, it could have been either.

Eventually, he left his vantage point in the cushioned chair in the corner, which he'd assumed soon after I'd sat down at the vanity.

"Leave." He dismissed the servants, and the buzzing stopped as they all shuffled out of the room, Leahnie alongside them.

She hadn't spoken to me, not even lifted her gaze to meet mine, as if she was afraid that any familiarity would bring Cyrill's attention to her, and I hadn't questioned her choice, unwilling to expose her to him in any way, no matter how small. At least, the bruise on her wrist hadn't gotten worse, so I had reason to believe he'd not hurt her after she'd tended to me the night before.

I didn't stand from my stool by the vanity as Cyrill approached, painfully aware the clothes he'd chosen for me put me at a disadvantage to move efficiently, the skirts tight enough down to the ankles to trip me if I attempted a long stride.

"Beautiful," Cyrill huffed, bending low enough for his breath to caress my neck. Not caress—assault, making the hair stand at my nape in anticipation of a knife in my back. "Not quite a queen"—he ran his fingers over the coronet of braids along the crown of my head—"but almost a saint." He reached into his pocket, extracting a clinking chain that, at first, had me thinking of shackles. But he slid it over my head, carefully placing a palm-sized, brass disk featuring two winged figures on top of the clean white covering my chest, and smirked at me in the mirror. "To honor your sacred connections with the Guardians, Saint Sanja," he huffed before he straightened and stepped back. "Stand." An order.

I debated shaking my head, but he grasped my nape with iron fingers, forcing me to my feet. My hands strained to reach his wrist, but the force of his grip made my vision blur. "I believe you don't understand what is at stake here, Sanja." His voice was smooth, anger simmering beneath the surface

77

like a ready branding iron to push into my flesh at his leisure. "One wrong step, and I'll have someone fire an arrow and make you a martyr."

Ice slid down my spine as he jerked his chin at the window where, on the battlements of the tower, a man was patrolling. Whether he could see what was going on inside this room, I couldn't tell, but I didn't put it past Cyrill to have someone storm in the door and fire at a signal.

He forced me to face the mirror where the bruise, still blooming purple and black on my chin, had been hidden under a layer of makeup Leahnie had applied first thing that morning before the other servants had joined us, covering up all evidence of just how mortal I was. "As you may have heard, I haven't yet officially accepted the crown, even though everyone calls me king." A self-satisfied grin spread on his face. "But with my wife having risen from the dead by the Guardian's mercy, no one will question my right to the throne—especially when you speak the Guardians' intent before the entire court."

My stomach turned at the thought of aiding him in even the smallest of ways.

"At my queen's side, of course." He let go of my neck, the absence of his touch bringing instant relief and allowing my breath to reach its destination in my lungs once more.

"What if I don't?" The words grated along my throat, barely working their way from my lips.

Cyrill merely laughed. "Then, my dear Sanja, you don't understand what lengths I am willing to go to secure what should be mine. I thought the wedding had taught you a lesson." His fingers casually wandered to the knife on his belt—a jewel weapon fit for a king who didn't fear his position of power would be challenged. An accessory more than a weapon, but deadly anyway. He placed the tip of the blade to my side near the scar that Dimar's knife had left there, and panic gripped me with a force, almost making me topple over.

Cyrill laughed and raised his hands. "Not today, Sanja." He tucked the knife back at his side, holding out an arm so gentlemanly that it made the moment before feel like a figment of my imagination, and smiled, the mask of the king about to present the saint to his court. "Shall we?"

I didn't place my hand into the crook of his elbow but joined his side with too-small steps restricted by my stupid dress, and, together, we walked out the door.

In the temple, a crowd of servants was waiting alongside the noblemen and women who had been dwelling in the palace since my father's death. And by the altar, dressed in gold and white as if blessed by the gods himself, the priest who'd married us then begged for my life when the rest of the wedding party had been slaughtered.

His murky eyes met mine across the corridor the crowd had formed to let Cyrill and me pass, *aahs* and *oohs* following us alongside whispers of a miracle, of a sign of the Guardians that their new king was blessed just as his wife.

I debated digging in my heels, turning, tearing the dress, and running. But where would I go? How far would I get before Cyrill's men fired an arrow at me? As if hearing my thoughts, Cyrill indicated toward the altar where, behind the columns framing it, two men with bows were positioned on each side, arrows loosely nocked as their eyes scanned the room for dangers.

Maybe the servants could be fooled, but both Cyrill and I knew they were there for me—to ensure I wouldn't follow my flight instinct and blindly bolt.

Cyrill leaned down, his features too kind, too harmless, as he pretended to be the grateful man who'd been gifted a second chance with a wife whose body he'd seen burned alongside the late king's. "They are all watching for my sign. But only one of them will shoot you, Sanja, while the rest of them will pick random people in this room and kill them until your last breath leaves you."

His arm yanked around my waist as I stumbled a step, horror making me forget to watch my strides.

"Kneel," the priest said, and the crowd lowered themselves to their knees, eyes on the marble floor as we marched past and climbed the stairs to the altar—where my father had once handed me over to Cyrill.

Cyrill gave me a warning glance before he released me from his arm and turned to face the room. "We all witnessed the tragedy of Princess Sanja's death, her funeral, the flowers the people of Cezux laid down for her. We all grieved for the jewel our realm lost to a wicked illness too soon. But the Guardians know ways that we don't. We've heard of saints before, of those who they blessed with a return from the dead."

I tried not to choke on the lies rolling off his tongue so easily, at the blasphemy of abusing the Guardians' blessing for his own vanity. I might not have cared for our deities the way the poor of Cezux did, but something recoiled in my chest at the thought of using their name for Cyrill's gain.

"Resurrected by the Guardians' will and brought back to us by our own King Cyrill," the priest said from his position at the altar, "I give to you Saint Sanja, Guardian-blessed, Queen of Cezux."

My eyes scanned the bowed heads, the courtiers' colorful collars, and the artfully done hair of the ladies. Between them, a tall figure stood, not bothering to lower his head, golden eyes directed at me like two daggers of precious metal ready to stab me if I so much as breathed. A dark breeze engulfed me, tugging on what few strands of hair had escaped the handmaiden's tight work. "Saint Sanja." He snickered, lips curling in disdain as he folded his arms across his chest.

I felt Cyrill's gaze on me as I sucked in a shocked breath at the sight of Prince Recienne the Second, in the middle of the Jezuinian palace, his attire not that of a fairy prince but typical Jezuinian finery.

By the way no one heeded him a look, I had to entertain the idea he was a figment of my imagination. But the dark breeze swept around me once more. "Scowls don't suit saints."

I was half aware of Cyrill murmuring something to me, of the tug on my arm as he led me one step higher toward the priest, who fell to his knees as well—not before his queen but before the saint Cyrill had made me.

But my eyes never left the spot where Recienne was towering over the rest of the room, his hair ruffled by a wind I couldn't feel, eyes glimmering in a beam of light that wasn't falling into the room.

"Speak," Cyrill hissed at me.

I jolted at his order, trying to orient myself, to remember what he'd asked me to say. But all I could think of was the smirk on Recienne's face, the darkness bracketing his lips as he mocked me.

"The blessing of the saint for her people," Cyrill reminded me as if we'd gone over this little ceremony multiple times when, in reality, he'd never told me what to expect other than his punishment if she didn't obey. "Speak your blessing for our people."

My jaw throbbed as I unlocked it to whisper something unintelligible, eyes raised to the ceiling as if beseeching the Guardians while I quietly prayed they wouldn't turn on me for playing Cyrill's game. On instinct, my hand flapped to my cheek, and I froze as darkness swept through the corner of my vision. When I glanced in the direction, Recienne was leaning against the altar, fury burning in those golden orbs. There and gone.

For a moment—only one tiny heartbeat, I thought his anger had been for me, but his face iced over as he stared directly into my eyes. "The Guardians don't take well to imposters, Sanja. Keep that in mind when you pretend to be their saint."

Why did no one else react to his presence? Neither the priest nor Cyrill seemed to be aware of the fairy prince's powerful presence.

"What a lovely prayer," the priest whispered in awe, and I needed to suppress an eye-roll at the lie. I hadn't spoken one actual word to our deities. Only syllables, whispers that had no meaning yet had left the room in reverent silence, all eyes now on me as the attendees slowly rose to their feet at a sign from their king.

"Yes, Sanja, very lovely," Recienne remarked with all the force of his cynicism and put on a grin that was both stunning and terrifying all at once.

No one turned even an eye toward him, as if he didn't exist, as if—

I swallowed, nodding my thanks to the priest before I shot a murderous glare at the fairy prince.

"Allow me to escort you back to your quarters, Sanja." Cyrill took my hand and placed it in the crook of his elbow, not giving me a choice this time as he led me down the stairs, and I didn't dare to pull away even when turning my back to the fairy prince left me wary.

I'd dismissed that sense of Recienne's dark breeze, when Cyrill's men had trapped me, as imagined due to my own exhaustion, but hearing him—seeing him—in the temple... It reminded me that he might have truly been the one to bind my legs so I couldn't run, that he was as responsible for my being here as my weak, human body. The smirk on his face most certainly didn't help me believe anything other than his mal-intentions.

Heads bent in bows and curtseys as we slowly made our way past—a prize pony shown off to Cyrill's court to snare them with a false blessing, with an untruth that would make them believe that him on the throne was something the gods insisted on. Something unquestionable.

I made it all the way to the threshold where two more guards with bows made way for us to pass.

Before I crossed into the hallway, I allowed myself a glance back over my shoulder at the empty spot by the altar where Prince Recienne had been standing. The priest was the only one I found, his face drawn as if from exhaustion. But the fairy prince—he was gone.

EIGHT

Cyrill discarded me in my room with a reminder that arrows would be ready to fly at any time of the day if I as much as indicated I was going to betray him. How he'd known of my intentions, I couldn't tell. So I turned my back to him without another word, aiming for the bathing room where I could look at the face of the liar I was while he locked the door from outside, leaving me to wonder if one of the servants would drop by to bring food or help me out of the dress.

It took me a short minute to decide I didn't care as I grabbed the huge pendant on my chest, now weighing on my neck like an anchor pulling me to the bottom of the ocean, and ripped it off. I heaved a breath, two, my heart racing as I allowed myself to drop the façade and admit that, as much as I'd have liked to believe there was anything I could do, I was very much trapped. And anything I'd do to free myself would put more than just myself in danger.

The bruises on my face were still as ugly as the night before, but the lack of throbbing in my head allowed for the full reality to crush down on me. This was it.

I hadn't even been able to say goodbye to the man I loved. If Tristan had found Zelia and Dimar, at least, he'd be with his family. My stomach hollowed at the thought of rotting here in Cyrill's claws. I'd been so foolish to believe there was anything I could have done against him—especially now that the fairy king was dead and he could do whatever he pleased with Cezux.

Taking a tiny step restricted by my dress, I almost stumbled into the basin. I doubled over and, with a scream, tore the seam open so I could move my legs. Then I dropped to my knees and vomited into the toilet until dry heaving was all that was left. Only when my body was shaking from exhaustion did I allow myself to think of what had happened in the temple, what I'd seen when the rest of the attendees had not.

Recienne's golden eyes flickered before me as if in mockery of my thoughts. I squeezed my own eyes shut, cursing violently when they remained right there as if permanently etched into my mind. With a groan, I pushed myself to my feet, rinsed my mouth, and trudged toward the settee, where I reached into the pillowcase after a glance over my shoulder to confirm I was alone and no one was watching from the battlements on the tower. When I found a figure there, I pushed myself back to my feet, savoring each long stride I took toward the window, and pulled the curtains shut.

Whoever was watching, even if they could never see a detail from that far away, made me decide I wouldn't leave anything to chance when I went back to figuring out how to make my Mage Stone work for me.

It swirled with that dull effect of a trapped rainbow the way it did every time I held it in my hands, but nothing apart from that play of colors happened—no tingling, no force. I would have even welcomed pain had it been a sign that something was happening. But ... nothing.

Suppressing another curse, I trapped the stone between my fingers and stared. Maybe that would do something.

It didn't.

By the time a knock on the door announced the arrival of someone other than Cyrill Tenikos, I'd whispered every potion spell I could remember having overheard Zelia or Tristan use. But that Guardian-damned little item remained as useless as a piece of jewelry to a pig. It didn't need extra mentioning that a pig was exactly how I felt—useful when looked at in the prospect of eventual slaughter. And Cyrill would dispose of me sooner rather than later. No matter how much he needed his *saint* right now, the day would come when he'd no longer have that need, and I'd be lucky if a knife to the heart was all he did to me.

I slid the crystal back into the pillowcase and sat on the edge of the bed, pretending to stare at the painting of my father.

The lock clicked, and the door swung open. On the threshold stood the elderly handmaiden, her expression bland as she dropped into a curtsey, balancing a tray in her hands. "Meal for Saint Sanja," she said, voice devoid of the excitement buzzing in the temple earlier, and entered the room. The door fell shut behind her, blocking the only path out. For a moment, I was reminded of the tower at the fairy palace where Prince Recienne had told me not to jump out the window.

A scowl stole itself back onto my features as I watched the woman's irregular footsteps. Her limp was slight, barely noticeable otherwise, but it was there.

"Are you all right?" I asked before I could think better.

The woman didn't dare look at me, too scared of the *saint* or of her husband.

Whether it was the habit I had acquired during my time at the sick house or a different instinct, I got to my feet and hurried to the woman's side to take the tray from her hands and gesture for her to sit.

If her horrified expression was anything to go by, I had grossly overstepped her boundaries. But if she was hurt ... I could help. Even without herbs and potions mixed with the last of Zelia's magic, I'd seen enough bones set and had wrung enough muscles to know where to touch to identify a sprained ankle. And I very well knew how to properly dress a wound.

The woman's eyes snapped up to lock with mine, but her fingers didn't let go of the tray, holding me in place for a moment. I noticed the tightness around her lips, the redness in her eyes. As if she'd cried.

"Your limp—" I didn't get any farther before she started shaking her head.

With a surprisingly hard tug, she pulled the tray back toward her, and I let my fingers slip off the wood as she turned to carry it to the table.

"You weren't limping this morning." She'd been bustling about my room, back and forth between the vanity and bathing room to get utensils or to wet the brush so she could tame my waves into neat braids. But now— "What happened?"

The demanding tone of Princess Sanja sounded odd in my ears, like a memory of a person dead.

I didn't allow my discomfort onto my features but instead forced myself to capture her gaze when she set down the tray and turned back from the table.

"What's your name," I tried when she didn't respond.

Hands curling into fists before her apron, she curtseyed and managed a tight-lipped smile. "Lord Cyrill wishes to see you in his study after you finish eating." She curtseyed again and turned to leave.

"Wait." I remained where I was, reluctant to intimidate her by approaching like I was so used to with my patients at the sick house, and gestured at her leg instead. "I can take a look at the injury," I offered.

A wary look was all I got in response.

"I don't know if you've heard, but ... I was a healer in the first ring of Jezuin." Focusing on my breathing, I waited.

The woman didn't speak, but something sparked in her eyes—something more than the fear that had made her stumble away.

"I thought—" She cleared her throat. "I thought he made that up, too." She shifted on her feet, wincing as too much weight landed on her right foot.

"Did you get hurt?"

She scoffed. "One could say so."

While I was still trying to figure out the meaning of her words, she hobbled closer, limp now clearly visible as she no longer tried to hide it from me. "How?"

She met my gaze, the fear suddenly wiped away as if she was seeing something she'd been looking for in my bruised face. "Cyrill Tenikos is not a good man, not a kind one, but that is not a secret. He is quick to punish whether accusations are justified or not. A lot of us have suffered since you disappeared, Princess Sanja. But none as much as the ones who questioned your death."

My heart did a painful thud at the thought that there had been people in this palace—in her home—who'd been willing to confront Cyrill about the truth of my timely death. And these women before me—

"You were one of them."

She didn't need to nod to confirm it; I could read it from her eyes, from the way her lips curled into a bitter smile. "You were so much like your mother that, somehow, it was hard to forget you weren't her. That you didn't *know*."

"Know what?" I reined in my commanding tone, which threatened to surface here in these halls where I'd been the princess and now had been made the saint.

But this woman—she knew something. And with everything Zelia had shared with me about my family history, I wouldn't have been surprised if there were more secrets hidden right under her nose.

"Who she was. Why she died. And how she—"

"Poison," I cut her off, my tongue loose in Cyrill's absence. Or simply too damn glad that someone was talking to me like I was a person and not a Guardian-blessed saint.

The woman pursed her lips and nodded.

"Though I don't know exactly what happened. But you... You've served in this court long enough to have been around for her death." My heart was now racing in my chest in anticipation of learning what Zelia had hinted at all those months ago.

The woman nodded again, hobbling one step closer and bracing her hand on the back of a chair. "Your mother was poisoned with a substance no Leeneae can remedy."

I had to remind myself to close my mouth and regretted it when my jaw throbbed as a result.

"Leeneae..." I forced myself to stop. It was one thing to let her reveal what she knew, but giving away my knowledge... If she was Cyrill's spy, this might turn into a disaster pretty fast.

"Is a fairy plant, yes. Native to the meadows and forests of Askarea and impossible to be found in the human lands." She glanced at the door, forehead creasing as she studied the carvings from afar. "I've been working in the kitchens since Queen Noa's death, and trust me when I tell you the bread supplier smelled of Leeneae the other day."

I didn't dare breathe, knowing what would come next.

"For the past weeks, her daughter delivered the bread, letting everyone know her mother was sick and being treated in a sick house in the first ring." She shook her head, holding my gaze as she read the truth from mine. "There are no sick houses in the first ring, Princess Sanja. At least, not until recently. And when Cyrill said he found you there, treating the poor like the saint you were, I knew."

I didn't dare speak.

"The old baker smelled of Leeneae. I don't know if it is you who used magic to heal her or someone else. But you know about magic. You know that Leeneae is a healing plant, and you know how to use it, or you wouldn't have been working at that sick house."

My mouth opened and closed, but no words came out.

"We don't have much time before they'll expect me to leave the room, but know, Sanja, that you're not alone in this palace. There are people here who never believed in your death and who are willing to take whatever punishment it takes to help you." With her free hand, she lifted her skirts enough to expose her ankle. A thin band of purple snaked around it, a bruise left by shackles.

I couldn't stop a gasp. I started to crouch before her, ready to examine the leg, but she shook her head.

"Unless you have magic at your disposal, there is little you can do," she said quickly before she dropped her skirts again. "Now, sit down and eat so you don't let the king wait. We both know what he is capable of if angered ... and Cyrill is angered easily."

With those words, she curtseyed, biting back a wince, and hobbled for the door.

I was still stunned into silence when the guards unlocked it from outside, glancing at me past the handmaiden with curious eyes. I didn't even get to thank her before she was gone.

So I followed her request and sat at the table, the boiled vegetables and slices of fruit mocking me with their colors as I felt the world turn to grays around me.

If the woman wasn't lying, I wasn't alone in this palace. I had never been—with Dimar just around the corner to look out for me. But even without him? There were people who'd known my mother's secret long before I had learned it and who knew about her death.

Poisoned because she was a Mage.

I shuddered as I sniffed my food, wondering if it was safe to eat anything that was served in Cyrill's court, and my mind strained around the possibilities of Cyrill knowing as well.

He'd been in league with the fairy king, after all, had warmed his throne until he could leave Askarea and rule over the human realm as well. But that border was protected by some ancient magic, Zelia had explained, that would rob any fairy of their powers and leave them to wither like humans.

Inevitably, my thoughts returned to the image of Prince Recienne in the temple. By now, it was safe to believe it had been a vision and nothing more. Maybe my own injured head was playing tricks on me, conjuring up the prince to escape Cyrill's presence.

I grunted in frustration.

"That's about as sightly for a saint as a scowl, Sanja." His chuckle startled me to my feet, and I cursed soundly as my lunch spilled over my dress when I spun to find Recienne leaning against the wall at the other end of the room, hands in his pockets and that familiar smirk on his features.

On instinct, I raised my fork before my chest—a meek weapon but a weapon nonetheless. If Zelia was right, and fairies possessed little to no power in this realm ... I might even stand a chance.

"Don't be ridiculous, Sanja." He pushed away from the wall, strolling to the foot of the bed where he eyed my ruffled sheets with a flicker of amusement before he faced me once more. "A fork? Don't you have better weapons to pit against me?"

For a moment, I debated screaming. Two armed guards could easily overpower one unarmed man. My eyes slid down his form, assessing for any sign of blades, and found none. When my gaze met his once more, a simmering flare of something I couldn't read awaited me before he blinked and shrugged. "Like what you see?"

I stuck out my tongue, unable to control myself, and threw my fork at him.

It sailed past his shoulder straight into the wall behind him where it bounced and, with a clang, landed on the floor.

Recienne didn't dignify my attack with even a cringe. Instead, he held my gaze as I was fuming for no apparent reason other than that he was here, smirking and grinning and mocking me—

"Better?" he asked after a long minute of enduring my seething gaze like the royal bastard he was.

I didn't even try to come up with a smart response since he'd twist and turn every word I said—or worse, make me say the words he wanted to hear with that cruel power of his. And I was convinced that part of his power worked. His control over my legs when he'd felled me in the street—

I folded my arms over my chest, ignoring as best I could the beautiful curve of his lips as they twitched with amusement. "Anything in particular you want from me, or did you just come to gloat?"

He stood like a statue, his human clothes unable to hide his powerful elegance, his obvious otherworldliness. It didn't slip my attention that I was still clothed in my ridiculous dress, lunch stains spreading on my stomach and thigh, and the bottom ripped apart in a long slit. I refused to feel embarrassed.

For a moment, he merely stared, golden eyes as unsettling as the first time they'd pinned me on the forest ground.

With a swish, he turned away, stalking back to the wall and studying the portrait of my father instead. "Good," he said as if speaking to the late King of Cezux. "Now that you've got that out of your system, how about telling me what, by the Guardians, you're doing in Jezuin?"

His words brought forth the irresistible urge to stick my tongue out again. But instead, I locked my hands into fists and made my tongue form words. "I could ask you the same."

He glanced back over his shoulder, black hair shifting with the motion. But instead of giving a response like a normal person, he chuckled. "I thought you were smart enough not to return into Cyrill's reach. Especially after what you learned about his ... motivations." His father's hunger for power in the human lands.

Killing the male who sold out his lands wouldn't make me a hero. It would make me a fool.

Our last conversation in the forest returned to my mind, and, for a moment, everything went still inside of me as I realized why he had to be here.

"You came to finish what your father started. You're here to take Cezux."

Turning, Recienne chuckled. "You seem to know a lot about what I'm up to, Princess." He stalked toward me in those measured strides I'd so far seen only in the throne room of the fairy palace. "Or should I say *Saint Sanja?*"

There was something predatory about him as he approached, too slow to be anything other than deliberate, too controlled to evoke any other impression than that he was internally preparing to bring down an opponent.

He halted a foot away, towering over me as I refused to shrink from him, and his gaze slithered along my face, the golden eyes solid and unreadable. "I've heard you were resurrected by the Guardians. Lucky you." He laughed without humor.

"May the Guardians send a bolt of lightning after you." Intending to ignore him, I turned to face the mess of vegetables on the floor before I continued to the window where I peeked through the curtains at the battlements of the tower.

A guard was patrolling, bow strapped over his shoulder. Great.

"A bit violent for a saint, wouldn't you agree?" His tone was anything but agreeable. Self-satisfied bastard.

"If there's nothing you want, you might as well disappear." And leave me to my misery. It was bad enough that Cyrill had made me a figurehead for his takeover of power.

"That would be a bit difficult, you know ... since I'm not even really here."

No matter how much I wanted to pretend his words didn't fluster me, I couldn't help but spin around to face him once more. "So you are only in my head." As if that were a good thing.

"Not quite, Sanja, but that's for another day." He stalked closer, eyes on the curtains shrouding the window as if he could see right through them. "If your *husband*"—he ground out the word—"knew you were having visions, he might feel emboldened in his endeavor to make you a saint. I've heard saints fantasize all sorts of beautiful things."

"Why exactly am I fantasizing about you, then?" I wanted to take the words back, ripping fertile ground for his next cocky remark from under him.

His eyes flashed in golden delight as I blushed.

But all he did was raise his brows and angle his head as if asking whether that wasn't obvious.

So I went back to tuning out his annoyingly penetrating gaze until he turned and stalked to lean on the bedpost.

"Next time you fantasize about me, make it something worth coming."

His chuckle lingered long after his form dissolved into mist and wind.

And I slammed my palm to my forehead as I realized what his words implied. I didn't care for the returning throb in my head. For now, that seemed dull, the anger at the fairy prince engulfing me so thoroughly that steam might have evaporated from my nostrils.

NINE

It seemed the supply of motion-restricting dresses was endless in the Jezuinian palace, for the servant who picked up the torn and dirty one already had another one slung over her forearm. Hanging the dress on the screen, she motioned me to the vanity where she made my bruise disappear behind that layer of paint that Leahnie had used on me before when we'd left the room, and it dawned on me that Cyrill must have ordered my injuries covered to perfect the image of the saint he was so determined to create.

After a second glance at the mirror, she gestured for me to step behind the screen to change, her eyes never meeting mine as she shuffled throughout the room like a devout crab.

"Where's Leahnie?" I asked, reluctantly sliding off my nightgown and replacing it with a beige version of yesterday's attire, and frowned down the front of my body.

"I haven't seen her today, Saint Sanja."

My frown deepened at the use of my Cyrill-given title. But I didn't correct her to call me queen instead. After the handmaiden with the injured ankle the night before, I was no longer sure whom to trust. With Cyrill's cruelty lurking around every corner already keeping me up at night, Recienne's unexpected appearance in my room had certainly not eased my sleep either. Day or night—it didn't matter—there was no peace for me, no sanctuary, no escape.

So I'd resorted to pacing the room until the candle stump burned down and I'd hit my toes on my bedpost. But my eyes hadn't closed when I'd lain down, the fury for the fairy prince soon smothered by that emptiness in my chest that only felt whole when Tristan's arms were around me. And how was I ever going to have that again when Cyrill had effectively locked me in what had once been my palace?

I knew the exact location of the room, knew how many flights of stairs I'd have to run down to make it to the main gates and how many to the side entrances. But what was the use of that knowledge when any attempt to free myself would result in the pain of others? My entire body trembled from helpless fury whenever my mind circled back to what he was capable of, how he'd snuck his way onto the throne.

Now, I was eyeing the servant over the edge of the screen separating me from the rest of the once luxurious room that had been gutted to the bed, the armoire, a table, and some chairs, trying to read from her smooth, brown skin if she would be someone inclined to help me or one of the many who seemed to blindly believe their new king's claim.

"I'd like to go see her." It was worth a try. Maybe, if I was escorted by guards, they'd let me roam the palace, and I could bide my time until I found an opening to slip through their fingers.

The woman's eyes lifted to my face, widening with shock when she found me gazing back at her, and she lowered them back to the marble.

Before she could form a response, the door opened, and in marched my husband, his gait far too cheerful for the master of torture he was. Waving a dismissive hand at the woman, he stopped a few steps from the screen, raising to his toes as if to peer for something worth seeing.

I bit my lip to hold back a comment until the servant had left and we were alone. "Have you come to make a spectacle of me again?"

Cyrill pretended to consider while he summoned me with a curl of his fingers. "Much as I enjoy the sight of you locked in this room, you are of little use to me behind closed doors."

I almost released a sigh of relief when he didn't indicate he would make use of me inside this room. At least, *that* I would be spared.

"You didn't follow my summons yesterday," he said drily, his eyes sweeping down to my ankles and back up again.

My heart stuttered a beat as I remembered what the servant had said. That she'd be punished if I were late. And Recienne—he'd distracted me so thoroughly that I hadn't even remembered I was to visit the king. "For what?" Trying not to panic, I counted to ten in my head—then backward.

He didn't respond as he frowned at my chest where the pendant was missing. "You didn't like my gift?"

Willing my limbs to remain still, I swallowed the fear of what he'd do to me if he learned that it had left a dent where I'd discarded the brass circle on the tiles.

"It's in the bathing room," I told him, voice surprisingly even. My lips twitched into a thin smile as I debated telling him I'd flushed it down the toilet, just to see if he'd snap and end me if I pushed him far enough. But this wasn't about my life as much as what he'd do to Leahnie, to the other servants, to Tristan or Zelia or Dimar if he ever got his hands on them. Swallowing back all the horrible scenarios of how that could go, I managed a shallow breath. "It was a bit heavy to wear, so I took it off for now."

The black of Cyrill's eyes sparked with danger as if he was about to plant a bruise on the other side of my face to match the already-existing dark, hidden blotch. But he collected himself, expression smoothing over, and marched to the bathing room to retrieve the pendant. His measured strides sounded through the room as he disappeared and reappeared, the chain dangling from his fingers as he marched around the screen.

"Why is it so important that I wear it?" I stared at the clunky necklace, at the rays of light etched into it—a symbol of the Guardians—and hoped that it would melt into liquid metal in his hands.

Cyrill's brows rose as he read the hatred in my features. "After the ... most unfortunate delay of our wedding," he said, smirk returning, "I knew that you'd be a handful to deal with, Sanja. But whatever you think up to defy me, even in the smallest of ways, know that someone has already paid for it. And more people will. Be it a necklace or refusing to follow my summons. I have ways to make you bleed without ever laying a hand on you."

My body locked up at the clear threat. There was only one person left in this palace who held my affections, and that was—"Leahnie," it slipped from my mouth, too late to bring back the word.

Cyrill closed the gap between us, draping the chain with the pendant back around my neck. "Oh what wonderful friends you have, Sanja. Leahnie is exquisite, and it would be a shame if her pretty face would be destroyed because you failed to behave yourself."

No.

Fear was a living, breathing beast between my ribs at the thought of Leahnie locked up in a cell beneath the palace. Even when, as a child, I'd never been allowed down there, I'd snuck into the dim corridors stretching beneath the foundation where the cells were mostly empty, but what few prisoners I'd spotted—

I wanted to close my eyes and disappear as Recienne had. Wanted to scream for someone to free Leahnie and take her far away from here where Cyrill couldn't lay a finger on her.

The fairy king had made a great choice in Cyrill Tenikos—the same wretched mind, same cruel malice. Only, now Cyrill was no longer warming anyone's throne. Now Cezux was his, and I, his path to blind acceptance.

"Fret not, Saint Sanja. Maybe the Guardians will help her, too." He looped his arm into mine, leading me to the door without another word.

◆

In the hallways, servants stopped to curtsey and bow as we strode by, my stupidly tiny steps so useless to gain ground if I decided to run. Not that I could with Leahnie in Cyrill's power and the guards armed with bows stationed at regular intervals along our path.

"You'll enjoy today's outing, Sanja," Cyrill purred. "It will be rather ... entertaining." It was all he said before he guided me to the empty throne room, taking a seat on the gilded throne where my father used to sit. He beckoned me up the two stairs to join him on a hard-wood stool. "Fit for a saint," he commented as he inclined his head at the guards at the end of the room—one of them armed with a bow—who opened the double door to free the view of a line of people, all of them waiting for something.

"They have come to see the Saint of Jezuin, Sanja," Cyrill murmured, leaning close enough to make my hair stand at the back of my neck as I took in the men and women approaching us in careful, reverent strides, eyes skimming the ornate ceiling and columns every other step, running over Cyrill, but never truly lingering on me. "Smile, and be gracious with your blessings. You did so well at the temple the other day. Show them that you support your husband and king with the Guardians' will, and I will allow you to see your friend."

My friend, who had both embraced Cyrill's truth and aided him in covering up traces of the violence Cyrill's guards had used against me. My hand itched to touch not my jaw, where the pain had subsided, but my chest, where I ached to show the people approaching us that I was as human as them, as mortal as they were, and not a saint at all.

"You've most certainly been busy," my words found me again at the familiarity of myself on the dais, of the people glancing up in awe.

Cyrill crinkled his nose in an almost genuinely amused gesture as he leaned in once more. "I've had months to mourn you, Sanja. And Jezuin had months to see me mourn. Now, they can see me elated at the return of my wife. At what a blessed husband I am." His words were like chalk trickling into my collar, itching and leaving a mark. "Now ... back straight and smile, Saint Sanja. Your devout servants are here to honor you."

I didn't cringe from his nearness this time, focusing on the weight of the pendant on my neck instead—and on the endless line of people streaming in, kneeling as they reached the dais. Not before their king, I realized as each of them spoke the greeting of the Guardians.

Cyrill's eyes lingered on me, grasping the armrests of the throne with white-knuckled fingers when the people of Jezuin barely took notice of their king.

And I—I took a steadying breath and lifted my chin, keeping my face impassive as I murmured words once more that no one would ever understand—because they had no meaning and would never bless anyone.

But my people's eyes lit up with awe as they left through a small door at the side of the room, motioned outside the palace by a set of guards. I didn't know their faces—Cyrill's men, then. Just like the guard with the bow patrolling the side of the room now.

Everything recoiled inside of me at the lie I had been made part of, at the betrayal of my people by supporting Cyrill.

For Tristan, I told myself. For Dimar and Zelia and for my people, I would endure this until I found a way out. And I was already searching. I let my gaze drift across the room as I continued to mumble, hand raised in front of me the way I'd seen the priests do. No matter how wrong every inch of my gestures felt, no matter how I ached to stand and scream and use my bare hands to throttle Cyrill, I endured. It was the only gift I could give my people, to prevail until I could free them. Even if playing the saint led them to believe exactly what Cyrill intended—that it was the Guardians' sign that his reign was their will.

I wondered if Eroth had an opinion on it or if I was the only one who found the whole ruse disgusting.

At the back of the room, hushed voices were urgently uttering as they proceeded in the slow-moving line. I allowed my eyes to wander to the source of the sound and, behind rows of colorfully clothed nobles, found a group of sand-colored dressed women. Peasants from the first ring, judging by their clothes. A guard was hissing at them to leave. Of course, they were. The palace was afraid of the peasants from the first ring. There was power in masses, and Cyrill couldn't control all of them by fear forever. Hadn't he spoken of uproars? Or defiance?

The conversation got louder, people before and after them stepping aside to get out of the way of a potential escalation—as if anyone would try something with armed guards around them. I shook my head as the group was escorted from the room, restrained by their elbows. Before the guards could drag them through the door, a woman turned and shouted over her shoulder, "Saint Sanja! Bless all of your people. Bless the ones who can't buy your blessings."

My stomach clenched uncomfortably as my eyes found Cyrill's, noting a warning hovering in the darkness of his gaze.

Ignoring all sense of self-preservation, I pushed myself to my feet and glided down the stairs as gracefully as my stupid dress would allow.

The room went silent. Even the peasants stopped fighting, and the guards stopped dragging them as the crowd parted for me. I sensed Cyrill stand and follow me to the edge of the dais, but he didn't dare move farther—of course, he didn't. He was a coward, killing his way to the throne, teaming up with another tyrant to gain power—and pushing me before him like a sacred layer of destiny.

The guard with the bow followed my every move, arrow nocked as he pretended to be looking out for me rather than awaiting Cyrill's sign to bring me down.

As if I could do anything against him in the role he'd forced me into. There was nothing ... nothing that I could do.

Except to give him what he wanted. Be the good saint the people adored. Maybe the day would come when that adoration could be used against my husband.

While I inclined my head at the men and women kneeling as I walked through the rows, my heart was racing in my throat. Any of them could hurt me. It wouldn't even take an armed guard to strike me down as I passed by within touching range.

None of them dared.

A smirk almost stole itself onto my lips as Cyrill's words replayed in my head: *Saints aren't for touching, Sanja.*

It took a minute to cross the room in this dress, a dignified air about me that I didn't quite feel. In the first ring, I'd learned to be invisible, to blend into crowds for the few times I'd left the sick house. But here—here, I had to become Sanja the princess once more. And something more. So I braved the final strides until I reached the guards and placed a slow and utterly harmless hand on one of their shoulders.

"The Guardians see your service to our king," I said to the man who eyed me with both upset and the same awe I'd found in the nobles' eyes. But not the devotion of the poor.

Applying the slightest pressure, I indicated for him to kneel.

Guardians bless the man, he let go of the woman he had been restraining and lowered himself to his knees. As did the peasants and the other guards, and the men and women behind them, out the door to the very end of the hallway where the front door was wide open, revealing the view on a line reaching far out into the streets. My legs wobbled for a moment at the expectations hanging in the air, the reverence, the *lie*.

It was then that I realized that Cyrill might have trapped me. But I had power within my cage. And I would do anything I could to use that power, even in the smallest of ways, so I could build toward the day I'd break free and rid the world of Cyrill Tenikos and his cruelty.

With a smile, I turned to the women in sand-colored linens, their faces half-hidden in scarfs the way mine had been mere days ago, and said for everyone to hear, "The Guardians be with you when you walk from these halls. They shall keep your safety and that of the ones you love in their gentle hands until the day you step before them."

A tear ran down the woman's cheek—the one who'd shouted for my blessing.

Bile rose in my throat at how, by playing along with Cyrill's plan, even if it was to save them, I had made them pawns in a game of my own.

TEN

I was lying on the settee, hand on the pillow where I'd hidden my Mage Stone and thoughts circling. Cyrill had escorted me back to my room after my performance in the throne room, the guard who'd bowed following closely.

Even though he'd complimented me on the nerve to walk through the crowd and my *skillful* convincing of them that I truly was the saint he wanted them to believe I was, he hadn't allowed me to see Leahnie. The conversation had ended with him ignoring my question when I'd see her if not that day.

Now, I was waiting. For what, I didn't know. Three days had passed with no more events—at least, none I was invited to. The handmaiden with the limp, the one who'd told me about my mother, had returned with a bruised jaw to match my own healing one, and I wondered if that had been Cyrill's punishment for me ignoring his summons the other day.

A glance at the table informed me that my dinner had long gone cold, the steam formerly rising above the bowl of plain soup dissolved while I'd been pondering my options.

The Mage Stone hadn't shown as much as a flicker of magic, and I hadn't dared ask the handmaiden if she knew how to get a Mage Stone to work. Without someone to actually help me use it, I'd be one tiny crystal necklace richer and had one magical weapon poorer.

At least, over the past days, my head had stopped aching, and the layer of makeup on my face had lightened, the bruise fading now to a cluster of yellowish streaks.

Cyrill had checked in every day to *keep an eye on his saint*, as he'd called it. But he hadn't shared his plans. However, the permanent smirk on his face and those knowing eyes that assessed me with an eagerness—not for my body but for the access to power I provided—gave him away.

Spending so much time alone with myself gave me plenty of opportunity to slip back into the dark corners of my mind where guilt was eating away at me—and I did have so much more reason than even a week ago. Wherever Zelia and Dimar were, I hoped it was far, far away from the palace. And Tristan...

I wrapped my arms around the pillow, pressing it to my chest, and allowed my tears to fall freely for the first time since our return from Askarea.

All of it—my running and enduring the fairies. It had been for nothing. Even finding my family had caused only more pain, more people to lose. And I had lost them once more.

And the worst of it, perhaps, finding love. Opening my heart to someone who could be taken from me as easily as the fairy king had. But this time, not even an immortal malice had been necessary to separate us. My chest ached to feel his heartbeat. My entire body ached for him, for his touch, his tender arms. Yet, every part of me hoped he'd never come close again if only to keep him out of Cyrill's reach.

I was about to let myself fall into the abyss of guilt entirely and vanish there until sleep swept me away when light footsteps sounded in the room.

I jerked to my feet, pillow tumbling from my arms as I reached for a knife that wasn't there.

"You should know better than to be surprised by my entrance, Sanja," the fairy prince said from the other side of the coffee table, eyes assessing me with hard gold.

Air rushed from my lungs in what could have been relief or exasperation as I let myself fall back onto the settee, shoving the pillow under my head. "It's you."

"It's me," he echoed, not moving an inch as his gaze wandered the length of my body all the way to my bare feet.

I rolled my eyes and turned my back to him. I wasn't in the mood for whatever games he was playing. Not with my heart raw and my thoughts jumbled. Deciding that he wouldn't disappear if I engaged in conversation, I ignored him.

"Aren't you going to ask me what I want?" Humor rang in his words, but he didn't sound half as amused as the last time he'd spoken to me.

I didn't even shake my head, instead allowing silent tears to continue streaming down my cheeks now that there was no immediate danger. And if Recienne believed I needed to die, perhaps I should welcome it. Facing him or not wouldn't make a difference when it came to the fairy prince.

"No smart words today, *Saint Sanja*?" The soft rustling of fabric told me that he was moving, but I didn't care to turn and watch what he was doing until, with a sigh, he perched at the edge of the settee, eyes heavy on me.

I didn't turn to face him but simply pulled my legs farther in so there was no chance I'd be touching him.

"Sanja." His voice was velvet and night, and something rough that reminded me not of the elaborate prince but of the bandit whom I'd given my name and who had full control over me if he so pleased.

"Go away." I wiped my eyes with my sleeve, wondering if, for once, he'd listen.

A chuckle told me he wouldn't. "I must say, Sanja, for a minute, you had me worried." He ran a hand through his hair, tilting back his head as he assessed the ceiling. "Anyway. I thought I'd do you a favor and check in before Cyrill springs the news on you."

Whatever it was about this fairy, even with my tears and emotions running high, he found a way to get me curious. Not that I'd ever admit it.

So I bit my tongue as I sat up and slid into the corner farthest away from him where I wound my arms around my pulled-up legs.

"When did you start doing me favors?"

"Perhaps, I feel gracious today." He angled his head, so he was gazing down at me with one sparking golden eye.

"You're a real bastard. You know that, right?"

He snorted, lips quirking in a way that revealed a hint of what may have lain behind the bandit's mask had he ever taken it off in the forest.

I felt my own lips do something at the gesture but clamped them into a tight line as I caught myself. So did Recienne.

"Not very creative, are you?" His features smoothed into a bored expression. "If you want to wound me, you'll need to come up with better insults."

Oh, I had insults. An entire queue of them. Ready to hurl them at him, I opened my lips, but a dark power snaked around my jaw, gently holding it in place so I couldn't release even one of them.

Ass. Prick. Son of a—

"I'll give you all the time in the world to call me names, Sanja, if you listen to me now." Something about the way his brows knitted together as he leaned forward, bracing one hand on the backrest of the settee, the way his chest heaved once as if to bring back a thought he'd accidentally let slip, made my blood still. His features turned hard as stone as he brought his face level with mine, voice a cold caress. "You need to watch your every move in the palace, Princess. Every last step, every last breath. I can't protect you here the way I can in my own lands."

His words registered, but my mouth was reluctant to open even when he'd released my jaw.

What he'd implied—

All warmth left my body as I unfolded my legs to brace my feet on the cool marble while he studied me with silent expectation—for what, I couldn't tell.

But the cold was replaced by a hot anger that I hadn't felt in a long, long while. "Protect me?" I shot to my feet, nearly colliding with his head as I turned to the side to face him. "Protect me, Recienne? That's what you think you did?"

His eyes widened a fraction.

But that didn't stop me. "You did not protect me in Ask-area, Prince, or I'd never have been summoned to the palace for Ret Relah." That first arrival in the royal residence in Aceleau rushed through my mind—the beautiful gardens, the fairy king, the males dragging me away from the celebrations. And *him* showing up in my path when I'd run. "Had you been protecting me, you would have never sent me back inside. You would have never allowed your father to take them and lock them up." Zelia, Dimar, and Tristan. My heart throbbed at the mere thought of them in cages, of Tristan's hopeless gaze when I'd made the bargain with the king. "You wouldn't have stood by—"

"I did what I could—" He stopped himself, realizing he was defending himself, and smoothed his jacket down his chest.

My eyes followed his fingers, the planes visible under his touch—and I looked away.

"I hate you."

With a startlingly effortless laugh, Recienne leaped to his feet. "Finally."

Because everything will be easier when you hate me again. His words from the forest shot through me, anger guttering at the sound of his laugh—a laugh that was cut off by a clearing of his throat.

"Remember to hate me the next time you see me, Sanja."

I didn't get to tell him that I didn't care to ever see him again when he dissolved into mist and wind.

The next day, I was summoned by Cyrill early in the morning. The elderly handmaiden was the one to dab a thin layer of makeup over the remains of my bruise, her own not yet half-faded. She didn't as much as glance at me when I tried to ask her if there was anything I could do for her. Instead, she shook her head, wincing when she opened her mouth to speak.

"Play your role, Princess Sanja. It is all you can do for now."

I watched her through the mirror at the vanity, her tired eyes, her drawn features. She'd been suffering because of me, as had Leahnie.

"Tell me more about my mother," I requested, keeping myself from pushing her even when every last part of me ached to learn what had happened.

The woman nodded after we both checked over our shoulders for anything suspicious at the door or the window. Nothing.

"What do you want to know?"

"Who poisoned her?"

The woman shook her head. "I don't know for certain, but there are theories."

Theories... Everything in my life had become vague, even death.

"Does Cyrill have anything to do with it?" It was a long shot, but it wouldn't surprise me if he did.

"Cyrill was a little boy playing in the streets of Brolli when your mother was killed, Sanja." She flapped a hand over her mouth. "Princess Sanja," she corrected. "I apologize."

It was I who shook her head this time. "Don't worry about the title. I've spent enough time in the first ring to sometimes forget I'm a princess." And no longer in Askarea, but I didn't add that.

"And now you're a saint."

I didn't say yes or no, but the look in her eyes as she met mine through the mirror spoke volumes about her opinion on the matter.

"What may I call you?" I asked her, unable to forget how little a name meant here in Cezux where it didn't grant anyone power or control.

"Erju."

"That's a beautiful name." It was.

"Thank you." She stopped the sponge at the side of my jaw. "Your mother said the same thing once. She confided in me a lot of things, Sanja. One of those things being her magic. A Mage in Jezuin—" She continued her work, checking for spots she'd missed. "Magic was banned then the way it is now."

"And Mages exiled," I added what Zelia had once told me.

"Exiled or killed." Sadness filled her face, and she laid the sponge down on the vanity, her free hand already reaching for a comb. "Your mother and father were a perfect pair. A marriage of love until, one day—" She glanced over her shoulder again as if expecting someone to be waiting there with a sword to slice off her head.

"It's fine," I told her. "I won't share your secret."

"You won't, but who knows how Cyrill learns all the news in this palace. He's been relentless in both knowing everything and controlling the situation since you disappeared—and I'm saying disappeared because you never truly died, Sanja. Not if Dimar was the one driving the knife into your side."

Words failed me, not because she knew but because, had I been not fully convinced that she wasn't Cyrill's spy, now all doubts would be erased. She knew, and she spoke to me about risking Cyrill's wrath when she'd already been punished.

"Your father found out that your mother had a frequent male visitor in her chambers—a Mage. Of course, the king suspected her even when there was nothing physical about their relationship. It was about something much worse than that. When your mother finally confided in her husband, the rumors had already spread that she was with child by the stranger. But your father knew better. He had someone follow the Mage and kill him to prevent the truth from coming out—to protect his wife. But the truth had leaked into the king's council, and there was nothing he could do when they slipped poison into her meal to keep that Mage-child from ever being born." She paused her combing, measuring my face with mild eyes. "I'm sorry Sanja. I'm so, so sorry. It was long after her death when I noticed the new boy in the king's guard—the one with the same rich eyes and lean build. The one who hunted you and brought you back when you ran from your wedding. The one who *killed* you at Cyrill's command. The Mage's son. A Mage himself."

I didn't think my heart was beating as I listened, eager to not miss even one syllable. Dimar's father. My arms ached to wrap around my cousin. To tell him I was sorry. And Zelia—

The woman continued her combing and braiding. "I never confronted him, glad for the rumors to end, for the truth about your mother never being brought to light. But it also meant keeping my secret. With Queen Noa's death and Dimar gone, you're the only Mage left in Cezux, Sanja. How we had been hoping to see you on the throne one day, and I even understood when Dimar brought you back, no matter how bad of a man Cyrill was. It meant you'd remain in our lands to be crowned one day. No one could have expected what would happen. That Cyrill would order everyone's death at the wedding, that with your reappearance, he would cover his tracks and fake your resurrection." She sighed, chest heaving heavily as if she'd freed herself of a burden. "And, no matter how bad he is to us... No matter the bruises and beatings, no matter the days in the dungeons when he's displeased with his supper—you're back. And if you're anything like Noa, you will find a way to bring him down."

She had relieved herself of a burden by sharing her knowledge; the weight now settled on my shoulders where it pushed like lead, making it heavy to breathe. I remembered my parents as loving and caring—at least my mother. Father had changed after her death and that had led to the arranged marriage with Cyrill which had started all of this messy *saint* business I was stuck in.

Erju... She was relying on me—just like the people in the first ring were relying on me. If not for my healing skills, then for my blessings as a saint, as someone to bring a better life for them. A sign that the Guardians hadn't forgotten Cezux.

The weight of responsibility crashed down on my shoulders as I was once more reminded how little I truly had to give while I was trapped in this palace at Cyrill's mercy, and I rose to my feet, barely making it out of her grasp and to the bathing room where I dipped my face in cold water to wash the panic away.

Cyrill awaited me in a carriage, his usual white suit impeccable and his dark eyes burning with delight as he watched me lift my skirts to my knees so I was able to climb the two small steps into the cabin to sit as far away from him as I could in the limited space.

"You look better by the day, Sanja," he said by way of good morning the moment the door closed behind me.

I ignored his greeting, Erju's words still swirling in my mind. And the guilt in my stomach hit full force.

"I might even reconsider not touching my saint," he drawled on.

I didn't deign to look at him.

"I'm playing your saint, Cyrill, because you have threatened me, not because I'm enjoying it." The burning lump of my conscience made it easy to ignore the danger he posed.

Cyrill pointed past me at the riders accompanying the carriage as we rolled out the gates. "We're leaving the palace today. But, besides my usual guards, there are archers with us. One wrong step and—"

"I die. I know." I didn't care if I was polite—not when there was no one to witness it.

"Good." He nodded to himself while I did my best to see past the lace curtains. "Since your grand success in the throne room, I thought we might bring more of the lowest in this realm to their knees with faith rather than steel."

More lying, more smiling and pretending.

I swallowed the urge to empty my stomach again.

Cyrill leaned in to study me from up close, his eyes dark pits with a direct connection to the gods' realm of punishment. "What's wrong, my dear? I thought you were rather fond of those lowly creatures. Or would you rather I did use my sword to silence their objections to my coronation? After the injuries you've treated in your little sick house, you should know very well where that leads."

I pressed back into my seat, bringing as much distance between us as possible, and held his gaze. "No steel."

He laughed, a melodious sound that brought back memories of the banquets at court, the politics and tactics of the courtiers' games. For some reason, Recienne's eyes flashed before me, the way he'd acted around his father, ever the obedient prince when, in truth, he was the most powerful fairy in Askarea.

I forced my gaze back to the window where the houses turned smaller with every street we descended from the first ring. Smaller and more humble, until we crossed the gate into the fourth ring where the streets weren't buzzing with activity the way I remembered it. Where smiles and barter had defined the streets mere months ago, now there was a caution to the way people engaged that had Cyrill's name written all over it. An effect of his threats, his way of depriving my people of even the most basic of things by taking their coins and their homes and their families.

What few were outside their houses were rushing from point to point, glancing over their shoulders and meeting others with distrust—it was in their faces, in the way coins changed hands in the market, where the carriage rolled along with little care for who had to leap out of our path to avoid being run over. In a way, it reminded me of Aceleau—only with less beauty and more poverty. Where fairies would have represented the carriage, the people in the streets would have been the humans. Not coveted like humans by fairies but treated as scum in the way the fairy king had treated me like scum. Like I'd taken something from him and he could wring it out of me to take it back.

We arrived in a small square not far from the sick house. I even recognized the low, narrow houses and the signs pointing into the side streets toward the few stores in this part of the city.

Cyrill climbed out the opening door, offering his hand to me like a true king the moment we had an audience.

"Time to meet the people you care so much about, Saint Sanja." He waited for me to collect my skirts and stumble down the steps, hand remaining extended despite my ignoring it.

The sun was climbing in the east, cutting the fourth ring of the city and the palace into the sky like a fairytale. The smell of dirt and rotten waste in the backyards and on corners assaulted me now that I wasn't wearing a scarf like during my time at the sick house, and I wondered how Cyrill could take everything from the people. Cyril's guards had spread out around the little square, forming a protective ring around their king and the saint he was presenting to a both curious and reluctant crowd.

Trying not to shout at my husband with the fury of the Guardians as he gave me a royal smile, I straightened and smoothed out my dress once more. "What am I supposed to do?"

"You know ... wave, smile, mumble your lovely prayers." He looped his arm into mine, pulling me along as the guards framed us, securing a corridor through the gathering crowd.

Though wary of the royal carriage, people were curious enough to stop and take a look at what was happening.

A few months ago, they would have waved at the carriage, would have stopped to curtsey or bow. How much had changed, and not for the better.

"Make them kneel, Sanja. For the saint and then for me." His whisper followed me like a set of claws on my neck as we approached the center of the square.

It was there that the murmurs started. "So it is true."—"The princess is alive."—"Not alive, resurrected. Haven't you heard? The Guardians brought her back."—"They say she spent months wandering the streets, without knowing who she is."—"My uncle visited the sick house where she tended to the ill and wounded."

I ignored the sickening feeling that I was a living lie, that whatever seed Cyrill had sewn into their minds about my sainthood was coming to fruition as they recognized me.

"Saint Sanja!" Shouts erupted from the back of the crowd. "Saint Sanja!"

Shuddering with every shout anew, I forced my gait to remain even, my hands steady.

I'd survived Askarea, I reminded myself. I could survive this.

I could—but how many of those praising me as a saint would survive the hunger Cyrill's reign would bring over these lands? How many would end up fighting anyway, only to be killed by his relentless guards?

"The king!" Someone shouted, and I could feel the tremble run through Cyrill's arm as he was noticed at my side, chest swelling with the ridiculous pride of the vain. "King Cyrill and Saint Sanja."

I swallowed my nausea, the crowd blurring before my eyes as Cyrill stopped us in front of the tallest building in the square and the people circled closer, eyes following my every move—like the fairies in the fairy gardens when I'd clawed at the Mage Stones, desperate to destroy our only way out of there. The fairy king's silver gaze awaiting my failure—my death. No, worse. He'd wanted me to live, to make me *his* so my throne would be his as well and he'd no longer need a placeholder on the Cezuxian throne.

"Saint Sanja!" A familiar voice caught my attention like a beacon in the night, and my head snapped to the side, finding him at the back of the crowd, half hidden by guards and peasants alike, but he was there.

My chest tightened, tears burning at the back of my throat that I couldn't risk releasing.

Tristan—

So far away I could barely make out his features. He was towering over a group of women, still in his travel shirt and hair tossed to the side by either the breeze or a morning of running his hand through it.

My feet itched to run to him, to safety, to the familiarity of his embrace, to crush my lips against his and drown there. But I forced my gaze back to the sandy ground where my eyes couldn't betray the flicker of hope that had ignited inside my chest at the sound of his voice, his presence, even so far away. He'd come for me, had returned from his errands and not bolted to save himself but remained in this Cyrill-cursed city to find me.

I couldn't stop a tear from falling into the dirt where it evaporated like a memory of something that never had been meant to be mine.

"Speak to them, Sanja," Cyrill ordered in the same quiet command as in the throne room.

ELEVEN

"Speak." Cyrill's command slithered down my neck, but my throat was tight with fear of glancing up and finding Tristan gone—or finding him still there with a guard's blade at his neck. "Now."

All right. I heaved a breath, stealing a glance at the back of the crowd where Tristan had called from.

My entire body trembled when I spotted him a few people farther toward the edge, towering over a patch of kneeling peasants who were mumbling prayers.

I see you, Tristan, I wanted to shout. *Get me out of here.*

But even if he could, others would suffer for it. And he couldn't get into harm's way, or he'd be the one suffering the most.

My chest ached at how easy it would be to march up to the people the way I'd done in the throne room, to let them scramble aside to let their saint pass. I'd have a path to my Mage in no time. But what then?

All it would do would be to draw attention to one more thing Cyrill could use against me.

It cost all my hard-earned self-control to lift my hands at my sides, palms facing upwards as if to receive the Guardians' blessing, and mumble something resembling a prayer. The shouts in the crowd stopped, more falling to their knees as Cyrill bowed his head as if in reverence in the presence of the saint.

In the front rows, half hidden behind the guards encircling us, a man was sobbing at the sight of me. "Saint Sanja," he called. "Help me."

My head snapped toward him, the desperation in his tone enough to put everything inside of me on high alert.

From the corner of my eye, I noticed Tristan shift toward the tall building at the edge of the square.

"Please, Saint Sanja. My wife's dying," the man continued.

The guard closest to him shoved down his head with a rough hand.

I winced at the mere sight of it and couldn't help but move closer.

Cyrill hissed a warning, but the man's plea was like a summons.

Murmurs ran through the crowd at my cautious, tiny step that was a clear indication I was willing to listen, to aid if I could—the way I had in the sick house.

"Let him speak," Cyrill commanded, appearing at my side with a self-satisfied grin on his lips as he pretended to be the merciful king he wasn't even if he wrapped his wretched character in gold and diamonds and dipped it in the sacred waters by the Horn of Eroth.

The guard stepped aside, hand on his sword, not leaving the kneeling man out of his sight for even a second as Cyrill led me closer.

"It's not like I'm a real saint who can heal with her mere touch," I muttered to him under my breath.

Cyrill gave me a beatific look that made me want to claw his eyes out.

But, the archers were following swiftly along the side of the square, arrows nocked and pointing toward us so skillfully that no one would realize they weren't here to protect me but to keep me in check when I could easily dive into the crowd and run—or could I?

My legs were fine, my head no longer affected by the brutal fall on the street. But I was shackled by that stupid dress, and Cyrill's grasp around my arm was like iron even when he was leading me along gracefully like the monarch he wanted to be.

A few feet from the pleading man, we stopped. Where there had been shouts and chants before, now, the square had fallen silent like a grave as all eyes were on me, all ears straining to catch a hint of that blessing I was about to speak.

"What does your wife suffer from?" I asked, keeping my expression empty while every part of me screamed to turn around and check for Tristan. He must have been near the carriage by now, and if he wasn't careful—

"She has been ill for months, Saint Sanja." The man gazed up at me with hopeful eyes, and I wanted to tell him what a fraud I was, that I could do nothing to help her. But Cyrill's hand shifted to the small of my back, a silent reminder that he was there, listening.

So I swallowed and extended a hand. The man hobbled forward, one of his legs not fully supporting his weight as if from an old injury. He kneeled in front of me, carefully grabbing my hand and placing a kiss on the back of my palm, weeping.

Beside him, the guard was watching closely, sword half-drawn.

I held up my other hand, gesturing to keep that blade where it was.

"The Guardians sometimes have plans for us that we cannot comprehend." It was all I could think of to say to him that wasn't a lie.

Kissing my palm once more, the man pressed his forehead to my wrist, his tears soaking my sleeve.

"That's enough." The guard grabbed the man's collar, pulling him away from me.

He stumbled back, ripping out of the guard's grasp, and stood frozen, wide eyes on me as he realized he was no longer favoring one of his legs.

Carefully, he took a step with his bad leg then with his good.

No wobbling, no grimacing—only wonder.

"I'm healed," he whispered, his words so loud in my ears as their meaning hit.

Healed. I hadn't done a thing other than try to console him about his wife's condition.

"Guardians-blessed," he said, taking a few more steps, running in front of the crowd, the eyes of which were wandering between the man and me. Back and forth until, eventually, they remained on Saint Sanja.

And I stared, trying to comprehend how the man could be healed when I had done nothing—*nothing*.

"Heal my daughter!" A woman shouted from nearby, standing with a little girl in her arms. "She's been coughing for weeks." The woman pushed through the kneeling spectators, through the ones getting to their feet, voicing who they wanted healed, whom I should bless.

The guards braced themselves, calling the people to order, and for a moment, they halted, desperate eyes lingering on me as I backed up a step.

"Saint Sanja will return to the palace now," Cyrill said from behind me, his arm snaking around my waist as he pulled me toward the carriage. But people were breaking away from the crowd, pushing their way past the guards, who'd drawn their weapons, ready to take down anyone who came too close to their king—and the saint who'd healed an old man.

"Get into the carriage," Cyrill hissed.

From the corner of my eye, I saw Tristan's tall frame slip behind the carriage just as I was shoved through the open door.

Help me, I thought at him. *Get me out of here.* For I couldn't just run. Not when the people of Jezuin would trample me in their frenzied attempt at getting my blessing—my healing. Not when my disobedience would cost Leahnie.

Catching myself on the bench inside the carriage, I peered out the window through a gap in the curtain—and spotted Tristan climbing the side of one of the lower buildings. By the Guardians, he was fast. The image of boy-Tristan climbing the roofs of Aceleau and curling up behind puffing chimneys so as not to freeze in the winters of Askarea flickered through my mind, and my heart broke a fraction for the man who had come for me, the man I so desperately wanted to hold in my arms while the rest of the world disappeared.

A scream tore my attention away from his skilled ascend. Cyrill jumped into the carriage after me, shutting the door, shouting at the driver to *go, go, go*—and a bloodied hand slapped against the window on his side of the carriage, alongside a pain-stricken face. The carriage set in motion, leaving the hand to slide in a trail of crimson fingers.

The carriage rattled across the even streets, the shouts and chants outside fading with every heartbeat. I debated just ripping the door open and dropping out onto the dirt road where Tristan might pick me up and we'd escape together.

But an archer was now riding beside the carriage, and my limbs turned into frozen attachments where I crouched by the bench.

"That went better than expected," Cyrill noted with no short amount of satisfaction.

Satisfaction that I couldn't share.

"The crowd was trying to trample us." I didn't turn to meet his gaze, too busy stealing glances past the archers at the roofs above us where I was hoping to spot Tristan's familiar face. But all I found was the glistening sunlight that seemed to be mocking me as my stomach turned into lead.

"The crowd wanted a piece of their *saint*, Sanja. Nothing more, nothing less." Cyrill shifted behind me, knee brushing my back, and I whirled on my toes, shooting up and tumbling back onto the bench across from where he sat, smirking. "An impressive show, Sanja. But what else should I have expected? You managed to pretend to be dead, after all." He leaned across the gap between us, his pale features and dark eyes and hair more stark in the sunlight filtering in through the curtains. "Tell me, how did he get you out of the palace?"

"Who?" I wanted to know, cursing myself for reacting so promptly—as if I had something to hide.

Cyrill's face froze over. "The Mage who was supposed to kill you."

Dimar—

I had to bite my tongue to not speak Dimar's name. Cyrill knew. And it didn't matter how he'd learned the truth. Only that Dimar was not safe in this city. Or anywhere Cyrill's reach extended to—which was all of Cezux.

Sending a quick prayer to those Guardians who'd supposedly blessed me that Zelia and Dimar had made it far, far, far beyond the borders by now, I swallowed all and any words lingering on my tongue—including those curses.

"What—nothing to say, Sanja? And there I thought your time with the King of Askarea had taught you some things."

I couldn't help a shudder, and Cyrill read in my eyes that the fear was paralyzing me enough that, in that moment, he could have done anything.

"Cezux and Askarea have had strained relations for a long, long time, Sanja. But with our new pact, there is a chance for ... something more." Greed flickered in his eyes. Greed and that hunger for power that I'd seen in the fairy king's silver gaze before.

It cost all my courage to speak the words, "You are a fool for getting into bed with the fairy king, Cyrill. He might have promised you the throne, but it will never be truly yours." Maybe, if I was lucky, he wouldn't know what had happened in Aceleau—that, together with the Mage who never truly killed me and the Master Mage of Aceleau, I'd helped slay the fairy king. That the male he'd bargained with was no longer around to collect his throne.

But the knowing glint in Cyrill's eyes was enough to make me bite my tongue once more.

"Well, how lucky that His Majesty is visiting Jezuin to prove you wrong, Saint Sanja." His words clanged through my bones like a clap of thunder.

He didn't speak another word for the rest of the ride back. Only when we arrived at the palace did he extend a hand to help me out of the carriage, a victorious grin blooming on his lips as he waited for me to climb out after him.

"Go to your room, Sanja." He gestured for an archer to escort me. "Because you've been so ... successful today, I'll send your friend up to clothe you for the banquet tonight."

"Banquet?" I hadn't meant to ask, but Cyrill met my gaze with a cruel one of his own.

"In honor of our returned queen and saint." He dismissed me with a wave of his hand, and I didn't look back as I finally had the chance to get away from him.

Leahnie joined me a few hours later, her face tight with tension and her hands shaking as she curtseyed.

"Thank the Guardians, you're all right." I rushed toward her, almost tripping in my stupid dress, and flung my arms around her neck, crushing her to my chest. "Did he hurt you?"

I let go of her to look her over, checking her bare arms and neck for injuries and finding none.

Leahnie eyed me with a caution I'd never noticed on her. "Is it true?" She adjusted her plain servant's dress at the shoulder.

"Is what true?"

She gestured for me to take a seat at the vanity, and I obeyed, knowing that, if I didn't, she would be the one to pay for my delayed arrival at the throne room where I was to appear in less than an hour's time. One of the guards in front of my room was kind enough to inform me of the requirement upon my arrival.

I'd spent the afternoon pondering what had happened with the man, if the Guardians *had* somehow worked through my touch and eased the man's pain, while I'd twisted the Mage Stone between my fingers, waiting for something to happen. I'd taken a short bath to rinse off the dust from the streets before I'd resorted to standing at the window and watching for any sign of Tristan, both hoping and fearing he'd come to the palace. One moment with him—it was all I needed. One moment to kiss him, to feel him, to convince myself he was real, that it hadn't been a dream and I'd never truly left Jezuin.

"The healing, Sanja. Did you truly heal a man?" Leahnie's eyes sparked with fascination, the initial wariness wiped away as more of my friend shone through.

I shrugged. "Who knows? Maybe his own faith healed him." He hadn't even asked for his own healing but that of his wife. Why the Guardians had chosen him instead, I had yet to understand.

"Or Cyrill is right after all, and you are a saint."

I almost snorted at the suggestion but reined in the urge before I could give her a reason to doubt, to put her in more danger than she already was for merely being my friend. For she couldn't be my confidante.

"Where did he keep you?" I asked instead, steering the conversation away from myself. "The dungeons?"

Leahnie's gaze met mine through the mirror, dark eyes haunted. "I had no idea how truly dark it could get down there..." She pursed her full lips, the gesture making her young face appear older.

My chest ached at the thought of her locked up in the darkness for days.

"He only came today to tell me I was a reward for your obedience." She sucked in a breath as if realizing she'd spoken something she wasn't supposed to.

"It's all right, Leahnie." I reached for her hand on my shoulder where she was pulling my hair from my braid. "I know you have noticed I'm not here out of my free will. If not before, then since he took you to the dungeons to have something to pressure me into obedience."

Her throat bobbed, swallowing words not meant to be spoken.

I couldn't help but turn on the stool and look up at her, taking both her hands into mine. "Much has changed since my father died, Leahnie."

She crouched in front of me, tears collecting in her eyes. "They didn't let me see you when you were sick. Cyrill was the only one to enter your room—and the priest. They were hoping for some sort of miraculous healing."

I almost laughed out loud. If she knew.

"I never actually saw you sick, or dead. And when Dimar returned—" Her cheeks flushed the slightest bit at the mention of his name. "The way I knew something wasn't right was because he never spoke of you as if you were dead. He was gone only for a day after the wedding, but it was enough for me to notice something was wrong."

"You and Dimar are close?" It slipped from my mouth, my mind focusing on the only fact not relevant to my staged death.

"Not like that..." Leahnie's gaze lowered to our joined hands, lips quirking the slightest bit. "It started a few weeks before the wedding," she admitted, and my heart did a tiny leap at this news. "Nothing ever happened, but sometimes, when he was on duty in front of your doors, we'd talk. You know ... just talk about nothing in particular. Just spend time together." A tear dripped from her lashes. "He hasn't returned from his trip to your sick house. Out of three men, one returned, and it wasn't him." Her eyes snapped to mine, fear flashing behind those tears. "Tell me that he's not dead."

What should I tell her? That he was on the run? That he was the one who'd helped me at the wedding and at the sick house again? That he was on my side and that of his family rather than on Cyrill's? That he was only truly loyal to the Mages?

I shook my head, that being the only response I allowed myself.

Leahnie read it the way I intended, relief relaxing her features, but her gaze remained serious, her voice hushed as she said, "I know that something is very, very wrong, Sanja, and don't try to protect me by sparing me the truth. Cyrill has already shown his true self the day after your wedding." She pulled her hand from mine to rub her wrist where, mercifully, no new bruise was blooming. "You escaped. Somehow, you escaped Cyrill, and Dimar was involved. So was something more that led to those glimmering freckles he's been trying to mask with makeup."

Leahnie had been so much more observant than I had ever given her credit for. And Dimar—he might have been a poor spy. Or made a mistake by getting close to someone who cared so much about my well-being that she'd start questioning everything.

"But I thought you believed Cyrill's story—the saint..."

"You are not a saint, Sanja. No offense." A bitter smile appeared on her lips. "And you've never been obedient to anyone, not even your father. You had to be dragged back to your wedding and forced into your wedding clothes. I wouldn't be surprised if Cyrill is playing a new game to force your hand."

She had no idea how right she was about all of it—and how her life would end if Cyrill ever learned about her suspicions.

I gave her a knowing look. "Whatever you think happened, keep it to yourself, Leahnie. Don't talk to anyone else about it." It was all I could say so as to not rouse her defiance. She'd already suffered enough because of me. I couldn't give Cyrill any more reason to punish her.

Something inside my stomach stirred at the thought of what had happened to Erju, the servant who knew all about my mother and my family history.

"The woman who tended to me while you were gone..." I started but let my voice trail away when I realized bringing attention to her might be another way of making Cyrill aware of just how dangerous her knowledge was.

"Erju?" Leahnie's face filled with horror. "She was found dead this morning after—" She stopped herself as if she'd shared a secret.

"After what?" The woman had just helped me dress this morning. And now—

"After you left the palace."

My heart kicked into a gallop. "How? Why?" I didn't truly need the why, for there could only be one reason, and that was Cyrill silencing her.

"Slit her own throat, they say."

My stomach turned at her words.

"But I don't believe it. Just like I don't believe you were dead and resurrected, Sanja. Something different is going on here, and Erju knew the truth. And now she's dead."

A knock on the door stunned us both into silence.

I hadn't fully turned to face it when it opened to reveal the sight of a young servant carrying a dress. "For you, Saint Sanja, from King Cyrill."

Searching for words, I motioned for her to leave it on the chair by the door where she dropped it before, with a curtsey, she disappeared and closed the door behind her.

Leahnie and I shared a look, both our breaths flowing from us with hesitant relief, but we didn't speak another word.

TWELVE

My feet moved with surprising ease in the monstrosity of a ball gown I'd been stuffed into. A loose layer of purple velvet covered me from collarbone to ankles, not so different from the white dresses Cyrill had insisted on before. But this one was flaring toward the bottom, allowing long strides in a way I hadn't been able to make since I entered the palace.

Leahnie and I hadn't dared to speak any more of Cyrill or the truth after the servant had interrupted us with the dress. Instead, her efforts had gone into making me presentable. Now, my lips were painted with a subdued berry blush, and my hair was pinned to the back of my head, no strands hanging loose. She'd refrained from framing my eyes with kohl the way she'd have done had I been *only* a queen—probably to keep the image of purity. Not that anyone had handed me a crown. I tried not to frown as I descended the stairs, followed, not by one archer but two this time.

Of course—in this dress, I could run, and Cyrill was prepared to catch me with an arrow before I made it three steps. What he'd tell *his* people if his saint was killed in her own palace, I didn't even want to think about. He'd surely make up a new lie to cover the old ones. Blame someone and have them executed, perhaps.

My mouth tightened into a thin line at the lovely music filling the hallway, announcing what awaited me in the throne room.

Not so long ago, I'd attended a different banquet—a fateful one where the fairy king had decided he wanted me in his possession and where the fairy prince had first used his control over me. A shudder worked itself through my body, up my spine, to the top of my head, where it made the roots of my trapped hair tingle. Trapped like the rest of me.

"Keep walking," one of the archers said, and I realized I'd stopped at the bottom of the stairs, feet frozen at the prospect of what would await me in the room at the end of the hall: more spectators, more people wanting *something* from me—be it my silence, my pretending, my *blessing*.

The tip of the arrow poked into the bare skin of my neck, startling me back into motion before I could inhale a steadying breath, and I didn't stop until I made it to the threshold where, at my appearance, all music stopped, and Cyrill rushed to hold out a gracious hand to receive me at his side.

With a warning look from Cyrill, the archers blended into the over twenty guards stationed around the room, their bows ready.

The assembly of people bowed and curtseyed, some whispering the way they had at the audience in this very room a few days ago. But no one cried and chanted the way the people in the first ring had.

Clasping my hands before my waist to keep them from shaking, I made my way forward, one step at a time. Finery and jewels sparked one corner as people rose at Cyrill's sign, and at the center of the room, right before the throne... I swallowed my nausea as I noticed the wide space that had been left free of tables to form a dance floor.

Not a banquet, a ball. Sweat broke out on my forehead at the mere thought of dancing.

I'd made it halfway to my husband when, at the edge of the standing crowd, I noticed a tall, dark figure—dark, except for those golden eyes fixing me with a bored gaze.

"Hello, Sanja," his voice carried toward me on a dark breeze, sweeping past my cheek, caressing the shell of my ear—and I had to bite my lip to not turn and run from the room at the coldness of his tone, the anger turning his eyes solid for a fraction of a second before he strolled to the back of the crowd, not heeding any of the nobles a look as they scrambled from his path, eager to get away from the fairy in their midst. I knew it then that, this time, he wasn't in my head. He was very much real, and the hatred in my heart flared as if his mere presence had stoked it with new embers.

I forced my eyes back to Cyrill's black gaze, wondering if taking an arrow might be a better option than taking his hand and allowing him to show me around like a prize pony. *His saint.*

"You look beautiful," Cyrill said to me for everyone to hear, and his words slithered down my back like an icy hand. He leaned in, grasping my shaking fingers and tugging me to his side before leading me toward the center of the room—the dance floor. "Sinful for a saint."

Music started, covering what had sounded like a growl at the back of the room. I didn't deign to turn my head for Prince Recienne, who seemed to be officially attending this banquet.

Something inside me—some little piece had hoped that perhaps there had been more to him than the cruel prince he'd been in his father's court. But his words floated back into my mind—*Remember to hate me the next time you see me, Sanja*—and that *something* crumbled.

"Do you like it, Sanja?" Cyrill wanted to know when he found me staring at the long table at the side of the room where Cezuxian specialties had been prepared, sitting with colorful decorations on gilded porcelain. Meats and fruit, and—my hands quivered in his—violets atop a sugar-coated cake.

"The King of Askarea mentioned you particularly loved violets," he murmured, following the direction of my gaze.

Of course, he had. It wasn't a surprise—at all—even when I couldn't tell how he'd looked into my mind to know what the flesh-eating plant had shown me in the maze, how it had used my childhood memories to make me hallucinate, lure me in—

"It's ... beautiful." I had to pause between words to swallow the bile collecting in my throat.

"Liar," Recienne's voice carried to me on that dark wind again, caressing my neck this time. "Pretty little liar."

I ignored him, locking my gaze back on Cyrill's as he swayed me into a dance.

My heart hammered in my throat, against my chest, feet aching with phantom pain of a night I'd danced through my shoes, had not dared stop even when I'd left bloody traces on the marble of the grand hall of the fairy palace, for fear of failing at my challenge to free one of my Mages. Whether Cyrill knew what it did to me, what I'd suffered through, I couldn't tell.

But there was one person in this room who did, and he didn't lift a finger to stop this, to offer even the slightest of help the way he'd done during the trial that had freed Dimar.

Within a few steps, my head spun from panic, and I barely registered Cyrill's words as he told me the rest of the attendees were joining on the dance floor to honor this first official dance between the King and Queen of Cezux—even when he was not yet crowned. That coronation was a matter of time with Saint Sanja blessing his claim to the throne with her presence at court.

I forced my eyes to find a point in the room and fixate on it, but wherever I looked, everything was moving, swaying, sparkling with the soft light of the chandeliers blending with the hues of pink and gold of the setting sun.

Out—I needed to get out of there, or I'd scream, or vomit, or collapse right there on the marble in a shivering bundle.

Every muscle in my body cramped as Cyrill led me over the dance floor in what felt like the swaying motions of a rocky ocean. But I could no longer tell up from down and left from right as panic closed in on me, pressing against me like a wall, pushing me to fight and hop from fear that I'd stop moving. For if I stopped, people would die—people I loved would die—Tristan and Dimar and Zelia—

"What a beautiful saint." Recienne's voice was a streak of ink through the glimmering, shifting world.

Cyrill slowed, stopping while the rest of the room kept spinning.

"Very true, King Recienne," Cyrill said, and his words almost knocked the breath from my struggling lungs.

King Recienne. Not *Prince*.

My feet stopped moving, the panic caged between my ribs stilling as Recienne's chuckle touched my ear—whether it was on that cursed breeze he used to communicate with me alone or his corporeal voice, taunting me as I near-slumped in my husband's arms, I didn't care. What I cared about was that coldness spreading through me, commanding me to keep my feet still. Not words but something else—his power, perhaps, or my own fear solidifying into icy petrification.

"And how lucky a king you are to call her your own." Recienne met my gaze as he stalked around us, the music fading from my perception when all I could see were those golden eyes simmering with quiet anger.

"Lucky indeed," Cyrill purred.

"So, how about that promised dance?" His gaze didn't stray from mine, and that ice in my body turned to something else—a creature prowling beneath my skin under the scrutiny of such power, such calculated politics.

He wasn't here to help me. No. Recienne Olivier Gustine—if only I could remember the rest of his name—the Second, was here to humiliate me, to remind me of the silence he'd demanded from me.

Cyrill shrugged and slid his hand from my waist, the trace of his warmth there like an oily sheen, and placed my hand in the prince's waiting one.

Not prince—*king*. That was certainly something to get used to. And something I should have figured out long ago—when his father's blood had been hot on my hands and I'd made him king the way my father's death had made me queen.

Cyrill stepped aside—all the respect he'd offer the new fairy king who'd so thoroughly betrayed me that I couldn't even fathom how to ever stop hating him.

But that was what he'd wanted. For me to hate him. And there, he had it.

"Take your time, King Recienne," Cyrill said before he turned away. "And then we'll talk about our business."

My spine turned into a rod under Recienne's touch as he reeled me in with a charmingly light tug on my hand. I nearly staggered into his front, catching my balance, and was swept into a dance too smooth for a human ballroom.

While I seethed up at him, he merely grinned as if he was having the time of his life while still keeping his royal grace.

A royal bastard, that's what he was. I gritted my teeth at the spin he led me into, trying not to think of the last time I'd been swirled around a room in his embrace. The throbbing in my feet returned as if summoned by a silent command, causing me to miss a step and stumble to the side while he was pulling me forward with him, and I almost lost my footing.

"You make for a poor dancer in this second-rate ballroom, Sanja." His grin widened unnaturally as he pulled me upright, turning me in a slower circle. Were the people around us laughing? I couldn't tell over the droning noise in my head as Recienne pulled me on and on.

"It's not like I had a say in whether I want to dance," I threw back at him, voice wispy, and I needed to focus to not let myself fall back into the panic-induced memories of exhaustion.

"And there we've had such fun before ... you and me, on the dance floor." He winked—actually winked—at me, speeding us up again while my feet struggled to keep the new pace. At least, this velvet dress didn't trip me like the white ones. Whether that was a mercy or a curse, I couldn't tell. The white ones, at least, would have provided a perfect excuse for me to stand in a corner and not move an inch while the rest of the room entertained themselves.

"Why are you even here?" I didn't bother to keep my voice down, the music drawing out the conversations in the room well enough to not fear being overheard.

"You could at least pretend that we're having a pleasant conversation, Sanja," was all he said in response. "Your *husband* and I have business to conduct, and he believes a dance with Saint Sanja will put me in the right mood for a bargain more beneficial to him than it is to me."

The way he exposed his teeth in a smile was more predatory than *pleasant*, as he'd called it. But I didn't give him the satisfaction of asking. Not yet. Not when sweat was beading my neck and forehead and the room turned hotter and hotter with every round he led me across the dance floor, my feet moving mechanically at his lead.

Only when the dance was over, and he bowed to me like to a real queen, did I deign to acknowledge again he was actually there, and inclined my head—*pleasant* but far from docile.

The rest of the room came back into focus, and I noticed the groups of nobles standing by small tables, watching us, the couples spinning into the next dance as the music continued, and Cyrill who was already marching up to us, one hand extended toward me as if to pull me back from Recienne's grasp.

"As always, Cyrill"—Recienne omitted the title, a sign of how superior he was in power, in strength. I didn't dare think what would happen if he unleashed his magic on a room full of humans—"your entertainment has been a delight. Who would have thought a saint could dance?" The midnight chuckle that followed whipped around me on that dark breeze meant only for my ears, and the hair stood on my neck at the sound of it—at the sheer power emanating from him beneath those *pleasant* words. And the rolling anger grumbling through the air as the chuckle turned into a hint of a growl.

"Let's get to business, then." Cyrill motioned for me to sit on the carved chair next to the throne and followed me up the two steps onto the dais.

"What business?" I asked what I hadn't allowed myself to ask Recienne—the new fairy king.

The latter raised a brow as he gazed up at me as if amused that I had asked after all.

"That is for you to find out, Sanja," he said on that dark breeze while Cyrill thoroughly ignored my question and shoved a hand into his pocket.

Two guards took up posts to my left and to my right, the ones with their bows remaining at the other end of the room from where they were tracking my every motion.

"Be a good saint, Sanja." Cyrill leaned in to place a kiss on my cheek, and it took all my self-control not to shy away. A display for this court—a way of keeping Leahnie safe, all so her life wouldn't end the way Erju's had.

The shiver that ran through me was owed entirely to Cyrill's cruelty and to the sword looming over my head, ready to fall into my neck at the slightest misstep. My chest constricted, my breathing difficult as I was once more the object of everyone's attention—only, no one was laughing at me now, their eyes curious rather than amused. Even Recienne, who gave me a brief, unreadable glance before he followed Cyrill toward the corridor behind the throne room, the one leading to my father's study.

And I sat alone before a crowd of spectators, a resurrected saint, a queen without a crown, a wife who hated her husband, a lover in despair. And the grandest failure in history.

ANGELINA J. STEFFORT

THIRTEEN

The stuffy air in the banquet hall didn't help my fading focus as I tried my best to keep my attention on the brocade tapestry behind the throne, on the dancing couples, the mingling by the buffet. Anything that happened and didn't involve Cyrill was better than those lonely days in my room—or the moments when Cyrill joined me there. Following the movements of the nobles and courtiers, I studied the dynamics, catching snippets of conversations when they passed before the dais. Some halted, bowing before they continued. Some even spoke a few cautious words to the saint before them.

I didn't dare speak for fear of what Cyrill would do to anyone I showed interest in, no matter how insignificant. So I merely inclined my head at anyone who came closer and waited until they moved on. At least, I was no longer dancing. The soles of my feet were slowly recovering from the memory of being ravaged by a night of dancing, as was the rest of my body. But I didn't try to stand or walk around. Not for a long while, until the crowd at the buffet tables thinned, revealing the view on the remaining section of cakes and pies, of fruit and pastries, and meats.

Lunch had been thin, and my stomach replied with a rumble at the thought of tasting the roast or the sliced melon.

For a moment, I debated asking the guards if I was allowed to get something to eat. But I remembered my role, the minuscule power I held through what Cyrill had made me, the remains of my status at court, and gathered my courage.

They didn't hold me back when I ventured down the stairs to the buffet, picking up a small plate at the end of the table, but remained a few steps behind me like true guards rather than Cyrill's bloodhounds keeping an eye on me. I could feel the archers' eyes on my back as I turned to pick up a piece of fruit.

A woman leaped out of my way, apologizing to *Queen Sanja* first, then to *Saint Sanja*. I gave her a bland smile, turning back to what would be my dinner, when he appeared on the other side of the table, dressed in Jezuinian fashion, a brown jacket threaded with brass and adorned with buttons high up to the collar. A white shirt peeked out from between the lapels and from the seam of his sleeves as he reached for the same piece of fruit that I was reaching for.

"Apologies—" Tristan picked up the plate, offering the melon to me with a careful smile on his lips that made him seem even more surreal in this place. Had my mind registered that it was truly him? I wasn't even sure. All I could tell was how my heart was beating in a frenzy, every inch of my body coiling to either grab him over the table and just hold him or to freeze in place and not let show I'd ever seen him before. "I believe you were first."

I shook my head. "It's yours." If he was found out... If he lingered too long around the saint... that would be his certain death.

From behind me, the guards already moved closer until they flanked me with their hands on their swords.

"I insist, Saint Sanja."

Of course, he did. He was Tristan. He'd do what he thought was best for me—be it feed me or risk himself to protect me.

Still, all I could do was gape at him as his troubled blue eyes met mine with an urgency that didn't leave room for debate—until he schooled his face into that of a courtier and inclined his head. "Queen Sanja," he corrected, or added, I wasn't sure. I was no longer sure of anything other than that he was here and alive ... and so, so very foolish to seek me out right under Cyrill's nose.

As my fear was climbing in my throat, I realized that Cyrill might not have been the most dangerous creature in this palace at this very moment.

Focus, I told myself. *Breathe. Think.*

Tristan had never been in here before, and Cyrill didn't know he was a Mage or even where he was from. What he meant to me.

I swallowed the tears burning behind my eyes, the impulse to throw my arms around his neck, and all those words I wanted to speak to him yet couldn't, and slipped back into my role.

The saint who graciously accepted the plate and turned to the next piece of fruit on the table.

Tristan mirrored my motions, moving along the other side with what I hoped wasn't obvious interest.

Reckless fool. He should have run from this palace, from the fate I'd been condemned to. The Guardians had been merciful to allow me to see him once more, but he needed to leave.

I was about to say as much when I remembered that all that would do was put him in danger. So I shoveled a few small piles of meat onto my plate and turned away, everything inside of me screaming as I told myself that I could do this, that I could walk away from my Mage, who'd come for me.

One of the guards gestured to an empty small table where I obediently took a seat and started eating, the observant eyes of the crowd keeping my need to glance over my shoulder for Tristan's familiar face in check. I didn't pay attention to what I was eating, my entire focus on trying to find a way to calm my breathing, to ease that ache inside my chest that seemed to be connected to the man who was risking his own life to get to me.

From the corner of my eye, I noticed him dancing with a noblewoman in a pretty blue dress—elegant and surprisingly not out of place at this court as he spun her around.

In and out. In and out, I directed my breath, each one of them shorter than the last.

When I was done eating, I stood, wondering if I could just march out of the room and disappear or if that would earn me an arrow in my back. But Tristan was suddenly there, bowing low the way he had to Lady Whithee when he'd first taken me on his errands in Aceleau.

"I don't think we've met, Lord..." I gave him an opening, words floating from my lips as his gaze met mine, and he straightened to his full height.

"Lord Tristan, Your Majesty ... Saint Sanja." He sounded different from the Tristan I knew, smoother, like a real courtier—like he'd spent days and days practicing those words.

My stomach was so tight that I wondered how the food remained down at all.

"Lord Tristan." Good—it felt so good to speak his name even when pretending about everything else. That little moment when I was allowed to call him by his name. *Tristan.*

I hid my shiver by locking my hands in front of my belly. "What brings you here, Lord Tristan?"

"Trade, Your Majesty," he said smoothly. "But also the rumors of a saint."

Fishing for a response, I glanced at the guard to my left, who was vigilantly eyeing Tristan, marking every last detail of his clothes, his slicked-back hair, his polished shoes.

My stomach was hurting by the time Tristan bowed again, gaze lingering on mine as he asked, "Is it acceptable for a merchant lord from Tavras to ask Saint Sanja for a dance?"

The guard moved half a step in front of me, sword half-drawn. Around us, the other guests were pausing their conversations, eager to listen in on what was happening.

With all the courage I could muster, I got myself to smile and place a calm hand on the guard's biceps. "Thank you, Lord Tristan. But I think I must decline your kind offer." Every word was like ashes in my mouth. Especially when his own smile slipped, letting a hint of the fear shimmer through.

But I couldn't—wouldn't—put him in danger by interacting with him more than I already had allowed. I stepped past my guard and continued to the dais, loosing a stuck breath as I bit back a scream, or tears, or both.

I was halfway there when Tristan appeared at my side yet again. "I insist," he said slowly, emphasizing every syllable.

My heart formed into a useless lump as I stopped and turned to fully face him. His eyes, so familiar, a safe haven while in the fairylands—here, he could do nothing to protect me. He held no power in this court, among these people who mercifully didn't know what he was to me.

And it wasn't enough. What he was trying to do, it would never be enough to get me out of there. Not without exposing himself and risking his own life by fighting our way out.

Absently, my hand wandered to my side where, in the pocket of my peasant clothes, the Mage Stone had been. Now, it was sitting in the pillowcase of the settee, stored away for a day I was provided with something to wear in which I could actually carry the crystal with me—no matter how little use I could make of it.

I felt the guards behind me, waiting for me to make a move or for Tristan to overstep the boundaries of what was socially acceptable in the Jezuinian court.

All he did was stare, devastation shining through the mask he had put up.

And maybe ... maybe if I danced with more nobles than him, we could get away with this one brief moment where he and I could talk, where we could touch. And maybe all words would cease in my head anyway when he placed his palm in mine, when his fingers curled around the edge of my waist...

I dipped my chin an inch at him, indicating that I'd agree, but turned to the guard closest to me, putting on a painfully sweet smile as I told him, "Find my husband's closest advisors. Bring them here. All of them. I want to dance with his favored court." The guard gave me a surprised and slightly uncomfortable look. But I rolled on, "And while I'm waiting, I'll entertain Lord Tristan here. Who knows, perhaps I'll learn something useful about trade with Tavras."

When I turned back to Tristan, his smile had become like stone, but his eyes had softened enough to tell me he understood my caution.

The guard bowed and shuffled away, stopping at a group of nobles at the back of the dancing crowd. I didn't wait for them to look up and find me across the room but extended a hand to Tristan, pretending to be in full control of the situation. "Very well, then, *Lord* Tristan. Let's dance."

He took my hand, leading me onto the dance floor where the moving couples made space for the saint and her dancing partner, and I almost laughed out loud at the irony that our first dance would be here, in my home, where I'd once hoped to dance with my future king.

My gaze found Tristan's as he stepped in front of me to bring me closer, swaying me into the animated music. A good dancer, without a doubt. Trained to survive in the cut-throat fairy court. His fingers grasped mine too tightly, though, as if his fear needed an outlet when he kept that smile pinned.

"It's good to see you, Saint Sanja," he opened the conversation, an edge to his tone that would have given him away had anyone been able to hear us speak. "I've heard quite some fabulous things about your miraculous skills."

"You shouldn't be here," I merely told him in a low voice. "If Cyrill figures out who you are, he'll have something worse than death ready for you."

I didn't care pretending anything other than the worst would happen even when I managed to keep my lips in a bland smile.

"I returned from my errands, and you were gone." His words were a bit breathless despite the comparatively slow pace of the dance, but he kept his neutral expression. "All of you. And there was blood on the floor and the cupboard. I thought you were dead."

Hearing the words—it almost made me forget to keep up appearances.

"That's why you shouldn't be here. Because it's enough that he got me. Zelia and Dimar are on their way to the Hollow Mountains."

Tristan shook his head. "There was no note when I returned. The sick house was empty. Beds and cupboards turned inside out."

Forcing my face to remain impassive, I wondered why I was even surprised to learn that. Cyrill knew about Dimar. He knew that I'd escaped with the help of a Mage. It would have been naivety to believe he wouldn't have gone after everything I held dear. And trashing the sick house, it seemed like something a man like Cyrill would order if only to erase all traces that I'd once lived there.

"I'm getting you out of here, San." Determination flared in his gaze, but as I scanned him—his chest and slim waist and hips—there was no sign of a weapon. No sword, not even a knife.

But maybe—"Do you have magic?" If he'd somehow gotten it back... It was the only thing that could truly save us since my Mage Stone refused to do a thing for me.

"No. But I can negotiate. I'm good with words. I've held my own in the fairy city long enough. I could—"

My chest deflated as that final spark of hope left me. But I gave him a genuine, if not sad, smile.

"There are no words to convince Cyrill Tenikos. He has *made* me a saint for a reason. I'm untouchable. No one can take me away. No one will dare offend a king who has the will of the Guardians at his side..."

"I don't care about the Guardians if I can have you back." His words hit like a punch to my stomach.

Of course, he didn't care. He hadn't cared in Askarea when he'd taken me to the fairy residences. He hadn't thought twice when he'd given away how much he cared about me at Ret Relah when he'd gotten upset about my absence in front of the entire fairy court. It had led us to misery and more misery. And a desperation that paralyzed me as much as it was screaming to be eased by a single kiss of his.

"You aren't invincible here, Tris. You're a human man just like I'm nothing more than a human woman."

He shook his head an inch. "I will find a way, San."

My smile hurt all the way to my temples as I kept it in place.

"Maybe, if I can get my Mage Stone to work, I can free myself."

At that, his eyebrows shot up, revealing too much of the intensity of our conversation. At least, this wasn't the fairy court, and human ears were oblivious to our words behind the veil of string music.

"You have a Mage Stone?" The slight tremble in his voice told me enough about the anger collecting in his stomach. Because he didn't. I'd destroyed his Mage Stone and taken his magic—and now I possessed what he could never again have.

"Zelia made one for me ... started in Aceleau after the Crow Fairy test," I quickly filled him in.

"She did what?"

For a moment, I thought he was going to let that anger jump the leash, but I continued, "She only gave it to me a day or two before I was captured by Cyrill's men." I left out that Recienne had played a role in that capture. "It's tiny. And I can't get it to work."

Tristan's emotions vanished behind a wall as he swayed us along, the music no longer meaningful in any way—not even the dancing or the closeness. "It takes a while to figure it out even with a Mage to tutor you. You need to get it to pulse in your grasp. If you feel that, you can access the magic."

"Is there a special word to unleash the magic? I tried *yetheruh*, but that did nothing."

Tristan shook his head. "I'll stay with you, here at the palace... find a way to make myself useful in Cyrill's court so I can help you unlock the Mage Stone."

"No," I interrupted before he could form a plan in his head. "If you're here, Cyrill will find out what you mean to me. He'll use you like he uses others at the palace to make me compliant. Worse, even. He'll use you to punish me, and we'll be no better off than in the fairy court." I didn't need to paint the image of the cage he'd been locked in. The flash of fear in his eyes told me he understood.

"You *can't* stay here," I emphasized my point.

Tristan didn't object, instead, swirling us in a fast turn with the music, and I grabbed onto his shoulder to keep my balance.

Tristan's hand slid more tightly around my waist, and my body ached to press against his. That familiar warmth... If I could drown in it one last time.

But the music changed, and, as if remembering his role, Tristan loosed his hold on me once more. "I can't leave here without you, Sanja. You're everything I have left. If I lose you—"

Every fiber in my body ached at the meaning of his words. Because he was—he had been everything to me, too.

He had been my rock in Aceleau. Had taught me most of what I knew about magic. He'd given me a home when I'd lost every last bit of my world here in Cezux, my identity, and in his care, I had become someone else. Someone stronger, perhaps, but also someone very different from the Sanja who'd run from Jezuin to escape her fate. This new Sanja, she saw the greater picture than her own happiness. And with that, she'd learned the meaning of sacrifice.

"I know..." Because I did... I did know how it felt to have my heart shattered, remembered those moments when I'd spotted him in a cage beside the fairy king's throne.

And when I realized I had to send him away so he could be safe, could live, my heart broke yet again in a long-running crack, pain echoing through my entire body.

"Listen to me," I said with all the court-trained grace I could find. "You need to leave while you can. You need to finish this dance with me then bow and walk away." His eyes turned harder with every word I spoke. Every single step the dance continued. But he didn't avert his gaze. "Find Zelia and Dimar. Make sure they are safe. Protect what little of my family is left. That is all I can ask for."

His fingers curled into the fabric of my dress, unwilling to let go, as hurt flashed in the troubled blue of his irises. "Is that what you want, Sanja?"

I want you, I wanted to scream. *I want to go with you. Take me away from here.* But not another life would be on my conscience. Tristan wouldn't give up anything for me again. He'd lost his magic because of me. If I couldn't give him that back, at least, I could give him his freedom.

So I braced myself for the storm of emotions that would come if he actually listened to me, believed me—and nodded.

The music trickled to a halt, and Tristan and I slowed with the rest of the dancers until we stopped in front of the dais where the guard obediently had lined up three men, each of them assessing me from a distance.

"You will be all right without me, Tris." Tears collected in my eyes as the fissure in my chest broke wide open while Tristan held my gaze in silent question. One word from him, one smile, and my body might betray me and fling itself at him, kissing him, tasting him, inhaling him for one last time.

But I swallowed all emotions until they lay in my stomach like an oversized rock in deep waters and indicated a curtsey.

"The Guardians' blessing may follow you wherever you wander, Lord Tristan." My words got swept away by a climbing melody, and Tristan backed away, hand slipping from my waist, from my palm, leaving it cold and empty. His eyes turned to ice as they gleamed down at me, scrutinizing me. "You're making it easy for yourself, San. And if you believe I'll ever stop fighting for you, you are wrong." And with a bow, he turned and walked away.

His words had barely registered when one of Cyrill's advisors took the empty spot in front of me, sliding his arm around my waist and pulling me into a dance. No respect for the queen, no reverence for the saint. Just a spin and a twirl and a closeness that made my skin crawl.

But I shoved it down, all of it, tuning out his words as I braved my best smile, until the dance was done and the next took his place, and the next, even when my eyes lingered on the spot by the door where Tristan's handsome face had disappeared after a last look over his shoulder. And with Tristan taking care of Zelia and Dimar, everyone I loved would be protected.

And I was truly alone.

Beneath my smile, a chasm filled my chest, and with every painful breath, I reminded myself that I needed to cherish it. It would be all I had left of Tris.

FOURTEEN

Cyrill returned without the new fairy king, the sly smile on his face that let me expect the worst. But, at least, I was spared Recienne's taunting and mocking as I fought to keep my facade up so the turmoil of emotions that had stirred at Tristan's departure wouldn't cleave me wide open and expose what was in my heart to this court of snakes.

If any of the men once loyal to my father had any interest in my well-being, or if they were so thoroughly ensnared by the tale Cyrill had spun they could no longer distinguish truth from lie, I couldn't tell. They all rushed to the king's side when he waved a hand and remained with him for the rest of the evening while I went back to sitting on my chair where, at least, I no longer needed to fake-smile at courtiers. At some point, one of the noblewomen approached me with a lowered gaze, her midnight blue gown sparkling as it bunched at the hem when she curtseyed before the saint queen, and I schooled my features into an expression of interest if only for the sake of keeping myself busy when Tristan's absence was slowly ripping through me, leaving a trail of destruction where I'd once believed in a happy end.

"What is your concern?" I asked the woman, who remained in a low curtsey, long black curls pinned at the back of her head spilling over her shoulders and covering the high lace collar, until I told her to "rise".

"Saint Sanja, Your Majesty," the woman said, voice trembling slightly. She adjusted her necklace of pearls. "I mean not to burden you, but I've been hoping to talk to you."

My hands gripped the armrests of my chair hard enough for my nails to leave dents.

"You wish to be healed?" I didn't have the energy to make my voice sound pleasant, the tone of Sanja, the princess shining through more than I cared to admit.

The woman shook her head. "I'm in good health. But—" She paused, looking left and right until her eyes lingered on one of the men standing with Cyrill. "But when I came to Jezuin with Lord Cyrill before your wedding, he had assigned me one task, and since you were dead and"—she paused again, eyes finding the guards that were my shadows this time— "there was no hope for an heir with the new king widowed..." She lowered her voice into a whisper as she took a small step closer, leaning in. And, Guardians help me, I leaned in, too, eager for anything that took my mind off Tristan, off the prison my home had become. And how I couldn't even fight back with everything Cyrill had proven capable of. "But now that you are back, saint or no, I was wondering ..."

"You were wondering what, Lady—" That chasm inside my chest turned into ice.

"Lady Garla, Your Majesty, Saint Sanja. I was assigned the task of taking care of the lord's queen once she was pregnant with his heir. And now that you're back, I was wondering if it is finally time for me to take up my task," she added quickly as if realizing just now that she might have offended the saint before her.

"I don't think this is the place to discuss this." The authority threatening to surface in my voice scared me more than the thought of what the people's expectations of an heir might mean for my sleeping arrangements in the palace. But all the pain and fear seemed to hone themselves into coldness as I stood, glancing down at the lady, who backed away a step from the angered saint. "If you will excuse me."

I stalked around her without another word, marching up to my husband, who was in discussion with his advisors, all three men I'd danced with and of whom I hadn't even bothered to learn the names.

"Apologies," I interrupted, wondering if I was supposed to use his title when I addressed him, his name, or something entirely other that he would make up just to give me something to fail at so he could punish me. But I didn't care. For that small moment, I didn't care.

Cyrill tore away from the conversation, his eyes turning darker, his features turning into that mask of pleasantness when I knew beyond which simmered pure calculation and cruelty.

"Excuse me, gentlemen, but my lovely wife and queen is demanding my attention." He grabbed my arm in a way that may have made it look like a loving touch, but his fingers squeezed my biceps with enough force to bruise.

I didn't flinch.

"What's so important that you have to intrude on a conversation with my advisors, Sanja?"

I almost snorted but remember to fear him before that devastation in my stomach could make me reckless, self-destructive. "I wish to go to my room." That I didn't phrase it like a question was purposeful on my side. If I had to live at his mercy, at least, I wouldn't beg for anything.

He laughed. "Too much excitement, Sanja? Some say that a saint needs a more secluded place to thrive. Perhaps they were right."

I didn't ask who had said it and what it meant. Instead, I gave him my sweetest smile and rose to my toes to place a kiss on his cheek while I wriggled my arm from his grasp. "Good night, my dear husband."

Cyrill stared at me with wide black eyes. "I'll talk to you later."

I heard it for the threat it was—the promise of something that would demand for my tears.

So I turned on my heels, enduring the gazes of his courtiers and the nobles who seemed to have forgotten they'd once been on my father's side—who had been betrayed just like my father had, and who believed that Cyrill was the victim of fate, pushed onto this throne by the Guardian's will.

Tears streamed freely by the time I made it to my room, the guards positioning themselves outside the door and locking it behind me. But, at least here, I could cry. Here, I could fall apart. Until the new day broke and Cyrill would call on me to use me to solidify his own power.

I didn't bother changing out of the velvet dress before I picked my Mage Stone from the pillowcase on the settee and slipped under the covers of my bed. There, I closed my fingers around the tiny stone, beseeching the Guardians to help me. To make that spark of magic flow.

The Mage Stone remained nothing more than a cool crystal in my palm, no resonating, no pulsing, no sign of anything.

After what felt like an eternity, I grabbed the pillow and pressed it to my chest, wishing it was Tristan. But my chest remained as cold as the crystal between my fingers.

Cyrill came to my room the next morning, Lady Garla following him on swift feet and wearing a smug expression on her features. She paused by the door, closing it behind them as Cyrill marched up to me, pulling the pillow from my hands just as I was about to stuff the Mage Stone back into the pillowcase and shove it into the corner of the settee before he sat next to me.

Heart pounding, I held my breath as I slowly wrapped my hand tightly around the Mage Stone and braced it beside my thigh out of Cyrill's sight.

Just as he hadn't bothered to knock, he didn't bother to tell me good morning. "You've met Lady Garla," he said and gestured at the woman in a floor-length blue chiffon gown who had approached me the night before.

A shudder ran through me at the memory of what she'd inquired.

And Cyrill had brought her to my room.

I didn't get to ponder the meaning of that before he turned to me, expression more serious than I was used to. "It has been brought to my attention that Cezux is waiting for an heir to protect the monarchy. With you dead, the people believed the House Lazar to be extinct, and they were reluctant to accept me on the throne, but with you back, I have a claim. And with you carrying my heir—"

He gestured at my front in general as if wondering if that was something to consider. Or to make it look as if I was already pregnant with his child.

Bile rose in my throat.

I didn't speak, knowing that anything I said could be wrong, could lead to more hours for Leahnie in the dungeons or for another servant to lose their lives at Cyrill's whim.

Had Dimar not mentioned that Recienne was the Cyrill Tenikos of the fairylands? I saw the parallels now, the deliberate cruelty that I'd feared so much in Askarea—and that had followed me all the way to this very palace.

"I have decided that it would be best if you went away to a more secluded place where our child will be protected."

So he was already pretending I was carrying his child. Now the bile did make itself known, and I leaped to my feet, lunging for the door to the bathing room where I heaved bile and a groan that carried the weight of all I'd given up within less than a day.

Lady Garla was at my side before I could heave once more, her fingers gliding over my back making me cringe.

"A good sign," she said to Cyrill, who was now standing by the door, a satisfied expression on his face. "A stable pregnancy if she is throwing up."

"Guardians-blessed," Cyrill agreed.

At least, if I didn't deny it, it would spare me the immediate necessity for Cyrill to visit my bed anytime soon. Because that was something I'd never be ready for.

"Where—" I cleared my throat, spitting the rest of the bile into the toilet. "Where am I to go?"

Cyrill laughed. "Somewhere *safe*," he said with that glint of malice in his eyes that told me he knew exactly that I would never carry his child. And hiding me away until a hypothetical heir could be born was easier than faking an entire pregnancy here in the palace. But where he'd send me... Would it be any better than where I was now?

"Go pack my wife's clothes," he dismissed Lady Garla. "I want you gone from the room when we come out." With those words, he closed the bathing room door behind the lady, leaving us in this too-small room where hiding my Mage-Stone-clutching fist was as hard as controlling my breathing.

"What an incredible actress you are, Sanja." Cyrill cut me an impressed look that had my bones turning cold. "But now that your people lay at my feet with your blessing ... with the announcement of an heir growing in your belly, I have no use for you in these halls. It will only attract more Tavrasian lords who want to steal dances with the saint"— my heart stuttered at what he implied—"and we cannot have that, right? Rumors that the heir of Cezux might be a bastard child."

"But there *is* no child." A fact, and a dangerous one, now that his mind had taken that turn.

"And there will never be one. For now, you'll disappear until you return with the tragic news of having lost the child."

Had I despised Cyrill before? Now I could no longer stand being in the same room with him. I backed toward the window, wondering if a fall from high up would be worse than being hit by an arrow.

But Cyrill grasped my wrist—thank the Guardians, not the one clutching the Mage Stone—pulling me forward. "When you walk out into the bedroom, your things will be ready, and your new keeper will be waiting. I don't want to hear any begging or whining. The business is done."

I ripped my arm from his grip, baring my teeth at him. "Will the archers follow me there, too?" I near spat at him.

Cyrill merely laughed. "There will be no need for archers where you're going." He reached behind him, opening the door to the bedroom where Recienne was leaning against the mantle of the fireplace, an expression of bored disinterest on his face.

"As agreed, King Recienne," Cyrill said as he shoved me toward the fairy male, "my end of our bargain."

I caught my balance a foot from Recienne, who smirked down at me while speaking to Cyrill. "After last night, I expected something ... more than a woman reeking of sweat and vomit." Something dark flickered in his eyes as I held his gaze, unwilling to quake with fear the way my throat commanded me.

"It is what we agreed upon. I never said what condition she'd be in." Cyrill picked up a small bag from the settee and dropped it on the floor beside me.

My belongings. All summed up in a bundle of the size that wouldn't even fill my arms.

"You can have her for eight months. And for those eight months, you won't push for the throne of Cezux."

So there it was. The business they'd discussed the night before.

"Exactly as agreed upon," Recienne confirmed and closed the gap between us, reaching to the floor to pick up the bag. "Shall we?"

His eyes didn't leave mine as he said to Cyrill, "I'll take good care of her." The feline grin on his face spoke the exact opposite, and I might have screamed when he grabbed my hand. But it was suffocated by the sudden blurring of the room and the tightening air when my surroundings melted and dripped until they were replaced by the polished, glimmering stone that was clearly of fairy architecture.

I ripped out of Recienne's grasp, stumbling a few steps away until my path was blocked by a wall.

"Welcome back, Princess," he purred, the sound making me whirl and assess the wide, open space, the tall pillars carrying a high ceiling, the carvings and ornamentations. The fairy palace.

A demand for him to take me back formed on my tongue, but where back? To Cyrill where I was a captive just as I was here?

"You know the way to the tower," he said, dropping the bundle on the floor, and turned to walk away.

But not without some answers. "You couldn't just have let me suffer in peace, could you? You had to come and make it worse."

At that, Recienne turned, his brows raised in question. "Worse? What exactly do you think I'm doing here?"

I opened my mouth, closed it. Opened it again. When no wild accusation made it past my lips, he chuckled, and the sound made me pause, assess him the way he'd assessed the night before: He was still wearing human finery, black, threaded with gold to match his eyes; his hair was ruffled and his face a hint paler, more tired than I remembered.

"I traded you in exchange for leaving Cezux alone—for a few months," he added, and the downward quirk of his lips made him seem even more dangerous. "Getting out of Cyrill's so-called *care* plus a guaranteed no-attack policy against your own realm, Sanja? I'd call that a win-win for you and you alone."

He turned again, ready to stalk away, but turned before he made even the first step. "As for your little merchant lord, Sanja"—every last muscle in my body tightened—"he made it out of the palace alive last night, courtesy of my generous care."

"I don't know what you're talking about."

Of course, Recienne wouldn't be fooled. He knew Tristan. Maybe he hadn't been in the room when I'd danced with him, but being a fairy bastard, he probably had other ways to detect people.

"Don't pretend he wasn't there, Sanja. I can still smell him on you." His nostrils flared as if in offense, and the gold of his eyes seemed to be burning. There and gone. He wiped his hand over his face, and when he was done, his features were once more schooled into that cool, calculated expression that I'd seen him wear beside his father's throne. "Of course, Cyrill's guards were easily distracted. Humans..."

Humans. Like me. I scoffed, fingers curling more tightly around the Mage Stone as I slid my hand behind my back. "It's none of your business who I smell like," I shot at him, something burning in my gut that I hadn't felt in a long time. Something other than that hopeless fear, that stagnancy of being Cyrill's puppet.

"No. No, it isn't." He pressed his lips into a tight line as he studied me head-to-toe once more, and I wondered if his fairy eyes could see through fabric and skin and flesh right to my ravaged heart where Tristan's absence yawned like a canyon. "Unless it gets you killed."

"Cyrill wouldn't kill me." Truth. He would torture others to make me complacent.

"Maybe not him. But now that you're a saint, Sanja"—a humorless chuckle escaped his lips—"there are others watching your every step. Not only the King of Cezux."

I shuddered when he called the tyrant that was my husband *the King of Cezux.*

"And who might that be? A certain fairy king perhaps?"

Recienne's lips turned white under the pressure of the words he was holding back. But he shrugged and turned, pointing over his shoulder as he walked away. "Make yourself at home, Sanja."

The air rippled, and he was gone.

FIFTEEN

I would have never admitted it to Recienne, but it
might have taken me a few solitary rounds through
the fairy palace until I found my way to the
stairs leading up to the tower. After the second time
of passing by the throne room where the fairy king
had caged Tristan and trapped me with a bargain, I'd
given up on the fear of running into anyone. Where I
remembered hordes of colorful fairies mocking me from
the sidelines, emptiness gaped in every corner of the
hallways, making it even creepier than the first time I'd
come here. But where that first time, at Ret Relah, the
beauty of the colorfully glimmering stone and flower
garlands had spellbound me, this time, it now felt like
walking through a tomb. The tomb of a Sanja who'd

hoped to escape fairy royalty and make it out of there unharmed. Now, I knew better.

Eventually, I found my way up the stairs to the room in the tower where I'd spent my captivity in this realm. But when, the last time, the furniture had been sparse, the bed narrow, and no commodities provided other than the bathing room, this time, I found a wide bed covered in throws and pillows the color of the sunset. A crystal jar of water sat on a small table under the window. A chair on each side provided enough space for two to sit and eat, or for the stacks of books that someone had discarded there. On the nightstand, white roses sat arranged in a glass vase, the scent spreading through the room like an intoxicating perfume.

I stepped inside, closing the door behind me, and inhaled deeply, waiting for the panic to hit, to drag me under at the sight of my former prison. But when I looked from corner to corner, discovering a new, unexpected detail in all of them, something different struck me—and it might have been the fact that I was tired to my very bones or the ache of how I'd had to push Tristan away to keep him from Cyrill's observant eyes, but a deep, mind-numbing sadness overcame me. And I slid to the floor right where I was, bundle and Mage Stone still in my hands, and wrapped my arms around myself as tears started streaming down my cheeks.

Only when there were no more tears coming and the sun was bending into twilight did I release the bundle of my things and unfold my fingers around the Mage Stone.

Help me, I thought at the stone, at Tristan and Dimar and Zelia, who were better off on their way to the Hollow

Mountains, to the Guardians. But not even a flicker of something happened.

The next morning, I woke to the sound of birds through the open window. While I couldn't remember having gotten into bed, I did remember that I was back in Askarea. The cold of exhaustion hit me a moment later—as did the fear.

While everything had happened so fast the day before—Cyrill's sudden interest in an heir, the bargain with the new fairy king, our departure—my mind and body seemed to lag behind when I tried to roll out of bed. A heaviness engulfed me that had little to do with the soft sheets covering me to my nose or the endlessly comfortable mattress swallowing me up.

I was about to convince myself to roll out of bed and had folded the covers back when a knock sounded on the door.

"Come in," I called, wondering if I'd invited a monster into my room—then quickly remembering that no door could hold back monsters in this realm where I was nothing more than a toy to a fairy prince who'd taken his father's place.

The door swung open, and in clopped the horned fairy with unnaturally pink cheeks and a mass of silver braids. Her smile reminded me that she'd come to this room to clean me up and dress me after my first challenge. She was even wearing the same black, knee-length uniform with a white apron.

"It's good to see you alive and healthy, Sanja," she said by way of greeting, her hooves painting the impression of a horse arriving in my room.

For fear of speaking anything she could use against me, I remained silent. Also—how had she learned my name?

Then, the fairy king had used it during my last trial. Perhaps, it was common knowledge now, and I would be the plaything of every fairy whose path I crossed.

Eight months—Recienne would return me after eight months. Even if I had no desire to return to Cyrill's court other than to kick him out for good, I felt equally little attachment to the fairy realm.

"Sleep well?" The fairy clopped to the window, pushing it open wider and inhaling a deep breath. "Summer in Aceleau is the best season of the year."

"Only in Aceleau," I wondered aloud before I could gather my wits and be appropriately scared, "or all of Askarea?"

In response, the fairy merely laughed, a chime of octaves that made me sit up straight in bed—and find myself still in that purple velvet *reeking sweat and vomit* as Recienne had so eloquently put it.

"You need a bath, my dear." The fairy phrased it a bit nicer as she crossed to the bathing room where I'd soaked after the first and second challenges mere months ago. I swallowed hard at the thought of dipping my body into the same tub. But what options did I truly have? I couldn't simply demand for a new room, could I?

"Come on. In with you." The fairy waved me toward the bathing room with surprising urgency. "He's waiting for you."

I didn't need to ask which *he* was waiting. So I obeyed, not eager to face whatever consequences Recienne would think up for me if I didn't.

The water was perfect. Not too hot, not too cold, and scented with the same white roses that had lulled me to sleep the night before.

"I found you on the floor when he sent me to help you get ready for bed last night," the fairy chatted on, her face friendly as she gestured for me to get out of my clothes. "So I took the liberty to put you into bed and tuck you in. No one wants a poorly rested human at their lunch table," she explained as she pulled a flask of oil from the shelf—rosemary and something else I couldn't quite place but liked very much.

Still edgy in her presence, I wondered if she'd put me in a ballgown that day or into something more practical that would allow for me to at least kick out when Recienne attempted to freeze me over the way some of the fairies at Ret Relah had frozen a woman.

A shudder raked through me, and I decided that closing my eyes and sinking under the surface was as good an idea as any in the presence of a fairy.

If only Tristan were there—he'd know what to do and how to deal with them. But without a Mage Stone—

My Mage Stone.

I shot to my feet, water sloshing from my body in a cascade as I hopped out of the tub like a crazy woman and rushed back to the bedroom, clanging to my knees by the door where I must have fallen asleep, and found the thin carpet there empty. I whirled around, hair dripping wet trails as I crawled on hands and knees, fingers searching every inch of the hardwood floor for any sign of my Mage Stone, the bed.

It had to be somewhere—

"If you tell me what you're looking for, I might be able to help," the fairy offered.

I bit my tongue, wondering what would be worse—her having found the Mage Stone and uncovering my secret while I'd been enjoying the sweet oblivion of sleep, or if I'd need to ask her for help. It would lead to another bargain, and I'd had enough of those.

But the Mage Stone wasn't there—not on the carpet or the wood. And certainly not on the nightstand beside the bed where another vase with fresh white roses was sitting like a bouquet of innocence.

"Nothing... I'm looking for ... nothing." No matter what the fairy would think about me—that I was insane, slithering naked across the floor after hopping from the tub—it had to be better than her knowing the truth.

"Well, get back in here then." Something about the way she said it made me look up and study her face—her round, friendly face with only a hint of scolding, and much, much patience. More than I'd seen in months from anyone—even from Tristan.

With a stinging heart, I lifted myself to my feet and slouched back to the bathing room. Once back in the water, I cringed as the fairy reached for my hair and started scrubbing.

"No need to fear me, child. I won't hurt you if you don't give me a reason to." I didn't miss the warning in her tone, no matter how kind her voice.

So I didn't move and let her finish her work.

Only when she motioned me out of the water again did I rise and dry off with one of the amazingly soft towels she handed me.

"Your clothes are in the armoire," she said, wiping her hands in her apron—"If you need anything, call for Naar."— and clopped out the door.

To my surprise, I found a set of pants and a linen shirt in the armoire. Beside it, a pair of boots my size had been pre-pared. But something else was folded on one of the higher shelves. I reached for it and pulled out a pink lace-trimmed gown—flowy and simple, and so, so soft.

I debated putting it on and falling back into bed. But Naar had said Recienne was waiting, and the anticipation of what he'd have in store for me if I ignored his summons—I was certain Cyrill's wrath would pale compared to what Re-cienne was truly capable of.

So I dropped the gown on a chair at the table and tugged on a set of underthings, the pants, and shirt instead, finishing up with the boots, which struck me as too hot for the summer, but everything was better than being stuck in silk slippers and too-tight-at-the-ankles dresses that kept me from running.

Not bothering to brush my hair, I towel-dried it enough so it wouldn't drip and left the room after one last fran-tic search for the Mage Stone—not under the bed or in the bathing room. Not *in* bed either.

The steep stairs leading to the main hallway were a hassle for the memories they brought alone. But the fear of what Recienne would do if I let him wait put even those horrors to sleep—for now. They'd find me soon enough in my dreams, I was positive about that.

I was halfway down the hallway when his voice swept around me, carried by that sark breeze. "Just a bit farther, Sanja. You're almost there."

Following the voice—the breeze that continued to guide me, I found him leaning at the end of a long dining table in a room a few doors down from the throne room. He didn't look up as I entered the room, oblivious to my presence or—more likely—uncaring that the insignificant human had arrived. So I cleared my throat and folded my arms over my chest.

"A very late good morning, Sanja." He turned slowly, his hair shifting as he angled his head and studied me from my wet hair to my boots with a predatory focus that made me want to leap out of my skin.

Shrugging it off, I sauntered closer, pushing my panic back as best I could, if only for show, when internally I was still crumbling.

"If you want me to be up for breakfast, I suggest you send the horned butterfly at dawn next time. Then you have a chance I'll be ready to watch you sulk over your tea when the sun comes up."

"That's a lot of words, Sanja." He shoved his hands into his pockets and put on a smile entirely too pretty for the bastard he was. "Do you have any idea what it is you are suggesting?"

In my mind, I went over what I'd said, finding nothing he could twist against me—apart from the obvious insult in them. "Please, enlighten me." *About what you want from me. Why I have to be the price for the freedom of Cezux from your cruelty.* I didn't speak those last words out loud, of course. There *was* a part of me, after all, that clung onto dear life—even when my being here meant that I might have mere moments before I'd be frozen over, or sent into a maze of flesh-eating plants, or lignified all over again. The dancing had already happened the night before, thank you very much, and my body was still exhausted. From swaying in various men's arms, from observing Cyrill's court and fearing to take a wrong breath. From pretending.

"Enlighten you—" He raised an eyebrow—perfectly groomed and in stark contrast to his tan skin—as he strolled closer until he came to a halt a few steps from me.

I refused to balk, refused to grab for the inexistent knife at my hip—or for the Mage Stone that would have been in my pocket had I not been so reckless to not hide it before I collapsed the night before. A frown paved its way onto my features, and I wondered if Recienne could smell the fear on me—and the shameless self-loathing for all I'd done, for what I'd taken from the people I loved.

"There are a couple of things I'd like to enlighten you about, Sanja. But I'm not sure you can stomach them without breakfast. So why don't we sit down and eat?"

He turned to the table where, at a flick of his fingers, a pastry-laden plate appeared right next to a bowl of sliced fruit and a pot of tea.

"I was more in the mood for lunch, but I'll indulge you since you asked so nicely." Sarcasm dripped heavily from his words as he pulled out the closest chair and gestured for me to sit before he unhurriedly walked around the table to take a seat across from me—from where I should have been sitting but didn't dare to.

"What will it cost me if I eat this?" I asked rather than try my luck.

Recienne gave me an insulted look. "Why, by the flicker of magic, would I give you food that harms you, Sanja? It's not like my sole purpose is to see you suffer."

"But it's one of your purposes?" I provoked, seeing an opening to gather some of the truths he was hiding.

In response, his lips twitched in a wicked grin, eyes turning to solid gold. "My purpose is something I'd rather not talk about over casual ... breakfast," he finished with a glance at what he'd conjured. "I guess it is breakfast after all." He gestured at the empty chair. "Sit, Sanja."

Fighting the urge to stick my tongue out at him, or scream at him, or simply run from the room in panic, I held my ground. "Make me."

The flicker in his eyes was like a brand—brief and searing but gone so fast I couldn't tell if he was debating ending me then and there. "I could."

"I know you could." *By the Guardians!* Why couldn't I stop talking? Every last word coming from my mouth seemed to dig a deeper grave that I'd be shoved into after those eight months.

"But what would that do to your lovely offspring if I controlled your body."

I choked on a breath. "Both you and I know I'm not pregnant. There is no need for me to be *kept away from the Jezuinian court,* as my husband would phrase it." There. There it was. He could decide to send me back. A part of me wanted him to if only so I could do something about the reign of terror Cyrill was building. But if he did—it would give him a free pass to take Cezux for himself after the bargain his father had made with Cyrill.

Wait—were fairy bargains hereditary? Did Recienne's father's bargain with Cyrill transfer to the Recienne before me?

"I wish I could read your thoughts," he said out of the blue, and when I gave him a quizzical look that I hated myself for—because nothing, *nothing* about the fairy male before me was supposed to stir my interest, especially not a statement like that—he added, "You seem to have a lot of convolution going on in there." He tapped his finger to his temple, and I wanted to spit at him. The smirk vanished as he read the ire in my gaze, and he gestured at the chair once more. "Sit, or stand if you wish, but please, Sanja, eat something. We've got a long day ahead of us."

The pastries did look tasty, and my stomach was still empty from my reverse-eating the night before. So I sighed through my nose and marched up to the chair, carefully sliding into it.

Recienne's chuckle reminded me to not let my fear show. He'd only spin it against me. Defying the urge to look up and study those features as he surely observed every last twitch of my body while I tried to get comfortable in the

Guardians-damned chair, I reached for curved bread that I'd never seen in my life.

The moment I'd bitten into it, Recienne leaned back in his own chair, flicking his fingers again, and a cup of tea appeared before him, steaming and smelling of herbs I knew from the Mages' House.

"Cyrill will be devastated to hear the news." There was too much humor in his voice, so my traitorous eyes snapped up to meet his gaze—and found not the least bit of humor there.

"As if you care."

"About what the King of Cezux believes? Not very much. About the actual likelihood of such a pregnancy"—he gracefully twisted his wrist to emphasize his point—"I might actually care about that."

"What do you mean?"

He didn't explain himself but lifted his cup to his curling lips and sipped, giving me time to figure it out on my own.

Care—about the likelihood of my pregnancy.

"You are aware that Cyrill knows as well, right? That he is using this to store me away so he can steer the people while they are smitten with their saint."

"*Smitten?*" His laugh drifted across the table, and I bit into the bread once more, this time actually tasting the sweet flavor of the soft dough.

"Smitten," I confirmed after taking my time to chew and swallow.

"Are you sure you don't want to call it a *mindless religious frenzy?*"

His words hit like a punch ... because he was right, and I would in no way admit to that. Ever.

"No pregnancy." It was all I had to say. "I would know if Cyrill had ever touched me, which he didn't. So unless you believe in the conception of the untouched, I'm not pregnant."

His chest rose and fell in what had to be the deepest, slowest breath in history, but his face was calm and composed as he met my gaze.

"So while we're at it," I continued, taking his lack of words as a good sign that he had lost a lever to rouse my fury, "why don't you tell me why I'm here."

Recienne held my gaze, cup in one hand, the other resting in front of him on the table. "Since the pathetic Mage you adore so much didn't have the balls to get you out, I thought it was time someone did."

I nearly dropped the bread in my hand at his impertinence. "Who asked you for help?" Most certainly not I. Especially not after how he'd mocked me, how he'd told me to hate him. And now he'd—a gust of air left my lungs, and I had to lean back in my chair. "Tristan would have done anything to get me out. *I* told him not to. I told him to leave and..." I stopped myself. In no way would I tell him about Zelia and Dimar, about where they were headed. That Tristan was supposed to join them.

"And you thought it was a better idea to remain Cyrill's little toy?"

I thought it was better for him *to be alive.* But I didn't say that. Instead, I ground my teeth and shrugged. "I thought you'd approve of that since you are the one working with him." I seethed at him from the safe distance the table provided—even when half a thought would have been enough for him to break my neck with that upsetting control he could summon over my body.

That calm silence settled over him once more, and it was more terrifying than the wickedness that sometimes showed. "There are very few who I despise more than Cyrill Tenikos, Sanja." He set down his cup and got to his feet, turning toward the window and leaving me with a view on his elegant back. Both jacket and pants were tailored to his tall, powerful frame. Powerful, though not in a way that spoke of brute strength but in a more athletic way that reminded me of climbing trees and leaping over streams and—the bandit. I'd seen him in leather armor, had noticed his build then.

Shaking my head, I absorbed the silence—the absolute silence. Not a pair of footsteps filled the hallways, no hushed voices of courtiers, no guards lingering in alcoves to oversee the coming and going of whoever it was that came and went at a fairy court.

I thought he'd forgotten I was there when he whirled around so fast I spilled the tea from the cup I was lifting to my lips and cursed as the hot liquid splashed onto my pants.

Recienne didn't seem to notice, eyes burning as he braced his forearms on the table, leaning over the breakfast plates, pinning me in place. "Maybe I underestimated you, Sanja," he purred, the sensuous melody of his voice setting my body on edge. Danger. Everything about this fairy was danger. Including the way his gaze made heat trapped beneath the cold in my body stir. Anger. Fury. Hatred. That was what I felt. And it snaked through my veins as I tried not to cringe.

But he pushed himself up to his full height, reaching into his pocket and extracting a familiar leather string with a tiny crystal attached to it.

"Did *he* bring you this? Is that why he came to the palace? To give you a chance of defeating Cyrill on your own?" Everything in his tone told me he was certain that would never happen.

This time, I did shrink away from him in anticipation of the fairy's ire raining down on me. I threw up my arms in defense, readying for the blow.

But Recienne laughed, a certain desperation weaving through the sound. "You think I'd strike you, Sanja? That's how high your opinion of me is? After everything—"

Blinking my vision free and lowering my arms again, I assessed his bitterly grinning face—beautiful, terrifying— and released a shuddering breath.

"After everything you've done to me here, and in the forest before, and ever since," I finished for him.

"You keep forgetting one little detail, Sanja."

"And what is that?" I asked before he could talk himself into a tirade. "That you stole my name? That you *made* me dance at the challenge? That you told me to hate you?" *I thought you were different.* I didn't say it, but from the way Recienne's face hardened, I could have sworn he had something to hide.

"Thank the Guardians you already know everything. That saves me a lot of time."

The impulse to grunt in frustration was only overpowered by the insurmountable need to call him on his bluff. "Do us both a favor and spit it out, Recienne."

Recienne stilled, his eyes guarded for once, as if I'd hit a mark without even knowing what I'd been aiming for.

"I got you out. Then and now." His words reverberated in my very bones, a truth that I couldn't deny, not even to a fairy bastard like him, not even when everything he'd done before it had been despicable.

He'd nothing to gain from a bargain that prevented him from seizing control over the human lands other than—

"You are doing this, not to help me but to hurt Tristan." I threw all my willpower into the accusation. He'd done it at the challenges, had smirked at Tristan while he'd forced me across the dance floor. Had delighted in my Mage's pain—no longer my Mage.

A heaviness settled over me that was only rivaled by the emptiness in my chest. "I want to go to my room."

"So you can wallow some more?" he provoked, and this time, his temper jumped his leash, and it was all written in his features—the worry, the anger, the emotion that had glimmered through before but I had no name for.

For a moment, I tried to read what it meant until the heaviness threatened to swallow me and I averted my gaze, draining my tea without tasting it. "Please, I'd like to go to my room." The words hurt, but I forced them out anyway.

Recienne dropped the Mage Stone on the table, right next to my empty cup. "Not that it will ever have enough magic to last longer than an hour, but maybe it will save your pretty ass one day."

He stalked away, running one hand through his hair. And from the way the room felt suddenly as empty as that canyon inside my chest, I wasn't sure if I'd demanded the right thing.

SIXTEEN

Naar brought me dinner that day. After a soft knock that had me leaping out of bed where I'd spent all afternoon staring at either the ceiling or the Mage Stone I hadn't set down for even a moment, she clopped inside, tray in hand, and asked me how I was doing.

I slid the Mage Stone into my pocket, putting on an innocent face.

"Where did he go?" It was all I had in store for a response since the pain engulfing me was none of any fairy's business.

"Out." Naar set the tray down on the nightstand and lifted a silver cover, and I almost sighed at the smell of roast greens filling my nose. "The king has business to attend to."

"Doesn't his court come to him like to a normal fairy king?" Not that I had any idea what a *normal* fairy king was like.

Naar chuckled at my interest in the fairy king's business—or at something entirely else I, as a meek human, couldn't understand. "Recienne has sent his court away for the next few months. He believes it a good idea to keep this palace safe for a human during your stay."

I was mildly aware that my jaw was hanging open but couldn't find it in me to close it.

Again, Naar laughed, a more genuine sound this time. "It has taken him quite a while to convince them all of a temporary leave."

"He cleaned out his palace for me?"

"I don't think he'd like to hear it phrased like that."

"How would he phrase it then?"

The smile faded from Naar's face. "That, you will have to ask him yourself."

I almost asked her "when" but thought better than to hope to see the fairy monster who'd been part of my torment in this very palace before.

"He said you didn't want to go with him today." She set the silver lid beside the plate on the tray and straightened, a question hanging in the air that she hadn't really asked.

I merely shook my head. I might never want to go with him anywhere. Perhaps, if I was lucky, he'd continue with his errands and forget I was even here, and at some point, I'd figure out the Mage Stone, and I'd be able to leave.

That reminded me that he hadn't ordered me to stay. Not that my natural affinity toward my beating heart allowed for the consideration of leaving this palace. But, maybe, if I

managed to get my magic to work and become a real Mage
... maybe I'd be free of both of them—Cyrill and Recienne.

"Thanks for dinner," I told Naar.

The fairy didn't curtsey before she left.

It took two full days for me to sort my thoughts enough to
want to leave my room—my bed to be specific. Recienne
didn't summon me again, and Naar left the meals on my
bedside table, cleaning up the room with some small magic
I hadn't seen at work during my first stay here. Where she
went, a trail of cleanliness followed until even the last speck
of dust disappeared in her wake. I watched her sweep it away
with her presence as she left after bringing me dinner again.
So much power, even in the hands of a servant. What abyss
of power was slumbering beneath Recienne's skin then?

As if in response, a dark wind licked up the column of
my neck, a whisper of a chuckle following the sensation. I
shook it off, sliding farther up against the headboard of the
bed. But a moment later, the fairy king was standing before me, golden eyes glimmering with mild amusement as he
took me in—rumpled hair and still in my nightgown.

"Perhaps I shouldn't have taken Naar's recent departure
from this room as a sign that you were decent."

I rolled my eyes, not bothering to pull the covers over
me. The nightgown covered me from collarbone to wrist to

ankle, and I wouldn't give him the satisfaction of shrinking away from him again.

"Knocking helps, they say," I retorted, spearing a green bean and imagining it were his head.

"I had been hoping you'd join me in the dining room again, but Naar says you haven't left your room since our ... breakfast." A muscle feathered in his jaw.

I debated ignoring him. But—"Any particular reason you are intruding on my meal?"

Recienne snorted quietly. "Am I not allowed to check in on my guest?"

"Guest?"

"What did you think you were? Prisoner?"

"It has crossed my mind." I held his gaze, regretting that I hadn't bothered to stand so I could at least pretend we were speaking at eye level.

"You are not my prisoner. But before you get all excited and ready to leave... there are some rules."

I groaned. Rules. I'd had enough of those at the Mages' House. That brought me back to Tristan and the gaping wound in my heart.

"The palace is safe for now. If you insist on wandering the streets of Aceleau, I or someone I trust will accompany you."

"Someone you trust? I thought you sent the entire court away." A challenge... That was what my words were. Yet, I couldn't help myself.

"And that should tell you everything you need to know about this court." Not an answer but another riddle. At my frustrated gaze, he sighed. "I have found, Sanja, that after decades of standing beside my father's throne, I've become rather ... tired of collateral damage."

Again, not a response. An explanation? An attempt at one perhaps. "But you had no problem with watching me become collateral damage when your father held me prisoner." *Me, and the people I loved.*

He flinched. King Recienne of Askarea actually flinched. With a few slow strides, he was at the window where he gazed out at the falling night. "I was going to see if you would join me for a walk in the gardens. Naar is ... concerned about you holing up in here."

"An invitation? Or an order?"

Recienne lowered his head, fingers sliding over the edge of the table under the windowsill, and shook it. "Does it matter?" As he glanced at me over his shoulder, his black-and-gold jacket shifting with the motion, hair ruffled by the breeze drifting through the open window, he looked nothing like the fairy royalty I so feared. And that, perhaps, made him even more dangerous.

It didn't matter. Not when he continued looking at me for one more moment before the air rippled and he disappeared from the room as fast as he'd shown up. But when I finally crawled out of bed to take a look at those gardens—to see if, perhaps, he was taking that walk without me anyway—my gaze snagged on the books stacked on the chairs and table that I hadn't bothered to take a look at since that first morning of my arrival. And my heart dropped to my knees.

Magic books. Those were magic books, and not just any but the very ones we'd had to leave behind at the Mages' House when we'd fled after the late fairy king's death.

And on top of it ... a folded piece of paper.

I reached for it with shaking fingers and unfolded it, both curious and scared what I'd find inside.

I saved these from the Mages' House before my father's guards destroyed all traces of the four of you from Aceleau. Hopefully, they will come in handy. —R

'R' like Recienne.

Something fluttered in my chest—a tiny sign that I was still capable of surprise.

Swallowing hard, I picked up the book on top of the tallest stack and flipped it open. I didn't recognize the contents, but the smell of old parchment and leather and dried herbs enveloped me as I browsed through the pages, trying to figure out why the most powerful fairy in Askarea would bother to save magic books.

I ran my fingers along the edge of the table just as Recienne had, wondering if he'd dropped the note just now or if it had been sitting there the day of my arrival. The books most certainly had. With a shake of my head, I lifted the books, one after the other, until I had an idea of what I was dealing with and was half disappointed that they were mostly on healing magic, on potions, and none of them on the actual use of magic. But they were more than what I'd had in Jezuin.

I mustered a deep breath, the scent of white roses mingling with that of the Mages' House, and something inside of me eased for the first time in months.

The palace is safe for now.

Safe. For now. Whatever that meant. But what else had he said?

And that should tell you everything you need to know about this court.

He didn't trust his court. Or his father's court. That was why he'd sent them away. Not merely because of me, but because...

I have found, Sanja, that after decades of standing beside my father's throne, I've become rather ... tired of collateral damage.

As I rolled his words over in my head, something else floated through my mind. Words he'd spoken that day in the forest when he'd told me to forget.

Killing the male who sold out his lands wouldn't make me a hero. It would make me a fool.

Sold his lands out to who?

As if the magic books could provide an answer, I stuck my nose back into the next best of them and started reading. Anything—anything was better than entertaining the thought that, in all this mess, the most powerful fairy in all of Askarea was afraid of something. And that *something* had been the reason he'd never spoken a full truth.

What felt like hours later, I was still sitting on the chair closest to the window, three books open side by side, and thoughts buried deep in the workings of human magic when a glimmer of light caught my attention from the gardens.

I peered out the window to find Recienne's tall form by the fountain where I'd once been granted a few minutes with Tristan before the disaster of my final challenge, his head tilted toward the starlight like a flower seeking light. The night disguised the details of his features, but the heaviness resting on his shoulders made me rise and lean forward so I could see all of him. Tired—he appeared so tired, like the absence of witnesses had lifted a mask from him. Or many. And left behind the male carrying the burden of a whole, immortal kingdom.

As, for a moment, pity infiltrated my heart, I rested my elbows on the windowsill, accidentally pushing a book to the floor. Before I could cringe at the thud, Recienne's head whipped around, and even over the distance, I could have sworn his eyes locked on mine. And that dark breeze whispered along as he got to his feet, sliding his hands into his pockets and turning away. "Good night, Sanja."

Whether he'd meant for me to hear it or it had slipped his control, I couldn't tell, but something about his voice was different—bare and exhausted—that I couldn't help that throb of sympathy in my chest where before the gaping chasm of Tristan's absence had dominated my days.

Stepping away from the window, I silenced it and returned to reading.

Trails of blood followed my ravaged feet across the dance floor as the fairy king led me at a relentless pace, his silver eyes gleaming with delight at every painful step, every wince when he spun us around, at every drop of sweat rolling down my forehead. I remembered vaguely why I was there, what was at stake, but apart from a pair of troubled blue eyes, everything else was blurry in the background of the brutal dance. The off-kilter music formed the metro of my torture, as did the chime-like laughs floating through the air—the air smelling of violets and sugar.

"So beautiful, Sanja. Such a prize," the fairy king murmured, leaning in so close I could feel his breath on my cheek. "But not durable enough to make for thorough entertainment."

I tried to pull my hand out of his grasp—tried and failed, his fingers like steel around mine. Heart pounding, I forced my breath to slow, to catch up with my need for air, to function at all. I needed a break, or I'd fall apart. Literally. The soles of my feet were already coming off, and the desperate beat of that useless organ in my chest—

Tears fell from my eyes as I realized that, this time, no one would be holding me up—no dark wind would sweep around me and keep my legs stable, my spine straight; there was no one to lean on. Only my human weakness and the superior, immortal strength of the beautiful and cruel people he called his own.

"I should take the offer and make you a vessel, Sanja. It would help me more than gathering my throne. But even for that, you are not enough. You were never enough."

Never enough. His words echoed through my mind as I tore away from his grasp—stumbling into a solid wall behind me.

With a gasp, I opened my eyes, drifting from my dream to a state of momentary stunning. My hand groped the floor beside me where I'd landed, falling backward with my chair. Gingerly, I rolled off it, legs reluctant but not aching like in the dream, and feet in a pair of slippers I'd put on when hopping out of bed earlier to find the books—the books.

I groaned and scrambled to my feet, cursing at the throbbing pain in my skull.

If I counted all the head injuries I'd suffered since the day Cyrill's guards had found us in the sick house, I would have needed to worry about my ability to think clearly. Whether it was from that or the nightmare still swirling in my mind, all I could do was hear those lines over and over again. *You are not enough. You were never enough.*

Tears flowed down my cheeks as I wondered if, perhaps, the late fairy king had been right. That I was truly not enough. Not enough to save them or to save myself. And most certainly not to master the skills needed to get my Mage Stone to work.

I didn't care who'd barge into the room or what time it was as I staggered through the half-light until I found my bed, dropping onto the mattress where I curled up and dragged the blanket over my head.

You're not enough, Sanja, I could almost hear Tristan's voice agreeing. That was why he'd come to the palace in Jezuin to save me. And I'd thought I'd stand a better chance on my own.

To protect him and everyone around me, I reminded myself, fighting the darkness in my heart.

But all I saw were Tristan's eyes as he stared at me from my memory with that hurt and that disappointment when I'd sent him away. Everything. I'd taken everything from him. His magic, his home. And when all he'd asked for was to protect *me*, I'd denied him that, too.

●

I couldn't tell when I'd fallen asleep, but bright sunlight greeted me alongside Naar's clopping footsteps what felt like a mere minute later.

"Out of bed," she ordered, pulling back the blanket.

"Go away." I fished for the corner of the blanket to pull it back up, but Naar captured my fingers and placed them beside my hip.

"Out of bed with you, Princess."

"I'm no longer a princess," I grumbled, squinting at the table and the tipped-over chair in front of it.

"What shall I call you, then?"

Her question at least got my brain to start working. Not *Princess*, but certainly not *Queen* either. And most certainly not *Saint*. "Just Sanja," I offered.

I groaned and rolled into a sitting position.

"Bad night, Sanja?" Naar inquired, and her cheerful voice almost made me tell her to mind her own business. Then I thought better of it and accepted the robe she held out for me.

In response, I shook my head even when my chest ached all over again with that echo of '*you are not enough*'.

I let Naar braid my hair and choose my clothes, listening to her chatter only half-heartedly. Until she mentioned the books on the table.

"Looks like an exciting read," she repeated when I gave her a questioning glance through the mirror. "Recienne brought them in the night you disappeared. I know he didn't expect you to return right away, but—" She stopped as if she'd caught herself saying something she wasn't supposed to, pursing her lips, pink cheeks turning even plumper as she seemed to hold her breath.

"He expected me to return?"

Shaking her head, Naar gave me a warning look. "Recienne doesn't expect anything from anyone. That's his problem."

Something in the way she said it reminded me of the exhausted king in the garden the night before, and I couldn't help that little throb of sympathy from coming back to life.

I smothered it with a grunt and held out my arms for Naar to slide the gown she'd chosen over my head.

"There, better." She looked me up and down as if assessing the outcome of a hard day's work, and I wondered if I'd looked as much a mess as I felt, but her transformative skills had well disguised it.

"Would you like me to paint your face as well?"

I cringed at the offer, the memory of the hidden bruise still too fresh, as was the kneeling crowd, the *religious frenzy* as Recienne had called it. Fresh yet like another life, now that the magic of the fairylands had swallowed me up once more.

It struck me then that I should have used the opportunity of Cyrill already bargaining with Recienne for my eight months' absence to negotiate some of my own conditions—not that Cyrill would have ever allowed for it. But, at least then, the guilt for leaving Leahnie behind wouldn't eat me up in addition to all my other failings.

"No." I tried a smile, meeting the purple eyes of the pale, pink-cheeked fairy, and, surprisingly, found her smiling back at me.

"Very well." She gathered her things, readying to leave, but I turned around, the rustling of my blue chiffon gown following my motions as I stepped toward her.

"How long have you been serving in this court?"

"One hundred and seventy-three years."

I wasn't sure if I should be impressed or pity her.

"You've seen Recienne's cruelty first-hand, have you not?"

"I witnessed how his father made a sport of finding creative ways to let humans die." She didn't add anything, expression guarded as she eyed me.

And I didn't ask any further questions as I slowly tried to piece together what information I'd so far gathered.

After a moment of awkward silence, Naar turned and left.

SEVENTEEN

That day, I decided to leave my room at last. But not until after a thorough few hours of browsing the magic books for anything useful that would help me with my Mage Stone—and finding nothing. Prior to leaving the room, I placed the little crystal in a hidden pocket in my dress before I smoothed out the skirts and made my way down the stairs.

At least, the fear of running into a random fairy who would then torture me had vanished with the knowledge that the palace was empty, and I found no evidence in days that suggested otherwise. Only Recienne and Naar—and the king himself seemed absent most of the time as well. So it was just me and myself when I made it to the long table in the dining hall, half expecting to find Recienne leaning against the edge and smirking at me.

Naar served me dinner there, but my own company soon became a burden I preferred not to shoulder, and I took a plate to my room, deciding that sitting by the window and reading would at least be something useful while I waited... waited for what, I didn't know.

For the eight months to pass, perhaps, and for Recienne to take me back to the human lands where I'd be treated the way I deserved.

Something tiny inside my chest objected, suggesting there was more I deserved than to be used for someone else's gain. But it quieted fast under the evidence that the voice from my dream had been right. That I wasn't enough. That I'd never be enough. Not to save anyone. So perhaps I didn't deserve the magic stored in the Mage Stone either. Perhaps I didn't deserve anything—

The heat in my palm came as suddenly as it disappeared.

With a gasp, I opened my fingers, revealing the view on the dim crystal sitting there, glimmering as milkily as always. But the heat returned for a brief moment. Returned and left. Like a beat of warmth ... a pulse.

My breath caught, excitement filling my veins, making me sit straight and focus on the small movements of colors beneath the surface.

There—another pulse. A stronger one this time.

The stone was now near humming in my palm, resonating with some energy that I couldn't place but had to be magic. I'd felt it in the Mage Stone shard Zelia had given me to protect myself at Ret Relah. But this was different. Where the shard at my throat had borne a fraction of magic, this was a real Mage Stone. A small one but capable of channeling magic, of storing it. Of being reused. And if I managed to use it properly ... I was already in the fairylands. What would keep me from earning magic to recharge it?

The next pulse was strong enough to zing against my skin, leaving me to gasp once more—with pain this time.

For a moment, I debated what I should do: try to continue with whatever was happening or try to stop it so I wouldn't make any mistakes. What if I used too much magic? What if I destroyed it and ended up without a Mage Stone the way Tristan, Zelia, and Dimar had?

Shuddering head to toe at the sensation of the pulling magic, I couldn't help but want it to continue. Let it lead me so I could finally stand on my own.

But as I stared, my eyes watering from keeping myself from so much as blinking, the warm pulsing ebbed until nothing but the memory of it lingered on my skin.

"Not now, not now, not now," I begged the stone. "Please. Continue. I need you."

But the stone had turned dormant once more.

What would Zelia have told me to do had she seen this? Or Dimar? Would Tristan have helped me?

Refraining from answering any of those questions for myself, I decided to call it a night and slid the Mage Stone into the drawer of my nightstand.

The next few days followed the same routine. Naar came every morning to dress me and make conversation. Not that I ever learned anything of substance, only that Recienne was gone most of the days, but that he'd been there some of them, and even when I left my room, I hadn't run into him. Whether that was a blessing, I couldn't tell. But after that night at the fountain—something felt different. Not in the way that I hated him any less, but, perhaps, I'd seen a side of him that felt more human and less monster so that I didn't cringe the next time I saw him.

I was on my way back from the dining room, bowl of stew in hand, and wondering if I should do some more reading. Going there to get dinner was more out of habit than expectation to find him there. But when I headed to eat in my room that night, he shot out of the throne room, a glower on his usually-so-smooth features and a growl on his lips as I noticed him a moment too late to prevent spilling the stew all over the floor as I veered out of his path.

Shit!

"And good evening to you!" I called after him as he'd already reached the top of the stairs, and I bent down to mop up the splashes with the cotton napkin in my other hand.

Recienne stopped, as if realizing only now that I was there, and turned. A smirk replaced the glower, and the growl turned into a chuckle. He prowled closer, coming to a halt a few feet away, grinning as he watched me on my hands and knees where humans probably belonged in his opinion. "You know it would take a mere flick of my fingers to clean that up for you."

Jerk! "You could have watched where you walked." It was all I really had to say.

But that only made him laugh. "Not that I don't enjoy seeing you do the dirty work, Sanja. But it's really not my fault if you don't take me up on the offer."

"Oh, you're welcome to join if you refrain from using magic." Nothing I'd like more than to see *him* get his hands dirty. "But then, I can live very well without your proximity." Most certainly, I'd done perfectly well without his presence the past few days. The bitterness in my tone surprised me more than I could have imagined.

He shot me an incredulous look. "And that is why?"

"Your proximity seems to only cause trouble."

"Trouble?" A challenge entered his gaze that sparked a new boldness in me. "If I remember correctly, my presence ensures your survival, Sanja. I saved you, remember? Repeatedly."

That hot sensation in my stomach flared, crawling through my veins as I seethed at him from my knees. Stupid. I was so stupid to even get down there before he disappeared to somewhere far, far away where he couldn't witness my adopted habits.

What probably upset me the most was the fact that he wasn't entirely wrong. And I hated him more for it.

During the dance, he'd kept me on my feet. At the very last challenge, he'd done something to help—I wouldn't have called it saving. But from Cyrill's claws—he'd gotten me out of there. Though, I was convinced he hadn't done it for selfless reasons. There was always something in the workings at the back of Recienne's mind. Some plan, some game. I wasn't even sure I wanted to know.

But as he pulled his mouth into that grin—"You were the one stealing my name. Had it not been for you, your father would have never been able to control me."

"Had it not been for me, you'd still be sitting in Cyrill's palace, playing the saint, or worse, scrubbing floors in the Master Mage's ramshackle home."

He might be the most powerful fairy in Askarea, but as he smirked down at me, insulting my family's home—something inside of me just snapped, making all that fear evaporate.

"While you might be worried you'll get your pretty fingers dirty, *I* don't mind."

He waited for me to pause my mopping and glance up at him before he said, "You think I mind cleaning the floor, Sanja?" He crouched beside me, pulling a silken handkerchief from his pocket, and wiped up a spot I'd missed a bit away. "But there are other things I can do even better with my *pretty fingers.*"

A wave of heat tinted my cheeks as I debated daring him to show me what exactly his *pretty fingers* were capable of. But something about the way he grinned at me made me want to slap his face instead. With a groan, I straightened. "Maybe I'll just stand and watch your *pretty fingers* do the dirty work, then." I folded my arms and stuck out my hip as I stared him down.

For a heart-stopping moment, I thought he'd use that control of his to snap my neck and silence me forever, but when I held his gaze, that heat spreading through my entire body like a harbinger of pain, Recienne laughed. Actually laughed and shook his head. "I'm not sure you even need anyone to save you, Sanja. Your words are sharp enough."

I wasn't sure if he'd meant it to be an insult or a compliment. My body, however, decided it was the former, and my anger pooled and pooled until that vast emptiness inside my chest was filled with it, a volcano ready to erupt.

"If you think that was sharp, you should have seen me with—" I broke off as I realized what I'd been about to tell him.

"I assume Mage Tristan used to enjoy the glorious torment of your words." He flashed a grin, and the heat in my chest flushed from me in a gust of breath.

Those early days with Tristan flashed through my mind when I'd bitten him with words more than I'd thanked him for picking me off the streets and protecting me from the fairies. The moment he'd first held my hand in the kitchen and healed my cut. The day in the meadow, the apple tart. All those small moments when he'd shed his mask and I'd learned what a caring being he truly was. And all those nights we'd spent together. Nights that would never be the same because I wouldn't survive this. A fairy taking a sudden interest in my survival wouldn't change that for long. At some point, the new toy would become boring, and he'd chuck me aside. He'd already started, leaving me alone in this palace. Who knew... one day, he might forget to have me fed.

Eight months—we were already close to two weeks. But eight months felt like an eternity in the prospect of what awaited me afterward—and what I wouldn't have now and after he returned me to Cyrill's court.

Recienne stood, making his handkerchief vanish with a flick of his fingers, his gaze of gold forming a question in the air between us—where nothing but emptiness was left.

"I don't care what you assume." I didn't pick up the bowl I'd set down on the floor before I stalked back to my room, the emptiness extending to the flow of my tears now.

Two days later, I was brooding over one of the magic books, my Mage Stone tightly clutched in my hand, and Naar's knock came early.

"Come in!" I slipped the crystal into the pocket of my pants, pretending to be focused on my read, when the door opened to reveal not the horned fairy but my least favorite fairy king in all of Eherea. I stifled a groan as I debated turning to the window and pretending he wasn't there.

"Good, you're up." He strode into the room, stopping halfway to the table.

"Good, you knocked," I retorted. It was a first after all. Until now, he'd taken the liberty to simply pop up in my room whenever he pleased.

His lips twitched. "Unlike what you might believe about me, I do have manners."

"On occasion," I jibed.

"On occasion," he echoed, "it is necessary to have manners. As on others"—he flashed a full-toothed smile that had me wondering if *on occasion* he merely sank them into people's throats for the fun of it—"I prefer to lead a less elaborate lifestyle."

As he folded his arms over his chest, stance widening just enough to make him appear less like an unbothered royal than a male ready for a fight, I could almost see the leather armor on him, the hood, the mask that had hidden those sensuous lips the first time I'd met him.

"So I've been told." I turned back to my book, gaze falling on the folded note I'd been using as a bookmark.

Recienne's eyes must have followed mine because he took a casual step closer, peering over my shoulder, and I could have sworn there was hesitation in his voice as he asked, "Are they helping?"

His question caught me so off guard that I turned in my chair, facing him—and finding his eyes clear, curious, his brows puckered the slightest bit. And maybe it was the fact that neither of us had expected to share a look like that— one that might have suggested he wasn't my enemy, *my keeper*, as Cyrill had called it—but, in that moment, it didn't feel like a betrayal to myself to gesture at the note and thank him. I opened my mouth to speak the actual words when he reached past me, his arm brushing my shoulder, which made me shrink back into the windowsill, and picked up a book from the stack in the corner of the table.

"I saved what I could. Thought they might come in handy at some point if a Mage ever came to spend some time in my palace."

What Naar had said the other day flashed through my mind.

Recienne brought them in the night you disappeared. I know he didn't expect you to return right away but—

She hadn't finished her sentence, hadn't added the reasoning behind his actions.

"Handy if a Mage knows how to use actual magic," I muttered under my breath.

Of course, Recienne's fairy ears caught it, and he looked up from flipping through the pages between worn leather binding.

"So you haven't figured it out yet? And there, I thought I felt magic the other night. Or was that just you dreaming of me?"

Choosing to ignore his bait this time, I adjusted his note in the book I'd been reading and closed it. "Why does it even matter to you? Your kind hates Mages—you more than anyone."

A thin layer of anger settled over his features as he watched me slide the book onto one of the stacks. "You know nothing about what I hate—or don't, for that matter." But it smoothed out fast, and that calm, composed expression returned, which caused a tingling in my stomach to warn me that I was missing something.

"I already asked you before—*enlighten me*." It was all I allowed myself to say. If he wanted to talk, he would. And he had come to me—"Or tell me why you're here."

"Just checking on your progress." He folded his arms over his chest once more, that casual grace of the bandit returning and making me painfully aware of the scent of nights under open skies weaving into that of white roses already filling the room. "Now that you destroyed all other Mage Stones, you seem to be the only Mage left, and it would be rather ... boring if Askarea was deprived of all human magic."

Boring. What else should I have expected than for him to see a human rarity in me that he could collect—not that it should have mattered at all what he saw in me.

"And what is in it for you if I master my magic?" A blunt question, but I was too tired to dance around it, to try to trick him into giving me information. Sitting at this very table since dawn after another fitful sleep filled with nightmares, I was just ... tired.

Recienne held my gaze, that grin gone for once. "I already told you I thought it was time someone got you out."

"Like you're the type to help someone without expecting anything in return." I debated biting the air between us just because it would give me something to do that wouldn't mean words he could twist.

"Again, Sanja—" He heaved a breath as if exasperated, but his features remained unreadable as he continued, "If I hadn't gotten you out, nobody else would. And I don't know if I could have lived with the outcome ... for my people," he added quickly.

"What do your people have to do with my being captured and tortured and used?" Not that his kin hadn't done exactly that before—tried.

"You will just have to take me at my word that they do." He tapped the book in his hand with a finger. "And the sooner you master your magic, the sooner I can take a break from worrying when I leave you all alone in this palace."

"Worrying? That someone might come and steal your toy?"

A glimmer of rage flashed in his eyes, and his voice could have frozen all summer as he said, "Don't push my kindness,

Sanja. I may be a patient male, but I'm still only a male. So if you want to make me your villain, by all means, do it. But don't pretend you don't see you are lying to yourself." He didn't give me a moment to comprehend his words, bracing his free hand on the table as he leaned down until his face was level with mine—and that rage fractured the gold of his irises. "Lie to yourself all you want. I don't care. But we both know that, without your magic, you wouldn't survive a day in the streets of Aceleau. And I need you to master it so my father's legacy won't smother us all."

Again with the crypticism. "I'm not lying to anyone." I didn't care how stubborn I sounded. "And you are not kind."

His eyes turned hard, rage contained behind a layer of precious metal, but I didn't budge an inch. Not when he'd had every opportunity to kill me, to hurt me, and hadn't. Cyrill or no.

If there was truly a connection between his people and me, he needed me, and I had leverage that I didn't know yet. So I needed to play this right until I understood what was truly going on.

"Think what you will, Sanja. This isn't about my kindness. This is about my people—and yours."

"Mine? How is this about mine?" Except for him holding off taking over the human realm of Cezux for eight months while he used me for whatever it was he needed from me.

It made sense—on a very abstract level, but at least that piece of the puzzle had settled now. He had traded taking control of Cezux through his father's bargain with Cyrill for something he wanted more—and that was something *I* unwittingly had.

"It is about your people—as in keeping the fairies contained to Askarea. And when I say *the fairies*, I mean all of them."

"Contained," I repeated as if I suddenly had no words of my own.

"I hate to be the one to break it to you, Sanja, but while my father was a cruel tyrant as much as your *dear husband* is, there are certain things he did not for the sake of cruelty but because he was hoping for an easy way out for himself and his people."

He picked up a pile of books from the chair across from me and set them down on the floor before he took a seat, settling in for what might become the longest conversation we'd ever endured.

Tempted to leap up and run at the prospect, my whole body tensed, but he was finally talking, and I needed answers more than I needed air to breathe. So I clamped my mouth shut and waited.

Recienne inclined his head as if understanding exactly how I felt. But he merely leaned back in his chair, interlacing his fingers and bracing them on the edge of the table.

"My father was a fool to make a bargain to extend his own power. After your *lovely Mage's* parents killed my mother, father never fully recovered to his full self. Despite his affinity for human toys, he'd ruled with relative justice for a fairy king. But when his mate was taken from him—he never came back from that. So every human became his enemy, and he desired for nothing more than to take control of the human lands for himself. But the magic protecting the human borders kept him from doing it. So he found himself a young, ambitious merchant eager enough for power to make a bargain with a fairy king."

Dread clanged through me as he was speaking.

"Cyrill Tenikos had only started his work when my father picked him out from the crowd, seeing the hunger for more, for power in the man's eyes, and offered a bargain: He'd get all the riches he ever dreamed of *if* he managed to overthrow the throne of Tavras." He gave me a meaningful look.

Tavras was the home of Tristan's parents, and, of course, the king had wanted to take everything from them—not just their lives and that of their son. I couldn't help but shudder.

"But he is Cezuxian, so my father made a plan. Start with the easy territory and bide his time until he had a human army large enough to invade Tavras. Since the fairies cannot survive outside the Askarean borders for long and their magic is reduced to scraps, he could have never invaded with his immortal army."

That, at least, was a relief.

"So Father gave him riches, helped him build a family history of trade, a wealth to match a kingdom. And when Cyrill was ready"—he met my gaze across the table, revealing a cold in his eyes that had me shuddering all over again—"he introduced himself to your father, Sanja."

Flashes of people dancing in Cezuxian finery, wine, and the taste of summer air. The sight of bruises on servants' wrists. I swallowed hard.

"You remember the day you met him. Probably curse it. But there was never really another outcome for you, Sanja. Your father needed the money. My father made sure of that as well, manipulated trade across the borders with his network of supporters." He paused as if deliberating whether he should continue. "My father could have walked into the human court and killed the king and easily brought Cezux's fall about. But this wasn't about an obvious shift of power, a public display of revenge. This was about sneaking into the human lands with an extended hand, and Cyrill was that hand. And your father took the bait all too easily. After the way he'd let his kingdom fall into misery following Noa's death, he needed the money, and he had you to trade with. So Cyrill was his saving—the saving of his kingdom, he thought. The fact that he didn't care what would happen to you in Cyrill's hands—" I could have sworn the room got a degree or two colder as the air turned almost too solid to breathe—as if Recienne's simmering rage had lifted the control on his power. The most powerful fairy in Askarea—what that meant, I wasn't ready to dissect. Only that he had known—so much more than I'd ever believed anyone could know about what had happened to me.

Yet, there he was, hands now splayed on the edge of the table, and gazing into the distance like he could see all the way to Jezuin where my *husband* was still carrying out Recienne the First's plan.

"If he weren't already dead, I might debate ending him." I didn't doubt it.

"For what he made you do. For everything that happened afterward."

I didn't point out that *he* had played a major role in what had happened to me *afterward*. Didn't need to. For he leaned forward, rage tucked away once more, and wearing an expression I'd never seen on his face—remorse?—battling for the upper hand.

"For what it's worth, I'm sorry, Sanja. For anything that has happened to you. For any part I played in it."

Shocked more than anything by his apology, I leaned back, mouth opening and closing as I fished for words.

When I didn't find any, he continued, running a hand through his dark hair and leaving it rumpled. "My father made a big mistake, though. After he had Cyrill on the Cezuxian throne, ruling from afar was no longer enough. He wanted to actually sit on the throne of Cezux before he'd one day sit on the throne of Tavras. And in his greed for power, for revenge, he asked the one people for help even we powerful high fae fear." He gave me a serious look that reminded me all too much of someone who was about to share a secret. Then a dark wind caressed my cheek as he opened his mouth to speak again, and I knew whatever would come was meant for my ears only.

"He asked the Crow Fairies," he whispered, and had I not been petrified already, I would have frozen over then and there, "and now, they are pushing for power in Askarea from their Seeing Forest."

There—there it was. A confession of weakness. Even brought about by his father. But he was struggling to keep power in his own lands. Even when—"If you are the most powerful fairy in Askarea, how can the Crow Fairies scare you?"

Recienne gave me a look so bare that the hollow in my chest began throbbing with sympathy once more, and I wondered what could possibly be so bad that even the master of masks couldn't keep a layer of disguise up.

"He promised them my sister."

I wasn't fast enough to ask him to repeat himself. Not that I hadn't heard clearly what he'd said—his words had caressed my ear in a dark, tormented murmur. He was already explaining, "When he reached out to the Crows to help him break down the borders between human and fairy realms, their price was the hand of my sister."

I sucked in a breath when I realized that, first—he had a sibling, second—that female had a fate similar to mine, third—Recienne had just given me a piece of information about himself that he might not have intended to give to anyone. And that was how much he cared about her. It was shining in his eyes as he spoke the word 'sister', and now that I'd gleaned that depth of emotion in him, it was difficult not to see it—even with his mask slamming back into place.

I didn't reach for his hand the way I would have with any human sharing such a detail. Didn't ask about how my ability to use a Mage Stone might ever be useful to him when it came to containing a whole realm of fairies to their own borders. Didn't even try to accuse him of having known all along what would happen to me and never once thinking of stopping his father before all of this could unfold.

I didn't speak at all. And whatever he found in my eyes, Recienne didn't speak either.

EIGHTEEN

I didn't eat alone that day. Not because I chose not to but because Recienne summoned me shortly before dinner, and I couldn't find it in me to refuse him. So I trudged down the stairs, still in my pants and linen shirt. Not fancy at all but practical—not that I'd done anything other than sit and read most of the days since I'd arrived in this palace.

Naar hadn't shown up to braid my hair or fuss in any other way as she'd adopted a habit of doing, and I hadn't taken the time to do more than swipe it back and bind it at my nape before I'd left the room. Now that I noticed the voices in the dining room—*voices* in plural—I wondered if I should return and change into something more appropriate for a royal court. Then again, it wasn't like I'd chosen to be a guest here, but I was more enduring my presence here for a lack of a better option. So I might as well look the part.

Stomach tight, I slowed my stride, hoping they hadn't heard me. They, meaning Recienne and a second, deep-voiced male who I couldn't remember having heard speak before.

"You don't think it's dangerous to keep her here?" the voice said, smooth despite the obvious concern ringing through. "What if they find out?"

"They can go to the Horn of Eroth for all that I care," Recienne retorted, but he didn't sound convinced, and the concern shimmered in his tone as well.

"She might be the last Mage in Askarea, but she is untested, untrained. She can't even summon an ounce of magic from what I understand."

"Then we train her."

"Train? You can't *train* a Mage. Not the way we train our younglings. It's an entirely different way of using magic. One not accessible to us, in case you don't remember," the other male grumbled, his response fading into something unintelligible.

I held my breath to catch the meaning.

"Don't think I don't hate the idea ... but I fear I don't have another option."

Whatever they were talking about, it made sense now that Recienne would want me to have those books to unlock the Mage Stone. Apparently, it was of vital importance, not only to him but to whoever else was with him in that room. I inched closer to the door, praying to the Guardians that their conversation would swallow the sound of my boots.

"Clio thinks a change of environment would be helpful. She has experience with Mages."

"Don't remind me." I could basically hear the eye-roll in Recienne's voice.

The other male chuckled.

My stomach used that very moment of silence following that chuckle to grumble audibly, and a sigh followed by footsteps told me they'd heard me.

"Come in, Sanja," Recienne called.

There was no point in hiding now.

Bracing myself for whatever creature I'd find in the dining room, I stepped onto the threshold, eyes scanning the room and discovering Recienne brooding over a plate of roast meat and what looked like some spice bread. A few chairs farther down the table, a male with wavy, shoulder-length auburn hair eyed me with an amused pale face.

"Goodbye, Astorian." Recienne didn't lift his gaze as he spoke to this Astorian but picked up his glass of water and drained it.

Astorian, however, straightened to his full height, flexing his long, powerful arms in a way that did nothing to hide the various blades sheathed along his torso, hips, and thighs. If anything, he reminded me of the bandit Recienne was hiding so desperately from the world.

He didn't bow as he walked past the new fairy king, and he most certainly didn't bow when he walked past me on the wide threshold of the open double doors. All he did was give me a curious look with eyes as auburn as his hair and raise his eyebrows before he vanished into thin air a few steps into the hallway.

"You don't need to worry about Astorian," he said, gesturing at the chair across from him where a second plate was waiting for me. "He is one of the few people I trust in this realm."

If I was honest, I was more worried about their topic of conversation, but I was also too scared to bring it up. Not because I feared what Recienne would do but because I was afraid of the truth—another truth he was hiding.

So I walked up to my assigned place and sat down, eyes on the food. And the smell of it—I suppressed a sigh.

When I looked up, a faint smile was placed on Recienne's lips. "I assume you heard every last word."

I couldn't help grimacing. "Not *every* word." At least, I could keep myself from wincing at the frown forming above the smile.

"So why doesn't Astorian want me to train?" I decided offense was the best defense. Perhaps I'd learn something useful.

"Because he doesn't understand the least bit about Mages," he said, sour.

"And you do?"

He lifted his gaze from his food again. "More than most fairies. Especially since two of them betrayed my family and killed my mother. I found it important to educate myself on the dangers of having a Mage around."

"And there I thought Astorian was concerned about *my* safety, not yours." It was a poor move, but something in the way his gaze wouldn't lighten made me want to push—push harder until his usual spark would return to his eyes.

"Oh, trust me, he is." He picked up his fork and started eating without further explanation.

So I did the same. Until the silence turned uncomfortable—and the questions in my mind had fully formed.

"Why exactly do you need a Mage? How am I useful against the"—I lowered my voice to a whisper—"the Crow Fairies?"

His eyes snapped up to me, a warning flickering in them at the mention of what seemed to be the unmentionable in Askarea. "How much did your Mage tell you about Mage history, Sanja?"

Fragments of my conversations with Zelia and Tristan wafted through my mind, the way Mages had been exiled from Cezux. The spying on the Jezuinian court in the hopes of forging a new era where Mages were accepted in the realm once more. My mother's death by poison. Erju's knowledge.

But also what she'd told me about the development of Mage Stones. How her ancestors had figured out a way to store fairy magic in crystals. I didn't know what was common knowledge and what a secret, so I shrugged. "The bare minimum, I assume."

He raised an eyebrow. "And you never thought to ask for more than the *barest minimum*?" There was no humor in his voice.

"It wasn't only *my* Mage who didn't tell me much, if I may remind you."

"You may," he said with a dry chuckle. "But considering how Tristan was prepared to steal you right from under Cyrill's nose and live with the consequences, I would have thought he'd have spent at least the same effort on preparing you for any and every danger you might face as a Mage—in Askarea or the human realms."

"You don't even know what I know," I retorted, hearing it for the meaningless phrase it was. If I was honest, it had been Zelia who'd told me anything at all. Zelia who'd filled me in about what had been done to my family and how we'd found a new place in Askarea.

His bitter grin was difficult to look at, so I averted my eyes from the painful realization that, maybe, I hadn't learned nearly as much as I could have. Not about magic, and not about this realm I'd been spending months in, too busy making moony eyes at Tristan.

No—no, that was not what it had been. I'd questioned everything, had tried, had pushed—and had gotten grumpy looks and pointers that it wasn't the time yet. That, as a Quarter Mage, I wasn't supposed to know certain things or *do* certain things. When in reality, what I would have needed was someone who'd prepared me to defend myself.

"Enlighten me," I demanded for the third time since he'd brought me here. And this time, it wasn't a taunt.

Recienne seemed to feel it, too, since, for a change, he indulged me with a nod and set down his fork. "Have you ever heard about the Ultimate Sacrifice?"

I considered pretending I knew just so he wouldn't find fertile ground to make me doubt what I'd gotten from my Mage family—the care, the protection, the knowledge—too little of it. "No."

Again, he nodded. "Have you ever wondered why there are so few Mages in Askarea, Sanja? Or why they are in hiding in the human lands? Have you ever wondered what made the blossoming population of magically gifted humans disappear?"

With everything going on—my escape from the fairy palace after freeing Tristan, Zelia, and Dimar, my focus had remained on my own family and kingdom more than on learning everything about Mages that I could—the way I probably should have. I picked up the water glass in front of me and sipped while I waited for him to continue.

"A long, long time ago, before the fairies were bound to their own lands so they couldn't harm the human realms of Eherea, human magic"—he reached for the napkin, absently playing with the edge of it—"*your* magic was the only thing standing between fairies and humankind." He said it as if there had once been many, many Mages—enough to control a realm of immortal creatures of power. I wondered if he'd seen those times, had once feared Mages. "Despite their efforts, fairies slipped through, taking humans in the night, whisking them into Askarea where they became slaves, entertainment—property. You can imagine that it didn't take the Mages long before they realized it. And, of course, they couldn't allow it. But despite their strength and numbers, they couldn't be everywhere at once to keep the human lands safe, so the Mages—your ancestors—decided to protect the human lands in a different way." He laced his fingers together, his napkin disappearing under his palms. "Instead of fighting for every single life the fairies took, every human they stole, and losing good Mages in every mission to rescue them, the Mages decided to make the Ultimate Sacrifice— and ban the fairies from their lands by other means."

Recienne paused, his eyes again fixed on a point in his memories.

"The Ultimate Sacrifice?" I almost didn't dare ask, but as Recienne turned silent, contemplative, I couldn't stop my words.

He gave me a long look—one of the sorts that made you regret having asked at all. "It took a thousand Mages to bind the fairies to their lands. A thousand good humans, who committed themselves to stopping the fairies—to save humankind from the threat lingering in Askarea.

"They weren't strong enough to kill the fairies, weren't enough in numbers to win a war. Stealth and intrigue were their friends, their weapons when they prepared, over generations and generations, an army of Mages willing to give their lives to protect their own and humankind." I gasped. "And when there were enough, they spread across the lands to perform the ritual that would bind the fairies, would tie our life force to Askarea and Askarea alone so that, when we decided to roam the human realms once more, we'd find ourselves withering and dying, so the one thing we valued above all else would be ripped from us if we dared come too close to your part of this world—our power.

"With their blood and their magic, they performed the ritual, soaking the soil with their spells—magic stolen from fairies, preserved in Mage Stones until they were full to bursting. They gave their lives so your kind could live in a world where they wouldn't need to fear for their families ... for their friends, their children to be taken in the dead of night by the fair folk."

I only realized I was staring at him when he stopped

speaking and his eyes found mine, cool metal hiding a wealth of emotions.

"You were in Cezux," I whispered, not even understanding why it mattered after what he'd told me about the Ultimate Sacrifice, the lives lost because of creatures like him, cruel and wicked, delighting in the pain of humans, despising humans.

"To get you out." The words were so low I could barely hear them. But he cleared his throat, running a hand through his hair. "I'm the most powerful fairy in Askarea, Sanja. I might have aged a day or two, and existing without full access to my powers is an inconvenience. But the border drawn in blood didn't affect me half as much as it does other fairies—weaker fairies." He paused, letting the full meaning set in. "Besides, I wasn't there for long. Only to remind Cyrill that his throne wasn't truly his so he wouldn't make any mistakes once he found you—and, believe me, I was counting on him to find you." The way he studied me made the little hairs stand on the back of my neck.

"Not to kill me." I knew that much by now. "But to ensure the bargain your father made with Cyrill would remain untouched."

Recienne shook his head. "I was counting on him to find you because I couldn't comb Cezux myself for weeks and weeks without the risk of losing my powers completely. Or even my life. Then Askarea would fall to *them*." He didn't need to mention the Crow Fairies for me to know who he was talking about.

"Not to *her*." I willed him to understand I meant his sister. If she was of the same bloodline, Askarea would be hers for sure.

"*They* would get her and at the next Ret Relah—" He wiped his hands over his face. "Well, you get the idea."

Beautiful human, pretty human. I have a fortress of bones for you to share.

The Crow Fairy's voice hissed through my mind; I could taste the fear like I'd tasted it that day when Tristan had first pulled me against him in the middle of the street. To show the Crow Fairy that I was already *taken*. The memory didn't make me shudder any less.

I have a lake of tears for you to bathe in. I have a crown of carved teeth for you to wear. I have a bed of skin for you to sleep in.

"They'd make her a bride?"

He nodded, fingers curling in front of him, and I could have sworn the air between them turned solid. "And there is nothing I can do to change it. Not if I am dead or powerless."

"And without a Mage to help you do *what*?" I prompted, the spot in my chest throbbing again, willing myself to use the opportunity to get more information. Anything that would help *me* survive—in this realm or the other.

"A Mage to help me redraw the border to the Seeing Forest that my father loosened." He leaned back in his chair, looking, again, so, so tired. "With the Ultimate Sacrifice, the Mages locked us fairies in Askarea, but they did more. The blood spilled over the soil of Askarea made the treaty with the Crow Fairies, which ended the Crow War, binding."

Tristan had told me about the Crow War. If nothing else, at least, I'd heard about that war before.

"In exchange for my sister's hand, they would help him increase his own power until he could cross the border the way I can—and prevail against the blood magic of the Ultimate Sacrifice."

"He'd have gone free," I realized.

"Free of all constraints of the borders protecting the human lands."

I swallowed the information, no longer finding space in my stomach for food or drink. And despite the pity for the fairy king before me, all I could think of was, "But why do you even care? You hate humans. You love to torture them."

The words tasted like ash the moment they slid off my tongue, and judging by the way Recienne looked at me, it was the one thing he hadn't expected me to say, for his eyes went vacant, and a muscle feathered in his jaw.

"If that's still what you choose to believe, Sanja, by all means, go ahead."

Just like that, the truce between us was over.

NINETEEN

I t didn't help that I kept replaying his words in my mind. Especially since they contradicted what Zelia had once told me. *We don't know exactly what ancient magic protects the borders, where it came from, and how it works, but we know that not even Crow Fairies risk roaming the human lands,* Zelia had assured after my encounter with the Crow Fairy. If she simply didn't know the truth or tried to keep it from me, I couldn't tell.

But the way Recienne'd spoken ... as if he was on the side of the Mages, the humans, rather than the fairies. It could as well have been Zelia telling me the story for the emotion he'd put in on the human side. But the emptiness in his gaze when I'd challenged his reasons... It haunted me long into the night and the next day when I was sitting at the table in my room once more, trying to focus on my Mage Stone in hope and dread of getting it to pulse.

I had yet to figure out what a fully *functional* Mage would mean for his attempts of redrawing the border to the Seeing Forest. Perhaps he wanted me to perform another Ultimate Sacrifice. A thing that would definitely never happen. Especially not if he was trying to trick me into it—or, worse, use his control over my body once I had the magic all figured out. He *could* do it.

He'd even admitted to having Cyrill hunt for me so he didn't need to.

A small voice at the back of my mind reminded me of what else he'd admitted. Something he had probably not intended for me to hear.

To get you out.

I wrapped my fingers harder around the Mage Stone, that hopeless emptiness gone for the first time in weeks and a solid layer of anger enveloping me instead.

Something vibrated in my fingers. Slowly at first. Then faster and faster. Not the muted pulsing of the last time I'd felt the Mage Stone come to life but something harder, more violent.

I braced myself for an eruption of magic, something as uncontrollable as the beast prowling inside my veins.

It didn't come.

Instead, the words Recienne had spoken manifested in my mind once more.

And the magic *got me out.*

My scream must have torn through the gardens like the howl of a sick cat, for both Naar and Recienne showed up a second later—Naar running from between the bushes and Recienne popping up out of thin air with amused surprise on his features and no trace of our earlier conversation clouding his gaze.

"That's what I call a surprise," he purred as he watched me roll into a sitting position and keep myself from brushing my hands over my behind where my pride had been thoroughly placed in the summer grass beneath the canopy of leaves and branches.

He held out a hand to help me up, and I ignored it if purely for the reason of no longer being sure of what to think of the male who'd *gotten me out*—but for what reasons other than to have me die somewhere else where it suited him better?

Naar was at my side in a heartbeat, her long, pale fingers brushing over my arm and back where little grass blades had caught on my linen shirt.

"Are you hurt?" she wanted to know.

"I'm all right." Despite the shock still stuck in my bones, I was. I truly was. Because, for the first time since the day Zelia had given me the Mage Stone, I felt like things might turn for the better after all—until I spotted the conflict in Recienne's eyes.

As if shrugging off a ghost of a memory, he took a step forward, shooing Naar aside with an elegant hand and picking a long blade of grass off my forearm. "I've got her," he announced, and together, we watched Naar clop back to the house.

"She can't ... step through the world like you?" I couldn't find a better way of phrasing it.

Recienne laughed, but the sound was hollow. "Site-hopping? That's for the strongest among us."

I couldn't help but think of Astorian. "Your friend did it."

"Astorian? He is strong. And by strong, I mean powerful magic—unlike yours, which won't last a minute if you hop through the world like a fairy noble."

"What?" I watched him watch me, waiting for whatever eloquent explanation he'd come up with this time.

"Your Mage Stone." He reached for my hand where I only noticed a slight soreness when he peeled my fingers off the stone and picked it from my palm to hold it up between us.

"What about it?"

"Isn't it a bit ... well, small?"

"It's sized perfectly," I objected, if only for the sake of not letting him belittle anything of mine. "Tristan's Mage Stone wasn't much bigger."

He considered me for a moment, a glint of something flashing in his gaze that I didn't miss even in the growing darkness of the gardens.

"Besides, it's not like size matters."

"You only say that because you haven't seen true *size*." That glint turned into a wicked grin, and I wanted to throw up my hands in frustration.

Instead, I made a sound between a hiss and a grunt and plucked my Mage stone from his fingers.

"It's only you men who are so obsessed with size." Whatever had made me say the words, I already regretted them.

For Recienne's teeth flashed white in the half-light as he angled his head at me.

"First—*male*, not *man*. Second—if you're ever ready to find out what's better with *size*, give me a shout."

My toes curled in my shoes, and I held on to the Mage Stone so hard it pulsed again, making little flames sizzle on the patch of grass between us.

Recienne's eyes widened a bit before he composed his face and said, "I think that's enough for today. We don't want you to burn through all your reserves the first time you use the stone."

"What? Are you an expert on Mage magic now?"

"*Mage magic*? Really?" He eyed me, the wickedness from before completely gone. "And, no, I'm not. But I've traded with the Master Mage and Mage Tristan enough to know how little magic even the bigger Mage Stones can hold. I don't know how much magic site-hopping or making flames take from a human, but I don't want to take any risk."

"Because you need me as a weapon against the *Crow Fairies*," I whispered the last words.

Recienne simply nodded once. "But more than that, I need you to be all right."

When he held out his hand this time, I didn't ignore it but studied it for a short moment—the long, strong fingers, the seam of his jacket grazing the end of his palm. An invitation to take it lingered so heavily between us that I almost did it. But he sighed and gestured toward the palace.

"I was going to site-hop you back to your room, but if you prefer to walk, I'd be happy to do that, too." He waited for me to join him before he started walking, leading the way to the back entrance of the palace where I'd once stood in a maze that had tried to swallow me whole.

I couldn't stop myself from shaking.

"Are you all right?" His eyes lingered on my face as I tried to breathe through the panic that came with the sight of the dense greenery surrounding us.

No. No, I wasn't. Without thinking, I reached for his hand, squeezing hard. "Site-hop me to the tower."

He didn't ask any questions but vanished us from the gardens back to the safety of my room where he let go of my hand, a tingling that had nothing to do with magic lingering in my palm long after he disappeared.

The nausea hit a sharp few minutes later. Not in full force the way it had that first time he'd site-hopped me from the borderlands to Aceleau and I'd vomited my guts up. And not as unspectacular as when he'd spirited me from Jezuin to the fairy palace. It was a mild sort of nausea, starting in the center of my stomach with a small squeamishness and spreading all through my body in shivers. Shivers, I realized, that had little to do with the actual nausea itself but with the sudden tiredness that crept up on me as if I'd run a long, long way uphill.

Without a look at the books I'd left scattered on the table or the Mage Stone in my hand, I dropped onto the bed and drifted into an exhausted sleep.

When I woke again, it was to the sound of muffled birdsong and clopping footsteps leaving my room. Blinking my eyes open, I tried to remember what had happened ... and found Recienne lounging in an armchair beside my bed, which hadn't been there the night before. I forced myself to keep still while he hadn't noticed I was awake.

His gaze was trained on the book in his lap, thick lashes hiding the gold of his irises and fluttering every so often as he blinked when he flipped a page. He had an ankle crossed over a knee and his head propped on a fist, elbow braced on the rolled armrest. His black jacket had been replaced by a creme tunic, which was unbuttoned to reveal a sliver of tan skin at the base of his throat, the sleeves rolled up to mid-forearm. Sitting there like that, just reading, features relaxed, near solemn, Recienne looked almost ... peaceful, and I could have watched the gentle curve of his mouth for the entirety of an hour had my body not betrayed me and my stomach growled—again.

"I know you're awake," he said without looking up from his book.

I tried not to smile at his sardonic tone. Even when his posture hadn't changed, his features had tightened, the planes and angles of his face no less beautiful, no longer that of *just* Recienne but that of the king, who was on guard at all times.

I rolled to the side, allowing my eyes to study him for a moment longer before I needed to return to the truths he'd shared the day before—and my own new reality of having used magic.

"What..." I cleared my throat. "What are you doing up here?" I tried not to make it sound like an accusation, but the words came out sharp anyway—and weak at the same time. Blame it on that damn exhaustion that hadn't really worn off.

Recienne's eyes found mine over his book, two golden suns tinted in hues of morning light. The intensity of the gaze made my throat dry up all over again.

"Someone had to make sure you wouldn't exert yourself with your newfound magic." So at odds with the weight of his gaze, the lightness of his voice—so casual. "But when I returned, you'd already fallen asleep..." He didn't finish his explanation, and something in my stomach told me that he might have been sitting there all night, watching over my sleep—or debating ways to offer me up to the Crow Fairies.

But the sensation was swept away by a wave of emptiness—and that guilt that had driven me into desperation long before I'd ever known Recienne had traded his rule over Cezux for eight months with me. Guilt—that my first thought after waking hadn't been that I wanted to tell Tristan about the magic, or Zelia, or even Dimar, but, instead, had marveled at the flawless face of the male sitting mere feet from me, not quirking a brow in question.

"How do you feel?" He closed the book and placed it on my nightstand right next to my Mage Stone, which, I was convinced, he had extracted from my grasp and placed there as well.

I swallowed the guilt burning in my chest, and the emptiness where Tristan should have been, and shook my head. "Tired. Hungry. And more tired."

His lips tipped up at the sides, and the guilt burned hotter.

"I'll have Naar bring you something." He flexed his arms over his head, rolling his shoulders as he got to his feet. "As for your magic, you used up most of the reserves stored in the crystal. If you want to try again, you'll need to recharge it so you don't risk draining it completely." And by that, destroy it. He didn't need to add that.

"Is that an offer?" I forced strength into my voice, but my throat was dry and my body so, so heavy.

He cocked his head, pulling down his sleeves as if he'd only now noticed they were up, and buttoning them at his wrists. "You tell me." He faced me, a challenge in his eyes that had nothing to do with the temper from our early encounters but a genuine prompt to ask him for help.

For a short moment, I debated giving him a vulgar gesture just because it was obvious there were only two fairies in this palace I could trade with and that he already knew I was dependent on him with my magic. But when he simply kept watching me as I rolled it over in my head, that part of me went still and attentive, listening.

"I'll give you some magic—however much your tiny Mage Stone can store," he eventually said when I didn't respond.

"At what cost." It was the only sane response I could give, and, thank the Guardians, my mind hadn't gone as numb as the rest of me.

At that, his lips curled into a grin that didn't promise anything good. "You come with me today, no questions asked."

"Where?" If I was to accompany him on his errands, I'd need to at least know it wasn't to the Seeing Forest.

"I said, *no questions asked.*" He flicked his fingers, and the armchair disappeared.

I made a mental note to ask him how that worked and if it was something I might be able to do myself—later. As for now, I struggled to balance the panic mingling with a new sort of excitement at the prospect of being let in on one more of his secrets.

"Promise me I will not get killed wherever you're taking me." I set a condition, my fingers wrapping around the Mage Stone as I tentatively lifted it from the nightstand.

And just like that, Recienne's grin broadened across his full face, making him look both awfully attractive and scary as sleeping alone and unarmed in a cave in the borderlands.

"Promise." He lunged for my hand, grasping it in a handshake while, with the other, he released a flickering stream of light dancing from his fingers to the crystal I'd just retrieved from beside my bed. And I couldn't tell what scared me more, the bargain I'd made or his calloused fingers around mine.

TWENTY

I didn't know what I'd expected, but it was not the sunlight-filtering greenery catching my fall as I stumbled away from Recienne when we hit the soft forest ground. His chuckle followed me right to the moss and roots, where I scrambled to get back to my feet. Not that I still expected him to ram a knife into my back the moment I turned it to him, but I still felt very much uncomfortable not having him in view—especially when he seemed to get a rise out of my human inadequacies.

"And there I thought you'd be used to it by now." He watched me brush leaves and dirt off the pants I'd put on after Naar had brought breakfast and pulled my shirt back into place where it had shifted to the side to nearly expose my shoulder.

In response, I grunted unceremoniously and stalked a few steps away just so I could mark every small movement that might indicate he'd grab me again and site-hop us elsewhere.

He hadn't informed me about our destination before he'd brought us here, only smirked at my question of where we'd be going and dared me to place my hand in his. After a long moment of hesitation, I'd decided that holding up my end of the bargain was essential if I wanted to keep him as my magic supplier.

Now, my eyes bulged, and I almost stumbled back into the tree behind me as I took in the changes that must have occurred sometime during the brief travel through the canvas of the world.

Where thin linen had spread over his torso, now a familiar leather armor was covering him up, a mask hid his mouth and nose, and those golden eyes had disappeared in the shadow of a dark hood. Behind his shoulder, a bow and a quiver of arrows were peeking at me, and the baldric of blades strapped across his chest invited the same dread I'd felt the very first time I'd run into the fairy bandit.

"Oh, don't look at me like that, Sanja." I could have sworn he lifted a brow in the shadows of his hood. "It's still me."

Wiping my fear from my features with a shaky hand, I did lean into the tree for support. "Of course, it's still you. Who else would choose to roam the forests and trick names out of unsuspecting humans." I hoped the words hit their mark.

Recienne chuckled again, and it was the same drizzle of sunshine and death that had once petrified me—only now, there was something more to it than that innate fear quaking to life inside my body. I wanted to peel back the mask and see those lips twitch with the sound, wanted to peer into those eyes and read whether it was real amusement or the mask I'd seen him wear countless times in the fairy court—before and after his father's death.

A shudder worked itself up my spine, and I hoped I hadn't made the biggest mistake of my life in trusting him.

"Should I even ask where we are?"

Much to my surprise, he shrugged, bow rising an inch with the motion, and pointed behind him. "You already know my biggest secret, Sanja."

"Your biggest secret?"

Instead of reminding me which of the many secrets he'd shared with me was the *biggest*—not that size mattered; I was going to stick by that—he leaned closer.

"My *biggest* secret," he repeated with that tone that made me want to throttle him yet, at the same time, triggered that spot in my chest to come alive ... with annoyance, I decided, since any other option would make me a traitorous human piece of garbage. And undeserving of Tristan's love. Had I not yearned for him not too many weeks ago? Had I not been hoping for him to find me? And now? So much had changed. But one thing hadn't.

You're not enough. You'll never be enough.

I couldn't tell why that dream was still haunting me. Perhaps because I still hadn't achieved any of what I'd hoped for.

Hadn't defeated Cyrill—no, I'd given him a weapon to work with by playing his little saint. Hadn't taken back my throne and freed my people, hadn't found a way to give Tristan, Zelia, and Dimar back their magic. Even with my Mage Stone finally reacting to me, I wasn't even an inch closer to achieving anything other than increasing my guilt.

He prowled closer until he towered over me, and those golden orbs pierced from the shadows right into my soul. "And if you decide to betray me, I can always find ways to make you regret it." As if in emphasis, his power slid over my body, reaching for my hand and drawing it toward him.

For a moment, I stood, paralyzed, but then I noticed the twinkle in his eye, proof of a different sort of mischief that had nothing to do with the violence I'd once expected from him.

Forcing down a slow, steadying breath, I pitted my will against his control and found my fingers wriggling free of it a moment before they landed in his palm.

Laughing, Recienne turned away, gesturing for me to follow. So I did. Not because his control made me but because, despite the danger he emanated, he was still safer than staying behind alone in the fairy forest.

We walked in silence, him bending aside twigs and branches when we got to a denser part of the forest. My human feet and coordination were enough to carry me through most of the path, but after what felt like an hour of walking, my patience left me, and I asked, "Where are we going?"

Recienne glanced at me over his shoulder, his eyes shimmering like real metal in the half-light, and I could almost feel the grin beneath the mask. "Where would be the fun in telling you?"

"I thought I already knew your *biggest* secret." I couldn't help but emphasize the word in a petty copy of him.

"You do. Doesn't make it any less fun to watch you guessing."

The fact that he hadn't really looked at me in the past hour was something I refrained from pointing out.

"And that is why?" I pushed my shorter legs to catch up with him.

"Do I need a reason to enjoy something, Sanja?" The way he said it made me stop asking—and it wasn't necessarily from fear—at least, not of him. But of that question in his tone—more than the one he'd voiced.

The forest grew denser and denser until, eventually, a wall of stone rose behind the thicket ahead. He climbed over a boulder, holding out his hand to help me keep my footing on the slippery moss, and, for once, I didn't think twice.

On the other side, underbrush and rocks tall as the fairy bandit himself blocked our path, and I was about to ask if he was just leading me through the forest for the fun of it. But he waved a hand, and the branches bent out of our path, leaving a narrow track winding between the rocks, straight to a slit in the stone wall, barely wide enough for Recienne to slip through.

Trying not to focus on the fact that he hadn't let go of my hand after the boulder, I followed him all the way to the gap where he stopped and placed a finger of his free hand to his lips over the mask. For a moment, I wondered what it would look like if he did that without the fabric covering up his mouth. "It might hurt for a brief heartbeat," he whispered. It was all the warning he gave me before he dropped my hand and slid in between the jagged edges of the rock.

My heart stopped for a beat as he was swallowed up by the inky blackness behind him, and I wondered if that was the brief pain he'd meant or if that was yet to come. I didn't scream when I finally stepped inside after him and all air was forced from my lungs in a painful squeeze that had nothing to do with the size of the gap. But a gasp surely followed as soon as it released me and I could breathe freely again.

"What ... was that?" I panted, suddenly worried that he had brought me here to end me after all. But in the darkness, a golden orb of fairy light was floating right above Recienne's head, gilding his hair where he'd slipped down his hood, and his eyes ... his eyes reminded me of the look he'd given me that morning.

"Welcome home, Sanja." He splayed his arms to the sides as if gesturing around the grand hall of a palace.

"Home..." I repeated, my breath still straining in and out of my lungs. Whatever that gap had done to me, it seemed to have a much worse effect on me than on him, for he seemed to be in perfect condition while I... Well, I was struggling to inhale deeply enough to curse him to the Horn of Eroth and back.

"Can you breathe?" He seemed to notice just now that I was indeed not doing well at all.

"Enough to tell you what a bastard you are, sure." It cost me a coughing fit to get the words out, but Recienne seemed immune to my jabs.

His arm slid around my shoulders, guiding me to a rock big enough to serve as a bench for two, and sat me down. "I didn't think it would affect you that much."

I didn't ask what exactly had affected me, but, for once, he offered the information anyway.

"It's a safety mechanism. When a fairy slips through, they feel like the gap is squishing them, and it motivates them to not push further. They simply think they don't fit through. I've never thought about what it would do to a human."

"Great." It was all I got out before I had to bend over when a new wave of coughs shook through me.

Could this have been any more humiliating? Perhaps if I'd vomited right at his feet instead, which, in fact, I'd done the very first time he'd site-hopped us. So there was truly no way I could sink any lower.

A warm hand smoothed back loose strands of hair, brushing them all the way to my neck, following down my spine.

"Breathe slowly. In and out." He continued the movement of his hand, up and down my spine—long, luxurious, soothing strokes that took my focus away from the vise on my chest and to the warmth spreading through me originating in his touch.

Slowly, gradually, my coughing ceased, and I managed to take a real, deep breath.

"I thought you promised I wouldn't die in your company."

That startled a laugh out of him, and his hand stopped between my shoulder blades as he considered me from the side. I only knew because I'd rested my cheek on my knee and was gazing at him in the half-light.

"Come." He stood, palm sliding off my back and leaving it surprisingly cold.

In response, the guilt in my chest brought back a new wave of coughs.

Recienne led me into a tunnel that I hadn't spotted at first since it was well hidden behind the wall of an alcove.

"So you live in a cave?" I eventually said when our footsteps had been the only thing cutting through the silence for excruciatingly long moments that made my mind drift to the Hollow Mountains, wondering if they were similar, if Zelia, Dimar, and Tristan had arrived there and were safe from at least Cyrill's reach.

"Sometimes."

His casual response drew me from my thoughts enough to acknowledge the outline of his shoulders before me—and the glow of natural light a few paces ahead. Recienne ducked through a low opening and waited for me to follow.

"But mostly, I live here."

Whatever I tried, I couldn't keep my mouth from hanging open as I took in the house that seemed built into the tree. As if made of branches and rocks carved from the cave, it wound along the tree trunk, climbing two stories into the treetop where a canopy of leaves hid what sort of roof sheltered it from the seasons. A beam of sunlight fell over the edge of the natural stone walling off the little clearing with the cave as the only entrance visible.

My feet carried me a step closer, my fingers itching to touch the braided walls, the glimmering stone that reminded me of the houses in Aceleau but so much richer in color. And the windows ... they seemed to be made of all hues of glass.

I couldn't tell how long I'd been staring when Recienne cleared his throat behind me, announcing his approach as if not wanting to startle me. "It's beautiful, isn't it?"

For lack of words, I turned to find his eyes not on the building but on my face. He'd pulled down his mask, and in place of the smirk from the palace, a hint of a smile graced his lips while his eyes... His eyes were near-solemn.

I turned away just in time to watch the door open and Astorian stroll outside in the same armor as the last time I'd seen him, his hair pulled back at the back of his head and bound into a bun. Behind him, a female lingered on the threshold, her copper hair flowing to her waist in lush waves.

I'd seen her before—at least, I thought I had.

"Good to see you again, Sanja," Astorian said, a grin spreading on his lips that I could only describe as feral and playful all at once.

I turned to Recienne, eyebrows raised in question. He shrugged innocently, and for the first time, I thought I glimpsed a fragment of his true self. Not the innocence, obviously, but something in his eyes had lit up, making them practically glow.

"You've already met Tori," Recienne said as he clapped the male on the back, apparently not an inch afraid of the brawn in his form and the danger and mischief in his face.

While Astorian scanned me like a particularly interesting opponent, Recienne strolled to the open door where the female had been observing the encounter with her arms crossed. I wasn't sure who to look out for more—the obvious danger of the male or the subtle threat that was the female. She had no weapon on her from what I could see from the distance, but that didn't mean she was harmless—in fact, it might make her the most dangerous of them.

Recienne wrapped his arms around her, pulling her into a tight hug. I tried to ignore the little spot in my chest that stung in response ... because nobody had embraced me like that in weeks. Because the only people who would still embrace me were the ones now fleeing to the Hollow Mountains without me.

"So you finally decided to bring her here," the female said as she pulled away from him, leaving one arm around his waist while one of his remained around her shoulders. A unified front—it was the first thing coming to my mind.

"I thought she could do with some company," Recienne said, face unreadable as he studied me from afar, eyes once more guarded as if monitoring what I'd do, how I'd react to the hulk of a male before me—or the female he seemed so protective of.

Protective—

My chest eased as I realized who the female had to be.

"He probably couldn't stand being alone with me anymore," was all I said. "Besides, it's a small palace for his big ego."

Astorian boomed a laugh while the female slipped out of Recienne's arm, taking a few graceful steps down the stairs and onto the mossy ground, until she was close enough for me to make out her intense green eyes, her beautiful features, flushed cheeks, and freckles scattered across her nose. Her full lips pulled into a smile as she sauntered forward another step. "I keep telling him his ego needs its own palace."

Behind me, Astorian snickered again, and Recienne's face pulled into an "are you serious" grimace as he lifted his hands at his sides in mock innocence.

"Get over yourself," the female threw over her shoulder as if she'd seen Recienne's silent protest, cocking her head as she assessed me very similarly to the way Astorian had. Only when her eyes found mine did her lips twitch into a broad smile and she lifted a hand in greeting—the least formal I'd ever seen a fairy. "So you are Sanja."

I nodded, wondering if her knowing my name, too, would mean I'd be controlled by three fairies in turn if I accidentally upset them all.

"It seems he has a problem with keeping secrets," I told her in a mock whisper.

Recienne prowled off what had to be the most elaborate, tree-made porch I'd ever see in my life and stopped a few feet behind the female. It was only when I studied their faces side by side that I fully acknowledged the similarities. Where Recienne was ebony and gold, the female was copper and jade. But the mischief in their eyes, the way their lips curved, the inherent grace—

"Sanja, meet Clio, my sister."

I swallowed as I stared at the smiling female before me. The female who had been promised to the Crow Fairies and whom Recienne had been trying to protect all those years. And she was *smiling*. Not quaking in fear.

Not that she had anything to fear from me. But I was a stranger, and even if all of them knew my name now and could surely smite me even without the control that name extended them over me, how could she know if I was trustworthy?

How had Recienne decided I was?

Between the fights—the sparring and banter—I'd missed the moment when we'd gone from enemies to something else. Something that had him bringing me into his hideout and meeting the one person he'd been protecting all along. The reason why no one could know about the bandit.

My eyes met Recienne's, and I knew I was right.

"It's a pleasure," my court-trained princess self came through as I managed to swallow my epiphany.

Clio rolled her eyes. "To meet me, perhaps. But I'm sure you already regret having ever met Rogue and soon will with Astorian."

"Rogue?"

Recienne shifted behind her.

Clio laughed a wind chime melody so at odds with the way she drawled, "You haven't told her?" She glanced at her brother, mock accusation in her jade eyes.

"Recienne Oliver Gustine Univér Emestradassus de Pauvre," she said with a white-toothed grin. "Or short, Rogue."

"Don't forget *the Second*," Astorian added from now next to me.

I wasn't sure if I should laugh or be afraid at the half-hearted growl *Rogue* shot at him.

In the end, I decided for the laugh, and Recienne's eyes found mine, lingering until the smile faded from my lips. It was then that I realized that, even when he wore a mask as the bandit, the true mask was that of the prince—of the king—roaming the fairy palace. And here—in this little hideaway the Guardians knew where, where Recienne became Rogue ... that was the real him.

Astorian prowled past him, clapping Recienne on the shoulder. "Do you feed her at the palace?"

Despite the way he said it, there was no condescension in his voice, only humor.

Recienne hissed, and a new sort of smirk spread on his features. "Perhaps not well enough." He turned to me. "Are you hungry?"

I didn't have it in me to say no. Not when, for the first time, there was something like joy in Recienne's eyes. And I couldn't place why it struck me so hard that the most powerful fairy in Askarea perhaps had lived in fear most of his life. Not fear for himself but fear for the ones he loved. And that was a fear I was all too familiar with. "Lead the way."

So he did.

TWENTY-ONE

The house wasn't small on the inside. Even when, on the outside, it was nothing like a palace, the interior was fit to host a large family.

After Recienne had led me through a small corridor and then a sitting room, we'd ended up in a dining room with natural wooden walls threaded with sparkling rocks. The windows filtered in soft light, its reflections from the colorful rocks and, in turn, tinting Recienne's hair in hues of deeper emerald, sapphire blue, and gold when he moved through the bright shafts falling across the long oak table.

I would have loved it right away had the table not reminded me of the one in the Mages' House, where Tristan used to sit across from me for breakfast and dinner.

Astorian and Clio were pulling out their chairs, settling down, when Clio flicked a hand the way I'd seen her brother do, and an assortment of foods appeared on the table. While Astorian grabbed for the nearest pot and started shoveling food onto his plate, Recienne was studying me over his empty one, a pensive look on his face.

"What's wrong?" The question slipped out before I could think better, and it hurt the tiniest bit to admit that, in this moment, I cared if he was all right. Because *he* cared that *they* were all right—his sister, hiding out here in the forests, and the male next to him whose role I yet had to understand.

Recienne shrugged and picked up a bread basket, offering it to me. "It's different."

"What is different?"

"Being here, with you, is different from what I'd expected." The look in his eyes didn't change even when he pulled up a grin at the conversation Clio and Astorian were leading on the other side of the table—something about the role of Leeneae in desserts.

I didn't ask what he'd told them about me before I offered, "Maybe I can help out with that." Astorian knew I was a Mage, that I was working on unlocking a Mage Stone. That much I had figured from their conversation the other day. But Clio?

"With Leeneae?" Clio prompted. "Do you have any experience with Leeneae desserts?"

"Some. What are you planning to make?" I wasn't exactly an expert. But I'd helped Zelia before, and perhaps one of the books Recienne had saved contained a recipe. I hadn't read them all cover to cover yet.

As Astorian explained a very specific sort of souffle, my mouth watered from the mere thought of chocolate and caramel and apple. "We're going to make it some time this week. You're welcome to join."

My glance wandered to Recienne, who was studying me again with the same pensive expression. He straightened an inch as he said to Astorian, "It depends on how you behave if I expose Sanja to the two of you again." A warning but with a smile on his lips.

Astorian just laughed while Clio jabbed a finger at him across the salad bowl. "Sanja can very well decide on her own if she can handle souffle with us."

She shot me a look as if in a prompt for my confirmation she was right.

All I did was shrug, my mind too full of thoughts already at the beginning of this encounter, and my heart ... my heart was swirling with emotions I didn't think I'd felt since I'd run from my own court what felt like a lifetime ago.

"Let's make a deal." I almost decided not to voice my suggestion when Astorian sat up, those auburn eyes narrowing in on me like on a target. But Clio placed a hand on his biceps, and his grin turned less predatory and more—friendly?

"What deal do you have to offer, Sanja?" Clio wanted to know, swishing back her copper strands over her shoulder and exposing the short sleeves of her low-cut shirt. I couldn't help noting the supple curve of her torso now that her waves weren't subduing them.

"Tell me your stories, and I'll help you with the souf-fle." Whether I'd be a real help or not—at least, this way, I'd learn everything to know about the people Recienne was hiding away in the forest, the ones he had given up his attempts to stop his father for. To protect them—pro-tect his sister.

"There is nothing much to know about this guy." Clio pointed at Astorian with her thumb, and the male bit the air an inch from it. I hid my shriek with a cough. "Only that he's the most annoying fairy in the history of Askarea," she added, and Astorian grumbled in partial agreement.

"Maybe not history," he corrected, "but I could if I practiced." Clio rolled her eyes again, and I couldn't help but laugh. Beside me, Recienne shifted.

"Astorian is the son of one of my father's advisors. True fairy nobility and almost too powerful to contain."

"Not that anyone has ever really tried," Astorian threw in over a bite of chicken wing which he tore from the bone with his teeth.

"Ugh—savage," Clio commented, much to Astorian's amusement. "Rogue has," she said to me. "And he didn't need to *try*. He kicked Astorian's ass—multiple times."

"With magic," Astorian retorted. "Hand-to-hand, he wouldn't stand a chance." A challenge sparked in Astorian's eyes, and, for a moment, I was curious what it would be like to see the two males roll in the moss and dirt until one of them surrendered. Somehow, I couldn't see Recienne being the one to ever give up. What I'd learned about him, the way he crafted his plans, the stealth and control—it would have surprised me if his strategizing wouldn't give him the upper hand in almost anything.

The fact that I admitted that to myself made me wonder if all it took was two witty fairies to raise my opinion of the male who *stole* my name and let me suffer at his father's hands.

Somehow, my thoughts must have shown on my face, for Astorian leaned forward, his hand reaching so close to mine that I prepared to pull it back, but he picked up a small bowl of pickles instead.

"We all have to do despicable things in order to survive, Sanja. Royalty makes you no different."

For a moment, I thought he'd meant Recienne, but I realized the king beside me wasn't the only royal in this room. And while I had no idea what Clio had ever done to deserve his words, I knew very well what I had done to protect the ones I loved. And it had left them bleeding without the most innate part of what defined them.

"Do you read minds?" Either that or the smiling and grinning and laughing and growling was the best mask I'd ever seen to hide a degree of empathy that would allow him to read people on such a deep level that he could guess. Not that I'd ever heard of a fairy being capable of either.

"Who knows with him?" Clio shrugged.

"*I* know." Astorian crossed his powerful arms over his chest, a chicken wing still in his fingers, and gestured with it as he said to me, "I don't. But don't ask me what else I do."

"What *do* you do?" I couldn't help it. Even when I'd watched him set the trap, I walked right in.

A feral grin was all the response I got, and I could have sworn even Recienne shuddered beside me.

Great. Another mysteriously gifted fairy.

"Astorian used to train my father's armies," Recienne said, and I wondered if he did it on purpose—leave out they were now *his* armies.

"Until the day that prick of a Mage killed the lovely Emestra," Astorian interrupted, and a cold filled the room that had felt inviting and homey before.

I didn't dare ask who Emestra was, already reading the answer from Recienne's eyes as I turned to him.

His mother.

"Everything went downhill from that point when the late Recienne Olivier Gustine Univér Emestradassus de Pauvre decided that he was going to use his soldiers to hunt down the Mages."

I noticed two things. First—Astorian didn't particularly like Mages. Second—he didn't agree with the methods of the late king. Where that put him, I couldn't tell.

But he was here, at this table, with a Mage, talking and behaving, for what it was worth, like I wasn't a reminder of the queen's death. I hadn't dared ask Recienne yet what she was like—if he'd loved her the way I'd loved my mother. And perhaps, I never would. Too much history sprawled between that conversation and the moment I'd participated in the king's death.

My stomach suddenly felt leaden, the usual emptiness and the occasional throbbing smothered by the weight of it as I realized that I might not have been the Mage who killed his mother, but I sure as Eroth's wrath was the Mage who contributed to his father's death.

I remained quiet for the rest of the meal, responding to questions with noncommittal phrases, polite but never sharing anything that could remind them of my role.

Astorian and Clio had an in-depth conversation about Leeneae and its usefulness for baking bread.

Eventually, Recienne announced that it was time for us to leave, and I didn't object. I managed a smile when we walked out the door into the falling night, and Clio and Astorian waved after us with threats at Recienne to bring me back soon. I merely thanked them for the meal and followed the fairy king back to the cave leading out into the forest.

We'd been walking for a while, Recienne with his mask back up and me with my lump of lead still wobbling in my stomach, when he slowed and eyed me from the side. "What are you thinking?"

I shook my head.

He stopped, facing me fully, that pensive, golden gaze of his making me halt before I could think about it.

"Sanja..."

"It doesn't matter," I told him, chewing on all the little dots I'd connected, all the ways I might have misjudged him even when he had done despicable things to me during the challenges. I didn't even understand how he could stand here, next to me, without seeing me as the failure I was.

Guilt burned hot inside of me as he leaned in until our faces were level. "Speak to me, Sanja."

"And what would you like me to say?" It was easier to pretend that I was angry because the alternative—allowing him to see into that dark depth of my heart—I didn't think I could handle that.

His eyes didn't twinkle, and none of those obnoxious chuckles sounded through his mask. All I could see was what felt a lot like an endless well of worry as he held my gaze through the near darkness, one hand reaching for my elbow then veering away and dropping back to his side. "How about how you feel?"

I shook my head. Not with him. Not when I knew one wrong look might make me burst into tears. Not when the way he'd watched me all afternoon made me question if perhaps my misery truly wasn't his top priority. When he'd shown me what was at stake for him if he let the Crow Fairies win.

And maybe it made me a despicable person. But a part of me wondered if, maybe, the only reason I didn't dare speak to him was that there was another man who should have been standing in his place, should have been asking me those questions back then in Aceleau when I'd closed myself off in my new identity. And he'd known. Tristan had known who I was and hadn't told me. He hadn't pushed for me to talk to him, hadn't waited for me to open up.

I gazed into the fairy king's eyes, a heaviness engulfing me that I wasn't sure I could shirk anymore because, when I looked at him, I knew he'd push and wait. Perhaps forever—until I spoke. Because he knew what it was like to be trapped in court politics, in royal intrigue, for his life to be determined by the choices of others. For his power to be meaningless when someone else was holding his reins.

"Recienne—" I started, but he interrupted me the second I'd finished his name.

"Rogue. Call me Rogue. At least when we're alone."

A weak smile was about to work itself onto my lips when hissing and screeching ripped through the trees above us, and Rogue cursed under his breath, drawing his bow and nocking an arrow as he turned away from me, slowly backing up and herding me toward a tree trunk until my spine lay flat against the rough bark.

"Stay still," he whispered.

I didn't dare so much as breathe as he fired an arrow, tip lighting up with flames as it zoomed into the sky—and the outline of a large, winged creature appeared over the treetops ahead.

TWENTY-TWO

Heart pounding, I pressed against the tree trunk, eyes following Rogue with both fear and fascination as he staked the space beneath the trees, a fresh arrow nocked and his eyes flashing in an echo of the flames spreading across the skies above us like a blanket. This was the first time I'd seen him use his magic for something other than to control my body or conjure food. And it blew me away.

Never in the months with the Mages had I witnessed magic like this—a floating carpet of fire over our heads, protecting us from the winged shadow. If anything had ever gotten close to this, it was Zelia's darkness when she'd concealed us in the hallways of the fairy palace. But this … *this* was something else. Rogue had set the sky ablaze with a mere thought.

The natural instinct should have been to quiver in fear from the creature hunting us and from the rogue king moving like a shadow in front of me, aiming for the predator above. But all I found was deep awe.

"It's a Ledrynx," he whispered on that dark breeze disguising his voice.

What's a Ledrynx? I wanted to ask, but Rogue was already continuing.

"Think of winged lions but smaller. And a lot more bloodthirsty." A dark chuckle carried his words. "They're rare creatures in the fairy forests down here in the flatlands. They usually live up in the mountains." His focus remained on the treetops. "They hate fire. So this should be enough to drive it away."

He had just finished his explanation when something slimy landed on my hair, dripping onto my cheek. I couldn't hold back a tiny squeak before I remembered to stay still. Holding myself in place was a lesson in self-control—especially when the gooey substance smelled of iron and salt and was most definitely not a raindrop.

Rogue turned—so slowly that the bark was drawing blood from under my fingernails where they now dug into it. "Don't move." His eyes met mine before glancing at whatever had to be sitting in the branches above me.

I swallowed, sweat forming on my neck, plastering my braid to my skin.

If I could use my magic, I would be able to defend myself, take care of the horror hunting us. The Mage Stone had even been recharged mere hours ago. Perhaps, if I could slide my hand into my pocket and reach it...

Letting go of the tree, I carefully slid my hand along my thigh, hoping I wouldn't make a sound to draw attention to myself. Not that it would make much of a difference. The Ledrynx was already hovering over my head—conscious of my presence after my earlier squeak, or oblivious to it, I didn't care.

I was halfway to my pocket when something large moved in the trees behind Rogue. I sucked in a breath, and he shot me a warning look. But I shook my head.

By the Guardians. There were more.

Wings. Those were wings ahead and moving along a massive branch leading right above Rogue's shoulder.

Instead of going for my pocket, I lifted my hand, pointing behind him.

A blur of roars and shrieks and growls filled the air as claws shot from the branches. "Watch out!"

He whirled at my warning, arrow finding its aim in a large cat sailing over his head directly at me. The creature went up in flames, pivoting and tumbling from the air and taking with it a multitude of little twigs and summer leaves, none of which caught fire even when the creature was burning like it had been dunked in grease first.

While I was still panting with shock, Rogue was already on the Ledrynx, one of his knives sunk into its neck while his other hand was holding onto both bow and arrow.

A second Ledrynx landed, saber-sharp teeth flashing in a maw wide open with a roar promising pain, and my heart skipped a beat as I assessed the chances of killing the beast before it could kill us—Rogue, specifically, since its yellow eyes were trained on him and it was pawing on the ground like a bull preparing to charge.

For a second, I just stood there, frozen, watching the male stare down his opponent while he ripped the knife from the flesh of the one he'd already ended. Then, my survival instincts kicked in, and I felt my feet itch to run, to take me anywhere but here; I didn't care where as long as it was far away from those creatures. But I had another weapon in my arsenal, and now that the Ledrynx were busy with Rogue, I could use the moment to get my Mage Stone and try—I *had* to try.

I didn't take my eyes off the danger ahead, monitoring each movement of both the fairy and the beast as they danced around each other like in an arena. Whatever kept Rogue from simply making the Ledrynx disappear, I couldn't tell.

Even with its minuscule weight, the Mage Stone lay heavy in my palm when I extracted it from my pocket, fingers curling around it. It pulsed to life alongside the fear when a new Ledrynx joined the dance between the trees. A growl reverberated through me, and I couldn't tell if it had been one of the creatures or Rogue. The next moment, he flipped the knife in his hand and sent it soaring between a Ledrynx's eyes. It dropped to the ground, another one taking its place while, from the ebbing fire in the sky, two more beasts circled in.

Why wasn't he using more of his magic to defeat them? If he was the most powerful fairy in all of Askarea...

Something caught me by the shoulder, and pain ripped through me as they pierced into my flesh like daggers, and

I managed a shriek before I was hoisted up, pulled toward a maw of saber teeth. My fingers almost dropped the Mage Stone. But I willed them closed while the rest of me was thrashing against the grasp.

"Help!" It was the last word I'd ever wanted to hear myself scream in the fairy king's presence, but the Guardian's be damned—who, if not him, should I ask for help now? But it came out more like a gasp than anything, my teeth gritted against the pain as I struggled to focus.

The fairy male, however, was already fighting four Ledrynx at once, his bow exchanged for a short sword, which was working its bloody path through the beasts who kept coming at him.

A warm, tingling sensation in my palm caught my attention through the pain. I tried to remember what I'd read, what I'd seen Tristan, Dimar, and Zelia do when they used their Mage Stones. But no words came to my mind, no spells, nothing but, "*Yetheruh.*" It came out strained and slurred by my struggle.

I didn't think to aim my hand anywhere the way I'd learned with the Mage Stone shard, but when a bright flash of light tore from my palm at the end of the arm pinned by the claws, I managed to yank it up so it faced the monster dragging me up the tree. A wince and a yelp, and the claws released me—which made me drop a few feet, tumbling on my ass and my head hitting the trunk as I bounced back against it.

A furry mass dropped from the branches, landing smack on my legs just as I was about to push myself back to my feet. And had my breath not been knocked out of me by the fall already, I might have screamed at the sight of the massive wildcat—winged wildcat—from whose maw blood was trickling onto my upper thigh, seeping into the fabric of my pants. Its eyes were gazing into a distant realm that thankfully no longer included the urge to tear out a piece of my flesh. It didn't as much as twitch as I attempted to slide out from under it—and eventually gave up, trapped under the weight.

Rogue's vicious curse came a moment later, the forest lighting up before it went completely dark. The sound of creatures plunging from the greenery above scared me more than the thought of the most powerful fairy in Askarea sneaking up on me while I wasn't able to move.

"Hold still," he said right by my ear, and I almost screamed again at the light touch on my injured arm where pain throbbed at every hole the Ledrynx had punctured into my flesh. "I'm trying to heal you."

Warmth flowed through my shoulder as a flicker of light brightened Rogue's masked features beside me—and the pain ceased as if it had never existed.

"There. Now get up."

Shifting and squirming under the dead Ledrynx, I did my best to follow his order, but even with my entire body on high alert, my legs didn't obey, still weak after the unexpected release of magic that had brought down the beast now draped over me. "What do you think I'm trying to do," I hissed, attempting to spy Rogue in the black of the night.

The metallic reflection of his eyes was hovering over my knees where the Ledrynx's belly was slowly lifting.

Guardians above, was it coming back to life?

Rogue must have sensed my rising panic, for he cut into the dark silence, "It's just me. I'm lifting the monster off you."

Just him. But my blood slowed, and I rested my head against the tree, closing my eyes for a moment. If he wasn't warning me to be quiet and pretend I wasn't there, at least, that was indication the immediate danger was over.

At least that of the Ledrynx.

"All right—" He didn't sound at all strained as the weight disappeared from my legs, freeing me to leap up and run.

A thud later, something touched the side of my head, and this time, I did scream.

"Just me again," he hissed by my shoulder, and I cursed the night as I strained my eyes to find that golden shimmer of his gaze. His fingers dug into my hair, probing my skull as if believing he'd find it cracked. "They're dead."

However he'd brought them down with one flash of light, I didn't dare ask.

"No head injuries." His hand slid down to the side of my face before he pulled it away. "Can you stand now?"

The simple fact that it was a request rather than a command petrified me for a moment longer, but his chuckle startled me into motion, and I scrambled upright, one hand on the tree trunk. "What just happened?"

I sensed more than saw Rogue move to my other side. "Let's get home before we talk."

"Your palace is not my home."

Rogue didn't respond. All he did was take my hand, and the darkness rippled out of existence, replaced by the glimmering stone of a fairy-light-filled hallway leading to the stairs of my tower. I blinked away the blurriness of my vision until his unmasked face came into clear view—and the expression on it...

I debated for a moment if remaining trapped under the dead Ledrynx might have been a better option.

But the fairy king's face smoothed within a heartbeat, and all that was left was the uncaring noble who had first brought me here. "Home or no—it's not like you have anywhere else to go."

He traced the lapel of his ornately embroidered jacket with a finger, the armor of the bandit replaced by the mask of the heartless fairy royalty once more.

"I do," I objected, ignoring the throbbing piece of my heart that ached to reach out and tell him that he didn't need to pretend—not with me. Not after he'd shown me his secret, the one thing he was willing to sacrifice his own happiness and peace of mind for.

His sister.

"And where is that lovely home of yours?" The fairy lights flickered as if swallowed by his invisible powers, and I remembered who I was facing. "Jezuin? The palace? Where you are someone's tool? Or the streets in the first ring? You certainly built something for yourself there, Sanja. A future among the starving." The cold fire lighting his gaze was more terrifying than the pitch-black and the monsters lurking that we'd just escaped. "Or in the rubble that's left of the Mages' House?"

I shrank away a step, realizing only now that he was still holding my hand as his palm slid off mine. He stared me down, words brewing like a thunderstorm. But he blinked, and it was gone—as was the fire.

"Next time, when I tell you to *stay still,* stay still. It will save us a lot of trouble." He turned to leave, but his words—all of them—kept swirling in my mind like little arrows of accusation.

"Should I have let the Ledrynx sneak up on you?" As his temper ebbed, I couldn't keep my own from rising. "I saved your fucking life out there by warning you."

Rogue laughed darkly, turning back to me—and it had never felt better and worse to have his focus on me. "I'm glad to know you have enough confidence in my abilities to trust I can handle a couple of minor nuisances in the forests I've been roaming since childhood, Sanja. Very glad." Sarcasm dripped from every word.

"Well... It didn't seem like you had the situation under control." It was a weak hit, but I couldn't help it. "You know, with the Ledrynx tearing my shoulder apart and all."

For a heartbeat, his lips twisted into an angry line at the mention of what the Ledrynx had done to me. "So you thought it was a good time to experiment with your magic?" He was now fully facing me, nostrils flaring as if scenting prey. "I thought you were smarter than that, Sanja."

"Maybe I'm not." I bit it out just to say something, to pull up a boundary that he couldn't penetrate. But his gaze did what not even a touch could have done, piercing right into those dark chambers of my heart where all my guilt lay like a well of misery. "Maybe I'm just a useless human who you should have never brought back to the fairylands. And maybe you don't care if a monster takes a piece out of me since you're planning to bleed me and my magic out, anyway. But maybe I'm not even enough for that, and I'll never be able to stop the Cro—"

Rogue's power curled over my mouth, sealing it before I could finish my sentence, and he stepped close enough for his breath to touch my face in warm gusts. "Is that what you think I want? To bleed you out? To sacrifice you?"

I don't know what you want, I was trying to say, but his control held me in a firm grasp—firm yet … gentle somehow.

"You really don't know me at all, then." His power coiled off me as he pulled back a foot.

But no words left my mouth anyway as I watched him compose himself, brows straightening and lines bracketing his mouth disappearing.

"Whatever my *plans* with you are, I'm not happy to see anyone hurt on my watch." The sincerity in his tone caught me even more off guard than the way he emphasized the word *plans*, for it meant that he had those, indeed.

A shudder ran down my spine.

Rogue sighed through his nose. "I told you to stay still so the Ledrynx wouldn't be provoked into attack, Sanja. The fire would have kept them at bay, and I would have snapped the neck of the one coming at me from behind."

"You killed them all in one blow of magic in the end," I pointed out. "Why not do that right away? Why wait until I was being ripped apart?"

"Because my power is recognizable, and in the forests of Askarea, I'm not Recienne, the king. If I want to keep Rogue a secret, I can't use that sort of power."

I couldn't tell what it was about the expression on his face that made me pause to think about his words.

He could have killed them all within the blink of an eye yet hadn't. Because if Recienne's power was detected in the forests, if he was recognized for who he was, that might lead to questions, might put his secret in jeopardy. And protecting his secret was more important than protecting the human he'd acquired from Cyrill to stop the Crow Fairies.

Anyone could have stalked the forests ... any creature could have witnessed his power. I'd spent enough time in Askarea to understand how dangerous any place in this realm truly was. Fairies of all sorts were roaming the lands—Rogue had warned me of them that very first day he'd stolen my jewelry—and if any of them reported to the Crow Fairies...

My epiphany must have shown on my features because his expression softened ever so slightly. "We were lucky no one else was around to sense the effect of my powers. But next time, we might not be so lucky. And I can't risk *her*."

He didn't need to speak Clio's name for me to know he was talking about her. And I understood. I did. She was all he had left of his family, and I'd seen the way he'd looked at her that afternoon, how he'd do anything to keep her safe. To protect her freedom and her happiness.

That spot in my chest tightened, making the void surrounding it seem even more vast.

"I can't risk Rogue's exposure. If anyone but my trusted circle learns what I'm doing, it will all have been for naught."

He'd spoken similar words to me before when I'd been near collapse at my second challenge and his magic had lifted me to my feet, had kept them moving until dawn.

Don't stop, San. For if you do, all will have been for naught.

All—his efforts to fight his father's insane plan of expansion, of protecting Clio.

But he was protecting more than her—the freedom of the human realms rested in his hands. For if he failed, the Crow Fairies would leave the Seeing Forest but spill over the borders with whatever dark magic they possessed. They had already found ways...

My hand was shaking as I lifted it to place on his arm. "If you don't intend to bleed me out in an Ultimate Sacrifice, what do you need me to do?"

And this time, I hoped he'd tell me something more than vague plans.

Rogue's eyes found mine, hesitation on his beautiful features, and I wondered if I'd made a mistake by asking. If I'd given him an opening to lull me into doing his bidding.

"Not tonight, Sanja." He gestured at my shoulder, the bloodied scraps of my sleeve. "You've exerted yourself with your use of magic, and resting seems like more of a priority than learning what I have or haven't planned. Another day, we'll talk, when you are rested and your distrust doesn't disembowel me." Inclining his head, he started to turn, but halted, sliding his hands into his pockets. "Regardless of what you think of me, how little you trust me, Sanja ... I do trust you. Enough to let you in on my secret. I hope it wasn't a mistake."

When he turned to leave this time, he didn't stop again. And I remained in the hallway, staring after his tall, dark shape long after he'd turned the corner.

TWENTY-THREE

Naar woke me the next morning, ushering me from my bed, pulling back the curtains, and letting in the afternoon sun.

Afternoon—

"You slept a good day and a half," she informed me as I crawled from under the covers. "It's time to face the degree of destruction you've done with your foolish use of magic."

I was about to object to her claim when she pulled the Mage Stone from the mattress where it must have slid from my grasp during my sleep. Falling asleep had been a challenge in itself with everything Rogue had given me to consider. But, most of all, his parting words.

Regardless of what you think of me, how little you trust me, Sanja ... I do trust you. Enough to let you in on my secret. I hope it wasn't a mistake.

Something about them stung in that tiny spot in my chest, but not enough to feel any more guilty than I already did.

"Give that back." I tried to grab the Mage Stone from her hand but caught thin air as she took a quick step back.

"I will once you're bathed and dressed and have eaten something." She pointed at the bathing room where the sound of water gurgling in the bathtub beckoned my sore muscles.

It wasn't like I'd exerted my physical strength the day before—or one and a half—but my limbs were heavy, anyway.

"And before you even ask," she called after me as I stalked over the threshold, eyes on the steaming bath, "Recienne told me what you did."

"What exactly *did* I do?" I shucked my clothes and dunked myself into the hot water, sighing as it sloshed over my body. The shoulder where the Ledrynx had gotten me seemed to be the only part of my body not drained enough to go right back to sleep.

"You wasted a whole charge of fairy magic on bringing down a Ledrynx Recienne could have killed with half a thought."

My body was too tired to even freeze at the depth of her knowledge. "Well, perhaps he should have actually killed it then, before it picked me apart."

Naar laughed heartily. "By the flicker of magic, Sanja. Do you not understand what he puts at risk when he uses his full power out there?"

Rogue's explanations of the day before came back to me. And, of course—*of course*—he was protecting his secret. If anyone found out their king was the bandit roaming the forests...

Then, how many of the fairies knew about the bandit? Did Tristan know? Did Zelia and Dimar?

My chest ached at the thought of all the things they'd never shared with me—out of a false sense of protecting me or lack of trust, it didn't really matter.

I wrapped my arms around myself in the water, keeping the warmth close when it seemed dead-set on drifting away from me.

"I do understand." At least, I thought I did. With Rogue, there were always more layers to the truth, and I wondered if he'd ever let me in on all of them. But then—he'd just told me I'd disemboweled him with my distrust.

"So do us all a favor and don't jeopardize the princess next time your self-control slips your grasp, will you?"

It hit me then... and I wondered if the strange feeling I'd had in Naar's presence during my stay for my challenges had already pointed me toward it. "You are one of his trusted circle."

Naar pulled a flask of shampoo on the rim of the tub for me. "About time you figured out I won't eat you alive." She gave me a meaningful glance. "And neither will he."

I ignored that last part. "You tried to help me during the challenges."

"Why, of course." She clopped to the mirror where she rummaged through various utensils. "Well ... in whatever way possible without tipping off the guards or the late king." She grimaced as if intending to add something more but stopped and offered, "Do you need help with your hair?"

This time, it was I who shrugged. "Sure." Maybe if she stayed in here with me she'd continue talking and I'd learn something useful about Rogue's plans for me.

Naar picked up the flask and poured out some shampoo onto my scalp then scrubbed my hair until it was a foamy mop atop my head.

"And Recienne?" *Rogue*, my mind corrected me, and I saw those golden eyes before me, peering through the darkness.

I shut the image out, focusing on the white rose scent of the shampoo instead.

"You are the one who knows best what he did to help you." She gestured for me to dip my head into the water to rinse my hair. "And even if I knew everything, I'd never spill his secrets."

"Because he'd punish you."

She laughed. "Because Recienne knows what he's doing, and even if sometimes I want to smack him on the head for being a foolish fairy male, I will never—*never*—take away his choice of what to share and with whom."

A little surprised by her words, I went under the surface, using the moment to sort my thoughts.

When I came back up, Naar offered me a towel, waiting for me to stand and wrap myself in it.

"I laid out a dress for you. Wear it if you like, or choose something different from the armoire, but be aware that you'll dine in company tonight."

I was about to ask her in whose company exactly when she gave me a warning look. "I don't know why he chose to do what he did, but know one thing, Sanja; if you betray his trust, you'll regret it later. Not for the reasons you'd think. He won't punish you for it. But you *will* regret it."

Her words hung in the air, a riddle in themselves, but she was out the door so fast I didn't get to ask why.

I was on my way downstairs an hour later, the setting sun gilding the stairwell and the flowers embroidered along the bodice of my chiffon gown. The fact that the neckline was more revealing than anything I'd worn since my second challenge was only half concerning. What bothered me more was the way more flowers seemed to grow from the seam of my skirts along the top layer of fabric all the way to my hips, and how much I liked it. How I could imagine it would paint a hungry smile onto Tristan's face if he'd ever see me in it. And the inevitable burning emptiness in my chest that followed.

He wouldn't. Ever. Because I couldn't risk his safety for anything.

I was so lost in thought that I noticed Rogue leaning against the wall at the bottom of the stairs only when he cleared his throat.

"Naar certainly knows what she's doing," he commented by way of greeting, no sign of the distraught fairy that had walked away from me the other night on his features.

"Whoever made the dress knew what they were doing. Naar simply has impeccable taste."

Rogue chuckled, stepping out of my path as I reached the bottom of the stairs, hands smoothing the front of his jacket as he started walking at my side.

"It's a bit early for dinner, still, but after one and a half days, I thought it was time I checked in on you."

"To see if I've died of stupidity?" I quizzed, earning a raised eyebrow from him.

"I never said you were stupid, Sanja. Just that I'd thought you were smarter than what you did ... well, in the forest."

"Protecting myself?"

"Not trusting me." A frown worked itself back onto his features as he studied me from the side, and something inside me wanted to find words to make it go away.

I didn't respond.

We were halfway down the hallway when he finally stopped, and my feet halted of their own volition,

I checked for his power, if it had snaked around them, forced them to still, but found nothing.

"I've been a fool to believe you would ... trust me," he said in that murmur that usually came on a dark breeze, but this time, it was just his normal voice, ravaged by a guilt not so different from what plagued me myself. "From the very first day, I've done nothing other than give you reasons to believe I am the horrible fairy Askarea believes I am. And with you trusting Tristan Bale—loving him—I'm not surprised you can't find it in yourself to believe I can be more than Recienne Olivier Gustine Univér Emestradassus de Pauvre the Second, fairy royalty delighting in humans' torment. He told me that would happen. Mage Tristan told me that, even if I got you out of Jezuin, you'd never trust me or help me."

It took a moment for his words to register, but once they did, my stomach turned, and I was glad we'd not made it to dinner yet, or I'd have gagged on more than just his words.

"What do you mean, he told you?"

When I studied his face for an answer, I couldn't help thinking that Rogue looked a bit sick himself.

"When did you talk to him?" By Eroth... There was only one time he and Tristan had been in the same place recently that I was aware of. "The banquet?"

Guardians above, he'd even mentioned Tristan had walked away at his mercy.

"You talked to him at the banquet?" My voice had climbed half an octave with a new sort of fear. "What did you do to him?"

Rogue lifted his hands. "Who said I did anything to him?"

"That's the thing. You don't say *anything*. If you'd tell me outright what is going on, I wouldn't need to jump to conclusions."

"And conclude the worst?"

"What else am I to conclude if you don't give me a reason to conclude anything better?"

Rogue exhaled a slow breath, eyes wandering the hallway behind me. I didn't turn to check what he was seeing. If it was the Guardians themselves, I wouldn't turn. This was about Tristan.

"Tell me," I demanded, and the defeat in his eyes was almost as shocking as the words that followed.

"It's no secret the quarrel I have with the Mage's bloodline. His parents killed my mother after all. And he hates me for what happened during your trials. So you can imagine the surprise when he approached me on the way out of the palace. I'd merely followed him to gloat for a moment—you know, how he doesn't even have the balls to get you out of there and everything."

I did remember he'd said that to me about Tristan after he'd taken me away from Jezuin.

Since the pathetic Mage you adore so much didn't have the balls to get you out, I thought it was time someone did.

"He begged me to help him, Sanja, even when he knew I was an enemy he could never defeat even with his magic." My chest constricted. "He went on his knees for me to help him get his magic back so he would never be so helpless again." My vision blurred. No. Tristan would never have done that. He'd never have—"I asked him what he'd be willing to give up in exchange for his magic." His eyes turned feral as he trapped my gaze with his. "And guess what he said."

I couldn't imagine the answer. Didn't want to, for it would destroy what was left of me in there. That tiny part of me that hadn't given up hope to ever get out of this mess. The part of me that was a void with Tristan's name written all over it.

"Ask me what he said, Sanja."

I shook my head.

He chuckled, a sound of midnight and pain. "Well ... too bad you don't want to know. I'll tell you, anyway."

My hand reached for my chest as I braced myself for the blow.

"You." He leaned forward, forcing my gaze not to leave his. "He gave up *you*." There was nothing beautiful about him now as he turned into the predator I'd always believed him to be—the predator for a moment. Then his face turned cold like the glaciers I'd once gleaned in the distance behind the fairy city. "And that emptiness you're feeling ... that's where you've known deep down all along that he would have given up anything for his magic."

TWENTY-FOUR

I couldn't breathe. Couldn't breathe as his golden gaze held mine with a force of ice. Not that control of his power but something different, harsher, making something inside of me violently toss and thrash.

"You're lying." My words were thin like the smoke of an extinguished candle.

"Am I now?"

I staggered back a step, and another, my heart beating like a war drum dead-set on drowning out every thought, *his* every word.

I hadn't told him how much I missed Tristan, about the guilt, or how I felt I wasn't enough. How Rogue had figured out what was going on in my mind and, even worse, the chambers in my chest, I truly didn't want to know.

Tristan couldn't possibly have given me up. Not when he'd come to the palace in Jezuin to get me out. Not when—

Hot tears ran down my cheeks, and I hated myself more than ever for what I'd destroyed by taking Tristan's magic with my final challenge. Or that I'd fallen in love, to begin with.

My back met the glimmering wall, the cool stone grounding me when all I wanted to do was scream at the stars. "You made that bargain with Cyrill before you talked to Tristan. He can't possibly have traded me for his magic. He would never do that." At least, that was what I kept telling myself in hopes of making it a truth.

"Perhaps he didn't. And perhaps he said it because he knew there was no way he'd get his magic back, no matter what he offered."

That was probably why. Because he knew there was no way.

"And yes, I made the bargain *before* I spoke with your Mage." He followed me to the wall, stopping mere feet away from me, his eyes piercing through my screen of tears, full of cold rage. "But you know what's truly wrong with all of this?"

I didn't even manage to shake my head, the pain in my chest eating up the void, making me feel where emptiness had ruled for so long.

Rogue continued anyway, "That it doesn't matter whether it can bring back his damned magic. You are not *his* to offer. You are *nobody's* to offer." The air became thick, tangible around him like a shield of invisible granite—like it had in

Clio's hideout—as he breathed in and out, in and out, the rage slowly fading and his hands no longer shaking. "What his offer says about him, I leave for you to judge."

Silence fell in the hallway, the sun illuminating the frosty air with rays of paling light, and I could have sworn he was waiting for me to speak even when his face no longer yielded any emotion. He could have been wearing the bandit's mask, and I'd still been able to read him better. But this Rogue—he was the keeper of a slumbering nightmare. And what he'd let slip onto his features, it was a wisp of what was haunting him.

But nothing inside my chest throbbed for him now, every last nook and cranny filled with the pain of crumbling at the possibility that this—that Tristan giving me up rather than remaining helpless—was the truth.

The image of boy-Tristan climbing the roof to curl up behind a puffing chimney flashed through my mind, and I knew that, even with the way he loved me—and he did, he really did—without his magic, without the Mages' House, he might as well have been that boy shoved back onto the streets. Of course, he'd give anything to never be that helpless again, to have to steal and hide and fear for his life. And had I not done exactly that to him? Had my foolish bargain with the late fairy king not taken it all from him? Had he not hidden in Jezuin and procured ingredients in sometimes more, sometimes less ethical ways? Had he not spent most of our time away since we'd set up in the first ring on the streets while Zelia and I had treated patients and created tinctures and potions?

Of course, he'd give me up to have back the only thing that gave him independence and freedom. Especially since I was the one who'd destroyed it in the first place. But Rogue had made the bargain to take me to Aceleau with Cyrill before he'd talked to Tristan—

By the time I found my voice again, I was already spiraling, and it came out as a rasp. "So I'm not here because of him?"

"Tristan?" He shook his head. "I already told you I made that bargain with Cyrill before. Even though I enjoy very much how much he hates your presence in my palace, no, you're not here because of Tristan."

My breath rushed from my lungs in what could have been a sob or half a wail of both relief and frustration.

Rogue raised an eyebrow as if to ask something but smoothed it out once more as he continued, "I did promise to help him get back his magic, though."

"You mean you made a bargain with him?" I held in every sound, even my heartbeat, as I listened for his answer.

"No. A promise, not a bargain. I promised I'd help him without asking for anything in return."

"Why?"

"Because you love him, Sanja. And, no matter how much I need you to hate me, I can no longer bear to make you."

Rogue disappeared in a ripple of air, and I returned to my room without considering who that company for dinner might have been.

I didn't see Rogue for two weeks, and by the end of them, I realized my second month in his residence was close to an end. Naar kept me company every other day, but mostly, I spent a lot of time in the library I'd discovered on my way to find Rogue on the third day of his absence, either working on my magic—without much success—or reading. After two full days of first ignoring his words and then thinking about them too much, I'd wanted to confront him—and, of course, had found no sign of him.

I'd taken to reading whatever book I picked from the shelves. He hadn't forbidden me to roam the palace or confined me to my room, so there would be no issue with me wandering the halls. Had he not said *Make yourself at home?* That's what I was doing.

A cup of tea Naar had brought me in hand, I made my way down the hallway, past the many doors leading to studies or empty rooms, until I reached the huge, carved double doors behind which an ocean of knowledge and imagination was stored on endless pages. At the center of the room lined with shelves, a low mahogany table surrounded by armchairs provided my usual reading nook. I set down my cup and picked up the book I'd left the night before, already opening it while sliding into my favorite velvet chair, when I spotted a folded note on the chair beside mine.

Lowering the book into my lap, I picked up the piece of paper and read, *I'll be gone longer than expected. I'm sending someone to keep you company.*

I barely had time to wonder how Rogue had slipped the message into this room when he'd been gone so long when the door opened, and concise footfalls that had nothing to do with Naar's clopping filled the room. Dropping the note, I leaped to my feet, the book sliding to the hardwood floor.

"Good afternoon, Sanja," Astorian said with a grin, and my knees wobbled at the sight of the swords sheathed at his hips, the knives strapped to his thighs, to his forearms.

Grabbing the backrest of my chair for support, I slid my hand into the pocket of my pants for my Mage Stone, ready to shout *yetheruh* if Astorian took one wrong step. But the male laughed, eyes tracking my every movement while he reached for his belt and unbuckled it.

"What—what are you doing?" I was almost certain my eyes were at least double their normal size.

Astorian removed the belt, including what had to be at least five different weapons strapped to it, and placed it on the sideboard by the door. "Better?" He strolled over, picking up the book from the floor and browsing through it while he plopped into the chair next to mine, completely ignoring my shaking.

"Recienne's recommended this one to me several times. Are you enjoying it? If so, perhaps it's time for me to read it after all."

Grateful for the chair between us, I followed the nimble movements of his fingers as he flipped the pages. At least, this one was a fairly neutral tale—not one of the heavy romance novels I'd found the other day—and ended up shelving before I was halfway through, sobbing Tristan's name.

"Perhaps you should." Assessing him—the bound auburn hair, the vigilant eyes of the near-same color, the leather pants and simple shirt so at odds with the number of blades distributed over his body. "Is there anything you needed?"

He lifted his head. "Recienne asked me to check in on you."

Awkward silence fell when I didn't immediately respond.

"You seem cozy enough, though—at least *were* getting cozy when I came in, so I guess I can tell him you're fine?"

Fine was far from it, but—"Tell him whatever you want." The words came out harsher than intended. It wasn't Astorian's fault Rogue had upset me so much the last time we'd talked.

"Oh, I'll most definitely do that. But that doesn't mean you really *are* fine, does it?" He lowered the book in his lap, boots shifting as he adjusted his knees so it wouldn't drop between his thighs, and gestured at my chair for me to sit. "Come on, Sanja. You know I won't hurt you."

"Do I?" He'd been nice enough when Rogue had been around—and Clio. But this male hated Mages and believed I wasn't safe to be around his king.

"Any friend of Recienne's is my friend," he simply said, and the way he shrugged as if it meant nothing to call a human Mage a *friend* made me sit down and pick up my tea.

"He's not my friend," I clarified.

Astorian's teeth flashed in a knowing grin. "My friends call me Tori, by the way." He shook a strand of auburn hair out of his face. "So, what are we going to do today?"

"What?"

"Today ... you and I ... together. Recienne *sent* me to keep you company."

"To babysit me," I corrected and felt like I would be clarifying and correcting all day if I didn't manage to get him off my back.

"Company," Astorian insisted.

"Where'd he go, anyway?" Not that I really wanted to know, did I? Perhaps I did. But I would never admit that to myself.

Astorian, however, didn't seem to care that I'd already admitted it to him. "East." He pointed over his shoulder at the wall between the window and a ceiling-high bookshelf.

"What's east?"

"Don't tell me those Mages of yours never showed you a map of Askarea."

When I didn't voice my thoughts, that I'd not been shown or told a lot of things during my time with *the Mages*, intentionally or unintentionally, he merely shook his head.

"And Recienne? Has he?" I didn't even get to say Rogue could shove it all up his fancy ass when Astorian laughed again. "You've got quite a temper, Sanja, don't you?"

"What?"

A smirk. "Nothing."

I studied him for a moment, trying to hold his gaze, but balked the moment he shot me a feral grin—a dare to ask him again, to push him.

"Why don't *you* show me a map, smartass?"

Astorian barked a laugh and got to his feet. "If you promise not to make him sulk again."

"I'm not making fairy bargains with you."

I watched him prowl to the far corner of the room, his shirt shifting over his broad shoulders as he reached high on the shelf to extract a large book. Turning back to me, he flipped it open, grinning at me over the pages. "Not a fairy bargain. Don't let Recienne know you thought I'd offer you a fairy bargain. He'd never let me near his—" He caught himself as if he'd been about to spill a secret. It was then that I noticed he hadn't called the fairy king Rogue once, but Recienne—as if here, in this palace, he was playing a different role the way Rogue did.

And then, it dawned on me that I'd been thinking of Recienne as Rogue this entire time, that the distance the name of the king brought with it diminished by those few letters.

A short name, Rogue, not the pompous long one of fairy royalty. Just like Naar's one syllable, Rogue had chosen a nickname with one syllable—a sign of the lowest fairy class.

Astorian watched me with a raised eyebrow. "I don't want to live in your head, Sanja."

I cringed into the backrest. "So you do read minds?"

Astorian just added his other eyebrow. "I don't need to read minds to see how crowded it must be up there." He tapped his index finger to his temple.

And I wondered what abilities Astorian truly held and what role they secured him in the fairy king's royal court.

When I voiced my question, he shrugged. "King Recienne Gustine Olivier Univér Emestradassus de Pauvre the Second has use for many talents in his court. Why do you think he chose *you* to join him?"

"As part of his court?" Disbelief flashed through me.

"What else?" That knowing grin again.

"I don't know... his pet, perhaps?"

At that, the grin slipped, and Astorian's knuckles turned white where he clutched the book. "I don't know all of your history with Recienne, but if you believe for one second he'd take a human pet, you don't know him at all."

The look on his face was enough to know that crossing this fairy was a bad, bad idea. With the grin gone, he could have very well been a warrior god glimpsing a pending battle of justice.

Awe and fear mingled in my stomach, but I didn't allow myself to be intimidated this time. "That's what he said the other day."

Astorian rolled his neck, fists relaxing, and strolled back to the table where he dropped the book in front of me, showing a giant, hand-drawn map. "This is Askarea." He ran his finger over the double page, stopping at a walled city near the western edge. "Aceleau." His finger slid east over a cluster of trees with illustrations of a stag and a bird—a crow, I realized—"The Seeing Forest." At last, he pointed at a harbor at the far north-eastern end of the continent—"Ansoli"—and on to the island beyond it, the castle drawn there. "Fort Perenis, the Askarean prison."

I stared, drinking in all details, memorizing them as best I could. Especially the mountain range in the west, beyond which my own kingdom was situated. My eyes followed the curved line of a river in parallel to the mountains all the way to the end of the map where the Hollow Mountains should mark the point where Askarea met Cezux and Tavras near the ocean. That's where Tristan was. Where Zelia and Dimar were.

"It takes a month to travel there by foot," Astorian commented when he noticed where I was looking, probably calculating that I was wondering if running made sense. How far I'd get if I even made it out of the palace.

"For a fairy?" I tried to cover my obvious thoughts. "I thought you lot traveled by site-hopping."

"The ones of us who can site-hop would be there in the blink of an eye. The fairies who can't would still need a week to get there." When I looked up from the map, a question shone in his gaze. "So are you planning to leave us any time soon, Sanja?"

His directness made me cough. "Do I have a choice? Recienne made it clear I wasn't to leave the palace without him—"

"Or anyone from his trusted circle," Astorian finished for me. "So are you up for a trip outside these walls?"

"To the Hollow Mountains?" I bit my tongue a moment too late to conceal the eagerness in my voice.

"Let's start with any place inside the city walls." I thought he was going to add that it was safer, but he didn't. All he did was flip the page to show me a map of all of Eherea, Askarea nestled between the human realms like a wedge.

My eyes fell on the Seeing Forest once more. "Is he there?" I asked, and this time, I wasn't surprised when Astorian said, "The Seeing Forest? Maybe."

What did surprise me was the uneasy sensation in the pit of my stomach that followed his very fairy response.

"So, where are we going?" He straightened to his full height, giving me an expectant glance that indicated he was willing to wait for not more than a moment before I made up my mind.

"I don't know... Recienne sent his entire court away to keep the palace safe for a human; shouldn't I better stay here to not put myself in danger?" The meaning of the words hit me only when I spoke them—he'd kept the palace safe for a human. For me. He was trying to keep *me* safe.

For his own, selfish reasons to contain the Crow Fairies once more or because he did care enough to actually want me safe. I stopped my thoughts right there.

"It's up to you. No one will attack you when you walk the city at the side of the king's advisor."

"You're an advisor?" A glance at the weapons still distributed on him despite the absence of his weapons belt fueled my doubt.

"Don't always believe what you see, Sanja. There is more to people than how they first appear. A warrior might be a scholar; a scholar might be an assassin; an assassin might be a general; and a king might be a bandit."

I rolled his words over in my mind. "So you dress as a warrior to hide what you truly are?"

He barked a laugh at that. "Everyone in Askarea knows I'm the king's advisor, Sanja. I also happen to be one of the best warriors Askarea has to offer. Why can't I be both?"

"Both—" I repeated, the way Tristan had been both, the man and the Mage. The way I'd taken part of his identity from him. My chest ached, and I had to take a steadying breath before I asked my next question. "The fairies out there... Do they know I'm in their city? Will they try to hurt me if we go into the streets?"

"Some know. Some don't. It's up to you to choose what you want to do. Except for wallowing in this pretty palace."

He jerked his chin, gesturing at pretty much everything surrounding him, and the grin returned to his features, making his auburn eyes light up. He was handsome in a more roguish way than Recienne. But there was no part of him that didn't scream fairy, immortal beauty, power.

"Of course, I'm happy to just stay here for the rest of the day and watch you read romance novels, but I'd rather you move your pretty legs for a bit, or you'll get lazy and out of shape. Not that your shape is any of my concern," he added quickly as if realizing what he'd said. "Except for where it impacts your ability to defend yourself."

"Aren't we safe in here?"

He cocked a brow. "The royal fairy palace is warded and protected. No one enters without the king's permission. It's a magic that passes through generations. He, Naar, I, and—" Again he cut himself off, and this time, I could finish his words for myself in my head.

And Clio can enter.

He nodded, seeing the recognition in my eyes.

"But, for now, entrance has been rescinded from everyone else." He waved a hand at me. "Except for you, of course."

"Of course," I repeated, trying to decipher what he was not saying.

"So ... are we going out?"

TWENTY-FIVE

We ended up staying in the library after all, him watching me read a book on Askarean history, and him filling in details whenever I prompted him where my human, Cezuxian upbringing and education failed me—which was pretty much every other page.

Apart from learning that the de Pauvre family had been ruling this realm for at least five hundred years, during which plenty of conflicts and uproars had risen and been smothered—one of them, the Crow War—I learned about social classes and a long, bloody history of Askarean rulers fighting to stay in power.

"With the borders locked through the Ultimate Sacrifice, the internal conflicts became more pronounced, and the crown was challenged. That was in the Crow War when the Crows intended to overthrow the de Pauvre rule and become the first non-high fae on the throne of Askarea," Astorian informed me as I brought up the topic. "Both Recienne and his sister were lucky to get away with their lives." Something dark entered his gaze, a memory, but he shook his head, and it was gone.

"They were alive in the Crow War? How old are they?"

"Recienne and I grew up together here at court. We will both be five hundred years in two decades. And the princess—" His features solidified as he met my gaze over the book he'd been reading in the armchair next to mine. "Princess Cliophera Clarette Tarie Amaryll Saphalea de Pauvre was killed a few decades ago. She would have been three hundred and two this summer."

I could see the lie in his eye, the plea for me not to call him out on it even with no one in the room with us, no eager ears following our conversation. But Rogue had refrained from speaking certain names in this palace, from bringing up certain topics, so I took it as a sign of caution when he told me the official story around what had to be Clio's real name.

"I'm sorry for your loss."

The way his eyes twinkled in response made me wonder if I'd said something wrong.

"Thank you." Those words were real, though. A real thanks for a loss that seemed to have come in a different form than her death—her absence from court, perhaps, or something entirely different that I couldn't yet understand.

"What was she like?" A neutral question that didn't demand for a lie, I hoped. And when I noticed the light shining in Astorian's irises as he seemed to ponder his response, I knew that whatever he'd say, the truth was that she'd been wonderful—that she still *was* wonderful in his eyes.

"You loved her?" It wasn't my place to ask. Not when I couldn't bear the thought of talking about love myself.

But Astorian didn't seem to mind, despite the pain in his eyes. "We were meant to be mated at Ret Relah. But everything happened a few days before the ceremony."

This warrior's eyes so full of emotion spoke volumes that there was a different story to tell about the end of their love. One that could never be spoken in these halls.

I reached over the armrest of my chair, placing my hand on top of his. "I'm sorry."

Astorian studied my hand on his for a moment then turned it over, catching my fingers and gently squeezing. A smile graced his lips when he looked up again, but the pain hadn't faded.

"You're human, Sanja. You don't understand what it means to have a mate and what it means to lose her. And maybe that's a mercy. One human lifetime is not enough to understand what it means to love like this—to suffer like this." The wisdom in his words struck me once more—just like at Clio's hideout where he'd told me that royalty made me no different when it came to doing despicable things in order to survive. There was the advisor, the educated male who would have been an asset in any court, and I could see why Rogue had chosen him as a friend and an advisor, as a confidant when it came to his sister's safety. His sister's mate—whatever that meant.

"Mates are something stronger than what you call a husband or a wife. They are soul-bonded, lovers, more than that even. Two halves of one whole." The way he said it—reverent—and the heaved breath following his words...

Maybe it was pity, or maybe it was my petty need to unload my own sorrow on someone who understood what it meant, but I laid the book aside and pulled my knees to my chin, bracing my shins against the armrest as I folded myself up in the chair and said, "I lost someone I love. Not the way you have, but I lost someone very important."

As I spoke the words, I knew they were true. With everything that had happened, I still loved him, even when he'd given me up for his magic.

"The Mage?" Astorian turned in his chair, placing his own book on the table as he gave me his full attention.

I nodded, unable to speak. I'd held it in. All those weeks, I'd held on to the numbness, the emptiness, until Rogue had told me ... told me about his conversation with Tristan. And now it hurt. It hurt so badly that I nearly screamed for the loss of all words.

"Recienne told me what happened. It's a shit move." A rumble of anger laced his voice.

The fact that Astorian knew could mean two things: One—Rogue had told the truth. Two—Astorian was playing along with whatever Rogue was scheming.

But the tear in his eye, the pain. And the deep, undeniable truth resonating in my chest, that Tristan *would* actually pick his magic over anything ... it sent a thin rift of acceptance through the pain in my chest, cleaving it in two.

"A mate would never do that. He would never give up on you."

"The way you'd never have given up on the princess?" *The way you haven't given up on Clio?* I corrected in my mind, and he seemed to understand.

"The way I will never give up on the star her spirit formed on the firmament." Something fierce pierced through his pain, and as I watched his face transform, I knew that he'd happily take whatever she'd give him for the rest of all eternity, even if it broke his own heart.

But Tristan wasn't a mate. He was human just like me. His own needs came first. While I ... I had put his freedom over my own, had sacrificed myself for him. Had wrecked myself in those trials so I could get him out—could get them all out.

Zelia had given the last of her magic to make me a Mage Stone. She'd accepted what had happened. Dimar, he'd been nothing but supportive since we'd left the fairy palace a few months ago. And Tristan—

Apparently, he'd struggled more than he let on, had quarreled with his fate even when he'd told me he was fine. He'd wanted me—but he wanted his magic more. Even in a world where the Crows and Cyrill were no longer a threat, that wouldn't change.

And Rogue... He'd offered his help. For free. Because he knew how I felt for the Mage and because he wasn't the cruel fairy I'd believed him to be. He cared. Deep down in the darkness of his fairy being, a part of him cared enough to not trick Tristan into another bargain and delight in his misery. For me.

I shut down the thoughts before they could take on a life of their own, find any meaning in what he'd said to me. For if I allowed myself to trust him and was betrayed—I didn't think I'd survive it.

"Is that where fairies go when they die? They become stars?" I responded to his earlier statement, just to keep myself from thinking.

He shrugged as he studied me. "It's a soothing thought to have a star with her name on it watching over me."

"With a *long* name on it," I amended, and he laughed, the sound lifting the stifling heaviness from the room.

"Indeed."

"What's up with all the names?" I asked, honestly curious but also steering the conversation away from the topic of Tristan. "I mean, if the length of a name speaks about the status in society, how come low-born fairies don't just give their children long names?"

Astorian gave me a look that suggested he was doubting if I knew anything at all about fairies. And had he asked outright, I'd have told him I didn't, because it was the truth.

"Because the law states the punishment for inappropriate name length is death." My face must have shown how confusing that was to me because he continued, "If a low-born fairy uses a name longer than a syllable, they can be executed."

That was horrible. Worse even than the taxes Cyrill beat out of my people when they couldn't pay.

"Don't look at me like that, Sanja. I didn't make the law."

"But you enforce it?"

"The late king enforced it. Recienne has taken a more liberal approach, but that's a conversation for another time." He glanced around as if expecting someone to crawl out from behind the shelves and call him out on what he'd shared.

Rogue—he'd chosen a one-syllable name to become a nobody in his own realm.

Again, Astorian nodded as if he could read my conclusion from the look on my face.

"So, tell me more about how that control works. You know my name. Can you control me?"

It might have been a dangerous question with any other fairy—even Rogue—but something about the way he'd shared about Clio even when unable to tell the full truth... It made me want to trust him.

"You gave your name to Recienne in a bargain. That's the strongest sort of control a fairy can gain. A strong fairy could still control you by merely knowing your name. But Recienne has warded you."

"He has *what*?"

"Protected you against fairy control. He used your name to prevent your body from listening to anyone other than you."

The fact that I could feel my mouth hang open didn't make it any easier to close it and look less like a surprised fool.

"You don't honestly think he would have left you unprotected. He's the most powerful fairy in all of Askarea, and even he was scared to leave you alone in this palace without warding you from name-control."

"How do I know you're not lying to me?"

Astorian shrugged. "I guess you'll just have to take me at my word about this."

It was easier to believe him than to believe Rogue had actually done that and not told me about it. He'd helped me—again—and not taken any credit for his aid, just like in the trials when he'd let me believe he was actually working against me. Until—until he'd saved me. He'd ripped me from his father's control, overruled it, had placed my hand in Zelia's so the magic could transfer.

He'd known. He'd known it was my only chance.

And he'd needed me to bring down his father so the Crow Fairies would never track it back to him. So he'd remain inconspicuous.

"Is he with the Crow Fairies?" I asked, a sudden wave of fear running through me that had nothing to do with the name-control or the cold expression entering Astorian's face.

"He's receiving orders, Sanja. And this time, it seems to be a lot of new orders, or he would have long returned."

Astorian didn't tell me more than that even when I debated begging for more information. Anything that could help me learn what my role was to be in Rogue's plan was a good thing. But as if he'd pulled up a wall, nothing leaked through, and I had to give up when Naar knocked, announcing that dinner was served in the dining hall.

So I watched him buckle his weapons belt on the way out the door, wondering how one fairy could carry that much steel on him. Astorian flashed me a grin over his shoulder as we turned the corner into the main hallway.

"What?" I prompted.

But Naar was waving from a side door, beckoning me to join her.

When I shot him a helpless glance, Astorian shrugged. "Whatever she says, follow her instructions. She is usually right."

The fact that he'd put it that way made me want to run back to the tower even when I already knew Naar *was* usually right. About the things she suggested regarding wardrobe and bathing soaps and oils at least. But something in her wide purple eyes told me this was about more than a bath.

"*Come-come-come*," she urged and waved me in through the door while Astorian continued down the hallway, not even half alarmed at the interruption.

"What's wrong?" I wanted to know.

Naar just sat me down in a chair, picked up a brush from a small table, and started brushing my hair. "Do you have your Mage Stone on you?"

I nodded, cursing when the brush tugged painfully on a strand in the process. "Is there a reason to believe I'll need it?" Not that I'd mastered the crystal in my pocket—even with the success at the Ledrynx attack. I'd also yet needed to recharge it. I hadn't asked Rogue about it, worried what he'd make me trade this time. "It hasn't been recharged in a while."

Maybe it was stupidity to admit that to her, then, she'd never led me astray since I'd returned to Aceleau—nor had she before.

"I can take care of that for you, even if it's not the same vast pool of magic as Recienne's." I glanced up at her from the side and found her face tight, lips pressed together.

"Are you sure? I don't want to cause any inconvenience—"

"You shouldn't bother what inconveniences you cause, Sanja. You need to think of your needs first—especially today." With those words, she held out a hand, waiting for me to pull my Mage Stone from my pocket.

The moment I did, a flicker of magic brightened the room, pulling my attention to the carved details along the glimmering walls. The light faded, constricting into a pulse beneath my fingers where I was holding the Mage Stone. Had I known a proper spell, I might have been able to conjure magic then and there, the adrenaline coursing in my veins pushing my connection with the magic beneath the smooth, glasslike surface. "Thank you."

Naar nodded, returning to my hair, braiding it down from the crown of my head in a long, dark plait. "That's better," she commented as she pulled me to my feet and turned me to face her.

"What's going on, Naar?"

She halted for a moment at the use of her name, as if it triggered a memory, but it was gone in a blink, and her smile returned.

"Why, the king is back. And he has a guest." *An uninvited one*, was what she didn't need to say. It was clear in her expression, despite the smile. "Now hurry, but not enough to be out of breath. When you get to the dining room, Recienne will be sitting at the head of the table, the king's place of honor. His guest will be sitting to his left. And Astorian will be sitting next to the guest." She blinked, a bit nervous, and I wondered if it was time for me to bleat and run to the tower. But Naar took my hand, closing my fingers around the Mage Stone. "You will sit to Recienne's right. And for the love of magic, keep quiet. Don't speak if you don't have to. It will make everything easier."

She sent me on my way before I could insist on knowing who the guest was that they intimidated her that much, and I wondered if there was a way for me to skip the dinner altogether, have her take something up to my room.

But Naar called after me, "Sanja."

I glanced over my shoulder to find her gesturing for me to pocket the Mage Stone. When I continued down the hallway, voices drifted from the dining room, one of them Astorian, whose tone had become all too familiar over the past hours, the other Rogue. But he sounded so bored, so calculated, so ... so much like the fairy prince who'd leaned against his father's throne—that I shivered at my approach.

It wasn't before I reached the threshold that the third voice spoke.

"Well, hello there, Sanja," Lady Moyen Shae Wellows said in her rich timbre, and from the gleeful expression on her face, I could tell she'd come here to see me more than she'd come for the fancy dinner spread across the oak table on silver platters. My stomach plunged to my knees at the sight of the female who'd taken Tristan from the Mages' House and escorted him to the fairy palace.

Recienne's gaze was already waiting for me when I glanced at him for information, support, aid—anything that would not make me look like a mute and very human fool.

He merely rose to his feet, gesturing at the place to his right, a perfectly polite smile gracing his features. The expression shocked me so much that I almost didn't notice how pale he was, how the side of his jaw seemed tighter than usual.

But I didn't let my observations show on my features, my court-trained princess-self surfacing as I followed his invitation and helped myself into my chair under the scrutiny of what had once been the late fairy king's torture master and might have just become the new one's as well.

From across the table, Lady Wellows's near-black eyes were measuring me like a pony for sale, smile turning serpentine as she leaned toward Recienne, who'd settled back into his chair and whispered something that made Astorian cough across from me.

I didn't let her trick me into speaking. Not with Naar advising against it.

"Well, well, my king. I see you have been busy collecting oddities during my absence." Lady Wellows's small, delicate hand slid along the edge of the table as she huffed a laugh. "What a fascinating little human you are," she said to me over a bowl of berries. "I thought I'd never see you again after the ... crimes you committed against the late King of Askarea."

"She is here as my guest," Rogue told her with little interest, reaching for a piece of bread from the basket before him. Astorian monitored every movement like a hawk, and I wondered what he saw—if he saw more than the rest of us, the way he seemed to sometimes read from my mind.

He winked at me as if in response, but his features remained like stone as he turned his attention back to the female beside him.

"Guest, you say." Lady Wellows swept her thick black hair over her shoulder, exposing the entire front of her dress—and what a stunning dress it was. Low-cut black velvet with thin, golden chains reaching from shoulder to shoulder, draped over her decolletage. Her long sleeves didn't remind of the late summer breeze drifting through one of the open windows but of the darkness of night. "There, I thought you'd mentioned a *prisoner* earlier. I would hate to be misled."

"And misled you shall not be," Rogue said, the mask of the king perfectly in place as he gave her a gracious smile—a smile that should have never curved his lips in the presence of the viper who'd taken Tristan.

I ground my teeth.

"Queen Sanja of Cezux has been keeping me company in my lonely palace, Moyen. She isn't here because she thought a summer trip to the fairylands appeared particularly enticing to her but because I made a bargain with the King of Cezux, her husband, who had a bargain with my father as you surely remember." Rogue dabbed a spot of wine off his lips with a luxurious napkin while swirling the goblet he'd drunk from in the other. "Cyrill has created a ruse revolving around dear Sanja's sudden return from the dead, and since her presence in Jezuin reinforced his power, I thought a break from her beloved city was just what she needed in order to restore the balance of power once more."

The balance of power. I did my best not to fall over the edge of the table with all the questions I had for him.

Before he continued, his gaze fell on me for a moment, assessing my face with those predatory golden eyes that seemed as cold as the first day I'd met him. But Astorian's words this afternoon had left a mark, and I couldn't help but look for that *friend* he'd mentioned.

"I have her for the next"—he paused to do a tally in his head—"six months. And when I return her, it's time to demand from Cyrill what he owes."

Lady Wellows gave him a satisfied smile that made me want to scream. But I swallowed all emotion and picked up a fork to help myself to some of the greens in front of me. Astorian tracked my every move.

"Good." Lady Wellows nodded to herself. "Very good. It's gotten rather boring in this city since all the Mages left." The way she eyed me as if she could see through my flesh to my very bones... "Now, what have you planned for her? And why haven't you called for me sooner? I'd been hoping you'd bring me into your inner circle since the day your dear father passed." Her fingers brushed the length of his sleeve from his elbow to the back of his hand. "And you"— she turned to Astorian, who gave her a bland smile, a perfect courtier in his element—"I'm sure I can find use for you during my stay here at His Majesty's palace."

The air turned thick, but Lady Wellows seemed oblivious to it as she was grazing Astorian's chest with her gaze.

Rogue, however, turned, opening his lips, a murmur drifting to me on a dark breeze as he whispered only to me, "I'm sorry, Sanja. I didn't know she'd invite herself. And I couldn't turn her away without raising suspicion." It was all he got out before Lady Wellows's attention returned to him.

"Maybe I'll find use for both of you."

I could have sworn, under the veneer of the king, Rogue shuddered.

Lady Wellows didn't pay much attention to me once she'd started finding Rogue and Astorian more interesting. Between bites of crisp waffle, she dipped her finger into the whipped cream atop her dessert then licked it off, eyes wandering to Rogue, whose politeness had slipped into the very much bored one I'd experienced during my first conversations with him. When he talked to me these days, more emotion showed. More anger, more of something else that seemed to be eating him up inside. But this bored king, he was gone when we were alone. Maybe that was a good thing. And maybe it was an even more elaborate mask than the one he was showing right now.

Tuning out Lady Wellows's sultry tone as she murmured to the fairy king, I focused on Astorian instead. His hand lay clenched beside his plate, napkin mangled between his strong fingers, and I wondered if he found the female as abhorrent as I did—not only because of what she'd done to Tristan.

I was able to refrain from speaking during the meal, glad to not be addressed by either of them. Only when

Rogue flicked his fingers, the food disappearing to the Guardians knew where, did the lady turn her focus from him back to me.

"Maybe, if Recienne is a good king, I'll invite you to join us later." The meaning of her words hit me like stones, and for the first time in a long, long while, I blushed. I actually blushed at what she implied, at Recienne's look following her announcement.

"Come, Sanja. I'll take you back to your room," Astorian offered, not in the kind way he'd spoken to me this afternoon but a calm, cold manner that reminded me too much of the way I'd been treated in this palace during my trials.

Recienne nodded once, all the confirmation he'd give in front of Lady Wellows, but he didn't speak to me on that dark breeze, even when lady Wellows turned to lead the way toward what had to be his rooms—or hers if she was staying in the palace the way she'd hinted.

Together, Astorian and I watched them march away, Lady Wellows looping her arm into Rogue's. Something inside me stirred at the sight, similar to the forests when the Ledrynx had appeared behind his shoulder. A natural reaction toward predators, I assumed.

Astorian's hand on the small of my back turned me away before I could give it another thought.

TWENTY-SIX

Through the window, a cold so untypical for late summer crept in that I rolled out of bed, intending to close it and roam the dresser for an extra blanket. I was half up, listening to the silence in the room, when a shadow moved beside the armoire.

"Who's there?" I blinked away the sleep, hand sliding under my pillow where I'd stored my Mage Stone the night before.

"Just me," Rogue's murmur told me on a dark breeze, and I couldn't help it—my body slumped in relief.

"What are you doing here?" My voice was gobbled up by that same dark breeze concealing our conversation.

"Checking in on you." He cleared his throat. Rogue *never* cleared his throat, but he did as he stepped out of the shadows. "Moyen said she'd drop by your room to have some fun with you. Even though I forbade her, I don't trust her to follow my orders. Especially since she no longer serves the de Pauvre crown."

I didn't know where to start with my questions, so I blurted, "And you didn't think to check from *outside* my room? How would you feel waking up to me spying on your sleep?"

At that, he shot me a grin that made me blush yet again, and I had to bite my lip to keep myself from screaming at him in frustration.

"I had to come in here because she can site-hop just like me. Even though this palace is warded, with her new master, I'm not sure about the limits of her power."

I swallowed a retort, finding all objections rendered useless. "Who does she serve if not *Your Majesty*?"

"The Crows." His curt response made the meaning even worse.

"You let the enemy into your palace?"

"*She* let herself in on behalf of the Crow King, who wants to see the kind of creature I've been hosting in my humble home."

"First, there is *nothing* humble about your *home*. Second, I thought you were the most powerful fairy in all of Askarea. How can she or anyone else dictate who you let into your palace?"

Rogue gave me a slightly twisted smile. "I am. But the bargain my father made with the Crow Fairies is binding. I cannot act against it—at least, not openly."

"So you'd rather sneak into my bedroom instead?"

The grin he gave me was nothing short of wicked. "I'd sneak into your bedroom happily whenever you ask me to, Sanja." He smoothed out a wrinkle on the front of his black tunic. "As for right now? Yes, I'd rather sneak into your bedroom in the middle of the night and upset you than knock in the morning and find you gone." No humor was lacing his words now, no twinkle in his eyes. "If Moyen gets her hands on you—and I don't mean her innuendo from earlier, that would be the least of your concerns—I can't get you back. Once the Crows have you, there is nothing I can do."

I didn't shrink away when he walked over to sit at the foot of the bed.

"Tell me everything, Rogue."

His head whipped around as I called him by his name, and as our gazes locked across the few feet distance, the gold of his irises seemed to burn in the darkness.

For a moment, he remained still like the glimmering stone making up his palace, and I thought he would simply disappear the way he had perfected. But Rogue shook his head, dark hair shifting on his forehead, and lifted a hand. The window drifted shut, and the moon and stars seemed to brighten as he pulled one knee onto the bed, ankle crossed over his other knee, fully facing me. His fingers rested on his calf, tugging on a loose string at the seam of his pants.

"Everything? That might take too long for tonight. You already know about the Crow Fairies and the deal my father made—the deal that I'm bound to fulfill by the cursed blood of a delusional male." His smile was bitter. "And there are things I'm not ready to tell you, Sanja. Just as you aren't

333

ready to fully trust me." A question lingered in his eyes, the same I'd seen there before.

I braced my hands beside my hips, suddenly aware of the thin nightgown I was wearing. But Rogue's eyes didn't stray from my face.

"There are things that you should be aware of now that you know about Clio and Astorian and the Crows. And about ... Rogue." He clasped his hands together to keep them from fidgeting, the most tell of nervousness I'd ever seen on him. "I assumed Rogue's identity long before Clio was ever in jeopardy. His home in the forest is as real as Recienne's home in the palace. Long before my father ever made the deal with the Crow Fairies, I was sick of watching humans die in his court. I was sick of fairies starving because of the way our forefathers set up the laws. And since Recienne couldn't work against his powerful father, he invented the bandit. That was long before my mother was killed by *your* Mage's parents." I waited for the anger to flare as he mocked Tristan with the way he emphasized that one little word—*your*—but nothing happened. Not even the emptiness that had carried me through so many weeks. Or the pain. In that moment, I wasn't Sanja the saint or Sanja the queen; I wasn't even Sanja the Mage. "And her power transferred to me," he continued, reading me through the distance between us.

"I did it to even out the social imbalance where I could, to steal from the rich fairies crossing the forests and from human merchants benefiting from their riches. I did it to scare the humans from ever crossing into our lands so they wouldn't fall victim to my kind and become trapped in this realm. And Astorian and Clio were with me from the beginning. A new generation of fairies waiting their turn to make changes when their time to rule came."

"You didn't scare me away," I pointed out, earning a chuckle of the smoothest velvet as he leaned closer.

"Perhaps that's because you have no sense of self-preservation, Sanja, or you wouldn't be sitting here with a fairy king who supposedly delights in torturing your kind."

"It's not like I have a choice," I drawled, bringing a bit more distance between us.

Rogue merely cocked his head. "On the contrary, Sanja. You have every choice with me. Want me to leave"—he pointed to the door behind him with his thumb—"I'll leave. Want me to stay, I'll stay. Want me to get you the hell out of here, I'll do that as well." Gleaming golden eyes unblinking, he waited for me to state what it was that I wanted.

"I don't believe you. I don't believe you'd let me go."

His lips twitched at the corners—not in a grin. "I'd go with you, that's all."

"So I can't run? I can assure you, I'm very good at running." At least, I had been until the day Dimar picked me up in the forests and dragged me back to Jezuin.

"I wouldn't go with you as your keeper." His hands tightened around his ankle.

"What would you go as then?"

Rogue shook his head. "How about I continue my story, and in return, you tell me about how very good at running you are in more depth?"

A genuine offer, not a bargain, I could tell by the look in his eyes, even in the dimness of the room.

"How about you conjure a dressing robe from those magical realms in-between, and I don't scream loud enough for Lady Wellows to come for me after all?"

In response, Rogue flicked his fingers. One moment, tiny stars danced at his fingertips; the next, a long, luxurious velvet robe dangled from his hand. "You dress, I talk?"

I snatched the piece of clothing from his grip without getting to my feet and wrapped it around my shoulders before I slid my arms into the soft fabric. The scent of summer rain and nights under open skies enveloped me, soothing my nerves as I inhaled a deep breath.

Rogue's face was unreadable as he got to his feet, pacing the room in measured strides.

"Where were we? Ah ... yes. A new generation of fairies waiting for their time to make changes." He halted, watching me tie the belt at my waist with a wistful expression. "Then my mother was killed, and I suddenly held true power. A power greater than even my father's.

"My father had always feared he might one day be challenged for his throne, but after my mother's death, he suspected enemies in every corner. Including me. I was who he feared most. And his fears drove him to make the pact with the Crow Fairies to break open the borders to the human lands once more that the Mages had sealed with the Ultimate Sacrifice." He paused at the window, leaving me with a view of the chiseled outline of his shoulders, the straight column of his neck, his muscled arms. A proud king—one with a multitude of burdens and sorrows that he'd never admit to.

Something inside of me stirred, wanting to reach out to him, to comfort him.

I quietly said, "I know what it's like to lose a mother."

He turned his head, his profile stark against the moon-tinted sky. "Tell me about your mother."

For a moment, I considered not speaking at all, but Rogue slid into the chair by the table, bracing his forearms on the edge, and the moonlight painted his features near-silver.

Beautiful. Surreal. But the sorrow in his eyes—

I gathered my courage, trying to forget what I could lose if he ever exploited what I was about to tell him, and said, "My mother was poisoned. I don't know who did it, but they knew she was a Mage."

"I'm sorry."

Shaking my head at him, I tugged the robe tighter around my chest and over my legs as I pulled them up on the bed. "It's been so long sometimes it's hard to remember." And it had been even longer for him.

"My mother was always the heart of the palace. With my father hunting for potential schemers and rogue lords and ladies, she was the one holding the court together." A faint smile played on his lips at some memory buried deep in his immortal mind. "Naar had served her for two centuries before she transitioned into my service. She used to say I was like my mother, that I *felt* too much, for a fairy. And when I started to apologize, she'd tell me that it was my strength, not my weakness."

Memories of my own showered through my mind of what Tristan had told me about fairies, how they desired human pets because they didn't feel the same way as we did.

"What are you thinking?" Leaning back in his chair, he scanned me, a thoughtful expression on his features that I hadn't yet seen on him.

I hesitated, but—"Someone once told me that fairies didn't feel the same way humans did... I mean, that hate was probably the only emotion we perceived the same way. But the rest—"

"You want to know if we burn the same way when we regret, Sanja? For, if that's your question, I can tell you, without a doubt, that we do. If we desire? I would be surprised if there was a single human who's been consumed by desire the way we are. And love ... love is an emotion for those who can afford it." He shut his eyes, breathing through his nose. "But hate ... yes, hate is probably the only feeling that works similarly in humans and fairies." He sighed and got back to his feet, gesturing at the thin line of light appearing above the palace roofs. "Dawn is breaking. It's time I return to my own quarters."

But I wasn't done asking questions.

Hate...

His words from before he'd left on his errands came back to me. "Why is it so important that I hate you?"

I could have sworn he cringed at my words. But when he opened his eyes, his face was smooth, unreadable. "Because then I don't need to wonder if things could be different."

"Different how? That we could be actual allies? Friends even? I don't even know if I can trust you. If anything of what you told me is the truth—or a big fat lie that serves your own purpose. The way it served your own purpose when you tricked Tristan into telling you he'd give me up for his magic."

There—there it was. Rogue had shown me his sister and his friend, had let me in on his dilemma with the Crow Fairies, his father's bargain that he was bound to fulfill with Cyrill. But he'd also brought me here to help him and hadn't yet given me a clue how. He'd mocked Tristan about him not getting me out of Cyrill's court, had implied that Tristan would give me up—

He hadn't even given a hint whether he could truly achieve it. If Recienne Olivier Gustine Univér—if only I could remember the rest of his name—the Second could truly give someone their magic back. A new Mage Stone? Or something else? Was it even possible? How could I truly trust him?

Because you know Tristan has never gotten over losing his powers, a small voice said deep inside of me, *and you've felt it for a while, even before Cyrill trapped you.*

"I never tricked your Mage, Sanja. I merely asked him what he'd be willing to give up to get his magic back. His response was 'Everything.'" He shrugged. "So is it my fault when he says that includes you?"

Whatever sympathy I'd felt for him went up in flames.

"But if you don't believe me, let's go ask him for *his* version of the story. I'm sure he'd be delighted to explain himself."

My body went cold at what sounded more like a threat than an offer—perhaps because I knew there was a chance Rogue was telling the truth. And that Tristan had long abandoned me.

"Tori said you showed particular interest in the Hollow Mountains today." He sauntered toward the bed. "Could it be a special someone has taken up residence there, waiting for the day his powers return?"

I ground my teeth, debating whether I could truly hide the truth from the fairy before me. "Since you seem to know everything, why don't *you* tell me?"

He chuckled, teeth flashing as he grabbed my hand and pulled me to my feet. "Don't complain to me when he asks questions about why you show up covered in nothing more than a nightgown and *my* dressing robe."

My objection made it half the way onto my tongue before we dissolved into rippling air and darkness.

TWENTY-SEVEN

I understood why people called them the Hollow Mountains the moment we materialized in a large, dimly lit cave. A cave filled with sediment columns the way a forest was filled with trees. They grew from the floor and the ceiling, slim and thick, in all shades of orange, yellow, and green. Rogue had landed us on what could only be described as a clearing at the center of the cave. He stepped away, graciously bowing to me. "Well then... Here we are. Feel free to call for your Mage." The dare in his gaze made me consider a trap or a trick or anything but the fact that he'd actually brought me to see Tristan—and Zelia and Dimar. *If* they'd made it to the Hollow Mountains.

The only thing I could tell was that we were underground—and it was hollow except for the strings of color framing us.

"Scared, Sanja?" Rogue leaned in as if sharing a secret. "Or merely worried I've been telling the truth after all?"

Damn all fairies to the Horn of Eroth and back. I gave him a smirk before I called at the top of my lungs, "Tristan!"

Rogue seemed to turn into a stone column himself as he realized I was going to actually do this—in his dressing robe or not.

When no one answered, Rogue grinned at me. "Don't be disappointed, Sanja. I'm sure there are others who'll appreciate the sight."

Ignoring him, I turned toward the echoes of my shout bouncing off the walls, the domed ceiling, to the fractured sound of my voice as it scattered across the place when I called for Tristan again.

Rogue folded his arms over his chest, face calm, composed, and jerked his chin toward the side of the cave. "This way." He started walking without checking over his shoulder whether I followed—probably not needing to with his superior fairy senses.

I trudged after him, unable to ignore the undeniable aesthetics of the place. The farther we went, the more detailed the patterns of color grew, witnesses of millennia of Eherea's history and yet never having seen the light of day.

"Pretty, aren't they?" Rogue commented as we made it to the cave wall. "Not that I'd panel my rooms with it, but the stone harvested in the Hollow Mountains is what most of Askarea is built of after all."

He flicked his fingers, and orbs of fairy light appeared above our heads, illuminating the cave into a glittering ensemble of colors. Blues and purples appeared between the greens and reds I'd initially noticed, reflecting tiny spots of light onto the velvet of my robe—Rogue's robe. My gaze found the back of his head, traveling the length of his spine, his legs, and it took me a moment to realize that he wasn't painted in light the way I was—as if a cocoon of shadows had wrapped around him, protecting him from being spotted in the sparkle of the cave.

"Beautiful, isn't it?" He commented without looking back.

I merely nodded. "Where is Tristan? And Zelia and Dimar," I amended with a flicker of hope.

"Sanja—" His voice almost brought me to my knees, rough and tired behind the layer of surprise—suspicion, perhaps. And behind Rogue's graceful shape … Tristan.

"Yes, yes. It's her." Rogue stepped to the side, gesturing at me with an elegant hand, and I almost wept at the sight of the Mage. Pale, exhausted … suspicious.

"Tristan." I clasped the front of the robe, trying not to stumble over the hem that reached all the way to the ground as I hurried toward him.

Tristan didn't spread his arms for me, eyes wandering back and forth between the fairy king and me.

"Tris—" I came to a halt in front of him, arms half raised to embrace him, but he stepped back.

"Is this a test, Recienne? Are you bringing me a vision to test if I was serious? Because if you are, my response remains the same. *Anything and everything.*"

I glanced back at Rogue, who gave me a curt 'I told you so' look that had my blood chilling before he sauntered to my side, placing a hand at my elbow as if he was going to escort me through the halls of the fairy palace.

"You should know better than to believe I can conjure hallucinations. So, unless you've nibbled from the mushrooms growing in the darker parts of the mountains, you can be very certain that both dear Sanja and I are real."

Tristan paled even more if that was possible, his eyes finding mine. "By the Guardians." His arms were around me, crushing me to his chest so hard my breath left me. But I didn't care. I didn't care about anything other than that he was here. That he was alive. And that—

Anything and everything.

"Did he hurt you? Did he—" He pulled away, holding me at arms' length as he scanned me head to toe. Confusion flickered over his features as he seemed to notice my clothes. "What are you wearing?"

Wrapping my arms around myself, I took a small step back, feeling Rogue's hard side against my arm.

"Now this will be interesting." His chuckle bounced off the glimmering threshold behind Tristan, which I was only now noticing. "What *are* you wearing, Sanja?"

Ass.

Ignoring the fairy king, I took a step away as I fumbled for words. "Are you all right? You look exhausted."

Tristan shook his head. "A month's worth of travel on foot through the fairylands will do that to a human. You should know; you traveled all the way from the borderlands to Aceleau."

I felt more than saw Rogue's eyebrow rise, a silent question if I hadn't told Tristan the truth.

"You forbid me to tell anyone," I said. But my words were swept from my mouth by a dark breeze as Rogue summoned them with his power.

"That has never kept you from doing anything, has it?" he drawled, but there was little bite in his words—more musing.

Tristan looked from me to Rogue and back to me, probably wondering what was happening, why our lips were moving and no sound was escaping. "What are you doing?" He took a step toward Rogue, hand sliding into the pocket of his pants—and my heart did a painful little jab at the sight of him reaching for his magic in reflex. "What are you doing to her?"

"Me? I wouldn't dream of doing anything to her ... at least, nothing she doesn't ask me for." Rogue's voice was laced with darkness and warning, despite the amused smirk on his face. "And she asked me for the truth about our little ... arrangement. Which, by the way, isn't a bargain," he said to me before he sauntered to the nearest column and leaned his shoulder against it, one hand in his pocket while the other gestured at Tristan, "but merely an agreement that I'd help Mage Tristan to become an actual Mage again."

There were no words for the throbbing in my chest as it settled inside of me ... the knowledge that, even now that I was standing right in front of him, Tristan chose to argue with the fairy king rather than kiss me.

And the fact that I wasn't certain I wanted him to anymore.

Tristan's troubled eyes met mine over the short distance, and the sadness there, the defeat... My heart broke all over again. But not here. Not with the smirking fairy observing my every move.

"And how are you going to actually help him?" I demanded, not taking my eyes off Tristan. His hair had grown longer, covering his ears, and his chin was stubbled—a good, roguish look on him. I grimaced involuntarily at the word *roguish*. Because there was already one rogue in our midst, and Tristan wasn't him.

Said Rogue shrugged, turning toward the threshold and strolling ahead. "I'd been hoping to have all my facts together before I tell you, but since you insist..." He stopped right on the threshold, turning on the spot so his ankles were still crossed as he said, "Since you love him so much, I'd been hoping you'd help me help him."

Tristan visibly flinched like at the crack of a whip.

"I thought I was supposed to help you with—" I didn't get any further since the control of Rogue's power coiled around my vocal cords, stopping them before I could finish my sentence.

"I told you that in confidence," he told me on that dark breeze, "not so you can blurt it to the Mage at your earliest convenience." His power slid along my cheek, not restraining me, not hurting me, but a gentle stroke—an apology. "Please don't let my trust be in vain, Sanja."

My throat bobbed, voice free again but no word leaving my mouth, even at Tristan's expectant expression.

"What were you supposed to help him with? Control Cezux the way his father had planned?"

I shook my head. "I'm not going to help anyone with anything before I understand what's going on here."

While Tristan glowered, Rogue's smirk told me how much he approved of my reaction, of my defiance to accept anything thrown my way. *Ask him*, his gaze seemed to say, *Ask him what happened. If I tricked him. Made him do anything. Ask him if I'm truly the big, bad villain you're trying to make me.*

"Is it true, Tris?"

"Is what true?" His expression became guarded.

All right. It was time to learn the full truth. "On the night of the banquet in Jezuin ... when I sent you away"—a flicker of pain in his eyes—"did Ro ... Recienne talk to you?"

Tristan hesitated.

"Tell her what we talked about, Tristan," Rogue encouraged. "I've got nothing to hide."

We'll talk about that later—I willed the words into his mind ... and a dark breeze came to collect them, carrying them back to him and painting a grin on his features.

"We most certainly will." His murmur was too close, too intimate as he chuckled against the shell of my ear even from so far away.

"Tris?" I reached for him, palm open, waiting for him to place his hand there.

Which he did. A heart-wrenching moment later, he grabbed my fingers, clutched them as if his life depended on it, and tugged me a step closer. "I'd rather discuss this in private, Sanja," he said, eyes pleading.

"And I'd rather we have this out once and for all. I can't have dear Sanja strolling around my palace, believing I'm a monster, can I now?" Rogue drawled from the doorway, audible for Tristan.

I gave him a damning look—which he answered with an innocent grin and a raised brow.

"It's all right, Tris. Whatever it is."

Rogue gave me an 'are you serious' look that I chose to ignore for the sake of Tristan's honesty, this moment when my world would either crash or be rebuilt.

Tristan pressed his lips into a tight line as he held my gaze, probably debating if it was a good idea to talk about this in the fairy king's presence—if there was any alternative, anyway. Then he wiped his face with his free hand. "I'd been in Jezuin for a few days before I heard that Cyrill was bringing his new saint to the first ring. A saint, Sanja, for the Guardian's sake—what did you think you were doing?"

I didn't correct him that it hadn't been my idea or my choice. Zelia and Dimar had surely informed him about that if they were here. Had they made it?

I didn't ask that either, making myself listen to what he had to say—the excuses or justifications, or whatever he'd come up with. Anything that would help me believe that he still loved me the same—that I could still love him the same and trust him.

"I'd been asking around, searching for you in the first ring from the day I returned. With the rumors spreading, there was no doubt Cyrill had you in his power. The question for me was how long would he manage to keep you locked up in the palace without using you to tame the peasants who hate him so much for his greed—and who adore you, *Saint Sanja*." A mocking chuckle escaped his lips as he eyed me like I was indeed a hallucination. Like what he'd speak to me would have no consequences. "When I saw you get out of the carriage by his side, that hideous dress on you preventing you from properly moving, there was no doubt I couldn't grab you and run with you. Even if we'd managed to trick the guards, you could have never outrun them with your legs half-bound like that."

The memory of the bag-like fabric restraining my ankles made me shift uncomfortably, made me strain to move around and stretch my legs. But I remained where I was, doing my best to ignore the way Rogue gave us his full attention—how his grin had faded and all that remained was a thoughtful expression.

"I thought if I could catch you by the carriage, I might be able to pull you out on the other side and get you to safety, but he had guards everywhere. They came to the square early that morning, scouting the area, placing sentries in strategic places." He shook his head, an endless sadness entering his gaze. "There was no way out for you, San. He had everything planned out. Even the man whom you healed with your blessing was bought by Cyrill's guards. I witnessed how they approached him before and compensated him handsomely afterward when the masses had scattered into the streets to go about their business. It was all an act to support his claim of what you are—and his claim to your throne."

Cold disgust spread in my gut, in my stomach, in my heart. I'd known what sort of man Cyrill was, had seen his cruelty. But there seemed to be a whole different layer of calculation to him that would prevent any loophole, prevent anything that anyone could possibly think of to get me out of there. Anyone but a fairy king with a hand-me-down bargain that bound him. And a cunning that made him so fearsome that no one would ever think to cross him. I shook my head. "So you chose to come to the palace instead?"

Tristan brushed his thumb over my palm, gaze dropping back to my velvet-clad form, and the sadness turned into bitterness. "I came to the palace to get you out. And if I couldn't, to find an entry into Cyrill's court and slowly bring him down."

"How... How could you ever bring him down without soldiers to fight or without ... without magic?" My voice became small, for my question already held all the answers I'd so feared. "You can't without magic. So you needed to find a way to use it again." I swallowed, my eyes finding Rogue's over Tristan's shoulder.

"I need my magic so no one can ever do that again," his voice was hoarse as he found my gaze again. "So no one can ever take you away again, hurt you, destroy you, control you."

"But most of all you need your magic so *you* won't ever depend on anyone again." I didn't know why I spoke the words. They weren't drawn from my lips by some magical force—Rogue's or otherwise—but merely that flicker of doubt that had grown since the day I'd first overheard Tristan's conversation with Zelia.

"So I'd never need to beg a fairy for help again," he corrected, glancing over his shoulder at Rogue, who had gone so still that I wasn't sure he was breathing. "So I could be strong enough to protect you and Zelia and Dimar. And that's what he offered. After I told him what I was willing to give up, he offered to help me get back my magic."

"For what price?" I swallowed the tears at the back of my throat, the impulse to scream at him, at Rogue, at the colorful lights dancing on Tristan's handsome face. But where would that get me? What would it change?

Tristan slowly shook his head. "No price at all. He didn't ask for anything in return." A smile finally spread on his lips as he'd finished his side of the story, and he curled his arms around my waist, pulling me in. "And now you're here." His breath washed over my hair and down my neck as he wrapped himself around me more tightly. "You're here, San. And everything is going to be all right."

But as I leaned my head against his shoulder, my breathing didn't slow; my heart didn't stop racing. Not a lie; Rogue hadn't told me a lie. Even if he hadn't let me in on all the details of his plan, this part hadn't been a lie. And as Tristan held me tight, my eyes didn't stray from Rogue, who merely inclined his head and disappeared into the corridor behind.

TWENTY-EIGHT

The cave felt empty all of a sudden, despite the presence of the man whom I'd bargained my freedom for. The pillars of glittering sediment were mocking me with their sparkle and shimmer, and Tristan ... Tristan was oddly silent as he slipped his arms up my back to circle my shoulders, a layer of protection that he could no longer provide—not when my Mage Stone made me more powerful than him. I only needed to master it.

Peeling my gaze away from the threshold, I leaned my forehead against Tristan's chest. "I understand, Tris. I do." And I did. This was no longer about me. This was about him surviving, about the life he'd built—and lost. "We'll figure it out."

His chest lifted in a deep breath of what could have been relief or resignation, and he shifted to glance over his shoulder to where Rogue had been standing a minute ago. "Do you trust him?" he wanted to know, and I couldn't help but acknowledge the calm in my chest as I lifted my head and locked my gaze with his.

"I do." No one was more surprised than me. "Do you?"

"I don't have another choice if I want to get my magic back."

"And he said he could truly help?"

Tristan pursed his lips, relaxed them, and pulled them into a half-smile that didn't touch his eyes. "I love you, San."

His words were like needles piercing into that calm.

Because I loved him. I did. But the fire, the desperate need to be with him … they were gone, finally extinguished like a candle when he'd confirmed Rogue's story. And what was left was cold smoke. Love of a different kind.

"I want to do what I can to help you get it back. And Zelia and Dimar, too. Are they here?" I glanced around, trying to spy another door that could indicate where my family was hiding. "Please tell me they're all right."

"They are fine." He slid an arm off me, pulling me to his side with the other in an all-too-familiar manner that used to mean something different to me—before I'd realized that what had happened in Aceleau had driven a wedge between us of a sort that couldn't be erased. It didn't change the fact that I loved him. I would probably always love him—for the man he was, the cautious, intelligent Mage who'd never depend on anyone. Who'd loved me freely and full-heartedly, if only for a while. Maybe that had been a gift from the Guardians for me to find someone like him, who'd take the bitterness in my heart and turn it into something beautiful.

He'd done just that. Had brought me to life ... the real Sanja, who wasn't restricted by her title and her obligations to her crown, but a Sanja who no longer shied away from the edges and scars she carried, instead acknowledging them as part of who she was. And part of them was that I'd taken something from him that he couldn't live without—and he'd admitted that he'd do anything and everything to get it back. He'd even give me up.

As he guided me toward the threshold, his arm weighed like lead on my shoulders, and I couldn't help but wonder if I was as much a burden to him as he'd become to me.

In silence, we made our way through a dim corridor carved from the same glimmering stone, but no fairy lights illuminated the walls here.

"Where are we going?"

"Just a bit farther. They're waiting at the heart of the mountain where we made our new residence." Tristan squeezed my shoulder in reassurance.

After two more turns, the corridor widened into a system of tunnels that spread into a small cave of the same stone. Here, there were only a few colors present—purple, to my amusement, the predominant one. How fitting for the no-longer Mages. And at the end of the cave—Zelia, Dimar, and Rogue were sitting around a round table large enough for six people. Rogue's back was to me, his hair shimmering like dark amethyst where he leaned his head against a pillar of stone behind his chair. He was listening to something Zelia was explaining. Zelia—

Despite the long journey, she looked healthy, refreshed. As if getting away from the poverty in Jezuin and back into the magical lands of Askarea had replenished her. And beside her, Dimar.

My cousin spotted us first, leaping from his chair and bounding toward us with a tight smile on his face.

"By the Guardian, Sanja. I thought I'd never see you again after what you pulled in Jezuin."

Painfully reminded that I'd shoved him behind the corner of the house to hide him from Cyrill's guards before I'd run into the street to give Zelia and him a chance to run, I detached from Tristan's side to wrap Dimar in an embrace. "So did I."

Behind him, Zelia had gotten to her feet and was walking toward us, disbelief tugging on her otherwise unreadable face. Rogue observed everything from where he'd turned around in his seat, face composed and back straight like the graceful king he was.

"I'm so sorry," I told Dimar as tears were rolling down my cheeks, soaking his shirt. "I'm so, so sorry."

Zelia's arms wrapped around both of us, and sobs shook me like an earthquake.

"It's all right, San." She stroked my hair. "Everything is all right."

But it wasn't.

I nodded into Dimar's shoulder anyway, reaching one of my arms around Zelia so I could hold all of my family tight at once, and the warmth in my heart reminded me that, with everything that had happened, Zelia had gifted me a Mage

Stone. She'd handed me the last of her magic rather than use it for herself. What she'd sacrificed—

For months, I'd been wondering if they'd ever made it out of Jezuin in one piece. I'd wondered if they'd come back for me to free me from the different sort of prison Cyrill had built around me. But they were alive. They were safe—considering Rogue knew their whereabouts.

I allowed myself a glance at the male still sitting at the table like a statue. But where his face had been calm before, emotions were fighting for the upper hand now. He held my gaze for a moment then stood and strolled toward us—past us—to stand next to Tristan a few feet away.

"What a neat little group, don't you think? And Sanja is the only one of you still in possession of a Mage Stone."

Tristan made an undefinable sound that could have gone with a shrug.

"Have you mastered it?" Zelia wanted to know.

It was I who shrugged as I pulled out of their embrace. "I'm not sure. *Something* has happened for sure. Just not at will the way it should once I truly master it."

I allowed Zelia to usher me to the table where she offered me a cup of tea from the pot sitting on a small stove in the nearby corner—corner might have been an overstatement since the cave had no straight wall, no even surface. Behind purplish pillars, a shelf and sofa were positioned against the wall under the lowest part of the ceiling. A hearth crackled next to it. I didn't think to ask how all of it worked, where the smoke went, or how it had been built to begin with. This was Askarea after all, and magic was at work wherever we went.

Dimar plopped down on the chair beside me. "Now that you're here, we can help you. It doesn't require magic for us to show you how it's done." He gave me a brotherly smile that made me want to wrap him in a tight hug all over again.

Zelia filled a cup for me then filled up Dimar's and her own and the one at the place Rogue had occupied. "You'll be staying with us for breakfast, will you not?" she asked, and I couldn't tell if the question was addressed toward me or Rogue, who sauntered closer and braced his hand on the back of my chair until Tristan had taken a seat across from me where another teacup was sitting. Then he slid into his chair, smoothing out his tunic.

I noticed only now the long nightgown on Zelia and the ruffled shirt and comfortable pants Dimar was wearing. I'd probably woken them from sleep with my shouting.

"We will," Rogue answered Zelia's question for both of us, meeting my eyes across the table. Something had changed in his features, and I couldn't put my finger on what it was. But it made him look ... younger? Different, for sure. Not as much like the king or even the bandit. But like a normal male sitting down for breakfast—even when everything about him was the opposite of normal.

Tristan cleared his throat, claiming my attention. "So, what have you achieved so far?" Even though I knew he was asking about the Mage Stone, I couldn't help noticing the undercurrent in his question. For his magic. What had I achieved for *his* magic?

Rogue had mentioned he wanted me to help with getting Tristan's magic back.

"I've managed to ... activate it, I guess," I said, not failing to feel under scrutiny the way I had those first weeks in Zelia's service when Tristan had instructed me on potions or herb collecting, or even simply cleaning a window.

Not enough—you'll never be enough.

My chest tightened, and I had to place a hand on my sternum to soothe the ache building there.

"Did you bring it?" Again Tristan, curious eyes grazing what was visible of my form.

No. I hadn't. Too busy with Rogue, I'd forgotten to keep my grasp on the Mage Stone.

"It's back at the palace in my bed."

At that, Rogue's lips quirked while Tristan's eyebrows knitted together as he glanced from the fairy king to me and back to the fairy king. Thank the Guardians, he didn't ask why Rogue had picked me from my bed to bring me here— that was a story I truly didn't feel like telling.

Instead, Tristan reached over the table to take my hand into his.

I didn't pull it back.

"You need to keep it on you at all times, Sanja," he told me with that serious face of the instructor—of the Mage teaching the Quarter Mage. Only, I was no longer that.

What had Rogue said? The stone was so tiny it wouldn't last more than an hour if I used it? Perhaps I'd turned into a Mage after all—an Hour Mage.

"If anyone else takes it—"

"I know," I cut Tristan off, aware of the sharpness of my voice, how even Dimar flinched a bit at it. "I know"—I leveled my tone—"I've been careless with your magic before. That has been made clear so many times that I can't even begin to forgive myself for it. But this is *my* magic we're talking about. And if I lose it, it's my problem I no longer have it, not yours."

Tristan let go of my hand, settling back in his chair as he eyed me as if I'd bitten him.

I could have sworn that dark breeze swirling through the room carried a sound of amusement on it. If the others could tell, I didn't know. All I knew was that Rogue was pressing his lips together into a flawless line, but his eyes twinkled the tiniest bit in approval.

"It *will* be my problem since you're supposed to help." The way he said it... as if I was a tool to be used rather than the woman he said he loved—and had been willing to give up on for his magic.

Of course, he'd care about my keeping it safe more than about what *I* wanted.

He hadn't asked me if I was willing to help, if I thought it was a good idea to agree to something I didn't know the conditions of—or the consequences, for that matter.

Dimar reached behind him on the shelf to extract a basket of bread. "Homemade," he announced in an attempt to break the tension.

"My home isn't here," Tristan hissed at him, and my heart broke—for the man before me who'd turned so bitter without what gave him freedom. There was so little of *my* Mage left that, behind the troubled blue of his eyes, I didn't even find the stars he'd quoted humans had when they heard the word magic. This was more—a need, a hunger.

As he quietly brooded in his chair, I knew Tristan would indeed do anything for his magic. Whether that made him dangerous, I had yet to decide.

"We've already talked about this, Tris," Zelia reminded him. "We can't go back to Aceleau even if you have your magic back. We'd be hunted, and the Mages' House is gone."

"If you take *his* word for it," Tristan seethed at the fairy king.

Rogue merely rolled his shoulders and picked up his tea. After a long sip, he hummed a sound of contentment. "It's up to you what you believe. I've always spoken the truth to you."

"About getting my magic back? You've said she would help. That's the only reason I'm not taking you apart for having her in your palace—because you're my only option."

"That's a bit of a harsh way to put it, don't you think, Tristan?" Rogue drawled. "Besides, without your precious magic, you can't even touch me." He swirled his tea, taking another sip.

"Stop it." I placed both hands flat on the table, considering getting to my feet to make them listen—but both their heads whipped toward me, Rogue's golden eyes alive as they met mine.

"Stop what, Sanja?"

Tristan growled for lack of words.

"This," I said, gesturing between the two of them. "Tell me how you're going to get him a new Mage Stone. And

while you're at it, why don't you enlighten us about the possibilities to get Zelia and Dimar one as well? They lost their
magic as much as Tristan did, and if I'm all ready to help,
then I want to do right for everything I took from them.

"Careful what you're asking for, Sanja." Rogue smirked
around the table. "The fact that I'm sitting in this room with
the man who'd trade you for a droplet of power any time is
solely because of your ... attachment to him."

"Well, I'm *attached* to my aunt and my cousin as well,
thank you very much."

Zelia and Dimar exchanged a concerned look that made
it hard for me to focus on being angry at all. Because this
wasn't about pride or guilt. This was about me not managing
to keep my tongue still in Rogue's presence, to let him stoke
that fire of anger burning inside my chest—and despite how
much I hated him right now, I understood that he did it for
a reason. And that I could trust his reasons.

The realization alone was enough to stun me into silence.

"We've talked about it," Zelia started, but Dimar placed
a hand on her forearm, stopping her. Zelia shook her head.
"No, son. She should know. Even when she's going back to
Aceleau with him."

I wanted to ask Rogue if I *would* go back. If he'd make
me. But the answer was already there in my mind—where
else would I go? Even when Zelia and Dimar were here and
I needed them to help me with my magic, there was no way
I could stay around Tristan. I couldn't see his familiar face,
couldn't tell him that I didn't want him to hold me or kiss
me or anything beyond; that by making his choice, he'd

broken something between us—even more than it had been broken before.

Swallowing the words building in my throat, I lifted my teacup and glanced at Rogue for help. He merely lifted a shoulder in a half-shrug.

"Dimar and I have talked about it. We've come to terms with not having our powers. Being a healer—even without magic, has been rewarding, and once Cyrill is defeated, we'll return to Jezuin to continue our work there."

"I still can't believe you're just giving up," Tristan cut in, his frustration evident in his features. And I saw how much he cared about them even when the way he showed it made it seem like he didn't.

"It's all about the cost, Tris." Zelia gave him a warm look—that of a mother he'd never known. "We've talked about the cost."

"We've talked about it being impossible for years—and now it suddenly is," Tristan corrected, and I could have sworn Dimar's body coiled for an attack at his tone.

Tristan's hand traveled to his pocket as if he could see it too.

"What's the cost?" I wanted to know if only to stop them from arguing.

Tristan's gaze snapped to mine.

"Tell her," Rogue encouraged, again with that slight amusement in his voice that I wasn't sure was entirely for show. "Tell her what the price is, Tristan."

"The Crow Fairies." Tristan lowered his head as if he was admitting a crime.

My heart leaped into my throat, pounding at the mere mention of the Crow Fairies at this table. "What?"

"I need to make a trade with the Crow Fairies."

"By the Guardians, Tris." Dimar was on his feet, pacing the small space behind the table. "I know that you want it badly. But is it worth going to the Crows?"

Tristan jerked his chin at Rogue. "He says it's the only way."

My entire body went cold. *What trade?* I wanted to ask, but Dimar was already responding. "And until recently, we thought there was *no* way, Tris. There has to be another way."

"There isn't." Rogue's calm tone was like a bucket of water over the table.

"Despite Tristan's faith in you, Fairy King, you're a questionable character, and I won't place my trust in you." If Rogue's words had been a bucket of water, Dimar's were oil in fire because Rogue adjusted the seam of his sleeve with unnerving calm, his eyes slowly wandering from Tristan to Zelia to Dimar, then to me.

"I will say this once, Dimar, and only once: I don't care what you think of me or my character. But I do care about what Sanja thinks of me, so do us all a favor and let her Mage make his own miserable choices so she won't complain about them to me later."

I gave him a seething glare. But he merely flashed me a grin that made his eyes sparkle.

"If he wants to throw his life away by going to the Crow Fairies, by all means, let's do it. I'm sure dear Sanja here will not talk to me again if I let anyone stand in his way."

"I won't talk to you again either way," I informed him, earning another grin.

"I'm not counting on it, Sanja," he whispered on a dark breeze, and this time, the whole room was aware there was something going on.

Tristan caught my gaze, questions written all over his features.

Just for the sake of staying true to my word, I ignored Rogue's quip and said to Tristan, "What do the Crow Fairies have to do with it? And if we need to go to them, it can't be anything good," I amended.

Tristan shared a look with Rogue that was way too conspiratorial for my taste, despite the way they seemed to despise each other otherwise.

"The Crow Fairies are not only the most powerful sort of fairy but also the keepers of an ancient magic that allows them to shape-shift."

"Into actual crows?" I blurted, virtually slapping my hand over my mouth for having spoken to him at all.

He gave me a roguish grin that was anything but. "Yes, Sanja. Into actual crows." He wiped the corner of his mouth with a finger after sipping from his tea again. "I thought you were never going to speak to me again."

I hate you, I thought at him.

The dark breeze swept my words up, transporting them right to him. "No, you don't," he responded with an even wider grin. His words brushed my ear in a caress of midnight, and I shuddered involuntarily.

Tristan's hand balled into a fist on the table, but he didn't say a word as he waited for Rogue to continue, and I folded my arms over my chest, painfully aware of what this had to look like to him—the nightgown, Rogue's dressing robe, the looks we shared that excluded everyone else from the hidden conversation we were leading. And I found I didn't care. For now, I didn't have it in me to care.

After measuring me for a long, uncomfortable moment, Rogue eventually continued, "Tristan will need to retrieve from the Crow Fairies one magical artifact—be it a tooth or a bone, but he'll need to retrieve it."

I shuddered at the mere thought of it. "And what does that look like exactly? Do they simply hand over a piece of their dead? Or will he have to fight?"

Rogue's eyes flickered with cunning and mischief. "That, dear Sanja, is where you come in."

TWENTY-NINE

"No." I paced what had to be the living room of the Hollow Mountain refuge for no-longer-Mages at Dimar's side, who'd been repeating the same word I had. "No. *No-no-no.*"

"You can't expect Sanja to go to the Crow Fairies with him. He just recently protected her from being taken in the streets of Aceleau," Zelia reasoned with Rogue, who was drinking his second cup of tea. He hadn't touched one of the dried meats Zelia had laid out on a small plate nor the bread. Whether it was because they were below his standards or he didn't want to take when they already had so little in this hideout, I couldn't tell.

"That"—he stretched his legs, crossing them at the ankles—"was at Ret Relah. We're far from end of spring, and the Crows aren't hunting for brides."

367

"I don't care," Dimar hissed, turning on the spot and marching back toward where Tristan was leaning on the wall, observing. "This is my cousin we're talking about."

"Aren't you the one who stabbed her?" Rogue drawled, but his fingers curled around the edge of the chair where the others couldn't see.

"He did it to get me out of there alive," I jumped in to defend the only cousin I had.

"What's so different about going to the Crows to save your Mage?" Rogue raised an eyebrow, waiting for me to come up with a response.

"The difference is that I didn't have a choice," Dimar hissed. "If I hadn't stabbed her, Cyrill would have. And he'd have made certain she was dead."

I winced at the phantom pain in my side where the faint scar was still visible beneath silk and velvet.

"I don't have a choice either," Tristan pointed out. "With Cyrill on the throne, Cezux isn't a place where we can stay without being hunted. And Tavras—"

"We don't need to fear Tavras now that we're no longer Mages. We can find a place there and—"

"No." Tristan prowled away from the wall, planting himself in my path. "I'm not going anywhere in the human lands without her."

His gaze, once so gentle, now burned like dark flames—and not the good kind.

I didn't balk. Not when this was about me—my life.

"And she won't go anywhere else than to Cezux where her throne is waiting," he finished, and I wondered if the loss of his powers had done something more to him than make him feel helpless. If it had broken him in a way that made him a risk to me as well as to the others—and himself.

"In case you haven't noticed, a tyrant is sitting on my throne. Cezux believes I'm pregnant with his heir—"

"Conception of the untouched saint," Rogue interjected. I gave him a forbidding glance.

"And I will be expected back in a few months with the story of having lost the child, Tristan. I am not free or yours to send to the Crows to do whatever. I'm still in Cyrill's claws, even so far away from his court."

Rogue's dark breeze brushed along my back as if in response to the implications of my words—soothing somehow. I shook it off. He was as much a part of this as I was. As was Tristan. "If a Crow Fairy is willing to give you a magical artifact, I'm willing to help you get it."

Tristan's eyes lit up while Dimar and Zelia were chanting their objections again. Rogue remained the only one silent as I amended, "*If* you are willing to do something for me in return."

Rogue's chuckle hung in the air like a little thundercloud, ready to release a storm, and I wondered if this was going off his plans entirely—that I was now shaping this situation to my own advantage.

"What do you want, Sanja?" It was all Tristan asked.

I glanced around the room—at my aunt holding Dimar's hand clutched in hers, Dimar's horrified expression at my decision to help, and Rogue's infinitesimal nod as he planted his feet back on the ground and stood.

"If this works, you'll help me get rid of Cyrill."

"Of course, I will." He was quick to agree. But he didn't know the conditions. Didn't know that Rogue needed me to defeat the Crow Fairies, that helping Tristan get access to magic might be one way to lead me onto the path of complying. And that only once Rogue's bargain with the Crow Fairies was broken could Cezux be free.

"You will do whatever it takes to get rid of Cyrill," I specified, not failing to hear the irony of the demand. *Anything*, he'd offered for his own magic. Including me. What he didn't know was that if he agreed to my own bargain, he'd seal the fate for his path of redemption. Not until I told him. And I wouldn't do that to either of us; I wouldn't let him step into a trap like the fairies he hated so much. So I inhaled a steadying breath and looked him in the eye. "If this works, you'll have magic again, Tris, but you'll have lost me." Because, while Rogue had asked a hypothetical question— what he'd be willing to give up—I asked him the literal one.

"You won't die at the Crow Fairies," Tristan reassured.

But—"That's not what I mean."

Understanding settled in his eyes, the blue turning dull and murky as he averted his gaze.

For a moment, he said nothing, the room entirely silent save for the thunderous beat of my heart.

"I need to think about it."

At his words, what had been left for us in my chest imploded. *Think.*

I inclined my head, placing my hand on his chest as I stepped around him. Just to memorize the feel of him, to remind him what he'd give up. And I could have sworn he shivered under my touch.

But the moment was gone, and I faced Dimar and Zelia. "Teach me how to use the Mage Stone. Teach me everything I need to know so I don't burn myself out or destroy the Mage Stone by draining it entirely."

Zelia and Dimar shared a look of understanding. When they turned back, they faced Rogue instead of me. "Bring her here for an hour every day, and we'll teach her. How she uses the magic will be up to her." Zelia turned to me. "Even if it will break my heart if you destroy yourself to save him."

I'd done it before. And I'd destroyed part of him as well, had taken what he held dearest. And now, I had a chance to rid myself of the guilt and provide a fresh start for both of us—just not together.

One look at Rogue had sufficed to let him know I needed to leave. He'd abandoned his observer's spot at the edge of our conversation for the benefit of taking my hand and dissolving us into thin air. Dissolving, at least, made the aching pit that was now my chest stop for a moment. Long enough to make it to my room in the tower where Naar was about to set down the tray in her hands and almost stumble into the table at our sudden appearance.

"By the flicker of magic, Recienne. Have you no respect for an old female?" she scolded him before a smile spread on her lips at the sight of my attire. "Long night?"

I frowned at her, then heavily at him, ripping my hand from his grasp. "The longest. And not necessarily in a good way, Naar."

She caught herself mid-flinching at the mention of her name, and I couldn't help asking just because that would push dealing with everything else that had happened a bit farther away. "What happened to you?"

"What do you mean?" She clopped to the window, opening it with one hand while she pushed a fresh vase of white roses to the center of the table.

"Your name. Has anyone used it against you?"

Naar gave me a long, sad glance that spoke volumes. "Almost any one-syllable fairy has bad experiences regarding the mention of their name. For me, it was before I ever came to this court that I was used as high fae entertainment. You don't want to know what things they made me do by controlling me through my name. You don't want to know anything from those years—nor do I want to talk about it. All you need to know is that there is a reason those wards were a smart move." She glanced at Rogue, who was perched on the foot of the bed, face unreadable as he stared out the window. "Recienne?"

He lifted his head, finding my gaze first before he turned to Naar. "I beg your pardon?"

Naar threw her hands in the air. "The wards, Recienne. You created wards to protect Sanja from the same fate."

Those wards... I had failed to bring them up with every-thing that had happened since I'd learned about them.

"They merely prevent anyone from controlling you through your name," he explained, not really paying attention to Naar or me as his eyes wandered back to the window.

"Except for you, of course." I reminded him that he *had* controlled me not even an hour ago. How that made me feel, I wasn't ready to think about.

"Except for me," he agreed. "But that can be remedied. Once you learn how to shield yourself from name-control with your Mage Stone, you'll be able to shut me out." He glanced at me long enough to notice how tired he looked. "That's what you want, isn't it? To get rid of me."

I'd never seen him so ... raw. So unfiltered and cold. Where usually cunning and teasing and wickedness lingered, a void seemed to have opened up. And if I dared look closer, I might find there was no end to it.

"Shush, little king," Naar said, heading over to fasten the top button of his tunic and smoothing out the fabric along his shoulders. "You've had a long night after a few exhaust-ing days." She gave me a meaningful look before she took Rogue's hand, tugging him to his feet; he let her. "Go to bed for a few hours. Rest. Astorian will be here shortly, and I'll watch over Sanja until you return."

"And Lady Wellows?" I remembered, a shudder of a dif-ferent sort running through me. "Will she be coming after me during the daytime?"

Rogue pulled himself up to his full height, not bothering to look at me as he said, "You can keep the dressing robe." And he was gone.

No answer, no goodbye. Not even one of those chuckles he so often left me with. And I remained behind with Naar, who held the most worried face I'd seen in months.

She eyed me with warm purple eyes and berry-flushed cheeks. "Sit. Eat. I'll do the talking."

I didn't even think to object, too tired to do anything other than plop into a chair and shovel scrambled eggs into my mouth.

"So he finally took you to see the Mage?" She measured my expression—which couldn't have been any better than the eggs on my plate. "I've been telling him it was time. But he kept finding reasons to hold it off." With a sigh, she sank into the chair across from me, her uniform so out of place between the books stacked at the sides of the table.

"He's been planning to take me to Tristan?" I asked around a mouthful, not daring to think what might have made him wait this long.

"He's been planning to do a lot of things, Sanja. But he's fairy royalty, and royalty doesn't always get to do what they wish."

The concept was all too familiar.

"He introduced you to the others, though." Her gaze spoke clearly that I wasn't to mention who she meant—I understood her, anyway.

Clio and Astorian. Both of them were a secret even when Astorian led a double life just like Rogue.

Naar watched me eat until my plate was empty then conjured another one full of pastries, and a bowl of fruit. "When I found the room empty, I thought Lady Wellows got to you." Pursing her lips, she shoved a hand into the pocket of her crispy white apron. "Be careful around her, Sanja." She didn't give any other warnings, careful of what she was speaking, for sure, with the Crow Fairies' ally in the palace.

"I'd ask what happened at the mountains, but Recienne's mood tells me enough not to pry."

The curved bread in my fingers suddenly became very interesting. "I have a lot to think about."

Naar didn't respond until I'd finished the bread. Then she flicked her fingers, and the armoire door sprang open. "Let's get you into something presentable, shall we?" With a sigh, she stood and reached into it, extracting a light dress from its depths. "Do you think he'll approve of this?" She held the powdery pink fabric up. "I'm sure anything is better than what you're wearing now. It might make people wonder if we don't clothe our guests properly."

I bit back the comment that the dressing robe of a king wasn't necessarily sub-standard—especially when said king had handed it to me himself. Inhaling deeply, I summoned the scent of rain and nights under open skies, of forests and something more, and where the black velvet had been meant to taunt me and to hurt Tristan, for sure, the feel of it suddenly gave me comfort.

That thought, however, drove me to my feet, and I grabbed the dress from Naar's hands before I hurtled for the bathing room.

"Need any help?" Naar called after me, concern tuning her voice slightly higher than usual.

"I think I can manage."

With shaky fingers, I peeled myself out of velvet and silk, letting the fabrics slide to the floor, and fished a washcloth from the shelf above the basin. I poured cold water over it, wiping my face, my neck, my shoulders and arms, my entire body, until I was shivering despite the balmy summer air. I wrapped a towel around myself and sat on the stool Naar usually used when helping me bathe. There, I remained until I was no longer shivering, and my mind gave up on the numbness and distraction. It hit me then—the all-consuming feeling of what I'd done. That I'd given Tristan a choice, and he hadn't known if he'd choose me over his magic. That hesitation—the look in his eyes as he'd hesitated—

I wrapped my arms around myself in an attempt to hold my chest together.

There was a rational explanation for this. He'd said it himself... that he'd intended to use his magic to get me back. And I—I didn't know if I wanted to cry or scream. Or if I wanted to do neither.

Pushing myself to stop thinking, to stop feeling, I changed into the dress.

The chiffon hugged me in soft layers like an embrace of flower petals, and I wondered if it was spelled to make me feel this way or if any shred of kindness would make me feel like this right now.

Naar didn't offer her help again. Instead, her movements continued around the room as she probably picked out my wardrobe for the next dinner with Moyen Wellows. Stopping in front of the mirror, I wiped away the tears threatening to fall from my lashes and steeled myself to bury the pain knocking on my heart so I'd be able to face her.

I'd taken about two steps into the room when the door opened, and Astorian swept in like an autumn storm, auburn eyes hard as he scanned the room for dangers. One look at Naar's surprised face and he composed himself, and a glance at me—

"I came as fast as I could," he said, sheathing the knife in his hand on his thigh.

Naar looked me over, the frown on her features disappearing at the sight of the pink against my tan skin.

"I'll head back to my own chores then," she announced and clopped from the room, but not without telling Astorian to be careful—whatever she meant with that.

"Hello, Sanja." Astorian sketched a bow, his features relaxing as he assessed me with a professional gaze. "How would you feel about going on a trip with me?"

I was about to demand what he meant and where he was intending to take me when he disappeared and reappeared at my bed, picking up the Mage Stone and holding it out for me. "Recienne told me not to let you forget to bring this."

"Where are we going?"

Astorian gave me an apologetic look. "I can't tell you where, but you've been there before."

THIRTY

The room blurred out of existence around us as Astorian took my hand, replaced with familiar greenery and rocky walls—and at the center, the house woven into the tree. Astorian let go of me, already stalking toward the house while I was still gathering my bearings.

"Are you coming?" he called over his shoulder as he leaped up the two stairs to the porch and knocked on the door.

"Show off," I muttered, earning a laugh from the auburn-haired male whose character I couldn't yet pinpoint. Not a bad male, for sure, but was he a good one? At least, a decent one when it came to not laughing at human women about their broken hearts. He was suffering from one of his own, so he understood. If that was the only thing we had in common, it would be enough to make me feel more comfortable.

Even with the eerie sense of having my mind dug through in his presence.

I didn't get to continue my thought when the door swung open and Clio stormed out, site-hopping a few feet toward me before she closed the gap and pulled me into a tight hug. "I'm going to kill my brother," she said into my hair, not letting go despite the way my arms awkwardly lay half around her—loose enough not to pull her in closer but tight enough to at least give the impression of hugging her back. The proximity—the feel of her leathers and weapons as she squeezed me once ... I was worried one of the knives would accidentally pierce through the chiffon of my dress and prick my skin.

"What did he do this time to deserve to die?" Astorian drawled from the porch.

Letting go of me, Clio huffed a laugh. "Have you taken a real look at Sanja? Because if you had, you'd have noticed that she looks like a Ledrynx carried her halfway through Askarea."

I shuddered at the mention of the winged predator cats I'd barely escaped, a phantom pain pulsing in my shoulder. The wound hadn't left a scar, thanks to Rogue's cast pool of magic he could draw from. A magic I'd only seen flickers of—but those were enough to make my skin crawl. The sheer power... he could wink Aceleau out of existence if he so pleased, I was certain of it. If he trembled before the Crow Fairies' power...

"Of course, I've taken a look." Astorian watched Clio drag me toward the house by my arm. "She looks delightful."

"Because she's wearing actual clothes," Clio retorted, and I could have sworn her humor was only partly because of Astorian's expression when he scanned the female's tight leathers. "Yes, Tori, I'm also wearing clothes, just not *actual* ones."

"What would you call those then?" I asked, my eyes following her supple curves from the side.

She raised a brow at me, the gesture so similar to Rogue's that my stomach did an upset leap. I couldn't think about what had happened at the Hollow Mountains. Not yet.

"A nuisance, Tori." She flashed her teeth in a predatory grin. "Necessary, but definitely a nuisance."

"They look good on you," Astorian commented, stepping out of our path as Clio led me up the stairs into the house. His footsteps followed us into the living room where comfortable armchairs of all colors were assembled around a short coffee table.

"Everything looks good on me." Clio's smile was directed at Astorian this time, and I could have sworn his eyes ignited with a forbidden sort of fire that would burn him with unimaginable pain if he ever gave in to it.

I didn't doubt it, though, that whatever she'd wear would look gorgeous on her, just because of those sparkling eyes of jade framed in long lashes, and the wild copper hair.

Clio waited for me to take a seat in a cerulean chair then settled into a russet one across from me. Astorian chose the seat next to her, expression carefully neutral as he studied the jar of water he conjured with a flick of his fingers.

"Tell us everything," Clio instructed while she poured me a glass and summoned a wedge of what looked a lot like apricot but in a much darker shade of orange. "Or do you need fairy wine first? You look like you might need a glass or seven."

Astorian shook his head. "If you give her fairy wine, your brother will be the one who'll be upset."

She handed me the glass. "It's safe to drink. No fairy wine—just water." She held up the fruit. "This is Askarean apricot. A specialty and completely harmless. Just like Tori."

Astorian cocked his head at her, but the nod of reassurance he gave me instilled more confidence than expected.

I drained half the glass, my thoughts tumbling into a spiral I'd been trying to prevent since the moment Rogue had brought me back to the palace—maybe sooner.

"Lady Wellows didn't visit you during the night, I assume?" Clio prompted.

Beside her, Astorian rolled his eyes. "Do you honestly believe she'd be sitting here if Moyen had gotten her pretty fingers on her?"

"You think her fingers are pretty?" Clio jabbed, and I could have sworn, Astorian's fingers twitched in response as if he was about to grab her hand from the rolled armrest of her chair and examine it for comparison.

"Considerably so." He drew his gaze away from Clio, studying me instead with that same concern I'd seen on him before. "How are you feeling, Sanja?"

Whether he was reading my mind, the circling images of Tristan's hesitation when I'd postulated that it would be his magic or me...

I'd made a mistake. Entire body shivering, I tried to not focus on the truth—that it hadn't been Tristan hesitating to tell me what meant more to him, it had been me putting him before that choice. Where I'd been wondering if he had his priorities right, it was I who truly felt like I could no longer be with him. Because of what I'd done to him. Because of what I'd tried to return to him. And because, between losing his magic, losing my freedom, and losing each other, we'd both lost enough. Zelia and Dimar would train me with the Mage Stone and I'd help Tristan regain his magic and become complete. And then, I'd think about the rest.

"All right," I responded as I avoided looking him in the eye.

"Lie," Clio said, earning a glare from Astorian. She merely shrugged. "What? She doesn't look like she feels *all right.*"

Astorian gave me an inquisitive look. "So ... the Hollow Mountains... Did anything happen there?"

"You told him about the Hollow Mountains." After the afternoon in the library... Rogue had mentioned Astorian had informed him about my interest in the Hollow Mountains.

Astorian shrugged, crossing his legs. "I wasn't aware it was a secret."

"Besides," Clio took over, "he knew. He's known for a while that the Mages are there."

I didn't know what to say other than, "And he didn't think to tell me?"

Clio's face sobered. "Why would he? You didn't trust him enough to share anything important with you."

"Except for introducing me to you," I pointed out. "His most important secret—one he'd let his father wreck the kingdom for."

The warning in Astorian's eyes was enough to silence me. But not enough to stop the sense of rebellion that tuned out all thoughts of Tristan.

"He told you why I'm here, right? He told you what the alternative would look like for me. And I'm not proud to be hiding in the forests. But, at least, I can do some good here."

"Nobody is doubting that you want to help, Clio. *He* knows that you'd rather confront the Crows with a sword and your magic and die trying than remain here forever."

The room was suddenly filled with a tension nothing like the thick air surrounding Rogue when his power gathered around him like a thundercloud. History—so much history lingered between them that I refrained from asking further questions.

"You can bet I would. If it wasn't for Father's bargain now lingering on Rogue's shoulders, I'd do it." Determination flashed in Clio's eyes as she held Astorian's gaze.

Astorian swallowed—probably a smart response—and sighed through his nose. "We all wouldn't be here if it wasn't for your father, Clio." And there was so much meaning to those words that I could feel the air go taut between them.

But I didn't dare ask when they seemed to have forgotten I was even there.

"And your brother isn't making things easier by involving an untrained Mage in this mess. This can go sideways any day if the magic doesn't do what he hopes it will."

"What?" I asked after all. "What is he hoping it will achieve?" Maybe they were more generous with their knowledge than Rogue. "Is this about the other Mage?" I didn't speak Tristan's name for both fear of giving something away they didn't know and what speaking the name would do to me.

Both fairies turned toward me, remembering I was still there.

"That's why he brought me to Askarea after all, right? To make me help him with the Crow Fairies."

"That's part of it," Astorian said, too quickly.

Clio shook her head at him.

"Do you know what he wants? He told me about the Ultimate Sacrifice. Is that what he needs from me to seal the borders again? Do I need to die?" I'd accused Rogue of exactly that before, and he hadn't denied it. He hadn't confirmed it either, so was it surprising that bringing up the topic to Astorian and Clio made my palms sweaty?

"He wouldn't sacrifice you," Astorian said. And that was the last thing he said before Clio rammed her elbow into his side with such force the male yelped and lurched for a glass of water instead of continuing to speak.

"He's not a monster, my brother, in case you haven't figured it out." Clio ran her hand through her hair, the strands flowing through her fingers like molten copper. I couldn't help but notice Astorian staring. "He might be a prick at times, but he wouldn't deliberately hurt anyone—human or fairy. Not if he can prevent it."

"He fought in the Crow War. And he's caused his fill of bloodshed and slaughter," Astorian took over, and the mere thought of Rogue drenched in blood—his opponents' or his own—made something stir uncomfortably beneath my skin.

"But he was a prince back then—a royal heir. Wasn't he supposed to stay safe?"

Clio looked at me as if she'd burst out in laughter any moment. "Have you ever seen Rogue sit back and let anyone else handle his problems?"

No. I hadn't. I hadn't truly seen him handle any of his problems since he hadn't trusted me enough to share how he'd handle them.

"Why do you think it's eating him up that he needs to depend on you for the Crow Fairies this time?" She didn't leave space for me to think about that. "Last time, he bled to protect Aceleau, to protect the outer regions of Askarea and the human borders. He fought, and he bled, day after day after day of the war, even when he only held a shred of the power he has at his disposal now. He was at risk as much as any of the soldiers in Father's legions. And had it not been for Rogue's efforts, the Crows might have never agreed to the treaty."

It took a moment to digest the meaning of her words.

"It's not my place to tell his story, so I won't go into details, but if you ever doubt Rogue, think of my words. This"—she gestured around the room—"was his idea. *He* built it with his magic and his bare hands—a place for us to become someone else. Perhaps our true selves when at court we were puppets, threats, or political assets." She swallowed, cheeks flushed, and grasped her armrests. "He wanted this place for us so we could help the ones in need in Askarea. If we couldn't change Aceleau for fear of being discovered, we could change the lives of the fairies dwelling in smaller settlements, could give back what the crown takes from them each year." Beside her, Astorian's lips pressed into a bitter line. "You've only seen the fairy nobles craving humans like they crave gold or diamonds or power—but you haven't seen our people's suffering. Their struggles."

She was right. I hadn't. But I had a people of my own who were suffering at the cruel hand of an unrightful king.

Clio slipped back into her chair, the fire cooling from her eyes.

"In Jezuin, the poorest people live in the outermost ring, far away from the protection of the palace and the guards. Cyrill takes what little they make as taxes, and if they can't pay, they get punished severely." I cringed at the memory of the injuries we'd treated at the sick house—and the 'thief' Cyrill's men had murdered. "I know what it's like to have a people you can do so little for, to be powerless in your own kingdom." Tears pricked behind my eyes, but I shoved them back the way I'd learned to do growing up in court. I was no stranger to the desperation of the hungry or the ill-treated. And how often had they not taken a copper from me in exchange for a loaf of bread or a bouquet of wildflowers...

"They never wanted to take my money... No handouts, no kindness from their princess," I told them after I explained in short what life had been like in Jezuin before *and* after my supposed death, their eyes growing wider with every time I mentioned Cyrill's tyranny, what he'd done to my friend Leahnie, to Erju—

Only when I'd arrived at the day Cyrill's men had captured me in the street did Astorian's face grow wary.

"He might be that heroic male here in Askarea, who wants to help his people, but he was something entirely different when he felled me like a tree with his powers to keep me from escaping Cyrill's guards."

Clio bared her teeth at what I implied. "Is that what he actually did, or is it what you choose to believe, Sanja?"

I held her gaze, ready to enter a fight—of words at least. But she blew out a breath, sweeping her hair from one shoulder to the other, and said, "When Recienne became Rogue, he chose to wear the mask so his people would take his gifts without feeling like they were in the royal family's debt—or they'd never accept them. He's not so different from you, Sanja. He also dreams of a better world for everyone in Askarea. Even the Crow Fairies. That's why he made the effort to bargain back then. And that's why he'd rather let them believe I'm dead than risk upsetting them by denying them what our father promised."

"I'm—" I uselessly searched for words at the reminder of what she was going through, what was at risk for her. Freedom. In a different way than my own freedom but still too similar not to feel her sorrow echo in my chest as she met my gaze. "I'm sorry, Clio. It must be horrible to cease to exist." Because it was. I'd lived through it. I'd been dead to Cezux. Dead to all of Eherea until I'd found a new family in Zelia, Tristan, and Dimar. A family—

My heart throbbed once, too exhausted from aching since Rogue had taken me to the glimmering caves in the Hollow Mountains.

"I didn't *cease* to exist, Sanja. I still have Rogue and Tori and—" She stopped herself, but this time, I could read her easily.

Me. Now, she had *me.*

I didn't know how that made me feel when I didn't truly know her. When all that had happened left me raw.

Astorian cleared his throat, and Clio picked up the jar to fill her glass with water and nibbled on an Askarean apricot.

"He stole from me that day in the forest," I whispered, and I had to brace my hands on my thighs to keep the exhaustion at bay. "He stole everything I had and left me to die in the forest."

This time, it was Astorian who responded. "But he saved you the next."

He wasn't wrong. Even when I'd traded my name in return. And Clio had been there, too.

When I dared turn to her once more, that swaggering female of our first encounter was gone, a young face with ancient eyes staring back at me with a truth I couldn't quite read.

"Talk to him about Jezuin, Sanja. Perhaps with everything you've learned, you'll be able to trust him when he tells you what actually happened."

THIRTY-ONE

A storian took me back at sunset, hues of orange rippling out of and into existence as he site-hopped us to the palace. The afternoon had given me a lot to think about—more things to sort through and figure out what I could allow myself to believe without shattering. Because with all I had lost, the next time I'd break, nothing would put me back together.

The aroma of raspberry pie lingered in the air when the male let my hand slide out of his with a tired look on his face. "Ask him," he said, gesturing behind me with his chin, and I only realized who he was talking about when the hair stood at the back of my neck as Rogue's presence announced itself with a touch of darkness.

"Ask me what?" Rogue stalked around me, cocking his head at Astorian, who gave me an encouraging grin before he vanished into thin air.

Rogue paced a few steps away, spun on his heels, hands in the pockets of his pants as he looked me up and down, approval glimmering in his eyes despite the mild unsettlement I didn't dare ask the origin of. Lady Wellows was still in the palace, to the best of my knowledge, and anything concerning her couldn't be good.

"Did you have an enjoyable day?" He gestured for me to sit at the table, the stacks of books disappearing at a flick of his fingers.

"Where did they go?"

"To a safe place." He waited for me to cross the room, and I did my best not to acknowledge the way his gaze followed me all the way until I'd settled in my usual chair. "Until the palace is ... safe again."

"So it's not safe now?"

Again, he cocked his head as if asking whether that wasn't obvious.

Of course. Hoping that Lady Wellows had left would be too much.

"Besides," he went on, "you won't need them if you have the help of an actual Mage."

I didn't wonder if the conversation was safe this time; the dark wind had swept up my earlier words and was delivering his to me.

The black of Rogue's pants and shirt gobbled up the fading light as he strolled over to join me at the table. He flicked his fingers again, and a bottle of wine and two glasses appeared between us.

I was about to object that I wouldn't drink fairy wine, but he explained, "Wine from Cezux. I acquired it from a merchant in the borderlands a while ago, on my way to Jezuin."

An invitation to ask those questions on my mind lingered in the air between us. But there were so many—too many. And most of them—"How long have you known ... about Tristan?"

Rogue understood without further explanation. Leaning back in his chair, he scanned my face, read what I couldn't speak—my cracked heart, the emptiness that had returned. The doubts and concerns that had been swirling through me for hours like birds of prey—

"He told me that day in Jezuin ... where he was going. If I'd help him, he said, he'd tell me anything I wanted to know."

A wave of disappointment flooded that void in my chest, and I had to suppress a gasp at the unexpected force of it—even after what I'd learned during those hours with Tristan, Zelia, and Dimar.

"I didn't ask anything from him, in case you're wondering."

"I'm not—"

"Of course, you are," he interrupted, a pensive expression on his beautiful face. "He told me where to find him when I figured out how to get his magic back."

Anything, Tristan would give for his magic. *Anything and everything.* Where allowing that thought had felt like betrayal mere days ago, it had settled in like a new truth. I heaved a breath, fingers following the edge of the table, feeling for the small dents in the wood that spoke of centuries of use. For a moment, I wondered who'd lived here before me, but Rogue continued, "I've been visiting them regularly, your Mages." And this time, he didn't emphasize 'your' the way he had when he'd spoken only about Tristan before. "While Tristan has been sitting on pins and needles for news about how to actually retrieve that magical artifact from the Crows, I've been using my political channels into the Crow Court to learn what I can about the location of their artifacts."

"And you're not going to tell me where that is, obviously."

"Wrong, Sanja. I'll tell you exactly where even when it won't help you much. At least, not until you can control your magic enough to not accidentally set yourself on fire." The grin he flashed me was everything but. "They aren't stored in a vault or in a secret dungeon, nor are they well protected by anything other than the Crows' power woven through the Seeing Forest. All one needs to do is dare to walk into their territory and pluck them."

Something about the way he said it made a shiver run down my spine. "Why hasn't anyone thought of doing that before? I'm sure there are plenty of humans and fairies desiring magic enough to make the trip."

"You think wrong, Sanja." He ran a hand through his hair, leaving his waves disheveled, and I couldn't help but notice how my fingers itched to smooth them back. "They aren't common knowledge. The only reason I'm familiar with them is the treaty—and because I've used them to recharge the Mage blood spilled in the Ultimate Sacrifice a long time ago. Their magic, the Mage blood, the

Crow magic, and my own powers together form a mesh of balance. I can't go in there and take an artifact away, or I will have broken the treaty, and whatever has been agreed upon will be void. They'll swarm Askarea and, if we don't manage to seal them in entirely, the human lands as well. Cezux won't be safe; Tavras won't be safe; not even the Southern Continent will be safe. And, least of all, Askarea. My throne will be eradicated so fast that I won't even have time to see my end coming."

"They're really that strong, then?" That they scared the most powerful fairy in Askarea.

"If they are free to leave their forest, they'll come in numbers. And while I can easily take on one or two of them, possibly even three, I can't battle an army and walk away. It would be my end—and the end of any bargain I made."

Including the one he'd made with Cyrill. Cyrill would be free to do with Cezux as he pleased. No more obligations to an immortal ally—no-longer ally. But the Crows would run Cezux over like a pair of boots stomping on ants.

All impulses commanded me to run, to fight, to do something—but there was no enemy I could fight, no immediate threat other than that of the fairy king before me. And he... He'd become something significantly more complicated than that.

Rogue eyed me as if he was going to ask a question, but he smoothed his features with a wipe of his hand and said, "I've told Tristan that I wouldn't be able to get an artifact for him and that he wouldn't be able to retrieve it on his own. You need magic to be able to detach them from the mesh of power, and the only person holding magic and willing to risk going to the Seeing Forest for him is—"

"Me," I finished for him. "The only one who'd risk everything for him is me." I'd done it before and had almost lost all our lives to Rogue's father.

"He didn't reconsider when I told him the potential price for his magic might be your life."

The flood had long retreated from my chest, making it hurt all the more when Rogue's words hit.

"How large is the possibility of me dying?" Holding my breath both kept my panic at bay and muted the pain in my chest.

"If you take enough time to train with Dimar and Zelia, not exceedingly high." He measured me across the table, the fingers of one hand absently playing with the collar of his shirt. "You are stronger than you think, human or no. That stubbornness of yours has saved you more than once."

I wasn't sure if that was meant to be an insult or a compliment, so I pursed my lips and stared him down until he gave me a useful response.

"I never knew humans could be as ... durable as you before I saw you fight the effects of the flesh violet in the maze at your first challenge, Sanja."

"That's what it's called?" Not that it made any difference now what the flesh-eating plant that had tried to lure me with the scent of sugared violets was called.

"That's what it's called," he confirmed. "You walked away from that challenge—with a lignified hand, but you walked away." He leaned over the table, picking up my perfectly human hand and turning it over in his. I didn't dare move. "I stopped the poison from spreading so you'd stand a chance at finishing those challenges and free your Mages. So Zelia would remain Master Mage and keep an eye on the developments in the Seeing Forest the way she's been doing since she took over the position from her parents." His thumb brushed a line through the center of my palm where I'd once felt nothing when it had turned into wood. But now—now I felt everything. And it was enough to make me pull back my hand and clasp it with my other under the table.

Rogue let my fingers slide out of his, holding my gaze as he said, "She used to hold dinners once a month, for influential fairies, so she could get her hands on valuable information about the developments."

I remembered—that day Tristan had come to my room to ... distract me when I'd intended to spy on the dinner conversation.

...hasn't been safe in years.

At least, not for a human.

We've been waiting long enough. It's time to do something.

We've already risked too much.

The fragments of an argument floated back into my mind, and I wondered if Zelia had known back then that the Crow Fairies were active again. That they were gradually weakening the border of the Seeing Forest, sneaking out and extending their reach through bargains with the fairy king.

It wouldn't surprise me.

"I'd hoped you'd walk away with all three of them and become a full Mage so I'd be able to take my pick from the four of you or use you all to defeat the Crows, but my father wouldn't have been my father had he let you go after you won all his challenges." His hands curled into fists where they still lay on the table between us. "You walked away eventually, and my father was defeated. And now I'm left with Father's legacy of terror and a Mage so eager for power that he seems to have forgotten he once loved you."

Like a rain of ice, his words hammered down on me, each of them stinging with their truth. *Had once loved me.*

"Perhaps, love isn't made for eternity," I told him, trying to erase the image of Astorian eying Clio from the side like he'd never seen anything more beautiful from my mind. "Or perhaps, seeing his Mage Stone being destroyed was more than he could bear." An excuse to soothe myself more than to convince Rogue of anything.

The gold of his eyes turned solid for a moment, but he exhaled a slow breath. "I shouldn't hate him for being willing to risk you, Sanja. Not when what I'm asking of you is equally dangerous. Perhaps even more so."

I quirked a brow. "You must be having a bad day to admit two things in one sentence." I attempted a grin.

He didn't answer it with one of his wicked ones but pulled his lower lip in between his teeth. When he released it, his gaze snapped to mine, a little bit angry after all—but not with Tristan.

"Do you think I'm enjoying this? Leading you toward danger to protect the lands of Eherea? Do you not think I wish it was different—that there was someone else I could go to for help? But with Tristan's hunger for his magic, I get to test your strength and your skill so I won't need to risk your failure when it comes to sealing the borders of the forest for good."

"How am I going to seal the borders?" I didn't even point out that I had never agreed to help him—even when we both knew I'd take myself apart gladly if it meant I could make sure the human lands would be safe from fairies for good.

"Crow magic, Sanja." His wistful eyes glimmered like the stones the palace was made of. "The power allowing you to wield magic as a human is connected to Crow magic."

"What?" I wasn't sure if I'd spoken or thought the word, but Rogue's lips curled the slightest bit at the sides.

"Always so curious, Sanja." And just when I was about to scold him for his comment, he added, "That's the reason I like you so much."

I had nothing to say to that, which only made his grin spread wider. "*One* of the reasons," he corrected, pulling his hands back toward him and lacing his fingers together at the edge of the table. "Where was I? Right ... Crow Magic." His grin faded as he went back into his tale. "Crow magic might be the origin of human magic—Zelia told me as much when we discussed her ancestors and how they learned to use and store magic. Crow artifacts are likely the inspiration for modern Mage Stones."

The fact that he was sharing all of this—"So you trust me enough to tell me everything now?" I asked for lack of any response to his revelation. For if that was the truth... Everything I'd learned about Mages might be wrong. If we could get our magic back once lost, more humans might be able to protect themselves against fairies, whether they were able to cross the borders to the human lands or not.

"I never said I didn't trust you, Sanja. Only that *you* didn't trust me enough."

I was still pondering his words when he rolled his shoulders as if shrugging off a weight. "What reason do I have to tell you an untruth?"

None. He had no reason. Not to share everything, yes, because I might be a liability. But apart from antagonizing me, there was no reason to lie to me. And no matter how unsettling his cryptic behavior might be, Rogue hadn't misled me. Not during the trials, not since he'd brought me back to Askarea. Only once had he actually worked against me, and that time—

"In Jezuin..." I cleared my suddenly dry throat.

"What about Jezuin?" The wariness entering his expression almost made me stop, but—

"Astorian said I should ask you about what happened in Jezuin that day when you tripped me with your magic." My heart pounded in my ears as I confronted him about his involvement in my capture.

Beneath that wariness, his eyes turned predatory. "So you're actually asking me? Not just accusing?"

My palms turned sweaty under his focus, and I wiped them on my thighs, grabbing the chiffon of my dress to keep from fidgeting. "I guess I am."

"Guessing is not good enough, Sanja." He leaned back, arms folding across his chest, and I couldn't help noticing the way the muscles flexed beneath his shirt where the fabric stretched tight.

"I am ... asking." I gathered my thoughts.

The air in the room turned thick, and I could have sworn Rogue shuddered before he smoothed over his face. "That day, I was with Cyrill's men. He'd asked for help with tracking down a certain healer who'd killed one of his sentries." My stomach tightened. "So I set out to hunt that healer down. I'd arrived in Jezuin a few days before, feeling out Cyrill's court for your official story. And let me tell you how very little amused I was when I learned the Princess of Cezux had died months ago"—his gaze turned solid, face a mask of ice—"at the hand of his guards." He shifted in his chair, biceps flexing as his hands balled into fists. He tucked them under his arms. "He told me that he'd done everything according to plan—the plan with *my father*. That he'd killed the King of Cezux, his inner circle, and ... you."

I didn't dare breathe at the contained rage working through his body.

"He hadn't known you were alive, Sanja. You were safe until those guards came to your sick house and you tried to save the thief."

"He wasn't a thief," I retorted, if only to keep myself from panicking at the power prowling beneath his skin, straining to break free. This—*this* was the King of Askarea, the most powerful fairy in all of the fairylands. Tendrils of power leaked from him like smoke and mist, constricting the air in the room even tighter.

"You're right, he wasn't. He was merely a guy unlucky enough to be caught trying to survive." I wasn't sure he was serious. But he added, "Stealing has consequences, Sanja. In the human lands as well as it does in Askarea. You, if anyone, should be able to tell a tale about it."

My throat bobbed at the indication that he knew—he knew what I'd done that very first day in his city. When I'd stolen the loaf of bread out of starvation.

"But what choice did he have when Cyrill is systemically starving his people, keeping them small, so they don't have the strength to fight him?" That wistful look returned to his features, and if anything, it made him even more beautiful ... and terrifying. "I went with the guards to find you and bring you to him because"—his teeth flashed in the settling twilight—"my father's bargain commands me to work with your *husband*." He bit out the word, letting me chew on it as he held my gaze, unblinking. My stomach folded into a tight knot. "There's no way around it for me. I *have* to help him in his endeavors to secure the reign over Cezux. And you are part of that securing."

"That's why you tripped me? To *secure* me for Cyrill? To make it easier for Cyrill's henchmen to catch me?"

"I did it to keep that arrow from hitting your back, San-ja. You hit your pretty face on the ground and earned some bruises because of me. Without me, you might no longer draw breath, and I don't know if I could live with myself." His eyes turned wild, crazed at the image of that arrowhead buried in my flesh, and for a moment—just a flicker of a moment—I could tell there was more to him. More than what I'd learned from Clio and Astorian about the fairy who wanted to make life better for his people, the bandit stealing from the rich to give to the struggling fairies at the bottom of society. More than the fairy who pretended to hate humans, to delight in torturing them. There was actual cruelty buried deep inside of him—and it wasn't directed at me but at the men who'd aimed an arrow at my back and ... and nearly killed me.

Because of the bargain by his father. Because he had to help Cyrill. Because ... because he needed me to secure the Seeing Forest and end that threat of the Crow Fairies.

"I didn't learn about your Mage Stone until the banquet when you informed Tristan about it."

So he'd heard our conversation? Even through doors and music? "Is that why you decided to bring me to Aceleau that day?"

"I won't lie to you, Sanja. It gave me one extra reason to take you. But"—he unfolded his arms to brace his hands on the table as he leaned in enough to make me shift back in my chair—"I would have brought you, anyway."

He heaved a deep breath and got to his feet, the tension falling away from him as he pulled up the bored mask of the fairy king I'd experienced in Lady Wellows's presence. "Make of it what you will, Sanja. I am not your enemy. I don't aim for your demise. And I most definitely prefer you alive and breathing. It is better for the complexion."

He winked at me and sauntered to the door.

"Where are you going?" It was the only thing I got out even when my mind was spinning with a multitude of thoughts. "We aren't finished."

Rogue stopped at the door. "We're far from finished, Sanja. But you'll have to bear without me for a while. The Crow's ambassador needs my attention."

How he knew, I couldn't tell. Probably something with his superior fairy senses. But he opened the door just as a light knock sounded, and I was ready to scream my frustration.

Rogue sent me a warning look, and I bit all and any emotions back as I watched him put on his most brilliant smile.

"Hello, there, Moyen. I was just on my way to you."

THIRTY-TWO

Rogue didn't return until two days later when he found me in the library, tearing me from a good book that had kept me from replaying his words in my head. They kept haunting me anyway.

I would have brought you, anyway.

Astorian hadn't returned to keep me company, so when I wasn't reading, I was twirling my Mage Stone between my fingers, wondering when he'd take me back to the Hollow Mountains to train with Zelia and Dimar. Not Tristan—the spot in my chest where our love for each other had once lived was still a vast wasteland, and I wondered if I could even be in the same room with him without my emotions breaking free and turning me into a version of myself nobody should ever see.

It seemed that moment was now since Rogue sauntered in, holding out a hand to me while he gestured with the other to put the book aside.

"Grab that tiny crystal and imagine the man of your dreams—it might take you right there."

I rolled my eyes, clutching my Mage Stone tightly, and lowered the book onto the table.

"See?" He took my free hand, tugging me to my feet.

"We're still here," I commented, just to shut him up.

Rogue gave me a mischievous grin. "Perhaps that should tell you something."

"That there no longer *is* a man of my dreams?" I offered.

Rogue merely shrugged, and the air rippled around us, folding us through the lands and spitting us out in a glimmering cave much smaller than the one we'd landed in last time.

In the far corner, Zelia and Dimar were bent over what looked a lot like a garden despite the absence of daylight.

At our arrival, Dimar lifted his head, a smile painted on his face as he spotted me next to the fairy king.

"I thought you'd forgotten your promise," he said by way of greeting, golden strands in his hair bouncing as he jogged over to crush me in a bear hug.

"I never forget a promise." I was surprised Rogue didn't sound more offended.

"Of course not," Zelia said from where she was weeding a patch of what looked a lot like Leeneae.

Letting go of Dimar, I scanned the cave for entrances and exits, for any hidden spot where Tristan could appear from. My stomach didn't relax until Rogue told me, "He isn't here." Of course, he'd noticed my searching. He noticed every detail even when they were none of his business.

"Tristan is in the kitchen, brewing a potion," Zelia informed me.

"Without magic?" We'd brewed potions in Jezuin, but Zelia had still had residual magic in her system then.

"The foundation of potions," she corrected. "*You* will provide the magic needed to make them fully functional, Sanja." She wiped her hands on her apron and stalked over. "I'd hug you, but I'm an earthy mess."

She was. A streak of drying soil graced her cheek, and blotches of splattered dirt were distributed all over her simple dress. Even her braid was full of crumbs of earth and rogue weeds.

"You look wonderful as always, Master Mage," Rogue said with a slight bow, and I couldn't help feeling like he intended to impress the woman who no longer held any power to use against him.

Zelia dismissed the compliment with a wave of her hand. "I'm glad you brought her after all. Whether or not she's determined to help Tristan, she needs to master her Mage Stone."

"I couldn't agree more." Rogue smiled at her, and Zelia actually smiled back, a sight I wouldn't have believed I'd ever get to see. But here they were, acting like accomplices rather than the enemies they used to be... perhaps never were—not in Rogue's book. Not if what he'd told me was true.

The latter turned to me, hand hovering in the air as if he was going to run it through his hair then thought better and lowered it. "I'll pick you up in an hour, Hour Mage," he said with a smile—one so different from how he'd smiled at Zelia that I was still trying to figure it out when the air rippled around him and he vanished.

"Have I ever told you how much this fairy puts me on edge?" Dimar commented as he beckoned me toward the door built into the side of the cave.

"If he puts you on edge visiting for a few minutes, try living with him." I looped my arm into his, savoring the sense of not being under fairy observation for once.

Dimar chuckled. "He's been visiting for more than a few minutes at a time, but yes, I can see what you mean."

Zelia followed us, taking off her apron and slinging it over her arm. "I can't believe he actually left you alone with us."

Nor could I. But what surprised me more was the way his absence put me on edge even more. A harrowing sensation of what could go wrong during that hour. He hadn't informed me of his plans—maybe I should have asked.

The tunnels they led me through were less glimmering than the caves but still a sight to behold.

"What is this place? Apart from a quarry?"

I could tell by the way the walls were partly smooth like the rock had been cut out and partly rough where natural bends of stone defined them.

"The entry of the first Mages into Askarea," Zelia said with a secretive smile as we entered the room where we'd had tea last time. "Part of the Hollow Mountains lies outside of Askarea on the Tavrasian side of the human realms."

"We're in the human lands?"

"This part is in Askarea. The caves and tunnels on the human side have long been collapsed—legends say the fairies did it themselves to keep the humans from entering unnoticed."

"As if we were threats."

I hadn't noticed Tristan in the corner, vial in one hand, bottle in the other. He was pouring some dark substance from one to the other, glancing up only long enough to meet my gaze and acknowledge I was there.

My stomach sank to my knees, heavy as the heart above it.

"Here for your magic training, Sanja? Happy to help."

Dimar's arm tightened around mine, and I could have hugged my cousin for his loyalty. But I detached myself and walked over to Tristan's side, placing a hand on his arm.

He stopped pouring, head whipping toward me, and his gaze was a swirl of guilt and hope.

"Hello, Tristan." I debated lifting to my toes to place a kiss on his cheek to acknowledge that, even with that new rift between us, he was still a good man. Instead, I let go and marched toward where Dimar'd taken a seat at the round table and where a long line of potions was waiting for added magic.

"We're starting over here." Dimar gestured at a small flask then lifted it from the table.

Zelia picked up a teakettle and poured tea for us.

"Is it true that he's been working with you regarding how to bind the Crow Fairies back in their forest?" I asked her as she leaned over the table for Dimar's cup.

I simply had to know her side after what Rogue had revealed the other day. Who knew when I'd have another chance to talk to her without the fairy's looming presence? It was bad enough that he'd been around to witness the nail in the coffin of what had been slowly falling apart between Tristan and me.

My eyes wandered to the man at the other end of the kitchen and found him staring back at me, expression thoughtful.

I turned away, searching for Zelia's gaze instead. "You've known for a long time that the Crows were active."

She nodded.

"Why didn't you tell me?"

She gave me a grave look. "At first, I didn't know if I could trust you. Then, when I knew you were truly my niece, I couldn't bring myself to confront you with another potential threat when we were just barely escaping from the fairy palace. I didn't know Recienne was aware of my monthly intelligence dinners."

"Recienne? You're on a first-name basis with the fairy king?" Not that it mattered.

"Aren't you?" Tristan asked from the other side of the room. "You seemed quite ... familiar last time." He ran his gaze up and down my body, and I couldn't help feeling the memory of silk and velvet there—Rogue's velvet dressing robe.

I didn't respond.

"He's visited us so often that, at some point, it no longer made sense to call him King," Dimar said with a shrug. "And he seemed fine with it."

"He called you Master Mage just now," I pointed out to Zelia.

"He does that sometimes. But it no longer feels like the truth. More like a memory." She set down the teakettle on the stove. "If what you're asking is if I trust him, I'll never fully trust a fairy. But Recienne has been vigilant in his efforts to do something that will put him in your favor, Sanja, so that's something I want to acknowledge."

"In his favor or in his bed?" I wasn't sure he'd truly spoken, but when I whirled to give Tristan a damning look, he was standing with his back to me, swirling a potion in one hand.

Dimar merely shook his head. "The fairy king seems concerned with a lot more than your perception of him, Sanja. He's been monitoring the development in the Seeing Forest as well, and let me tell you, he isn't happy about it."

Perhaps I hadn't expected their stories to match, but it was a relief so stark it made me slump into a chair with a sigh.

Dimar raised his eyebrows, golden freckles glimmering in the fairy lights. "He offered to work together— combine our knowledge for the good of all of Eherea. He made a promise that his intentions are genuine and that he'll renounce Cezux once the Crow Fairies have been taken care of."

They didn't know ... about the bargain his father made with the Crows. About Clio and Astorian and the little house in the woods. But he'd let them in on some of his plans long before he'd ever told me anything—because I'd been a hateful creature who'd done anything to get away from him.

And now—now I didn't know what had changed. But when I thought of Rogue, his golden eyes were the first thing that came to mind rather than that fear of months ago, the terror of the challenges in his father's palace.

I couldn't help but glance over my shoulder at Tristan again.

"Shall we push the talking to later and use the time to do some actual magic?" Dimar asked, setting the flask in his hand down in front of me. "What have you learned so far?"

So I told him—I told all three of them—about that initial time I'd used the Mage Stone, how I'd accidentally magicked myself into the palace gardens. How the stone kept reacting in moments of anger or panic. How *yetheruh* had worked when fighting off the Ledrynx.

"A Ledrynx?" Tristan interrupted, finally joining us at the table. "What business do you have being out in the forests?"

I didn't know why I still cringed at Tristan's tone.

"It doesn't matter," I told him. "What matters is that my magic worked because of it, and now, let's get this over with. If I ever want to step into Crow Fairy territory to get you your Guardians damned magic back, you shouldn't be asking why it's working, only whether it is."

With those words, I turned back to Dimar, a silent plea in my eyes to let it go.

Thank Eroth, he understood, pointing at my left hand where the leather string of my Mage Stone was peeking through my fingers. "I've got this, Tristan. You can go back to your potions." I didn't fail to recognize the frustration in his tone, the mild anger that might very well have come from that same protective instinct that had driven his arm to tighten around mine earlier.

Much to my surprise, Tristan let it go, returning to the potions while Zelia left the room to clean up.

"Thank you," I whispered at my cousin, who smiled at me, the skin around his eyes crinkling a bit.

"Of course. I will always try to help you, Sanja. You're family."

That reminded me... "Leahnie sends her regards."

The smile faded. "Is she all right?"

"She was the last time I saw her. Now that I'm gone, Cyrill has no reason to punish her or use her to keep me in check."

The look he gave me told me he understood exactly what had happened—and how sorry I was about it.

"We'll get rid of Cyrill, Dimar. And then, she'll be free, the same as all of Cezux. She is tougher than you think. She knows the palace, knows how to disappear for a few hours if need be. She'll be all right." Not fine but all right. I couldn't promise more than that.

"Thank you." Sincerity made his words weigh more heavily than they usually would. "I would hate for her to get hurt."

"So would I."

Dimar gestured at the Mage Stone again. "Let's get started."

I opened my palm, exposing the stone to the glimmering room, and couldn't help noticing Tristan's attention wandering back to us—to the crystal.

"Can you feel it pulse?" Dimar asked. "Close your hand. Try to sense it."

I did.

Indeed, a weak pulse emanated from the milky surface of the stone.

Dimar's face brightened as I nodded. By the potions, Tristan went very still, as if listening for the magic, trying to feel it through the distance.

"Today, we're going to focus on releasing tiny amounts of magic. We don't want you to exert yourself every time you use the stone. So potions are a good training ground." He pushed the flask before me an inch closer. "Grab the potion, focus on your breathing."

The flask was cool and smooth but felt somehow ...empty, despite the brown brew swirling inside it.

"You feel the missing magic, don't you?" Dimar nodded his encouragement.

"I do." My eyes slid to my closed hand where the crystal had started to glow. "What's happening?"

"Your body is channeling the magic. It's answering the call of the potion. The missing ingredient is what you need to add by releasing a sliver of magic." He demonstrated a deep inhale and a slow exhale.

"Think of it like a leash. You give an inch, it takes an inch. You let go of the leash, it will take everything you have."

I could do that; imagine a leash connecting the magic stored in the stone to myself, holding onto it, letting go an inch.

"Good." He watched me more than he watched the stone or the flask, as if he could see the magic flowing through me. "That's enough."

I'd barely felt the magic move by the time he stopped me, and part of me wanted to do more, to let it swish and lash through me in whatever way it wanted. That rush I'd experienced when I'd brought down the Ledrynx—

"It needs some getting used to. The control, I mean. It's more a control of yourself than of the magic you wield. If you let it slip, you might destroy rather than help, hurt rather than heal."

That alone was enough to silence that impulse, but—

"What if I spend all the magic in the stone? What happens to me then?"

It was Tristan who responded, "Of the Mages who are known to have drained their Mage Stones so they can no longer wield them, most merely fell unconscious for a few days. But there is a chance you might not wake up again if that happens."

I didn't ask if he meant me specifically or Mages in general, too busy marveling at the silken glow that now emanated from the flask between my fingers. I'd observed all three Mages transferring magic into potions plenty of times in Aceleau, had watched Zelia do the same in Jezuin. But it still took me by surprise how it was possible at all.

And that, now, I was the only one of us left to be able to do it.

"Well done, Sanja," Zelia praised when she entered the kitchen, clothed in a fresh shirt and pants, her hair tucked into a bun at the back of her head. "Dimar is an excellent tutor, isn't he?"

"He is." I smiled at my cousin, and for a moment, I forgot Tristan's presence, the weight it put on my chest, the guilt and regret and pain. It was just Zelia, Dimar, and me, and we could have as well been sitting in the sick house in Jezuin.

Except, the light was an assembly of reflections off the glimmering walls, flowing in all hues across the room, and this wasn't Jezuin.

"Again." Dimar took the flask from my fingers, handing me a new one. "Focus on the pulsing. Breathe. Release."

I followed his instructions, finding it easier this time. Easier to sense the channel, the 'gap' of magic in the potion. I released the adequate amount, and the liquid began to subtly glow.

"Am I not supposed to use some incantation to get the magic flowing?" I asked around the focus on my task.

Dimar nodded. "With potions like these, it's not necessary. Only with more complicated things. For advanced Mages, sometimes thinking the incantation is enough. I chose this task so you can focus your attention on one thing at a time."

Dimar kept pushing new flasks at me every time I was done with one until finding the path of magic through me no longer felt like a challenge and more than half of the potions were now sitting in a neat, glowing cluster.

By the time Rogue sauntered back into the room—stepping out of thin air as if he'd decided he wanted to site-hop mid-walk—I'd gotten tired, and my Mage Stone barely responded.

"Just in time," Dimar said by way of greeting, gesturing at the crystal in my hand. "We need some replenishing."

Rogue gracefully slid into a chair, scanning me from the side before he flicked his fingers and the magic swirled from him into the stone.

"I thought you needed to shake hands in order to do that," Tristan commented from where he'd taken up post against the wall, monitoring my progress

"That's when you give magic in a bargain or trade." Rogue shrugged, flashing a toothy grin that was more scary than anything. "I am giving my magic to dear Sanja freely—nothing expected in return."

A part of me wanted to throw my arms around him just to let him know how much I appreciated that, for once, something in my life didn't come with a price. I opted for giving him a smile even when he didn't deign to acknowledge it. But his eye widened a bit as I studied his profile, and his hand twitched an inch toward me on the table. He leaned back in his chair instead, studying the potions in front of us.

Tristan's gaze wandered between the two of us, a familiar anger rising behind the troubled blue of his irises.

"What did you learn today, Sanja? Anything worth changing the world?"

"Maybe not the world," I said, that smile not slipping even when he was pretending to be that grumpy, unpredictable fairy king. I'd glimpsed a piece of him before, and that piece had chosen to not trap me with another bargain and put me in his debt. "But it's a start."

"That's what I'd hoped to hear." He inclined his head to Dimar, to Zelia, and to Tristan last. "A bit more patience, Tristan. Soon, we'll all have what we want."

I didn't get to ask what he meant by that before he huffed on that dark breeze, "Let's go," and site-hopped us out of the caves, back into the bright sunlight of the balcony overlooking the palace gardens.

THIRTY-THREE

I was about to thank him for recharging my Mage Stone when he whirled on me, that composed fairy male vanished.

"Don't do that again," he hissed, golden eyes molten as he scanned the confusion on my face.

"Help to make potions?" It was really the only thing I had done.

"Use me."

"What?" I wasn't sure where the Rogue I knew had retreated to, but the one he showed me now was one that seemed ... hurt. There was hurt in his eyes.

"You know Tristan hates me for keeping you at the palace even when he asked me for help. He wants you, Sanja. But he wants his magic more." His eyes flashed, gold solidifying once more as he composed himself. "I'm Tristan's only

419

way of getting what he wants, and you quietly delight in seeing that little spark of jealousy in his eyes."

"What are you even talking about?"

"You are using me, Sanja. To punish him for picking his magic over you. And I don't particularly enjoy being used."

"In what way am I using you? *You* are using *me*. With your scheming and secrets and plans that you don't share with anyone."

"Because I don't dare give false hopes, Sanja. The same way I don't enjoy hoping wrongly." His gaze pierced through the layers of glimmering rock I'd built around my heart, right to the core of myself. And what he found there? I wasn't sure he wouldn't shy away if he saw that darkness, that pain in me.

Silence filled my head.

"That smile—" A muscle feathered in his jaw as he seemed to debate whether to speak at all. "That smile you gave me." Everything went still inside of me. "You did that to punish him."

I couldn't look away from him even when every last sense of self-preservation commanded me to close my eyes so as not to fall into that abyss of ... *him* lingering behind the metal of his gaze.

And I didn't think when I told him, "I smiled at you because you did something nice for me, and I wanted to let you know I'd noticed."

Rogue's mouth opened, closed ... opened again. He went rigid as I placed my hand on the side of his arm and squeezed. A neutral thanks, a way to ground him, perhaps.

Or just something I'd never considered doing for him when I'd normally have done it for any friend had he so wildly misread a situation.

His stone-like stillness melted, and he stepped closer, fluid and graceful like a mountain cat, his front coming almost flush with mine. Behind me, the rail of the balcony kept me from backing away more than a few inches. His rain and nights under open skies scent enveloped me alongside that of white roses as he leaned closer, hands braced on each side of my hips on the handrail, and brought his face level with mine.

"So you are telling me you don't care what he thinks when you show up in my dressing robe?" His breath touched my face. "That you don't delight in that spark of jealousy that flies whenever he sees you at my side?"

Whatever dark corner of him those words were coming from, I didn't shy away from him, not anymore. I'd been afraid of the calculated fairy male, but this one—this was a feeling one. And who'd ever thought that was possible for a fairy?

I let my hand slide down his arm all the way to his wrist, squeezing again. "Tristan made his choice."

A shiver ran through Rogue, making his breath shudder. "And you're good with that?"

For a beat, we stared into each other's eyes.

"I will be."

His gaze wandered over my face, probing whether I was serious. Lingering on my mouth for a long, long moment. "Ask me again why I tripped you in Jezuin."

My chest rose and fell too rapidly for simply standing still at the edge of a balcony, even when it was with the most powerful male in Askarea and his warmth radiated between both our layers of clothes. A breeze ruffled his hair, making the face of the fairy king turn into that of the predator he became in the forests, tuning out the palace and the dangers lurking there.

"Why did you trip me in Jezuin?" I breathed, heart thundering in my throat. I was sure he could hear it. The birds in the bushes below could probably hear it.

But Rogue's face twisted the slightest bit, providing me with a glimpse of the pained creature beneath the mask—the male who'd suffer so his sister wouldn't need to, who would rather be hated and feared than let anyone see the real him.

"Because I've lost too many things in the past, and I couldn't afford to lose anything else."

"Your kingdom... the bargain with Cyrill..." My voice died in my throat as he placed a finger to my lips to stop me from speaking.

"We both know my kingdom isn't what I was talking about."

Before I could give it a second thought, he was gone.

And the blinding brightness of the summer day hit me like a club to the head.

Astorian came to pick me up the next day. We spent the morning in Clio's hideout, playing a Cezuxian card game.

Astorian informed me it was part of a bag Rogue had stolen from a wealthy fairy when he'd been a youngling. Human objects that fairies coveted—a part of me would never understand it.

I'd won five out of ten games, uncertain whether it was due to Astorian's and Clio's kindness or actual skill. Both of my companions were lazily lounging in their armchairs, not bothering to tell me any new stories about the fairy king; the memory of whose finger was still lingering on my lips like a phantom touch.

"So you come and go at court," I eventually said to Astorian when they decided they were tired of playing.

Astorian lifted a slice of cake to his mouth, biting into it like there was no tomorrow.

Clio shot him a warning look. "We have company, Ass," she told him, and I coughed at what I thought was an insult.

But Astorian merely laughed at my reaction.

"When he behaves like one, I shorten his name to the essence of what he truly is," Clio clarified.

"You call him Ass?"

"Lovingly so," Clio retorted, flopping her arm half over Astorian's shoulder and chest as she leaned over.

My heart ached for him—and not because of the name.

"I'd prefer it if you called me Tori," he said to me before I could ask. "Astorian only in formal settings. It sounds better in a royal court—no matter how many royal asses are around."

"We call you Tori only when you're a good fairy," Clio sweetly said.

I involuntarily laughed, startling myself with the clear, chime-like sound.

Clio cocked her head. "It seems, spending time with my brother has worked wonders for your mood."

Shuffling the cards, I hid any potential response in the focus on the silver-decorated deck.

"I come and go like any other advisor," Tori replied to my earlier question, and I could have hugged him for it.

A glance at him confirmed he'd noticed Rogue wasn't my favorite topic. "Before Rogue cleared out the palace after his father's death, a lot more advisors and courtiers used to roam the halls. My coming and going didn't draw much attention then." He shifted, allowing Clio's hand to slide right over his heart, and he paused, blinking a few times.

She seemed to notice only then what she'd been doing and reeled in her rogue limb. "Ever since Moyen turned to the Crow's side, we need to be more careful. She's reporting everything to the Crow King, and if he suspects even the slightest deceit, there will be death and destruction."

"And when she says *death and destruction*," Astorian took over, "she means the kind where you'll find no identifiable bodies after the slaughter."

My insides went cold. Those creatures—if they were released upon Askarea or the human lands... I didn't even want to think what would happen to humans if fairies feared them so fiercely.

"I want to help him, you know."

Astorian raised a brow.

"With sealing the borders. I don't care if it's a risk. I need to do it for my people."

Neither Astorian nor Clio questioned my decision.

"He'll be delighted to hear that." Clio sat up in her chair, eyes behind me.

"What will I be delighted to hear?"

Rogue's voice slithered down my spine like a lick of sunset-gold, and I jerked around in my chair to find him leaning on the threshold, leather armor in place and hood up. I couldn't make out his eyes in the shadows, but his mouth—with the mask down, the feral grin he gave me made my toes curl in my boots.

"Always so nosy, brother." Clio hopped to her feet and crossed the room, arms ready to wrap around the bandit in her living room.

Rogue's face turned softer as his sister hugged him around the waist, sunlight penetrating the shadows of his hood when he angled his head to drop a kiss on the top of her head. So at odds with the male who'd tackled me off the horse and pinned me to the forest ground that first day. So little like the mask of the king he pulled up whenever he walked the halls of his palace.

I only noticed I'd been staring at him when Astorian cleared his throat and Rogue's golden gaze snapped to mine.

Clio slid out of his arms, breezing from the room to do whatever, and Astorian excused himself with a pat on Rogue's shoulder. "We took good care of her all day—it's your turn."

"Don't bring me over if I'm a nuisance," I called after him as he swaggered up the narrow stairs behind Clio, and he turned to flash me a grin.

"Oh, not at all, Sanja. I wouldn't even consider bringing you here if you were, no matter how much little Rogue here begged me to." With a few mighty leaps, taking a few steps at once, he was gone.

"*Little Rogue?*"

Rogue rolled his eyes. "If we're back at the size discussion, I can assure you it *does* matter."

Holding back a grin, I nestled into my chair, watching him tug down his hood to reveal the touches of deepest copper and gold coming to life when the angle of the sun illuminated his hair.

"Is that why he calls you *little Rogue?*" I couldn't help it, the delighted grin on his face was too precious not to tease him into it.

"Want to come see for yourself?" The grin turned predatory—not so different from the day before, and if the sudden rush flooding my system was anything to go by, we were on dangerous ground.

Ignoring my racing heart, I managed a shrug and a casual tone as I said, "I'm sure there are enough females in Askarea I can ask for confirmation."

Rogue took a few steps toward me, that fluid grace impossible to conceal even in the garbs of a bandit. He braced a hand on the backrest of the chair next to me, fingers digging into the cerulean upholstery. "Do you *want* confirmation, Sanja?"

The way he locked my gaze to his, how his focus had narrowed in on me ... I no longer knew what sort of confirmation we were talking about.

The light shirt I'd chosen was suddenly too hot, the air stuffy.

"Is there a special someone I should ask then? Moyen, perhaps? She seemed quite eager to escort you to your quarters the other night."

His grin faded so fast I wanted to ask if I'd said something wrong, but he leaned over the chair, a stark warning in his tone as he told me, "I might have taken lovers, Sanja. And I'm happy to point you in the right direction in case you want to compare notes. But never—*never*—indicate that I'd take Lady Wellows to bed." *Not if I can help it.* The words were written so clearly in his eyes that I almost didn't dare ask.

"So ... no special someone?" I held my breath. I'd never thought about it before, but he was King of Askarea. Certainly, females would line up to marry into the royal bloodline. In Cezux, I'd never had a shortage of men interested in my hand—and more. But mainly for the power. If anyone had ever been interested in me as a person, it was Eduin. And he'd been more a friend with benefits. And Tristan—

Tristan had been just right for me when I'd been just San—not a princess, not yet a Mage. When I'd tried to find my place in my new life and had to come to terms with never again asking for more.

But I'd failed at disappearing from that old life. And Tristan had failed at realizing I was so much more.

I swallowed.

"So far, no one I've been with felt like a good enough choice to consider spending an eternity with them." The tension left his body, and he circled the chair to flop into it instead of using it as a prop.

"Eternity is a long time."

"You want to consider well who you share it with." That wistful look had returned to his eyes, making me wonder how many times he'd wished someone was out there for him. "But I'm the most powerful fairy in Askarea. Even before my mother's power transferred to me, I was more powerful than most. And it was difficult then ... to find someone who'd consider *me*."

"Consider you?" I looked him up and down, the powerful legs stretched out under the coffee table, the arms strong enough to ward off enemies or nightmares. That face seeming to become more beautiful with every mask he shed.

"It's not an easy thing being loved by fairy royalty, Sanja." His eyes met mine as if he knew exactly what he was speaking about. "And it's even harder to be loved by me."

I rolled his words over in my head for a moment.

"Because you're an annoying bastard who never says what he actually means?" I offered, hoping to wipe that pensiveness off his features, to bring back a smile.

Indeed, he smiled, but it was a bitter one. "Because who should stand a chance at surviving being loved by me?"

"Survive—" I whispered.

Rogue rested his head on the back of the chair, gaze wandering the wooden ceiling. "It's bad enough that the Crows are merely waiting for me to make a mistake so they can rid Askarea of me. Imagine if I loved someone—if they *knew* I actually loved someone." He placed a hand on his chest, on the leather and buckles there, as if he were holding in his heart. "They'd use it against me before that someone could ever love me back. And she wouldn't survive."

For a while we sat there, each following their own train of thought—mine running back to Jezuin, to Eduin's unseeing eyes when I'd hit the marble next to his corpse. Would he have survived had he not been close to me—close, not even loved?

Eventually, Rogue sighed, folding his arms across his chest. "So, what will I be delighted to hear?"

I dove out of my own little world to answer the question he'd asked long before our conversation had gone off track. "That I've decided to help you with locking in the Crow fairies."

Eyebrows knitting into a tight line, he faced me. "Are you sure you want to risk that much for me?"

"For my people," I corrected.

His eyebrows pulled together even more tightly. "Of course." He studied me with those golden eyes, every breath turning heavier in my chest than the last as I read what could have been a hint of disappointment there.

"And perhaps a tiny little bit for you," I added.

"*A tiny little bit?*"

"Let's be precise with dimensions while we're at it," I said with a halfhearted grin. But it was all I could do to push him out of that mood that had befallen him.

"*Tiny?* Not *small?*" His lips quirked at the sides, but it wasn't the same as before. Better than nothing, though.

"Perhaps a bit more than tiny. I'd need to measure to be sure."

At that, Rogue laughed. And the sound was so unexpected, so beautiful, that my breath stopped for a beat.

"Let's go back to the center of Askarean power, Sanja." He held out a hand between our chairs, glancing sideways at me. "I'm sure they're missing a *big* pillar there to uphold it."

"Who are *they*?" I asked with a grin, placing my hand in his.

He squeezed once—"Some things are better left unspoken, Sanja"—and spirited us back to the palace.

THIRTY-FOUR

Rogue took me back to the Hollow Mountains that afternoon. Dimar was already waiting with a new set of potions ready to have magic added. Tristan had been busy, as had Zelia, who was standing at the stove today, boiling a large pot of Leeneae in preparation for healing potions.

"So, what exactly do all of those do?" I gestured at the line of colorfully filled flasks. "They aren't all for healing, are they?"

Zelia shook her head over the steam of Leeneae extract she was condensing in a pot for lack of other tools.

"Some of them are for healing, but some are meant for strength. Some are sleeping draughts, and, of course, we have some that will block magic. You know ... just in case one of the fairies who visit us on a regular basis gets any ideas."

"There's only one fairy visiting you on a regular basis," I pointed out, earning a sideways glance from Tristan, who'd been brooding over a purple tea that smelled of licorice and cinnamon.

"I doubt a simple potion will be enough to block his powers." It wouldn't. Nothing would be enough to truly silence it.

"A man can dream," Tristan retorted, and I wondered if this was more meant for me than for Rogue.

"A man can stop sitting on his lazy ass and help me plant potatoes," Dimar said from the other side of the table where he had set down a bag of old potatoes to lay into the soil in the other cave. With every time I came here, I was baffled anew at what was possible in these caves. Grow greens without daylight, have actual plumbing and a stove and a small bath; I learned when Zelia beckoned me to follow her to the residential area of the cave system.

The fairies had built it for the overseers of the quarry hundreds of years ago, she'd told me. And that human slaves had done most of the work in these mountains. A short walk toward the edge of the pretty and inhabitable areas of the caves was all it took to reassure me that helping Rogue with the Crow Fairies was the right thing to do.

Piles of bones lay at the bottom of steep pits—mass graves where the sick or weak humans had been discarded so they didn't take up space when new workers could be brought in.

My stomach still tightened into a sickening knot at the memory of those few parts of the caves that hadn't been collapsed by the fairies to block humans from entering the fairy realm decades later—perhaps to cover all their tracks as well.

Tristan shot Dimar a damning look before he said to me, "Can I talk to you for a moment?"

I turned over a hand in front of me, gesturing that he should talk if he needed to.

"Alone," he added.

Dimar's eyebrows shot up—first at Tristan, then at me, a silent question in his eyes.

"It's all right," I told him and nodded at Tristan, who immediately got to his feet, beckoning me to follow into the tunnel leading to the massive cave where Rogue had brought me that first time at the Hollow Mountains.

I followed on sluggish feet, half anxious about what he'd have to say—or what he wouldn't.

As soon as we cleared the darker parts, he stopped, spinning on his heels.

Crossing my arms over my chest, I waited.

"I'm not taking it for granted that you're helping me."

Not an apology then, no cordial words. Just a fact.

"I love you, Sanja. I still do, and I might always love you. But I learned in Jezuin that, without my magic, I'm powerless to protect you. To protect my family." Zelia and Dimar—*my* family. Ours. "And I can't be helpless. Not after everything I've lost. After months of hiding from fairies, of living off handouts and stolen remains. After being dependent on others..." His shoulders relaxed as if someone had lifted a weight off them. "I can't be dependent on anyone."

"I understand." And I did.

"You don't." He ran a hand through his hair. "You have never been dependent like this. You grew up in a palace on top of the food chain in Cezux. You had everything you needed: food, shelter, safety. And when Cyrill took your throne, you had someone who had your back. Dimar first, then me. You've always had someone who cared for you, someone who fought for you. You don't understand what it means to truly be alone. To depend. To gain freedom after years on the run."

Everything inside me tightened as he tried to explain to me how I felt. But I blew out a breath, putting aside all the ways he'd misunderstood what my life had actually been like. How royalty didn't equal safety or freedom. How that hadn't protected me from becoming a pawn and a target.

And I wasn't the only example. My mother had been killed for being a Mage—the Queen of Cezux, for the Guardians' sake. Clio had to hide in the forests of Askarea to keep safe from the Crow Fairies. Tori had given up his freedom to go with her. And Rogue—

Rogue was the one who kept sacrificing and sacrificing—for his family, for his friends, his people. And even for mine.

Something eased in my chest as I allowed myself to lift that veil of the fearsome creature I'd believed him to be for such a long time.

I smiled at Tristan. "It's all right, Tris. I won't hold your wish for freedom against you. As long as you don't blame me for wanting the same."

The glimmering reflections of the fairy lights in the cave walls painted patterns on his face, paler than it had been a month ago when he'd come to the Jezuinian palace for me. I couldn't tell if those were tears in his eyes, for he lowered his gaze. "Once I have my magic, I'll make sure we both are free."

I didn't tell him he didn't need to do anything. That I had already found freedom—there, inside my heart. The freedom of my people I'd fight for alongside him as agreed.

"Thank you for not giving up on me in Jezuin," I said with a smile.

Tristan's lips curved into that half-smile that had become so familiar, yet its meaning was now so different. He wrapped his arms around me. I let him until my cheek rested against his shoulder. There, I remained for a moment until I drew back.

"We should return to the others. I've got some magic to learn."

The smile widened then faded. "We should."

And I knew there would remain no hard feelings between us. Even when he'd picked his magic over me. I understood. And I was ready to help him as best I could. For the sake of the boy who'd slept behind chimneys in the winter and the man who'd cared enough to give me a chance even when I'd been a nobody. For what we'd had and what he might find in his future.

He led the way back to the kitchen where he picked up the sack of potatoes and headed off while I settled into my usual chair, ready to channel some magic.

"Everything all right with you two?" Dimar wanted to know.

I nodded. Because it was. Not in the way it used to be. But it was.

"Let's get to work, Dimar."

For the next few weeks, I spent the mornings with Dimar, improving my magic, and the afternoons with Tori and Clio or with Rogue. The latter was away on errands every other day, unwilling to leave me alone in the palace when Lady Wellows was still roaming the halls.

She hadn't sought me out alone so far, but she did make comments whenever I was forced to sit through a meal with her. And every time, Rogue assured me before and afterward that he felt the exact same way.

The days had started to blend into each other, with my Mage Stone being half-drained every morning and refilled by Rogue again. He never asked for anything in return—and, having learned my lesson, I didn't try to thank him again.

Dimar was juggling a particularly difficult potion when Zelia sat down beside me in the kitchen of the Hollow Mountains and told me that she believed it was time for me to move on from potions and try something bigger.

Tristan merely lifted a brow from where he was reading one of the books I'd brought from the stack Rogue had saved from the Mages' House.

"Bigger?" A part of me wished Rogue was there so I could secretly watch him chuckle at the quantification of size.

"Something using more magic in a less controlled way," she specified.

Eager to know what I'd been upgraded to, I peered at the piece of paper she was smoothing out in front of her on the table.

"This"—she gestured at the scribbled lines—"is a spell."

My pulse picked up pace at the thought of spelling something. Just the idea—

"It is a minor one, but it will come in handy in the future." She shoved the paper toward me, and I silently read the words—instructions, really. And one word. "Memorize it. You won't always have a book or a Mage at your disposal to help you."

For the potions, I hadn't needed spells, but this was different. This was something more active than merely channeling magic from one point to the other. It would *bring* me an object.

"*Dasteris*," I repeated aloud what was written. "What am I going to summon?" The instructions said to think of the object you wanted to summon then speak the spell.

"Small things," Dimar threw in, joining us at the table. "The larger the object, the more magic is required."

"I don't even know if, with your tiny Mage Stone, you'll ever get beyond basic household tools and foods. But if that's all you can manage, it might be key to survival."

"You can build impressive things from little ones," Dimar said with that grin I'd come to love so much.

In those few weeks of helping me train, he'd become like a brother to me.

"How about a pea?" Tristan offered.

"Why not?" Zelia got to her feet, reached into the cupboard behind the table, and pulled out a jar of dried peas.

"Where did you get those?" It never ceased to amaze me the supplies they conjured even without magic.

"Recienne dropped by the other day with a bag of peas and a sack of flour, fresh eggs, milk, butter, spinach... Did I forget anything?" she asked Dimar, who'd taken the jar from Zelia's hands and was extracting a single pea.

"I don't think so. But who knows? He shows up with something new every other day." He placed the pea in front of him, handing the jar back to Zelia. "Now, take your Mage Stone, feel it pulse, think of the pea, and speak the word."

Very well...

I did as I was told, focusing on the pea. "*Dasteris.*"

A zing of magic flicked through me, and the pea disappeared before Dimar to pop up in my open palm instead. Gaping at it, I tried not to squeal with excitement at having performed actual magic—and how easy it had been.

"Well done." Tristan had looked up from his book to monitor the situation. "I knew you'd figure it out in no time."

"You pushed to give her bigger tasks weeks ago," Dimar said with enough bite to inform me there had been an argument about it.

"Because you underestimate her."

"Because I'd rather she learned the foundation so she can make her own choices about what she can handle than making those decisions for her."

Zelia shook her head at both of them—and at my quizzical glance. "We have a whole jar of peas," she announced. "Let's burn through them before we move on to something bigger."

I didn't need to think twice at her suggestion but merely popped the pea in my hand into the empty bowl beside me and grasped my Mage Stone harder. "Ready."

We'd gotten halfway through the jar when Rogue popped up in the chair beside me, making all four of us jump. "We need to go," he told me without heeding the others a look.

He held out his hand, gaze speaking of an urgency the source of which I wasn't sure I wanted to know. But I abandoned the pea in my hand, pocketed my Mage Stone, and placed my fingers in his palm.

"What's wrong?" Zelia wanted to know, but Rogue and I were already flickering out of existence and into a room I'd never been inside before.

Dark, carved furniture stood against crème-colored walls—an armoire, a desk and chair, and an oversized bed covered in golden silk.

"Where are we?"

"My bedroom. It's the safest place in the palace." He took a step away from me, looking me over as if for damage.

"What's wrong?" I echoed Zelia's inquiry, my eyes lingering on the cluster of half-cut white roses on the nightstand.

"Sanja—"

My heart leaped into my throat at the sound of my name—a plea rather than a request.

Slowly—so slowly, I faced him, his eyes the color of the sheets on the bed already on me.

"What happened, Rogue?" Now, fear entered my system, spreading like a wildfire at the sight of his distress.

"A Crow escaped Askarea."

My blood turned to ice. If it wasn't in Askarea, it had to be in—"Which territory?"

"Cezux."

I was once again caught in a hedge, twigs and branches grasping my chest like a vise.

He took my hand, rubbing soothing circles on the back of my palm. "Moyen informed me a minute ago. I came right away to get you."

"How can it have crossed the border?"

"We don't know yet. But the theory is that the Crow King is getting stronger by the day." He shoved his free hand through his hair. "I've used the past weeks to feel out what's going on in the forests. My *errands* there were to speak to my sources—in and out of Crow territory. But it seems I haven't been the only one."

I cocked my head, still gathering my thoughts.

"The Crows have been monitoring, not only the palace, through Moyen. She was a distraction—something to keep me busy while they were sneaking around the borders of their territory, as far out as they could get, and made new allies."

"And now one got out?"

"One got out," he confirmed. "And it made it all the way across the Cezuxian border. It's on its way to Jezuin to take the throne before I can."

Something roiled in my blood. "I thought you were going to help me free Cezux."

"I *am* helping." He took my second hand, tugging me a step toward him. "I need to take the Cezuxian throne from Cyrill. It's part of the bargain with the Crows. If I don't, they'll see the bargain as unfulfilled, and there will be nothing restraining them from coming at us once they break open the borders of their forest for good."

"Why are they going after the throne now? I thought they knew you had a couple more months until you'd return me to Cyrill and fulfill the bargain." I couldn't believe I was actually speaking the words—was actually hoping they'd come to pass.

"They learned what I'm trying to do with you, Sanja."

"Seal their borders?"

"They know you're my only chance. There is no other Mage left."

"You mean I'm the only one willing to help you."

He shook his head. "They disappeared, Sanja. Every last one of them. What few of them were left in the remote corners of Askarea—all gone."

"What do you mean, *gone*?" I'd known there were others. Had learned about them from Zelia and Tristan. But I'd never met a single one of them. His words hit me in the chest, nonetheless.

"Whether the Crows found a way to kill them or they'd simply gone into hiding, I cannot tell. But there is no other Mage left for me to turn to."

"They aren't after my throne... They are after me, aren't they?"

Rogue pressed his lips into a tight line. "They are after anything that could prevent them from getting out of the Seeing Forest. If you're the last Mage, no matter what little magic you have at your disposal, you're a threat. And they will do whatever they can to eliminate threats." He let go of my hand, pacing between the bed and the desk across the hardwood floor. "I negotiated the treaty to end the war, Sanja. They know I'm not thrilled to see them try to get out again. But they can't act against me— not unless they find me breaking the bargain they made with my father. Or by destroying any tool I could use to lock them in."

A tool. That's what I was.

I blinked away the surprise at the pain that came with the realization. A tool for him to use—and a willing one, for the good of the human lands.

"We need to get that Crow out of Cezux before it wreaks havoc, Sanja. If it gets to Jezuin, to Cyrill, there is little I can do. But before—" He stopped, glanced at the window, and continued pacing. "Before it reaches Jezuin, we can do a whole lot. But I'll need your help."

"Anything," I blurted. Anything that would keep my people safe.

I almost didn't notice the flash of recognition across his face.

That word—the same one Tristan had used. I'd do anything to save my people, not myself. That was the difference.

I schooled my expression into careful neutrality as I told him, "Tell me how to stop it, and I will."

With two long strides, he was in front of me, eyes burning with anger, with something more.

"We need to work together if we want to catch it, Sanja. It can't site-hop, so we're at an advantage. It will take the Crow days to get to Jezuin. Valuable time we can use to go to the Seeing Forest while the Crow Fairies believe we're already hunting it. You and I need to retrieve that artifact for Tristan so he can use magic again. Then we have more magic at our disposal when we get to the human lands."

"By retrieve, you mean ... steal?"

"What did you think? That the Crows would simply hand one of their precious artifacts over?"

Of course not—of course, I hadn't believed it would be that easy.

I shook my head, hearing every word, yet not understanding how that would work out. How I could get the artifact when my magic was still so fresh, so unreliable.

"I'll be there with you in the Seeing Forest. I won't leave your side. But when we go to Cezux, you and Tristan will need to finish it on your own. If I interfere, I'll have broken the bargain, and a broken fairy bargain comes with a steep price. My life would be the least and a small price compared to what could happen."

I could read it in his eyes, then, that he'd have paid that price a long time ago had he been certain it was the only one. But with that element of unpredictability... He wouldn't risk anyone else to break free of the stronghold of a villain.

"The Crow's magic will be diminished in the human lands, more so than a normal fairy's since they need to break free of two borders to get there. With luck, your combined magic will be enough to defeat it before it can reach the capital."

"If it's after me... Why go to Cezux? Why not come here? Why not track me down in the forests or the Hollow Mountains?"

A shudder visibly worked its way through his body. "They won't attack my property. It's against the bargain as well. They won't risk that—no intelligent fairy would. And they won't attack you in my presence. You're part of the bargain with Cyrill, which is part of the bargain with them, so attacking you without cause will break it as well. No... their best bet is to lure you away from me, to make you act against them on your own. You didn't make a bargain with either of us, so if you attack, for them, it's self-defense, and it won't affect the bargain."

While my mind reeled to follow him, my heart was trying to catch up with the panic flooding my entire body.

It didn't matter what I needed to do. Once Tristan had his magic back, we'd do it together. He'd already promised as much.

"When are we leaving?"

"Now." He flicked his fingers, and two packs appeared on the floor beside him. He shouldered one of them, handing me the other. "We'll go to the hideout first. Tori is already tracking the Crow into the human lands. He'll report back, and he'll be checking in every other hour to keep us informed of the Crow's progress." At a flick of his fingers, his kingly clothes changed into his bandit uniform, hood, mask, and all. He made for the nightstand, pulling open a drawer and extracting something small that I couldn't see before he slipped it into his pocket. "You can change your clothes at the forest house," he said before he picked up a rose from the nightstand.

Returning to my side, he offered the blossom to me. "It would be a shame if it went to waste just because you won't be spending the next few days in your room."

I didn't dare ask if he'd been the one to put fresh roses on my table every day but took the blossom from his hand, the panic easing for a moment as his eyes warmed as if, beneath his mask, he was smiling at me.

"Thank you, Sanja."

"For what?"

"For trusting me."

He wrapped a hand around mine holding the stem of the rose, and the gold, black, and creme of the room blurred away, blending with the greens of the forest, the blues of the sky, the slate gray rock protecting Clio's hideout.

THIRTY-FIVE

Clio was a sight to behold in her fighting leathers. Even when I'd seen her in her bandit uniform before, this was an entirely different thing. A warrior fairy with a braid of liquid copper and eyes of sharp jade that would shred opponents with a gaze alone.

"Tori popped in a moment ago," she said by way of greeting. "The Crow is following the stream south."

Rogue dumped his pack in a chair, gesturing for me to do the same. "Smart move. That way, it won't need to search for water and food." He paused, glancing around the room. "Do you have a vase?"

Clio cocked her head. "Are you intending to throw it after the Crow?"

Rogue's chuckle was midnight and stars, cold metal and cunning all at once. "Perhaps."

I realized only then that his hand was still wrapped around mine, the blossom of the rose sitting right above our wound-together fingers.

Understanding crossed Clio's face, and she waved a hand. A brass vase entirely too big for the lonely flower appeared in Rogue's open palm.

"Thanks." He set it down on the table, letting go of me to extract the rose and place it in its new home. "Now, on to more practical things." He gave me a once-over. "Sanja needs clothes that won't get her killed at an encounter with the Crow...s."

"Crow...s?" Clio prompted.

"Crows. As in the plural of Crow." Rogue gestured at my loose shirt and linen pants. "And yes, I'm serious. She can't fight in that."

The jade of Clio's gaze seemed to attack Rogue like little daggers. "You're serious. You're going to take her to the Seeing Forest."

Rogue's humorless chuckle ground against my fragile composure like sandpaper. "When am I not serious, Clio?"

Oh, I could have named countless times when he'd teased me, taunted me, and none of it could have been serious. Because if it had been—I didn't dare go there or I'd need to confront myself about why his touch lingered on my hand like a phantom caress.

"I'll take her to the Seeing Forest to get the artifact for the Mage. Then we'll go to Cezux. As soon as Tori has new coordinates for us."

Shock was an understatement for what flickered across Clio's face. "She's trained only for a few weeks, Rogue. She'll burn out her Mage Stone. Do you want to risk that?"

"She's mastered control. For the Guardians' sake, Clio—she managed to survive Father's trials. She can survive the Crow."

"*Could*, Rogue," Clio corrected as if I wasn't even there. "*Could* survive."

The exasperation in Rogue's eyes was more emotion than I'd ever expected to see on him, so it hit double as hard as he said, "There are risks I need to be willing to take in order to gain something. If it's a lost cause, it is. But I need to at least try."

Clio closed her mouth, swallowing what she'd been about to say, then turned to me. "There are more leathers in my room. Pick whatever you like. Rogue will help you adjust them."

Unsure if a thanks was in order or a cutting glance at Rogue, I remained silent until Rogue eased the pack off my shoulder and ushered me up the stairs.

"It's the last door on the left," Clio called after me as I reached the top of the stairs.

Rogue was right behind me when I entered a plain room with walls paneled with wood to the height of my hips and painted in forest green up to the ceiling where the color faded into a buttery spring yellow.

"Clio likes green," he commented. "In case you haven't noticed."

His gaze was on the equally green carpet at the center of the room. Beside a chair covered in a fir-green throw with a green-bound book atop.

With a few strides, he was by the armoire on the other side of the room. He extracted a pair of leather pants and a jacket similar to the one Clio was wearing. "Try these." He held them out to me. "I'll tighten them for you where necessary."

His gaze wandered down my form, pausing on my chest, on my waist, my hips, and I felt more naked than if I'd stood there in my underthings. Where Clio was supple and strong, my body wasn't that of a fighter. Yes, I'd learned the basics growing up as a princess in Jezuin. Self-defense mostly. But not the strength and stamina of a trained fighter, the way Clio and Rogue and Tori were. My body was that of a woman who'd spent too many months sitting on her ass and waiting for a chance to run ... and then no longer trying.

Rogue's eyes met mine, and I could have sworn he could read my mind in that moment. "I'll wait outside. Call me when you're ready." Handing me the clothes, he strode from the room, leaving me to change in privacy.

I didn't hesitate to slide out of my linen trousers and into the leather pants. Then I shucked the shirt and put the jacket on over the thin undershirt I was wearing. It hung loosely around my shoulders and chest, so I didn't even try to buckle the front before I called Rogue.

Staying true to himself, he didn't walk in the door but rippled into existence right in front of me, making me yelp.

"What have we got?" His eyes jumped straight to the too-wide pants then wandered up to the sleeves, a few inches too long, all the way to my shoulders, to the front of the jacket where the overlapping sides were covering my breasts. "You'll need to buckle that."

I grasped the metal and leather strings, tugging things into place until I was a lost human caught in fairy armor.

"Good." He stepped forward, and I was tempted to shy away. But he placed a careful finger on my shoulder. "I'll need to touch the seams to make them pull in."

Trying not to grimace, I nodded. "I thought you were the most powerful fairy in Askarea. Can't you just conjure new leathers from that brilliant mind of yours?"

His eyes flashed. "You think I'm brilliant." Not a question.

And I didn't deny it. With all those bargains in place, the restrictions on what he could or couldn't do to protect his realm, his people, his family, he had to be brilliant not to miss something, accidentally destroy the carefully crafted balance he was trying to uphold until the opportunity arose for him to break free.

I was that opportunity.

His fingers slid down the length of my arm so lightly I could barely feel it, but underneath his touch, the leather tightened, molding itself to my form.

"I might be powerful, Sanja, but even I have limitations. I can't create matter, can't put things into existence, or I'd have conjured an artifact for Tristan and been done with it."

Tristan. Not *your Mage.* And the mention of his name no longer hurt.

His attention followed the path of his hand as it worked its way along the inside of my arm back to my shoulder. I didn't flinch. Instead, I held my breath as his fingers brushed along my side, all the way to my waist, halting.

"What's wrong?"

When I looked down, his gaze lingered on my chest. "I'll need to do the front next."

Was that—

"Are you embarrassed to touch me?"

I reached for his mask, tugging it down so I could see all of his face. His eyes snapped to mine, those golden irises solid. "Of course not."

"Go on then."

When his fingers moved to the center of my waist, leather stretching tight over my form, I could suddenly feel the warmth of his touch, the gentle graze as he slid along the seam running up to my breast. My heart kicked into a gallop as he stopped right beneath, throat bobbing, those eyes never leaving mine. The leather formed a layer like a second skin, and I was suddenly very aware of how close to my curves he was, how nothing but that leather and the thin fabric of my undershirt were separating his skin from mine.

But I didn't move an inch. Not when he slid his fingers up then over the buckles to my other side, tracing the same path down with a trail of heat in its wake. Only when he reached the side of my other arm did he seem to breathe again.

"Pants next," he announced, placing both his hands on my hips in a featherlight touch.

The leather molded itself around my body where his hands moved lower, lower, until he needed to kneel in order to reach my knees, my calves, my ankles.

"We'll set out for the Seeing Forest after eating," he said, probably to distract me while his hands reached the inside of my thighs.

I swallowed, ignoring the unexpected rush that pushed my pulse into my throat. Just a touch to adjust the leathers. It meant nothing.

"Since we can't site-hop all the way there, we'll need to take a couple of hours to rest before we enter the Seeing Forest."

"What if they find us before we can get the artifact?"

His hands stilled mid-thigh, the leather stretching taut beneath his grasp.

"They won't. We'll lie low. I won't use my full powers, so they can't track me. We'll be in and out in no time."

How he could speak so casually, so reassuringly, when my focus had narrowed to where his fingers were sliding a few inches higher...

I stiffened—and he dropped his hands.

"I'm sorry." I didn't even know what for. The way my body seemed to have a mind of its own when it came to the unfamiliar closeness? Or the shame of reacting at all, craving to feel him trace that path all over again when I'd just broken free of Tristan.

Rogue sat back on his heels, clearing his throat. "I think that's enough."

Whether he was referring to touching me or the way my attire had changed, I couldn't tell. But the air had become thick and his gaze blazing gold.

He blinked, and it was gone. "Clio will be waiting."

Indeed, Clio *was* waiting with a full table when we came downstairs, Rogue trailing me as I tried not to let on how self-conscious I was in my new outfit.

"Well, don't you look stunning?" Clio flashed me a toothy grin as she gave me a once over. "Rogue must have paid very close attention to detail when adjusting those."

Rogue muttered something at her that sounded a lot like telling her to shut up.

Clio just laughed, offering me a glass of juice and a bowl of greens. "Help yourself to whatever meat you'd like." She pointed at the various slices distributed on simple plates.

Rogue chose the chair next to me while Clio sat in her usual spot, glancing at the empty one beside her every now and then.

"He's fine," Rogue commented when he caught her for the fifth time.

"You can't know that," Clio said around a mouthful of what looked like lamb.

"Clio always gets edgy when Tori is gone longer than a few hours," Rogue explained with slight amusement that I couldn't place.

I raised a brow at him, fork with speared green beans pausing in front of my mouth. "And you aren't?"

"Astorian is one of the best warriors this kingdom has to offer—and that was before he decided to leave our father's military and train with us instead." There was no pride in his tone, no jealousy. Just the raw acknowledgement of skill— Tori's, Clio's, and his own.

"I haven't seen you fight," I noted. Not with blades. With his power, yes. He'd battled his father for the upper hand in control over my body. I'd felt the raw force there, the abyss of power slumbering beneath that composed face.

"Then let's keep it that way," he suggested. "I'd hate for you to fret for my life."

"I thought you were one of the best." A challenge.

In response, Rogue smirked.

"He's most certainly one of the most obnoxious," Clio interjected. "And Tori *is* the best."

"You certainly like to use superlatives, Clio."

Clio stuck her tongue out at him, and I had to grin.

"That's not funny." Rogue shot me a look I couldn't quite place.

I laughed anyway, and the feeling of laughing, that even in this desperate moment of waiting for disaster to hit, they made me laugh... An unfamiliar sense of safety spread through me. The safety of a home, because of the life filling these walls, the obvious little family bickerings. The worry and concern for a friend's well-being. The way Rogue used his humor to distract Clio from it. All of it.

Rogue was still watching me when I finally led my fork to my mouth and continued eating.

I couldn't tell how much time passed as we finished the meal in silence, Clio and Rogue sharing glances of understanding that only people who were as close as they were could share. The sun hadn't reached its pinnacle when we finally shouldered our packs again. I patted the pocket of my jacket for my Mage Stone and pulled it out, just to make sure it was still there and glowing in dim rainbows.

"You'll need all the magic you can get," Rogue said, flicking his fingers and releasing a shimmering cascade of magic into the crystal.

I nodded my thanks.

From the threshold to the kitchen, Clio watched us with weary eyes. "I don't like staying behind."

"I know you don't." Rogue gave her a tight hug. "But you can't come to the Seeing Forest, and you can't go anywhere near the Crow in Cezux. Plus, you know Tori would lose his mind if you weren't here when he checks in."

The reluctance of leaving her here alone when she was obviously worried about Tori and would be worried even more about her brother was a subtle undercurrent in his voice.

Clio bobbed her head. "Be careful, Sanja. I'd hate to see him lose you so soon."

Before I could ask what she meant by that, she strode over, throwing her arms around me. "And I'd hate to lose you, too."

We left the cave on foot, his hand finding mine in the darkness of the tunnel and not letting go until we made it to the narrow gap that squeezed my rib cage into a miniature version of itself for a breathless moment. Then we were out, trailing the edge of the rock concealing Clio's home—Rogue's and Tori's true home. And a place I could consider calling home myself one day.

If we managed to bring down Cyrill—managed to grab that artifact from the Seeing Forest for Tristan and get ourselves a magically capable and experienced ally.

Rogue was unusually quiet as we crossed through the underbrush, not even his cocky grin falling into place as I complained about how hot those leathers were and told him that perhaps I should take them off and go for a swim in the nearest stream.

His focus remained on our surroundings, fairy ears picking up a whole world my human ears couldn't.

"We'll site-hop in short distances," he informed me as we came to a less dense part of the forest. "Your human legs are slowing us down too much." Not an accusation but a fact. If we wanted to get to Jezuin in time to stop the Crow, we couldn't afford to wait until my shorter, human legs caught up with his long, powerful fairy ones.

Rogue stopped, holding out a hand, and I placed mine in his without hesitation. The world fell away as he took us from the sun-flooded green of this forest to a darker, wilder part that had to be west of where we'd started, where I'd seen the Seeing Forest on the map of Askarea Tori had shown me what felt like a lifetime ago.

Rogue didn't let go of my hand this time, pulling me closer as the whispering of the leaves and branches folded around us like a canvas of magic.

"We'll hop another few miles then walk a few more before we rest." His eyes slid to mine, two golden orbs above that hood he'd pulled up before leaving the hideout.

By the time we arrived at a small clearing, it had gotten near dark, and I had to hold onto his hand not to stumble over the fallen tree trunks overgrown with moss and ferns. Rogue's grasp never faltered; he never got impatient when I had to climb over rocks he could simply leap over.

Only when we made it to the other end of the clearing did he stop, gesturing at a gap between three tall, thick trees. Rocks lay scattered around them, forming a narrow space shielded from view.

"We'll rest here." He released my hand, dropping his pack, and got to his knees to extract a bedroll, which he unfolded along the side of a long, slim rock.

When I didn't move, he glanced up, questions in his eyes.

"It's not a *lot* of space," I pointed out, gesturing between the trees and the boulders. Not more than the golden-sheeted bed in his room at the palace, I noticed.

Rogue seemed unimpressed. "It's all we need for a few hours. And I'd rather have you within arms' reach with all the dangers lingering in the forest."

The feel of blood and saliva dripping onto me from above flashed through me as I remembered the last time we'd been in the forest together after nightfall.

"Ledrynx?"

"Those and worse," he said without emotion. "And I can't risk drawing attention to us today. So no fires, no magic unless it's life or death."

Something in his tone told me that was a real possibility in this part of Askarea where everything seemed wilder, untamed—even more so than what I'd seen before.

He held out his hand for my pack, but, failing to see how there would be any alternative, I let it slide from my shoulders, getting to my knees to unfold my bedroll at the other side of our shelter.

Rogue watched me arrange the blankets, carefully leaving the most possible space between his bedroll and mine. Yet, no matter how many times I checked, the room didn't get any bigger, the distance merely enough for a pair of feet to stand.

So I did. I stood, Rogue unfolding to his full height next to me, his presence suddenly powerful, primal, overwhelming in this wild space of fairytales and nightmares.

I exhaled a slow breath, trying not to acknowledge the way my pulse thundered in my ears, how the phantom touch of his fingers lingered on my sides, my thighs—

"I will keep my hands to myself, Sanja," he murmured, scanning the surrounding treetops. A gust of air swept through the narrow space, cool after a day of travelling. "You can sleep."

I made a noncommittal sound that should have hidden the nervousness collecting in my stomach, driving me to splay my hand there—and become all too aware of the tight leathers all over again.

I'd taken care of my needs before our last hop, had washed my neck and face at a stream instead of bathing the way I yearned to do. So, besides gulping down a sip of water from the waterskin he offered and nibbling a few dried apple slices, there was little left for me to do than settle down and lie on my bedroll.

He remained on his feet for a few more breaths, monitoring the forest until he had convinced himself it was safe, then stretched out on his own bedroll, closing his eyes.

I wasn't sure what shocked me more—that he'd actually gone to sleep or that he felt comfortable doing so in my presence.

Perhaps, after everything we'd gone through together, he no longer felt the need to keep up his guard with me.

In the falling darkness, his brows and eyelashes seemed pitch black, his skin paler than in the sun. I wondered what he looked like under his mask—if his mouth was relaxed or if the tension from the day left it set and bracketed even in his sleep.

"I can practically feel your eyes on me, Sanja," he said on that dark breeze he hadn't used all day. But now—now that the night was creeping in, the dangers of the forest circling us, hopefully oblivious to our presence, it caressed the shell of my ear again as if he was laying right next to me—closer than he actually was. He didn't open his eyes, though.

And I couldn't look away. Not when, for the first time, we were working toward the exact same thing. We'd get the artifact; we'd defeat the Crow—*I'd* defeat the Crow. While he, with his immense power, was to stand by and watch me succeed or fail—and wouldn't be able to do anything to change it.

"You know that you're placing an unreasonable amount of trust in me," I told him, my voice whisked away by the dark breeze. For a moment, I considered what it had to feel like for him, to have my voice brought to his ear—if he could feel it the way I could with his.

The fact that he still didn't open his eyes as he said, "My life, Sanja. I trust you with my life," was enough to show me how serious he was about it.

"What if I can't get the artifact?" Because it was a possibility—one that made me so desperately want to succeed that my stomach tightened.

"We'll find another way." He rolled to the side so he was facing me, but his lids remained shut. "There's always another way. One that may result in more bloodshed than I initially hoped, but I'll find a way. Even if it takes another century."

A century. I'd be in a grave by then.

"What is it like to be immortal?"

My question hung there in the darkness as Rogue sighed beneath his mask. "Lonely... It used to be very lonely."

I curled my arm under my head as I shifted to my side as well. So little space between us. Even when I slid back until I felt the cool stone against my spine.

"What changed?"

His eyelids fluttered, and he gazed at me from hooded eyes. "I ran into a stray human in the borderlands and stole her jewelry."

My stomach did a nervous flip. Dangerous—this was a dangerous game we were playing.

His hand wandered the length of his ribs, over the belt loaded with blades he hadn't bothered to take off, and slid into the pocket of his leather pants where it lingered as if debating something. But he dropped it back to the blanket right in front of his chest, fingers grazing the edge of the stipe of forest ground between us.

His gaze strayed to my own hand, curled against my chest as if to keep warm even when I was only slowly cooling down enough to feel comfortable now that the sun had hidden for the night.

"We have a few hours before we need to continue." He folded his other arm beneath his head, mirroring my posture. His hood slid back, exposing a slight crease between his brows.

"You don't expect things to go well," I concluded.

For a long time, he said nothing. Then—"Depends on what you mean."

"What do *you* mean?"

He blinked, tugging on a young fern between fallen leaves. "There's a lot that can go wrong, Sanja. Not getting the artifact is just one of them."

"The Crows could detect us," I picked up his thought, running with it.

"That. And they could take you."

"What if they did?" He couldn't risk interfering when it would affect the bargain so badly and breaking it could demand more than just his life in return.

I wasn't sure he was breathing as he considered my question—considered what was safe to share and what wasn't.

With his life—he trusted me with his life. He would trust me with something as trivial as the truth.

"I would shred anything and everything standing in my path to get you back."

My mouth was suddenly dry, the leathers too tight around my body as I fidgeted for a comfortable position.

"Sometimes, I lie awake at night and wonder what it would be like to forget my obligations, Sanja."

"What would that be like?"

His gaze locked on mine, gold turned pale in the fading light. "I'd forget I'm not supposed to want you, Sanja. I'd forget, and damn the consequences." My breath caught, and his gaze flicked to my mouth. "I'd forget we are about to enter Crow territory. And spend the entire night making you forget, too."

The space between us had suddenly become too warm, the air too thick. My heart leaped into my throat, speeding uselessly as I tried to figure out what to do with my hands to prevent them from reaching for his mask, tugging it down to properly read him.

"Things might go wrong enough to demand both our lives tonight," I reminded him, voice shaking. "Perhaps forgetting is exactly what we both need."

That dark breeze brushed my cheek, my neck, driving a shiver up and down my spine.

"You don't know what you're asking for," he murmured, propping himself up on an elbow and glancing down at me from the shadows.

"It won't matter what I asked for if neither of us lives to tell the tale." My traitorous hand wandered to the edge of my bedroll where I curled it around the blanket to keep it from crossing that invisible boundary between us.

"So you expect to die, Sanja?" Worry, perhaps a hint of fear.

"I expect to not think about potentially dying until it's time to find out whether we'll survive the night."

Now, my hand did move. Slowly, it grazed the moss and tiny ferns between us, the rough material of his bedroll, the length of his arm—almost the way he'd touched me mere hours ago.

A hiss escaped his lips—surprise perhaps, but something more. "So you want me to make you forget?"

I found his biceps, his shoulder, his collarbone, the fabric of his mask—was about to grab it and pull.

He caught my hand before I could tug it down.

Make me forget I'd ever feared anything. Make me forget I was going into an unknown future where I could lose everything—including this new thing that had been growing between us. A tiny speck of more than his teasing, our banter. And I wasn't ready.

Keeping my hand trapped in one of his, he reached over the gap between us, pulling me onto his bedroll, my side flush against his front. The steel of his weapons pushed against my hip, my thigh, and he chuckled as I wiggled a few inches away.

He snapped his fingers, and the blades were gone—laid out between our bedrolls, a barrier I had no intention of crossing again, now that his warmth was radiating through my leathers—and he reached around me with both arms, freeing my hand as he purred, "I promised to keep my hands to myself, Sanja. But I never said anything about my arms or my fingers. If you want to forget"—he curled me against him, my back to his front, arms banding around me like a sweet layer of protection—"I can either hold you and hope you don't have nightmares about the Crows"—his mask slid over my cheek as he whispered in my ear—"or I can use my fingers, Sanja."

My body went taut in his embrace, heat flooding me that had nothing to do with the summer night. A small sound escaped my mouth as his fingertips brushed the side of my neck, my collarbone.

"Whichever you choose, Sanja, I can make it worth your while."

My choice—

His fingers stilled at the base of my throat, right above the first buckle of my jacket. My breasts turned heavy beneath the leather, and I arched into his touch, trying to get his fingers to slide lower.

I should tell him to just hold me, that his arms were enough to ward off the darkness and the fear. But the closeness, the tone of his voice, the way each word was more breathless than the last. The scent of rain and nights under open skies—

I glanced at the treetops above us, the star-scattered night beyond.

This might be our last night—and the darkness wouldn't mind if I gave in to that ache pooling in my core, commanding me to move closer, to feel the hard planes of his body against mine.

"Fingers," I whispered, barely able to believe I'd actually spoken.

His chuckle caressed the skin of my neck despite the mask—perhaps that dark breeze that was part of his power.

"What do you want me to do with them?"

Had I said I didn't whimper at his question, it would have been a lie. "Anything," I panted, pressing my knees together.

Rogue's laugh wasn't like anything I'd ever heard from him. A purr and a command all at once—and as his fingers retraced their path from this morning on the front of my jacket, I could have sworn he was shivering against me. "Anything?"

He lingered on my peaked breast, lazily circling as if he had all the time in the world. I arched into his touch, trying to get them to slide across that sensitive flesh—

"How about this..." He followed the line of buckles, each of them falling open under the graze of his power.

Night air rushed my skin through the thin undershirt as he peeled the sides apart enough to brush his knuckles over my nipple. I cried out a bit, my teeth catching the sound as they pressed into my lower lip.

Rogue's voice turned guttural as he traced my stomach all the way to the waistband of my pants with his other hand, the tight leather there. Lower. Until his fingers skimmed the point at the apex of my thighs. "Or this..."

More. I wanted more of this. More of him.

I rolled onto my back, trying to get him to slide even lower. But the steel length of him pushed against my hip, sending a thrill through my heated body. And every thought left my head as his fingers pressed down on the seam of my pants at my front, shifting until the friction was enough to forget who I was, where I was, where I'd be going in mere hours. He squeezed my breast in time with the circling between my legs. My hips ground against his fingers, brushing against the front of his pants again. Again.

He groaned, low in his throat, the sound summoning my gaze to his, to the gold that was nothing more than burning metal lost in shadows—and the mask beneath—

Once more, I was tempted to tug it down. But this time, I didn't care what was written on his features. I just wanted that mouth on mine, his tongue—

"Sanja—"

I pressed closer up against him, needing to feel that hard length of his. My hand grabbed for his hip, not quite able to reach without moving so much his fingers would be thrown off track between my thighs.

"This..." I slid my fingers down an inch until the leather of his pants stretched beneath them, and under that—"I want..."

His mouth crashed down on mine, mask still in place, preventing me from feeling more of those lips than the pressure, the movement. But his breath—

His breath was hot even through the fabric, mouth molding over mine.

He rubbed over my core. Faster. His hand continued roaming my breast, the leather of his half-gloves scraping over my nipple as he slid beneath my shirt, and I could barely make out the sound he made in his throat. A moan, soft and low. "I—" He detached himself from my lips, but I reached behind his neck, straight under his hood to where his hair was curling at his nape, pulling him back down, inhaling the scent of him until it filled my entire being.

Heart thundering in my chest, I splayed my hand on him, but he caught it, pinning it to his chest, a wicked chuckle all the explanation I got before he returned his fingers to massage that bundle of nerves that was throbbing for release.

"This," he said, his own breath cut short by that inconvenient kiss ... that only made me want him more. "It seems *this* is what you want me to do with my fingers." His voice was the open sky and the forest ground all at once.

I didn't get to tell him that *this* wasn't all I wanted, that I was far from done, that I wouldn't sleep before I got out of those leathers and had him inside of me.

My hand wandered back to his pants. Rogue swore, rolling me to my side so I lost access. But his fingers were relentless between my legs, the wetness there letting the leather slide enough to put him right back into that perfect spot.

I ground my ass against him, grasping the bedroll at the feel of granite against me.

"Fuck—" Rogue abandoned my breast for a brief moment, reaching behind my head, and his breath hit my skin in a gust of heat. I almost screamed with pleasure as his tongue licked up the column of my neck, his fingers returning to stroke and tease. "You'll be my demise, Sanja—" His lips traveled the side of my throat, my jaw, the corner of my mouth, until they molded mine into a kiss.

And the taste of him—

Release cascaded through me, turning me into a shivering bundle in his arms while his tongue thrust into my mouth. His fingers continued, gentle now that I'd become heavy, boneless. And his lips lingered on my mouth for a moment longer after his arms folded around me, tucking me against his chest even when that hard length of him remained solid against me.

I wriggled my hand free, reaching for him again, but he stopped me, gaze not leaving mine. His ragged breath caressed my face as he studied me in the dim moonlight, that predatory focus turning softer. "Next time, Sanja. Next time, you can touch me. But grant me this one memory where, for once, I did nothing for myself and all for you."

I had no words for him as he kissed my forehead before he pulled me in tight, chin resting on the top of my head, and lulled me to sleep with a quiet hum that reminded me of those golden sheets on his bed.

THIRTY-SIX

I was roused from my sleep by the efficient sounds of
Rogue packing up my bedroll.

"Is it time?" I yawned, limbs still heavy as though
the pleasure had freed the strains from the past months, and
relaxation carved its path from my toes to my fingertips.

"You can rest more." Hands stilling on the pack, Rogue
glanced at me over his shoulder. "We have an hour before we
need to leave."

"But you're not resting?"

His face was near-unreadable in the now fully settled
cover of night, even with the mask down.

"I've never been a good sleeper." Perhaps I imagined the
darkness in his tone, but something told me there was more
to it.

"Tell me about it." *I'm here,* I wanted to say. *Talk to me.*

Rogue closed the pack and returned to the bedroll we'd shared, kneeling by my hips. "One day, Sanja, I will tell you everything there is to know. Tonight, I'd rather leave the nightmares where they belong." His eyes wandered the length of my body, my open jacket, the places he'd touched.

Heat returned to my veins at the mere memory of it.

Rogue cleared his throat, hand on his weapons belt, which he'd buckled at his hips once more. "Perhaps we should just leave early and get it over with."

Anything that would stop my mind from returning to the feel of him against me, the taste of his lips—

My eyes drifted to his mouth, to the serious line it had become.

"Let's go," I agreed, sitting up and fiddling with the buckles of my jacket.

Rogue didn't offer to help, and I didn't ask.

A deep drink from the waterskin later, we were on our way through the thicket, Rogue's feet near-silent on the leafy ground while my own boots made plenty of noise that made me wonder why we hadn't summoned another Ledrynx.

"How much farther?"

"Not much."

Rogue bent aside branches in our path, ducking around thick, ancient trees and helping me over roots and boulders.

The occasional hoot of an owl mixed with the sounds of nocturnal creatures scurrying and skittering around us reminded me that this was the wilderness—and even the company of a powerful fairy wasn't enough to put me at ease.

We didn't speak for what had to be an hour or longer, until we got to a slow stream, its water gleaming silver where patches of moonlight filtered through the treetops.

"This is the border to the Seeing Forest," Rogue murmured.

Beautiful would have been an understatement. This glowing thread was like a necklace dropped in a mossy meadow and forgotten—illuminated by the open night sky above, it lay half overgrown with ferns, and a thick tree bent over it at the nearest bend like an ancient bridge. Eager to take a closer look at what could have been coincidence or of deliberate making, I took a step toward the tree.

Rogue caught my hand, a warning in his eyes as I faced him. He'd tugged his mask up before we'd left our little resting place, and, for some reason, it bothered me more than usual that I couldn't read all of his face.

"Don't let anything lure you in this forest. There are ancient forces at work whose attention you don't want to draw."

Of course not. The mesh of power, the artifacts, the Crows who were lingering in this place.

The fuzzy feeling of post-pleasure sleep had long left my body, and where release had made me shudder not too long ago, shivers of fear were now taking over my body.

"How do we know where to find the artifact?" If nothing else, it would be helpful to know at least that.

Rogue pulled me closer, pointing into the darkness ahead with his free hand. "Do you see the faint glow?" I shook my head. "You will once we cross the border. The artifacts are scattered throughout the forest. I can feel them through my powers. You should be able to sense them with your own magic as well."

Taking his words as an invitation to try, I pulled out my Mage Stone and focused on the pulsing that had become the crystal's familiar reaction to my touch.

"Let's cross the stream first," he said, letting go of my hand and backing up two steps before he took a powerful leap right to the other side of the silver band.

For a moment, I lost his shape in the darkness, and panic stirred in the bottom of my stomach. But his voice sounded from the other side. "Your turn."

I was about to ask him if he was serious. If I jumped in the darkness, I'd surely slip and stumble into the water or break my neck on one of those Guardians-forsaken rocks I'd tripped over along the path.

"I'll catch you." And when I didn't move? "I promise."

A fairy promise. Very well.

My stomach didn't feel any better when I backed up at least double as far as he had. I gave the stream a warning glare, hoping that—if this forest was sentient—it would help me get to the other side safely. It wasn't even that wide—a few feet. In broad daylight, I'd taken the leap without a second thought. But this was the Seeing Forest, and I was a human in the darkness. And I really didn't want to break my neck before I'd had a chance at getting that artifact for Tristan.

I tried not to think as I ran and jumped, the line of silver glimmering beneath me as I sailed over and—

A pair of arms caught me out of the air, and Rogue's scent wrapped around me as I landed against his hard front, almost tackling him to the ground.

I could hear the smirk in his voice, even when both the mask and the even thicker darkness on this side of the stream were concealing it.

"I should be insulted that you doubt I'd catch you—with or without promise." He let me slide down until my toes met the ground, hands lingering on my waist while I was catching my breath.

"Let's go." His hand found mine, and he led me toward a faint glow in the distance.

The Mage Stone continued pulsing between my fingers, picking up pace as we entered the Seeing Forest. Why it was called *Seeing*, I wasn't sure I wanted to know, but perhaps I should have asked.

As we made our way farther in, the light grew brighter, revealing massive branches crisscrossing between moss-covered trunks, shielding the root-scattered ground from the stars above. This was a world of its own—ancient and sleeping, and dangerous, more so even than the rest of Askarea—of which I'd seen so little.

Rogue's fingers tightened around mine at every crack in the underbrush, making me flinch, his voice a low murmur as he reassured me that we had nothing to fear as long as we stayed undetected.

So I breathed and kept setting one foot in front of the other, trusting *him* with *my life* for once. I didn't even let the fears of what could happen if the Crows noticed our presence take form. He'd done too good a job at putting me at ease earlier. If I wanted to stand a chance at using my magic to extract the artifact, I needed to keep my wits about me—or the chances that this indeed was our last night would increase.

"We'll take the artifact to Tristan as soon as you get it and we're out of this forest safely," Rogue narrated as he guided me around a fat tree trunk blocking our path. "I hope he really is as powerful as he says he is because, if he doesn't master that magic soon, we'll be too late to intercept the Crow in Cezux."

Cold that had nothing to do with the wind playing with my hair filled my body at how little time we had left.

The stone in my hand kept pulsing, gradually picking up pace as we neared the artifact, which was now a pale yellow spot on the horizon. I couldn't figure out its shape, but the sight, even from a distance, was enough to make me shudder.

"When we get there, all you need to do is grab the artifact while you channel your magic," Rogue explained. A bit late for my taste but better than not learning at all how to get it done.

"Channel it where? Do I need a spell? Or do I just think about that spot where the artifact is strung into the mesh?" Not that I had any idea how that worked—or what the *mesh* even looked like. So far, I'd not spotted any lines of magic that wove together in artful patterns—or even simple ones.

"We're going to take from the Seeing Forest. So we need to give back."

The glow was now strong enough to illuminate Rogue's face beneath his hood. Instead of following his gaze into the trees ahead, I studied his profile, the mask hiding that sensual mouth.

"Could you be more specific, please?"

His gaze locked on mine, stride never faltering as he led me forward. "Since you asked so nicely." The gold of his irises twinkled like rising suns. "You grab the artifact while you fill the empty spot with your magic."

I ignored the teasing tone. "And how am I about to *fill* it?"

"You channel."

Our hushed conversation was swept away on a rustling wind. Rogue stopped, holding a hand to his lips above the mask. The sound faded as if carried away on soundless wings, and we set in motion once more, Rogue's pace faster as if he was suddenly eager not to waste a moment.

Anxious not to lose my footing on the moist ground, I scrambled after him, clinging to his hand more for support than for direction. Rogue didn't comment when I tripped and stumbled into his back but simply waited until I stabilized myself before he continued at a slightly more moderate pace, his shoulders tense beneath the leather of his armor.

Then I saw it. Like haze dispersing with the first rays of sun, the glow took shape in front of us, and what I found—

I swallowed.

Rogue noted the horror on my face with a frown.

"I am to bring Tristan a human skull?" I wasn't sure I'd had enough breath in my lungs to make my words audible.

"It's not the worst we could have found," he commented, tugging me forward the final few feet.

I didn't dare ask what the worst could have been.

"Do they discard their brides by making them into artifacts?" A shiver ran down my spine at the look he gave me.

The skull was woven into strings of buttery light, the hollows of its eyes brightened where the magic ran through like an ornate spiderweb. I followed the threads to where they faded into nothing between the trees.

"So they just leave those *artifacts*"—I almost gagged on the word—"hanging around in their forest?"

He didn't answer my question. Instead, he said, "I can't touch it, or my magic will be detected. I can't even refill the empty spot once you pry it out."

I'd need to touch a skull. "How much magic is stored in this—" I gestured at the skull rather than naming it.

"A lot."

That thought alone made me nervous.

"It's not like I'm an expert on magic, but..."

"But what?" he prompted when I didn't continue.

"Well... It's a *big* skull, and I have a *tiny* Mage Stone."

"So you decide *now* is the time to acknowledge that size *does* matter?"

I gave him a humorless laugh.

"A tooth is all we need."

Not that it made me feel any better.

"How do I get it out?"

Rogue let go of my hand, pulling a tool from his belt that I'd only seen blacksmiths use to hold red-hot iron in the forge. Just much, much smaller.

"What's that?"

"Pliers. You use them to pull the tooth."

My stomach turned.

"Can't I just use magic?"

He raised a gilded brow. "I thought your Mage Stone was too tiny to fill that hole. Now you want to waste magic pulling the tooth?"

My response was a grimace, not a laugh. "Thank the Guardians, I have you at my disposal. I'm sure you won't mind refilling my stone if I drain it while extracting the tooth." A *tooth*. Tristan would use a human tooth for his magic.

I tried not to think about it as I shifted my gaze from the pliers to the skull, wondering which of them would be easiest to take—and settled on the last molar in the upper jaw, if only because I wouldn't need to worry that I'd rip off the entire thing the way I feared with the lower jawbone. Besides, it was only slightly bigger than a pea.

With a deep breath, I studied myself, fingers clasping the Mage Stone harder.

"*Dasteris*," I whispered into the light.

Rogue turned so still he could have been made of stone.

Nothing happened. Not even the slightest flicker of magic.

"Perhaps try the pliers after all?" he suggested.

Begrudgingly, I picked them from his hand and sighed. If I hadn't even been able to summon the tooth, how could I channel magic into its place once it'd been taken out?

"You'll need to be fast," he added. "Once the tooth is out, your magic must flow there immediately, or you'll trigger an alarm."

I didn't ask if there would be horns and trumpets announcing their presence or if the Crow Fairies would simply sweep in on silent wings and throttle us.

He jerked his chin at the skull suspended in midair by nothing more than visible magic, and I knew that I couldn't wait any longer—not if I wanted to reach Cezux in time with help. However we'd defeat the Crow there was for later, when I didn't need to pick a tooth from a dead person's fleshless mouth.

"All right..." Hand shaking, I lifted the pliers to the skull.

About a hundred things that could go wrong rushed my mind, making it hard to focus on the task at hand. What if the skull dropped from the mesh? What if the tooth didn't come loose? What if I damaged it? What—

"Focus." Rogue's voice brushed up against my ear. "You can do this."

I had to at least try. For Tristan, for Zelia and Dimar, for my kingdom. And for ... Rogue.

The last molar was easy to access without having to move the lower jawbone. The pliers slid over it from the side with a sickening *clack*. All I needed to do was fasten it and pull.

You can do this. His words echoed through my mind, and a warmth filled me at the thought that he might have said it, not to get me to do this because he had no other choice but because he truly believed in me.

I gritted my teeth, grasped the pliers hard, and pulled.

Like held by steel, the skull didn't move, but the molar loosened slightly under the strain. I pulled again.

In my other hand, the Mage Stone came to life, heating against my skin.

"Keep going," Rogue was now right behind me, hand on my back as if for support.

I held my breath as I threw all my strength into it and ripped the tooth out clean.

The crunch of it reluctantly sliding from the bone reverberated through me, making bile collect in my throat.

"Channel the magic."

Like with the poisons, I focused on where I wanted the magic to transfer, but as I eyed the hollow spot in the skull's denture, I could feel its pull, its demand for power. And the gap was vast.

The heat in my palm spread to my arm, along my shoulder, until it collected near the pliers in my other hand. Unable to bear the searing sensation of the metal against my skin, I dropped them, tooth and all. I couldn't tell if Rogue had noticed. His hand didn't leave my back.

"Channel it," he said, the urgency in his voice barely contained.

I trained my focus on the hole the tooth had left in the bone and let the magic flow.

The tug was instant, rough, and painful. But I ground my teeth, suddenly all too aware of the feel of the last molars rubbing over each other. Like a current of water, the magic streamed from me, from the crystal in one hand, through my body, leaving me through my other hand. Strings of light wove into each other where they met at the skull, braided and folded into one another until they formed something solid. A fraction at first, then more and more of a familiar shape grew from the bone. Grew and grew until what I'd ripped from the skull was glowing there once more—a magical, translucent tooth.

And my knees buckled.

THIRTY-SEVEN

Rogue's hands caught me at the waist as I swayed, but the flow of magic stopped, and I stabilized myself. I whirled out of his grasp to my knees, searching the ground for the tooth. Between moss and leaves and roots, it would be easily lost—

The pliers lay right by my toes. I pocketed my Mage Stone to have both hands free for searching, not wasting a thought on how much magic I'd spent on refilling the hole in the mesh. As long as it was done and I was still conscious, it couldn't have been a critical amount.

Cursing colorfully, Rogue joined me, his fingers nimbly combing through the leaves.

It would take forever to find it in this half-light. And with him being unable to use his powers...

"I dropped it when the heat—" As if that made it any better. It didn't matter why I'd dropped it. Only that it had disappeared somewhere by my foot, and I wasn't even standing where I had been when I'd dropped it.

For all that I knew, one of us could have already stomped it into the loose soil.

"Summon it." More command than I'd heard in weeks reverberated in Rogue's words.

I didn't think as I extracted the Mage Stone once more with shaky fingers, whispering, "*Dasteris*," and hoping the tiny thing would float into my open palm.

Nothing happened.

"Try again." Rogue had abandoned his search to monitor the trees surrounding us, tinted in the light of the woven magic.

So I did. "*Dasteris*."

Nothing.

Again and again, I whispered the word, scanning the blur of brown and gray that was the ground.

Rogue placed a hand on my shoulder. "We need to get out of here."

I heard the swish of wings only then, the rustling of leaves and twigs, and I knew that, this time, I wouldn't find a winged wild cat when I looked up but something more birdlike.

Shit. *Shit-shit-shit.*

Whatever had triggered the alarms, the crows were on the move—and Rogue couldn't be found here, or the treaty would be violated.

I debated for one heart-stopping moment.

"Go," I told him. "I'll be right behind you." At least I knew the direction we'd come from. It wasn't such a far walk. If I ran—considering I wouldn't break my legs stumbling and tripping over roots and rocks—I could make it out of Crow territory before they figured out what was going on.

"I can't leave you here. If they get their claws on you—"

"Then *I'll* be very dead. But you'll get to save Cezux for me."

He was about to argue.

"Promise," I pushed, looking up from the ground to meet his stare.

Uncompromising will stared back at me. "Summon it again."

I didn't move.

"Do it, Sanja. And I'll leave." Not a promise, but good enough.

"*Dasteris.*" Still nothing.

Rogue got to his feet. "I'll get out of sight so I'm not detected. But if you're not on your feet and running within moments, I'll come back and get you out. No matter the cost."

That, I could tell, was a promise.

He grabbed my hand, squeezing it.

Then he was gone. Not site-hopped away but running so fast all I could make out was a dark shadow blurring into the darkness that marked our path out.

"*Dasteris,*" I tried again in a whisper. "*Dasteris-dasteris--dasteris-dasteris.*"

The whisper of wings crossed over me again, circling. All I could hope was that the treetops provided enough cover to protect me from the Crow's prying eyes.

Please-please-please. If I'd ever prayed to the Guardians, it was now as my hand frantically ran over the ground around me while I kept repeating that magical word that should have brought the tooth to me.

Nothing happened.

Nothing—except for the murmur in the branches high up. I froze.

"Look what I found."

I knew that voice.

"A thief in our lands. A thief of magic."

My skin crawled as the Crow Fairy spoke again. "What has brought her here? Ret Relah is a long while off."

I could only hope Rogue had made it out now that the Crow had spotted me. If nothing else, I could be a distraction while he fled. Tristan wouldn't get his magic back, and I wouldn't be able to fight the Crow in Cezux with him. But Rogue would find another way to seal the borders and free his sister, his realm, and the human lands.

I'll come back and get you out. No matter the cost.

He couldn't. If he did, the bargain would take his life, mine perhaps, and strike in unpredictable ways I didn't even want to think about.

And just like that, the part of me that had already given up sprang back to life, growing claws and teeth and the will to fight.

My eyes snapped to the canopy of leaves, hoping to spot the crows large or little, I didn't care. Wings or no. But darkness was the only thing I found, the glow of the skull before me near blinding now that I focused on the absence of light.

"What does the thief want?" the Crow mused, and I could feel a pair of eyes on me like a deadly weight. "Or is she a tribute? A gift of the high fae for the masters of the forest, of the sky, of the night?"

My blood chilled in my veins as I debated running. But that day in the streets of Aceleau came back to me. Tristan's fear when he'd pressed his lips against mine, the apologies.

This bride is already taken.

"A tribute perhaps ... or an early bride."

I swallowed, scrambling for anything I could do. Anything that could give me an advantage.

I was weak, human, slow, my magic nearly drained. Not even the summoning spell worked.

But there was one spell that had worked before, even when I hadn't known what I was doing. Almost on instinct.

I grasped my Mage Stone harder.

"Let me see your face, little human," the Crow hissed from atop the trees. "Stand and show me what a lovely thing you are."

In my skin-tight leathers, with Rogue's scent all over me...

"Come see for yourself." I couldn't help the trembling in my voice.

Blindly, I dug my free hand into the ground, praying to the Guardians that the tooth would be in the loose soil between my fingers, and was about to get to my feet.

The Crow swept from the crown of leaves, wings spread wide as it banked to land on the other side of the skull.

Not a normal bird but much larger, wings as long as my arms ... and growing as it landed, head slowly turning human—part human. A beak sat where the nose should have been, eyes as black as a crow's filling the entire space beneath his lids. He was tall—almost as tall as Rogue, but his arms—they remained feathered, and his bare chest—

I struggled not to turn and run at the sight of the chain of teeth dangling from his neck to his navel.

By the flicker of magic.

"How good of you to already be kneeling. You will again once you fill that empty place in my home where my bride died so timely."

A muscle twitched in his powerful thighs, leather pants reflecting the glow of magic.

If he came a bit closer... Perhaps it was worth a try. At least, it would buy me some time to run.

"I haven't kneeled for anyone in my life," I seethed at him, not even trying to hide my disgust.

Crackling laugh hatching from his throat, he stalked around the skull, strings of magic parting where he crossed and knitting back together behind him.

I didn't back away, no matter how my instincts commanded me to. If I didn't handle this, the Crow would hunt me, and I'd be too slow. And Rogue would have to save me.

I was tired of being saved.

"Oh, you will be a delight to have at my home." The Crow stopped a good few strides away. Close enough to make my heart stutter a few breaths with peril. But was it close enough to strike?

I didn't dare wait another moment, for it would only allow the Crow to figure out that I wasn't petrified by its mere presence, that I was preparing to hit and run.

"What's your name?" He cocked his head, a flash of light crossing his black eyes.

But I had learned better than to give anyone my name.

"*Yetheruh*," I said instead.

A flash of light ripped from my palm, and I opened it just in time to direct it at the Crow. Had the tooth been there, it would be lost for good.

The Crow hissed a long curse that ended in a whimper.

I couldn't bring myself to care when all I could hope for was to incapacitate the Crow long enough for me to hurtle into the darkness, toward the Silver Stream, across it—to safety.

To Rogue.

The Crow screamed a caw, contracting into a much smaller form that was even less human, more bird, and fluttered a few feet closer. The scent of burnt hair and skin filled the air, and I knew I'd hit it. Perhaps not strong enough, but my magic had worked, and I'd gotten it enough to draw blood.

A thick streak of it trickled down the Crow's chest as he transformed back into his near-human form.

"Not a pliant bride then," he cawed.

I grabbled at the ground, my Mage Stone near sizzling in my other hand. *Come on—*

"*Dasteris*," I tried one last time, now that my magic had proven it still worked.

Something cool slid into my palm—not the tooth I'd hoped for, but the pliers.

I aimed and hurled them at the Crow, right at his face.

I didn't look back to see if it'd hit its mark but turned on my heels and ran. Across roots and rocks and slippery moss, blindly toward the stream which I could make out in the distance, a silver band, beckoning with the promise of safety. I didn't question why I was so much faster now than when I'd groped my way into Crow territory on Rogue's hand, but kept going, going, going faster, until my breath burned in my lungs and my face was strewn with little cuts from branches and twigs I couldn't avoid.

Behind me, the Crow's footfalls spurred me on, each step a whip promising a future of pain and devastation. A predator herding his prey.

I'd lived both. Had lived pain at the hand of Rogue's father—had gone into his challenges, knowing they'd be torture—and devastation at Cyrill's hand. Every new day as his saint was a day of helplessness, of choices that would only hurt others.

Did that make me fear them any less?

If anything, they made my feet fly, my heart push to its limits, and my legs pump along the path, fingers painful around the Mage Stone. Above, the rustling of leaves and quiet groans of wood followed me like a presence of its own, and all I could wish for was that, if another Crow had joined the hunt, they would make it quick.

Before me, the stream stretched wide, bathed in moonlight and shimmering what had to be eons of stars. Unnatural, stronger than when we'd crossed into the forest. Had I not feared for my life, I might have taken a moment to marvel. With the Crow on my heels, I pushed myself the final few steps, lying to my weak, human body that it could rest soon.

"Wait, little bride," the Crow said from too close behind me.

I staggered right as I nearly jumped out of my skin, losing my footing enough to not make the full leap but crash into the water, shoulder and knee hitting the stones beneath the surface. But I managed to hold my breath.

Like icy, silken arms, it wrapped around me, dragging and shoving with its currents that seemed to flow in both directions. My shoulder screamed with pain, and the leather on my knee had probably scraped off alongside my skin. Yet, I scrambled to my knees until the water didn't reach higher than my waist. My fingers curled more tightly around the crystal—the last defense I had—preventing it from slipping from my wet grasp.

A snapping twig drew my attention.

The Crow sat, crouching by the side of the stream. The feathers on one of his arms had been singed off, leaving the view of powerful muscle beneath angry skin. In a voice more human than I'd ever heard him, he said, "I have a dry bed for you to rest in, bride. You won't need to kneel there."

But in his eyes, malice gleamed—that, and vengeance.

I gave him my best, vicious grin as I lifted my free palm toward him and said, "*Yetheruh*," and silver shooting from my hand speared him like a spike of hot iron.

The Crow's black eyes grew wide, a scream tearing from his beak. Taloned hands clawed at the light, reaching through it as if it were nothing more than a beam of starlight. But he howled in agony, knees buckling as blood oozed around the light. I could have sworn a curse wove into his screams, but I was too shocked to speak or move or even think. All I could do was stand there and stare, mouth open and heart racing in my throat.

I was still gaping when he toppled over, face first, to the ground, no longer heaving painful, rattling breaths, and a pair of hands pulled me from the water.

Panic seized me all over again, and I was thrashing against the grasp, legs kicking blindly, uncoordinatedly. My clammy fingers secured the Mage Stone in a fist, ready to strike, and a scream built in my lungs.

It had worked its way half into my throat when the scent of rain and nights under open skies hit my nose, and everything inside me went silent. He murmured, "Be quiet, Sanja. You'll wake the entire forest."

Before I could sigh a breath of relief, Rogue gathered me in his arms and ran.

The forest turned into a blur of darkness around us, my head swimming with exhaustion ... and a bit of nausea, perhaps ... at the swaying of his movements. He didn't stop until we left the dense patches of trees and made it into a clearing.

He didn't set me down as he surveyed the seam of underbrush surrounding it—for danger or the right path, I couldn't tell. But my stomach eased as the swaying stopped, and his strong hands grasped me tighter.

"Your knee's bleeding," he said without looking at me.

The pulsing pain made itself known as if called back to life at his mention. I gasped.

Rogue's gaze slid to mine. "What, by the flicker of magic, happened?"

A loaded question—the answer to which I didn't know. "I got us out alive," I mumbled.

Once more, I wished I could pull down that mask and study his face—for his eyes yielded nothing.

He didn't ask again before he site-hopped us to the base of a rock—Clio's rock, I realized—and carried me to the narrow gap that was the entrance.

"Why can't you site-hop me inside the way Tori does?" I asked as I braced my hand against the cool stone to take the weight of my injured leg.

He merely gestured at the entrance and said, "I don't want to leave a trace that could be detected. Astorian is strong, but the power of royalty is so much stronger. While he leaves a pale line of ink that blurs into water, I leave a solid streak of gold on iron if I use my full powers. I won't risk it."

"But you risk site-hopping *to* the hideout?"

"I could be in this forest for many reasons. One of them the nearby lake—perfect for taking a naked bath in the moonlight by the way." His tone gave away the feral grin behind his mask. But his eyes fell to my fisted hand, the leather strings of my Mage Stone dangling from it where it pushed into the rock, down to my shoulder, my knee. "Let's get inside."

ANGELINA J. STEFFORT

THIRTY-EIGHT

Clio was sitting by the window overlooking the small meadow behind the house when we arrived, teacup in hand and a tight expression on her face.

She took one look at me as Rogue carried me in through the door and opened her arms for him to dump me into—which he didn't. Instead, he carried me to the settee by the wall and gently laid me down.

"Knee, shoulder—head, potentially," he said to Clio, his gaze never straying from mine.

He'd scooped me up once I'd pushed through the rib-crushing magic of the cave entrance ... dismissing my objections that I could walk on my own once he'd watched me limp and wince a few steps.

"Just because you *can* doesn't mean you *should.*" With those words, he'd lifted me into his arms, and I hadn't found it in me to be upset with him.

Instead, I wondered how many times he'd told himself those same words. When he'd debated ending his father's power over Askarea and shaping the bargain with the Crows into something less dangerous? When he'd watched his father torture me, knowing that a flick of his fingers could have spared me? When he'd hesitated before leaving the shelter of the cave, gaze wandering my face and golden eyes blazing?

Clio rushed to his side, her hands diving behind my neck, gently probing the base of my skull with her fingertips—and her magic, I realized as warmth spread beneath my hair, trickling down my spine, into my limbs.

"Move your leg," she instructed. I did. To my surprise, the sharp pain was gone.

Clio turned to her brother. "You could have done that yourself in the forest."

Rogue pulled down his mask, frowning.

"Yes, you could have," I seconded Clio's statement. "Or is healing also one of those powers unique to royalty that make you traceable? I've seen you use enough magic around this house to doubt it would make any difference."

It would certainly have spared me needing to hobble through the gap.

"It's not that. There are different types of magic, Sanja. Some, like site-hopping, only warp the world around us, but there are others that enter the body when applied. Like healing magic. Rogue is just careful not to—"

Rogue cut her a glance that silenced her.

I didn't dare ask what he'd been careful about.

"How about you tell me what happened?" Clio offered instead, face softening as she looked me over, hair still wet and leathers torn at my knee.

She flicked a finger, and a towel appeared in her hand. "You could have thought of this, too," she told Rogue with a sideways glance, who was again studying me with that un-readable face.

Taking the towel from Clio's hands, he perched on the edge of the settee, lifting my head with one hand while he placed the towel beneath to catch my dripping braid.

"You can grab whatever you like from my wardrobe as soon as you tell me what happened," Clio said with little patience for her brother's silence—or mine—as I observed the set of his jaw, the curve of his mouth unwilling to speak. And the questions in his eyes.

"A Crow found us and—"

"A Crow?" Horror filled Clio's features. But she flapped her hand over her mouth to stop herself from launching into a tirade.

"I don't know if we triggered wards or if he was there by coincidence—"

"You really believe in coincidences when it comes to the Crows?" She couldn't help it.

I merely nodded, and Rogue again gave her a silenc-ing look.

"Since I wasn't there the whole time, I'd like to know the rest of the story myself, Clio. So if you don't mind—"

Clio cut him off, eyes wide, "You left her alone in the Seeing Forest?"

Before Rogue could grind out more than a growl of warning, I said, "I sent him away."

Now, Clio gave me a look as if I'd lost my mind.

"The Crows couldn't find him there, or the bargain would be broken," I reminded her, reminded myself, and Rogue, whose face had turned mildly green. "I couldn't just let that happen, could I?"

Clio's gaze wandered back and forth between Rogue and me, a question building behind those Jade irises.

Rogue shook his head at her, and whatever she'd been about to ask, she let it go.

"I extracted the artifact." It was easier to say than *tooth*— from a *skull*. "And then I accidentally dropped it. The Crow showed up only moments after Rogue disappeared. It wanted to take me back to its home as a bride, but I attacked it with my magic."

Rogue's face hardened, a flicker of that powerful fairy king flashing in his eyes, the gold near-liquid in the soft fairy light illuminating the room. "I told you I'd come back for you..." His voice trailed away.

"I didn't want you to have to come back, Rogue. You shouldn't be risking your life, your realm, your entire people for me."

I could have sworn the floor trembled as he said. "Let me be the judge of what I'm willing to risk."

For me—what he'd be willing to risk for me.

His hands squeezed water from my braid into the towel before letting go.

"When my magic wasn't enough, I threw the pliers at him and ran." An echo of panic flooded me, making me shiver in my wet clothes.

Clio conjured a blanket, draping it over me.

"Then I fell into the stream, and the Crow almost got me. But I used my magic again and it"—I met Rogue's gaze, reading the wonder there—"was so much more than the Mage Stone could ever hold."

Clio cleared her throat. "You fell into the Silver Stream?"

Rogue nodded in my place. "And she channeled the moonlight within it into a solid spear of magic."

Had I not felt the power thrum through me, not seen it pierce the Crow's heart, bringing it down, his words wouldn't have made sense to me. But they felt right. True. And that was perhaps scarier than the fact that I'd killed a creature even the most powerful fairy in Askarea feared.

Clio and Rogue shared a look I couldn't read.

Exhaustion made my voice weaker than I'd hoped when I asked, "Can anyone explain to me what happened there, in the stream?"

Rogue sighed through his nose. "You're from an ancient bloodline of Mages, Sanja. The very line who first learned to use magic and store it. The magic of the Crows might have something to do with it, but it's more likely the blood of your ancestors ran through you when you dropped into that water."

"The way it's running through my veins now," I clarified.

Both Rogue and Clio shook their heads. "At the Ultimate Sacrifice, the Mages bled into the very soil of Askarea. Some say the Silver Stream is one of the few places left where their blood remains on the surface."

The water soaking my leathers, my hair, my skin, suddenly felt like grime. I'd bathed in blood; in magical blood.

Nausea made itself known with a jolt in my stomach. I shot into a sitting position, gagging.

"I've never seen anything like it before," Rogue admitted. "And I don't know if this was a one-time occurrence or if you could do it again."

"I'm not going anywhere near the Seeing Forest ever again ... until it's time to seal the borders for good," I amended. Letting him know I hadn't forgotten my promise. "If that Silver Stream is the answer to our problems, so be it. I'll happily take any help I can get." As a human between immortal fairies, between power and mighty magic ... I'd take any ounce of aid so I'd survive. "Especially when we won't be able to count on Tristan," I added in an afterthought.

Rogue raised a brow, and his lips twitched as he reached into his pocket, extracting a tiny, ivory object.

"How—"

"I went back when you bolted from the fairy and led him away. I'd seen your magic, what you are capable of, how creatively you assaulted him with the pliers. It was right there in the moss, waiting for me to pluck it."

My mouth fell open as I took in the sight of the tooth between his long fingers.

Not in vain—this trip hadn't been in vain, and I hadn't risked all our lives for nothing. Breath rushed from me in a choked laugh.

"It's tiny," I said, meeting Rogue's gaze over the tooth.

"But powerful. If you know how to wield it."

I didn't point out that he'd failed to inform me about anything regarding size. But the dark breeze of his power caressed my cheek, the shell of my ear as he murmured with less humor than expected. "One can achieve incredible things with something tiny if they know how to use it, Sanja. But imagine what can be done when size and skill match..."

I couldn't help but blush at the tone, at the memory of him granite-hard against my backside. A chuckle licked down my throat then faded.

Clio rolled her eyes. "Have the decency to speak out loud in the presence of others, brother."

Rogue winked at me, pocketing the tooth again. But the humor had already left his features. "Any news from Tori?"

The fidgeting of Clio's fingers was the only reason I noticed how worried she was about the male—the mate she wasn't able to be with even when she was with him every day. "He reported back half an hour ago," she said, leaning over to wipe a smudge of dust off the nearby shelf. "The Crow is fast. But it hasn't gotten near Jezuin yet. That will take another day or two at least."

The tension in my stomach eased as Rogue let out a slow breath.

Time wasn't on our side, but it wasn't breaking our necks yet. We'd returned from the Seeing Forest before dawn *with* the artifact for Tristan. Now we could get to the Hollow Mountains and craft a plan.

As if having the same thought, Rogue held out his hand. "Let's get you into something dry," he said, but I took one look at that face, the soft golden glow of his eyes as he scanned the length of my wet body where the blanket had slipped—and decided that Clio was the safer option.

In her room, Clio pulled out an assortment of pants and shirts, all good for lounging in a chair and reading, but not for what lay ahead.

"You should take a rest before you set out to the Hollow Mountains," she explained when I asked why I didn't get any dry leathers. "Besides, we'll need to recharge your Mage Stone." She eyed my fist—the one I hadn't unclenched since the Seeing Forest.

She flicked her hand, and a cascade of light spiraled into my fist like swirling stars. Different from the raw power of Rogue's glimmering magic; more bubbly, crisper somehow. She gave me a knowing look. "I've had a lot of time on my hands over the past decades," she said with a shrug.

My heart turned heavy at the thought of what this female had endured, at how she'd done so all by herself, even with her brother and Tori holding her hand on occasion. She was still mostly alone.

Like me, a voice whispered deep inside me.

"I'm sorry, Clio." I placed my free hand on her forearm.

She gave me a half-smile—one that came from the bottom of her voluminous heart that had opened up to a human with prejudice and distrust and so much fear ... and never once judged.

"Don't be sorry," she told me, the second half of her mouth curving as well. "If there's anything to be sorry about, it's usually Rogue's fault ... or Tori's. Or both."

I laughed, and the sound startled me so much that it turned into a cough.

Before sending me to take a hot bath, Clio helped me peel out of the leathers when I got stuck at the legs. She sat on the edge of the bed, chatting with me while I soaked in the water, if only for a little while to battle the heaviness in my bones.

"It's from the excessive use of magic," she explained when I told her how often I'd used my Mage Stone. "Using spells will always drain you—some faster than others."

"Is it the same for fairies?" Perhaps a silly question, but no one had ever truly explained the difference to me, except that fairies had magic at their disposal without needing any external *storage*. And that Mages could create potions in a way fairies couldn't.

"It's the same with all magic, Sanja. It's about balance. If we exert ourselves, we need to rest and rebuild our strength as well. Sleep will help, the right foods. But eventually, every magic has its limit."

"Even Rogue's?" As the most powerful fairy in Askarea, he had to be different in some way.

"Even Rogue's. But he could raze all of Aceleau, perhaps all of Askarea if he so wished, before he'd even need to take a nap."

Something shuddered awake in me. So much power. Yet, he didn't use it against his enemies.

"Has he ever considered doing just that? Wipe the board, including the Crows, and start over?"

Clio was silent for a long moment as I closed my eyes, trying to tune out the images of the Crow approaching me, of the glowing skull, the searing heat of my magic when it had attacked. When I turned my head, she was gazing out the window.

"He would never do that. Even one innocent life lost is too much for Rogue. That's why he'd rather become the one-syllable bandit than the mighty king. Here, he has the free-dom to take from those who have too much, to give to those in need, to help in small ways without assaulting Askarea with his power."

Her words made me think, weigh what I knew about the male who'd once stolen from me ... who'd kissed me mere hours ago.

You'll be my demise, Sanja.

I sank under the surface, trying to rinse off the feel of his touch ... the way my body seemed to come to life at the mere thought of it.

Grant me this one memory where, for once, I did nothing for myself and all for you.

I scrubbed at my scalp, just to keep my hands busy, keep-ing my head under water one moment longer.

When I came up again, Clio had lain back on the bed, staring at the ceiling.

"He used to run from his power, Sanja, you know? But things have changed since you arrived in Askarea. *He* has changed."

I didn't dare ask in what way, and Clio didn't offer any more information.

The bathwater had turned lukewarm by the time I heaved myself out, exhaustion making it almost impossible to get to my feet. But Clio was there with a towel and an encouraging word. At least, my knee and shoulder no longer hurt, thanks to whatever magic Clio had infused in me—that Rogue had refrained from. I'd need to ask him about that some other time.

"Tell me about Tori," I said when I was finally dressed in a long pair of pants and a soft, breathable long-sleeved shirt and curled up on her bed where she'd beckoned me and draped a blanket over me.

Clio tossed her copper braid back over her shoulder, slipping onto the bed beside me where she folded into a cross-legged seat. "There is nothing much to say."

"How did you meet?"

Her eyes grew softer, nostalgic perhaps. "When Rogue and I were little, we played hide and seek in the palace all the time. Much to our parents' chagrin. Father was more interested in politics than family, and Mother... She was a sweet soul. So much like Rogue, except for the hair. I have her hair." She gave me a meaningful glance, but all I could think about was that someone had called the most powerful fairy in Askarea, the male the realms shuddered from, a sweet soul—and that it no longer shocked me.

"Tori's father spent most of the time with ours, leaving Tori in the care of his governess." She leaned in an inch as if sharing a secret. "A bitchy creature if you ask me. So it's no wonder he ran and hid at every opportunity." Her lips curved. "I wasn't even old enough to wield a knife when I was searching for Rogue—and found Tori instead. Imagine Tori, gangly and entirely out of proportion with his slow transition into adolescence."

And I could see it—the powerful male, his limbs more boy than man, his eyes unsure, his features softer, rounder. And that auburn hair like a shock of fire atop his head.

"I'd seen him in the palace plenty of times but always in the presence of his governess. Or he'd been playing with Rogue, and I wasn't allowed to join because I was too young and a female, and all those stupid conventions that ruled my parents' court when we were young."

So similar to my own court, to what little voice I'd had as a princess, despite the inheritance of the throne lingering in my future.

"He pestered Rogue to let me join for playing until Rogue gave in, and the three of us were inseparable for long decades. We started working on this dream ... of a free Askarea, of a just realm where fairies had equal rights, no matter their gender or color, their power or background. And together, we grew into adults. And that friendship with Tori turned into more."

A hint of pain tugged the corners of her lips down, and she fell silent.

"And now?" I knew what had happened. Tori had told me the quintessence. But she'd been there for me; both of them had. And there was nothing I could give back other than a few moments of listening to her speak if she needed to talk.

Clio sighed, a smile forming on her lips that didn't meet her eyes. "He has a life outside these walls when mine will be confined to them for the foreseeable future. I don't want to tie him down."

Not wanting to pry, I didn't ask any further questions, but her words echoed inside me again as I drifted off, nestled into the soft blanket in the safety of their home.

THIRTY-NINE

The low murmur of voices from downstairs greeted me when I woke to an assault of bright morning light. I remembered immediately what had happened: the forest, the Crow, the Silver Stream, the tooth.

Shaking off the heaviness in my bones, I rolled out of bed, padding to the open door and peering over the banister of the stairs to spot Clio, Tori, and Rogue—the latter with a glass in his hand and a frown on his features.

"It's been making faster progress than expected. I've been following it at a good distance so I won't get detected, but it's hard to keep up with my magic restricted in the human lands," Tori's voice drifted toward me.

"If he does this much longer, he could suffer severe damage," Clio said to Rogue—to her king, who'd given the order for Tori to follow the Crow, I realized.

An interesting balance of friendship, family, and hierarchy, where Rogue would need to weigh what he could lose against what he could gain.

Because I've lost too many things in the past, and I couldn't afford to lose anything else.

The memory of his words brushed something dark and tired inside of me, stirring it, and as if in response, he lifted his head, finding my gaze across the length of the stairwell.

"Sanja risked everything to get that damn tooth for the Mage. The least we can do is help her stop the Crow before it destroys Jezuin."

Tori hummed his agreement. "I'm all right, Clio. A couple of site-hops to the human lands aren't enough to bring me down."

Rogue was still studying me when I descended the stairs and joined them.

Indeed, Tori's face was drawn, and he looked a little worse for wear. But he grinned at me anyway.

"I've heard you pinned a Crow to the forest ground. Good for you."

I wasn't certain if thanks were in order, so I merely inclined my head at him.

"When are we leaving?" I wasn't sure if I was asking Rogue or Tori, but Tori waved a hand, indicating that he'd be leaving on his own, and Clio hissed at him as if that could stop the male.

Rogue, however, continued to study me even when Tori popped out of existence after a dismissive gesture of his hand and Clio's sudden eagerness to find minted water.

"What's wrong?" I eventually asked when we were alone and my stomach threatened to tear from tension.

He cocked his head. "You look tired. Perhaps we should wait."

Wait—"For what?" Until my kingdom was doomed and the Crow would wreak havoc. "I slept enough. I'm even wearing intact clothes." I gestured down my body where Clio's pants and shirt were hanging loosely around my form.

Rogue raised a brow, and I noticed that he looked like he hadn't rested at all.

"I brought you new leathers that should fit," he said, snapping his fingers, and a pile of dark fabric appeared on the nearest chair from where he was leaning against the wood-paneled wall. "Change, and we can be on our way. Tristan will be delighted to get his new magic source, and you'll have someone who can actually help you defeat Cyrill." The disgruntled expression on his features made me want to ask again what was wrong.

But, he gestured at the leathers, and I picked them up, heading to Clio's room to change.

When I returned, Rogue was standing by the window, arms folded across his chest and eyes on the rock at the end of the meadow. I cleared my throat, and he turned, scanning me top to bottom, the tight fit of the leathers, the belt at my hips with enough room for three blades on each side.

An emotion flickered over his features, but he pulled up his mask and strode to the door. "Let's get it over with."

Whether he meant the Crow or Tristan, I couldn't tell. But when I marched outside behind him, his shoulders were tight, his fingers curled at his sides.

As we entered the dim tunnel leading to the gap in the rock, he took my hand, thumb sliding over the back of my palm as he led me out of Clio's hideout—his *home*, as he'd once called it.

Outside the stone walls, we marched along the thicket framing it until we were far enough away for him to deem it safe to site-hop.

But I asked, "Aren't you worried anyone will track you to the Hollow Mountains if you use your power to get us there?"

He halted, turned, his front so close that I could feel his warmth overpowering that of the late summer morning. "There are many reasons for me to go to the Hollow Mountains that have nothing to do with the Mages dwelling there."

I didn't balk at his tone, the darkness filling his eyes. "Like what?" I prompted, wondering if I'd been wrong that one moment when he'd ripped off his mask and kissed me. That there had been more than the mere distraction from what we'd been about to do, the danger we'd submitted ourselves to. Perhaps I should have hoped that had been all.

His gaze was unreadable as he said, "I'm the king of these lands, Sanja. I need to keep myself informed on the state of my quarries in case I want to build a new palace ... or a city.

No one will follow me there from suspicion. I've even sent craftspeople to the Mountains before—long before the Mages ever settled there, don't worry—to have them figure out how to revive the quarry for a huge construction project."

"You want to build a city?" Not that it mattered.

"Perhaps it's time someone built one. Aceleau has been the seat of power for a long time, but imagine an Askarea where humans are welcome and trade with Tavras and Cezux is not life-threatening for merchants... How would you feel about a settlement in the borderlands that belonged to both humans and fairies?"

I didn't know what to say. So I grasped his hand more tightly and waited for him to spirit us away.

We hit the glimmering floor of the large cave mere moments later, my heart hammering hard at the anticipation of bringing Tristan what he so desperately desired and gaining the aid of his power to kick Cyrill out of my palace.

Neither of the Mages greeted us this time, probably busy elsewhere.

Before I could move away from him, Rogue wrapped that dark breeze around us, holding my gaze as I raised my brows at him.

"I was there last night before you ran ... in the trees nearby, you know," he said. "I saw everything ... heard every vile word, every threat the Crow made." His voice trembled. "I was ready to eradicate him with my power, no matter the cost."

I swallowed at the glow in his irises, a reflection of the lights bouncing off the glimmering stone. But it could as well have been a fire of its own.

"I followed you in the treetops, debating when to drop and take him out."

So it had been him—the sound above me when I'd been running, fearing to have attracted another Crow. It had been Rogue watching over me—risking everything by staying close enough to step in.

I swallowed, sliding my hand out of his.

The fire in his eyes guttered, and for a brief moment, I could see him. The real him, deep down, buried behind walls and masks and carefully crafted pretenses—

"Thank you." I rose to my toes, stabilizing myself against his biceps as I brushed my mouth to his cheek. It was brief, and the mask separating our touch was rough against my lips.

As I pulled away, Rogue's eyes closed for a silent moment.

Then, he stepped aside, gesturing at the tunnel to the kitchen.

We followed the smell of cinnamon and Leeneae announcing that we'd chosen the right direction. Rogue didn't speak the entire walk, letting me enter the kitchen first, and Tristan's eyes found me immediately, followed by Dimar's wide ones and Zelia's skeptical ones.

"Thank the Guardians, you're all right." Dimar folded me into a hug the moment he leaped up from his chair and met me mid-room. "We assumed the worst when you just disappeared during our last training and didn't return yesterday."

The worst—

My eyes slid to Rogue, who was leaning against the stone wall, a thoughtful expression on his face. For a moment, he held my gaze. Then he slid his hand into his pocket—the one where he'd stored the tooth. I noticed only now that he was no longer in the clothes of the bandit but in his finery. He must have changed them with the help of his near-infinite power while I'd already stepped into the kitchen and he'd remained in the darkness a moment longer. When he spotted the silent question in my eyes, he cocked his head as if asking why I was surprised.

Of course, he'd hide the bandit from them, no matter how we were working together to free Cezux and end that damn Crow Fairy bargain. The Mages might have been his allies, but they were not his friends.

"What happened?" Zelia wanted to know. She'd gotten to her feet behind the row of bowls with dried herbs. They'd been restocking their supplies over the months they'd been spending here. Months... I could barely believe that I'd been separated from them for such a long time. And Tristan...

Tristan studied me from his chair, eyes wary. "You look different."

An assessment of my new attire, perhaps; but his gaze lingered on my face, not on my leathers.

I mustered a shrug under the scrutiny of those eyes that had been my world until not so long ago. "A lot has happened since I summoned a pot-worth of peas."

From the corner of my eye, I watched Rogue's lips twitch with amusement—for a fraction of a moment. Then his face iced over, and he pushed away from the wall, strolling to my side. "While you've been peeling potatoes, my dear Sanja has been fighting Crows and summoned dental residues from the unholy place that is the Seeing Forest."

I could have sworn Tristan paled before he got to his feet, eyes glimmering almost as much as the walls as he completely dismissed Rogue, turning to me instead. "You got the artifact? I thought I was supposed to go with you."

"Change of plans," Rogue informed him without offering any further explanations.

Dimar cleared his throat. "It seems there's always a change of plans with you, King."

Rogue chuckle, the sound slithering down my neck, my spine, like a cold caress. "Would you rather I'd have stuck to the initial one and left your precious human territory to the mercy of the Crows?"

Horror flickered across Dimar's face while Zelia braced her hands on the table, the voice of the Master Mage snapping back into place as she demanded, "Tell me everything, Recienne."

To my surprise, Rogue left out no detail when he indulged Zelia with the story of what had happened since we'd crossed the Silver Stream—except, of course, the little secret he'd admitted to me only when we'd arrived at the glimmering caves—that he'd returned to watch over me, that he'd have ripped the Seeing Forest to shreds had the Crow touched me. He also left out that I'd channeled their magic from the Silver Stream—the blood of my ancestors.

I shuddered.

Dimar sat down halfway through the story, his hands balled into fists and assessing Rogue as if for a weak spot to ram his curved knife into.

"You left her behind all on her own?" Tristan prompted, fury burning behind those troubled eyes. "In the presence of a Crow?"

Rogue merely flashed his teeth. "I wasn't aware she was still your concern, Tristan."

Tristan made a rumbling noise that reminded me of the growl of a wolf.

"As far as I remember, my dear Sanja here has made herself very clear regarding where she stands." Rogue grinned—*grinned*—at me before he pinned Tristan with a gaze that made the room turn a degree or two colder. "And as far as I remember, all you care for is getting your magic back. So here it is." He pulled his hand from his pocket, flipping the tooth at Tristan, who wasn't quick enough to catch it and watched it roll over the floor with near-inaudible clicks.

The sound drove a chill through my body.

"Is this—" Dimar didn't get any further, spellbound by Tristan dropping to his hands and knees to crawl after the answer to his lost power.

Something like pity pulsed through me, but it was gone when Tristan's fingers closed around the tooth, and his eyes met mine—the eagerness there, the greed. As if he were a starving man going after a piece of roast meat.

"A human tooth? It is," Rogue informed Dimar, who was still gaping at the tiny item in Tristan's hand.

"How does it work?" Tristan wanted to know, still on his knees as he twirled and twisted the tooth that now replaced his Mage Stone between his fingers.

"Really? That's your first question? How does it work?" Rogue took a casual step toward Tristan, staring down with hard golden eyes. "Not, 'Whose tooth is it?'"

Tristan lifted his head, gaze meeting Rogue's with equal hardness, and I could have sworn the troubled blue turned a shade darker. "Does it matter?"

It didn't—not in the greater picture.

Rogue continued anyway. "It was a *bride's*. A human woman who was unlucky enough to spend Ret Relah out of her home and lacking the company of a male companion to claim her as *his*." The bite in his voice was enough to draw my gaze—and find him measuring me. "She was taken to the Seeing Forest and made a Crow bride. Was bathed in a lake of tears, crowned with a crown of carved teeth, slept in a bed of skin, and"—his throat bobbed—"the rest is history. So ... congratulations, Tristan. You are now in the proud possession of a Crow artifact. A new source of magic that will be keyed to you once you get it to respond—almost like a Mage Stone." He turned on his heels, strolling back to his observer's post by the wall, and shoved his hands back into his pockets, amending, "You're welcome."

Scrambling back to his feet, Tristan ignored him. "You did it, San. You got the artifact."

"A tooth, Tris," Dimar said coolly from behind him. "She got you a tooth."

"Try to get it to work," I encouraged. Because there wasn't much else I could say. I needed him. Needed him to rid Cezux of Cyrill. But first, I needed him to help with the Crow. And that wasn't anything he'd agreed to. Also, it was helping Rogue as much as it was helping me, so, of course, I was worried whether he'd agree to do it.

Zelia rounded the table, fingers sliding along the backrest of a chair as she stopped next to Tristan. "Let me see. It should start pulsing like a Mage Stone when you focus."

"So, it's not keyed to anyone yet?" Dimar asked. "Zelia could use it, or I?"

Rogue dipped his chin, the only response he'd deign to give.

But his dark breeze brushed up against my cheek, summoning my attention. "Let's hope your Mage is smarter than he looks," he spoke on that intimate channel that belonged only to us when I met his gaze. "I'd hate for our trip to have been in vain."

"Nothing is in vain," I responded, the words swept up by the breeze and delivered right to his ears.

A brief smile cut through his otherwise distant expression. "I guess we'll need to see about that."

While I was still trying to figure out what he'd meant, Zelia, Tristan, and Dimar had gathered around the table, the tooth sitting in Tristan's open palm.

"I don't want to be a spoilsport, but we have an issue to deal with that cannot wait," Rogue announced. Unsurprisingly, all heads turned toward him. "There is a Crow on the loose in Cezux."

I could have sworn Zelia and Dimar held their breaths while Tristan's fist curled around the artifact as if in reflex.

"How did it get out?" Zelia was directing the question at me more than at Rogue; I could tell by the way her eyes flicked back and forth between the two of us.

"We didn't let it out, if that's what you're asking, dear Master Mage," Rogue responded smoothly. "There have been ... issues with the borders of the Seeing Forest. I've told you as much, but not about the recent issues with the borders to the human lands."

And he wouldn't tell them all of it. The bargain in which he was trapped, what was at stake if he interfered with the Crows. Clio and Tori and his hopes of making both Askarea and the human lands safe again.

"The Crow's headed straight for Jezuin." I didn't wait for Rogue to take over again but rushed on. "I'll need your help to defeat it, Tris, or it will rip apart the city."

Dimar was the one who said, "I'm ready to leave now." Because it was his city as much as it was mine. Even when the crown was supposed to rest on my brow and Dimar had grown up in Aceleau for most of his childhood and youth, he'd spent a major part of his adult life protecting me, spying on the Jezuinian court for the Mages.

"You can't go, Dimar." Zelia rested her fingers on his forearm as his hand twitched to his hip. "Not without magic. The Crows are too dangerous."

She glanced at Tristan, who gave her a weighing look. He didn't have any connections to Cezux other than the three of us.

But he lifted his gaze to me after a silent moment and nodded. "Give me a few hours to figure this out—"

"We don't have a few hours," I cut in, hand sliding to my pocket where my Mage Stone was waiting to be used on the next Crow. "If we don't go soon, the Crow will be close enough to the city to leave severe damage." And I wasn't speaking about the walls and houses and the roads connecting the villages to the capital but about the people; the closer to Jezuin, the denser the settlements and the busier the streets. "Please, Tristan."

I was ready to beg him even when I hated to need anything from him. He'd chosen a side: his own.

The look Rogue gave me was cold and hard, but in his eyes, I could read how much he hated what had to be plain on my face—that I'd do anything for my people. Including begging the man who'd put his own power above me.

"Give me a few moments, at least. I'll do my best." Of course, Tristan would. Because he wasn't bad even when he wasn't who I'd believed him to be. He still cared.

So I nodded, retreating a few steps to Rogue's side as I watched him focus on the tooth, Zelia and Dimar observing from up close and offering advice.

After a short while, a crease so deep it made him appear a decade older was etched between Tristan's brows, and another few moments later, his breathing had become heavy. He was trying—by the Guardians, he was trying. I remembered those moments I'd brooded over my own Mage Stone, attempted to feel as much as even a slight pulse—and nothing had happened.

But Tristan was a full Mage, a powerful one, and experienced. So I wasn't surprised when, in his palm, the tooth began to glow, and his eyes flashed dark blue as his features lit up in a victorious grin.

"It's working," I whispered just as Tristan launched to his feet, mumbling silently, and whipped a blow of magic right next to Rogue's head.

Rogue didn't as much as flinch, his own power shielding him from minor assaults like that, but it was the gesture that counted. And Tristan had just declared war on the male beside me.

"I'll help *her*, King of Askarea. I'll help Sanja. But don't expect anything else from me."

My stomach dropped as Rogue slid his hands out of his pockets to brush away the glimmering dust of pulverized stone settling on his shoulder and angled his head at Tristan, who stared him down, a wicked glint entering his features.

"Wait ... you weren't expecting anything in return for my magic, anyway. We never had a bargain. So I don't have any obligations."

My stomach dropped to my feet.

No. This couldn't be happening. We had bigger problems than this. I'd thought we'd gotten past this hatred and learned to work together—even Dimar and Zelia were staring with shock at this new Tristan who had access to his powers once more.

"Have you lost your mind, Tris?" It was all I could bring myself to say. "This alliance isn't over just because you have your powers back. We need Ro—Recienne," I corrected myself, "to get to Cezux. If we take the human route, Jezuin will be destroyed by the time we get there."

"Let the Crow take care of Cyrill," Tristan said with a shrug. "It would be the answer to all your prayers."

I couldn't tell what hurt more—the way Tristan had turned from the kind Mage who'd helped me and given me safety in a fairy city to the broken boy he'd been a moment ago to ... this. This man, hungry for power and uncaring of the collateral.

"If the Crow takes Jezuin, we'll soon be fighting not one of them but a horde. And two Mages won't be enough."

I wouldn't say anything else, for everything beyond that was Rogue's story to tell, not mine.

"Why does the almighty King of Askarea not come to your aid the way he's prided himself in doing so many times?" The bitterness in Tristan's words... Something inside me splintered.

From the corner of my eye, I spotted Dimar's hand on his knife.

"Because," Rogue said with a deadly calm that made the air in the room hard to breathe, "if I so much as touch the Crow, everything we've worked for will go to shit. And I doubt you want your beloved Tavras to be next." A warning in those words. Subtle but sharp like honed steel. "So do yourself a favor, *Mage* Tristan, and pull yourself together long enough to handle that escaped Crow, or the human lands will very soon be very much under fairy power."

He didn't need to specify that, if the Crow wouldn't take the human lands, he would. Because that was something he'd be willing to do to protect them. He'd need to take Cezux at Ret Relah anyway and be the Crows' proxy on the Jezuinian throne. But he'd take Tavras to prevent the Crows from spreading. If I'd learned anything about Rogue during the past months, it was that. And that he'd do anything to keep the ones he loved protected—Clio, Tori. The only family he had left. Even if it meant he'd have to wreck himself.

FORTY

"Stop." I didn't know who I was addressing, Rogue or Tristan, or both of them. But the flash of hurt in Rogue's eyes as he straightened away from the wall was enough to tell me he thought I didn't see what he was doing, didn't understand. Later, I'd take a moment to be upset about his lack of confidence in me. As if I hadn't just placed my life in his hands last night. I didn't allow myself to think about what else had happened. "Tristan—" I placed a hand on his chest, summoning his attention as I stepped between them. "I *need* your help to finish that Crow. And we *need* Recienne to take us to Cezux. There, his powers won't work the same as in Askarea, but he at least can site-hop us and drop us off."

Tristan's lips turned into a cruel smile that hit deep in my stomach, even when not directed at me but at the male smirking at him over my shoulder.

A weakness, I realized. I had presented Tristan with a weakness for Rogue.

"Don't look so excited just yet, Tristan," Rogue said, tone icy despite the grin. "I could still flatten you to the ground with the scraps of my powers."

Tristan had the good sense to pale.

"I didn't bring you up to be like this, Tristan," Zelia reminded him, and for the first time, I understood that she had been so much more to him than just a mentor. He'd lived with her for over ten years, and she'd become probably the closest thing to a mother he'd ever find since he never knew his own. My heart cracked yet again for the broken man before me.

"I got you what you wanted, Tris," I said, using that moment of clarity that had entered his gaze at Zelia's words. "You can use magic again. You'll never be powerless again or dependent. I fulfilled my end of the bargain, Tris. Now, help me save Cezux."

Tristan blinked. Nodded. "For you, San. Only for you." He opened his fist around the tooth, the glow fading as he loosed his grasp on the power stored within.

How much, I'd failed to ask Rogue—or how long it'd last. But it didn't matter as long as Tristan would be able to help get rid of the Crow. He'd never need to look at me again afterward. I wouldn't even hold him to helping me with Cyrill. As long as he didn't turn away now.

I nodded that I understood—that I respected it. "For me," I said, voice turning hoarse as I felt Rogue's power touch my shoulder, caress the length of my spine. "For me, you'll let Recienne take us to Cezux. And once we find the Crow, you'll help me take it out."

Rogue didn't wait for Tristan's response but grabbed my hand, and with a, "Get ready, Mage. We'll be back within that hour you requested," spirited us away.

The world crumbled into pieces around us, wobbling and swirling, and my stomach turned the way it hadn't in a long time. When we hit the forest ground, I doubled over, expelling bile and curses.

"What just happened?" I asked as Rogue caught my braid a moment before it could slide over my mouth as I turned my head enough to find him staring down at me.

"Your Mage is an untrustworthy bastard is what." His mask was up and his armor in place—not only the physical but the one that had been shielding his emotion gloriously from the day we'd met in the forest.

I remembered vomiting in front of his feet then—things hadn't changed so much after all.

Yet, they had. Everything had changed. From the way his fingers rubbed a soothing circle between my shoulder blades, the end of my braid still tight in his grasp, to the way my body no longer recoiled from the touch. Instead, warmth spread from that spot, calming every muscle and bone and tendon. Only my blood—that didn't calm. It remembered too vividly how he'd touched me under the canopy of trees, made me forget.

"He will help me," I insisted. Because Tristan had loved me the way I'd loved him, and part of us would always be connected through what we'd gone through—even when now, with his magic back in place, he'd no longer have need of anyone's help. He'd be free. And who, if not I, would understand what craving freedom meant?

"You trust him?" Rogue said, smoothing my braid down my spine as I straightened, the nausea ebbing.

"I wouldn't trust him when it comes to you," I said truthfully. "But what reason does he have to betray me? I've paid my debt." And as the knowledge settled in, the guilt eased and I could finally, finally breathe.

I'd taken his magic, destroyed it. But I'd given it back to him now. Whatever would come of it was for the future. At this moment, all I could worry about was the Crow and getting there in time.

But Rogue's hand lingered on the small of my back, right under where my braid ended. "I don't want to rule Cezux or Tavras. I hope you know that."

That hurt crossed his eyes again, and I was glad I couldn't see his mouth, for I might have wanted to ease the expression from his features with my lips.

"You'd do it to save them." I stepped out of his touch, the mild air cold where it replaced the warmth of his touch. "You'd do it to keep us all safe."

He didn't deny it.

Calm silence fell between us as we walked back to Clio's house. Rogue's near-silent footsteps a steady reminder of how much of his abilities, his powers he kept hiding. One day, I'd ask him to show me what he was capable of... If there ever came a day when he could use his powers without attracting trouble.

I'd seen the rock in the kitchen blast beside his face, had seen the splinters crumbling to the ground, the dent Tristan had left. And Rogue hadn't as much as flinched at the impact.

I didn't ask him about that either.

Tori was there when we entered the house, shoveling some steaming, leafy greens from a bowl into his mouth. Beside him, Clio was fidgeting in a chair, so at odds with the confident princess I'd gotten to know over the past weeks.

Both lifted their heads at our entrance, Clio shooting to her feet to throw her arms around Rogue first then me.

I'd forgotten what it felt like to be embraced like that— by a friend. Leahnie had been the last one, and she had done so looking over her shoulder for Cyrill. And Dimar and Zelia were family—

Tori gave me a look that indicated he knew exactly what I was thinking, and his gaze drifted to Rogue, who was silently watching the exchange.

"Clio told me what happened," Tori said after swallowing a mouthful of greens, his eyes sliding back to me. "But something more happened at the Mages', didn't it?"

Clio let go of me to wait for our report, and Rogue gave no short amount of cursing as he explained exactly what an unreliable, fairy-hating Mage-bastard Tristan was—and how we needed him to eliminate that Crow.

"So where exactly is the Crow?" he eventually asked, his breathing calm as if he'd gotten most of his anger off his chest. But I could still see it there—the spark of anger coming to life in the gold of his eyes when he glanced at me.

"It is making too-fast progress, Rogue. The two to three days were a gross overestimation of how long it'd take to reach Jezuin. I fear it will get there tonight."

By the Guardians.

"I'm ready to fight," Tori added.

Rogue shook his head. "I cannot risk you being exposed. With or without your mask. If anything happens to me—" He finished the rest of the sentence in that strange form of communication I normally was on the receiving end of, his lips moving ever so slightly—as did Tori's, as his features turned from angry to hopeful to resigned.

Clio gave me a knowing look. "They do that all the time. Doesn't matter how often I tell Rogue it's rude."

I didn't laugh at her obvious attempt to put both of us at ease at the tension lingering in the room. A king exacting command over one of his subjects—over a friend, who was willing to give his life. A life Rogue would never be willing to risk. Not when he knew Tori was Clio's mate—together or not. He couldn't take that last piece of hope from his sister.

The silent exchange between Rogue and the male made the air sizzle with power. But eventually, Tori sighed, and I knew he'd given in.

"You'll be keeping an eye on the palace," Rogue told Tori for all of us to hear again. "Moyen didn't say goodbye or leave a note when she departed a few days ago."

So she was gone? The female who was in league with the Crows...

I wondered what her position in the Crow Court was. If she was a bride...

As if reading my thoughts, Tori shook his head. "A bride never leaves the Seeing Forest," he told me. "At least, not alive."

"In pieces of teeth and bone splinters," I offered.

Rogue laughed, but it was rough and more for me than because he found it funny. But the sound grated along my skin, awakening that part of me that had reveled in his touch in the forest.

"So I've heard," Tori said, measuring the air between Rogue and me.

And for a brief moment, I feared he'd responded to my thought rather than my words.

But he tilted his head toward Clio. "She filled me in about all the details you left out this morning," he said to Rogue.

The way Clio's lips curved for a moment, how Tori's eyes lit up at the gesture, how his eyes grazed her linen shirt and leather pants as she turned away to pick up her own bowl from the table—it was easy to forget that this was the Princess of Askarea and the male in his bandit armor a fairy nobility. This was indeed their home—not the lavish palace in the fairy city where intrigue and hatred lingered in the hallways like tripwires.

But Rogue—as he stood there, mask down and face unreadable, eyes hard as he studied his sister and his friend the way I had—he was the fairy king whose power made the realms tremble. Because for them, he'd unleash all of it upon the world.

We didn't stay for lunch, tea, or even a bowl of berries as Clio insisted. Rogue claimed all he'd wanted was to see if he could discover the latest information about the Crow's position, which he'd gotten from Tori. But I could have sworn it was to get away from Tristan before he decided to snap the Mage's neck with a touch of his power.

Now, we were standing in the forest, a good mile from the entrance to the hideout, his extended arm an invitation for me to step closer so he could site-hop us back to pick up Tristan.

The way he looked at me when I hesitated made a fissure in his invisible mask.

We hadn't talked about the night in the forest—not about the part before we'd gone to the Seeing Forest. But every other look he gave seemed to be a question I had no answer to. His arm was now accompanied by one of exactly those looks, his fingers of his half-gloved hand elegantly curving as if for a dance.

Steeling my spine against the assault of his scent, I took that hand—and nearly stumbled into him as he spun me into his arm exactly like in a dance. One of those dances of our very first encounters—when he'd been the Prince of Askarea and his power had controlled my movements.

"We're going back into danger, Sanja," he purred on that dark breeze. "Care for a moment of escape?" His other hand traced the length of my arm all the way down to the back of my palm.

Before I could tell him to keep his fingers to himself, his whole hands, and his arms—bring myself to even want to tell him—he chuckled, and the world blurred, the transition softer this time, not as nauseating.

We hit the solid cave ground in the Hollow Mountains a moment later, my knees like jelly from the way he'd been pressing me against his front—even if it had been mere breaths. Breaths laced with his rain and night under open skies scent. And white roses.

I reached for his mask and pulled it down. Rogue didn't stop me.

For a long, stuttering heartbeat, we stared at each other, those questions in his eyes silently challenging questions of my own. His fingers slid down my back, lower, lower, until they grazed the seam of my jacket at my hip where a hunting knife was attached to my belt. "Tell me that you won't die today, Sanja," he murmured, that gold turning liquid. "Tell me that, if they come after me, you'll outlive me."

I didn't know what to say, so I laid my hand against his warm cheek.

His eyes shuttered, and I was about to draw it back. But he let go of my hip, securing my hand to his cheek with his large, gloved one. "Promise." A mere breath.

I hadn't realized that he was leaning down, the way his face had come close enough to feel his breath on mine.

"Promise me, Sanja."

I traced his cheekbone with my thumb, savoring how the hardness left his expression, how heat infused his gaze, widened his pupils. "Even if I promised... A human promise means nothing."

He leaned down another inch. "Your promise means *everything*." Whether he'd spoken or I'd imagined it, I didn't know.

My breathing had turned heavy, my chest aching with the longing in his words, the loneliness speaking from the depth of his soul as he let that mask of the unimpressed fairy king slip for a vulnerable moment.

Footsteps echoed in the tunnel leading to the kitchen, and I pulled away so quickly I almost fell on my ass.

Rogue caught me by the wrist, tugged me upright, and let go, expression smooth, even when I could have sworn a flicker of hurt appeared at the sudden distance I'd brought between us.

Because I was embarrassed to be found so close to him. Or wasn't ready to admit to anyone how good it felt. As long as no one witnessed, it wasn't real—and I wasn't hopping from Tristan's arms to Rogue's, uncaring of what had happened with the man I'd given my heart to half a year ago.

Even when the guilt of destroying his magic had faded, a part of me recoiled from what might happen if Tristan saw us together like that.

"I thought I'd heard something in here," Tristan said as he prowled into the glimmering light, his gait powerful, confident, much like the Mage I'd first met in Aceleau.

Rogue took a casual step to my side, his bandit's armor still in place. Just the hood had disappeared, and the mask gathered beneath his chin—that was gone as well.

"Zelia is preparing a few potions for us before we head out," Tristan informed me, buckling his weapons belt and ignoring Rogue altogether. Whether it was to get under his skin or simply because he felt like I was the only one who needed to know would have to remain a mystery.

FORTY-ONE

We were ready to leave the Hollow Mountains mere minutes later, a bag with potions slung over Tristan's shoulder and my Mage Stone tied around my wrist so I couldn't lose it the way I'd lost the artifact. Normally, I'd keep it in my pocket, well out of sight and where I couldn't accidentally touch it or trigger it. But we were headed into a battle, and I'd need the stone accessible and secured. The same was valid for Tristan's Crow artifact.

In the short period of time that Rogue and I had been gone, Tristan had somehow managed to attach a silver chain to the tooth, which he was now wearing around his neck.

Rogue eyed him sideways, hand open for Tristan to take it so he could site-hop us out of there. "Interesting choice of jewelry," he commented with that gloriously bored face, and I would have laughed had it not been for the slight teeth-baring between Tristan's lips.

The Mage placed his hand in Rogue's, looking uncomfortable enough to vomit at the contact, while Rogue grinned and took my hand, tugging me gently to his side in that dance-like motion that made heat run through my body.

Swallowing it down, I gritted my teeth to match Tristan's expression.

"Ready to pick a Crow apart, Sanja?" he murmured on that dark breeze.

Had Tristan not been around, I might have stuck out my tongue at Rogue.

"Let's get this over with," I said for both of them to hear, wondering if I'd ever get to see Dimar and Zelia again after the brief goodbye in the kitchen earlier.

The world fell away, and I clung to Rogue's hand as I tried to prepare myself for what was to come. Tristan shot me a nervous glance around Rogue's chest, one hand on his artifact. Rogue had said he'd recharge it for him after we were done with the Crow, but the residual magic in it would last a while. That reminded me of Zelia's magic, how it had lingered in her tissues for weeks after my last challenge.

Nothing could have prepared me for what was awaiting us when we hit the ground moments later.

The tang of salt and iron hit me first. I squinted into the midday sun above my lands. Gravel crunched beneath my boots, and Rogue's fingers tightened around my hand.

"By Eroth—" Tristan said, and where I'd dreaded finding a dead body or two, the sight of destruction greeted me in the center of the village we'd landed.

The roofs had caved in, walls crumbled in places, painted crimson in others with the blood of the people the Crow had ripped apart, limbs strewn across the ground, discarded on the flight to its next victim. My stomach turned. But what was truly disturbing was the utter silence. This was a tomb. A reminder of what happened if a fairy got out of Askarea. Of what they were capable of.

Tristan loosed a vicious curse, turning on the spot to survey the entire village. A Guardians-damned village had been taken apart by the Crow and all its people killed. If this was the sort of trail it left through Cezux... I didn't want to think of what it might do once it reached Jezuin where, by one blow, it could destroy hundreds of lives.

"Is it still here?" Scanning the area, trying not to cringe from the sight lest I miss something, I waited for Rogue's response.

So much blood—

"It was sighted a few miles back from this place." He didn't say by whom, didn't allow for Tristan to hear a name that could give away who Rogue worked with, whom he trusted. "It's sheer luck that we came to a place it has visited. At least, now we know we're on the right track."

The way he spoke—unfazed by the carnage—I could have sworn the way his fingers kept gripping mine indicated he was as equally affected as I was. But with centuries of perfecting a mask, Rogue played his part easily. Didn't let Tristan see a flicker of that emotion, of that guilt that now wound around my wrist, snaked up my arm, a dark wind that had nothing to do with the remorse eating me up at the sight of what our delay had cost Cezux.

When I measured him from the side, he let go of my hand, strolling a few steps ahead where he craned his neck, glancing at the sky. "I can take you a little farther, but not much. The Crow can't see me," he amended, reminding us that we'd be on our own once the Crow came within view.

"No need," Tristan said from across the little square where we'd landed. I noticed the open stable door a moment after the stomping of horseshoes on wooden planks. "We're going to ride."

Two horses were pressing into the back corner of the dim stable when we peeked through the half-open door.

To my surprise, Rogue praised, "That might be an even better idea."

He waited for Tristan to cross the threshold before he grabbed my hand. I halted, turning, finding his molten metal gaze resting on my face. "Be careful, Sanja," he whispered on that dark breeze, and it didn't stop where it had carried his voice to my ear but slid down my neck, around my shoulders in a phantom embrace that I didn't think he'd ever given me in person. With everything we'd gone through, I hadn't embraced him either.

Throwing overboard all caution, I closed the gap between us, winding my arms around his neck. His body went rigid under my touch, as if he hadn't been held like this. Not by anyone other than Clio and Tori—his only remaining family.

"Promise me you won't do anything stupid that will jeopardize both our realms," I said instead of all of the other words I might have needed to say to him—words that had been building at the bottom of my stomach for a while. That he was not to blame for his father's choices, that he deserved to reign in times of peace and that what he was willing to sacrifice to achieve it was nothing he needed to apologize for. Because, these words... I might have needed to hear them myself. And if I dared speak them, I might find there were things I was no longer willing to sacrifice.

His shoulders eased, and one arm wrapped around my waist, his quiet chuckle grating along my skin and bones. "I promise not to do anything stupid."

His words reassured me until he drew out of our embrace, leaving my arms cold and empty. Eyes guarded, he studied me over the foot distance between us. "Ride southwest, along the water." He gestured at the stream following the road to Jezuin. "You should catch up with it by the next village."

It was an act of willpower to turn away and follow Tristan into the stable where he'd managed to calm the horses enough to gear them up with saddles and bridles hanging on the wooden wall behind the stalls.

I didn't look back as I crossed onto the half-light and took the saddle Tristan handed me.

My horse, a brown mare, huffed into my palm as I petted her nose, her body no longer shaking, and it was a comfort that I wouldn't need to be using Rogue's help to get to the Crow. He'd risked enough. Even come to the human lands again, where he was weakened and not in possession of his full powers. He'd made Tori site-hop here, over and over again. And Tori wasn't as strong as him. Crossing into the human lands probably affected him a lot more than the fairy king and in ways I couldn't even imagine. I'd thank him the next time I saw him—*if* we defeated the Crow Fairy.

For a hollow moment, I wondered how long we'd need to wait until being in the human lands affected the Crow enough to reduce it to mere human strength—then I remembered the bloodbath it had left behind for us to find in this very village. If it had been flying for over two days and was still able to do *that*, waiting for it to slow and weaken would mean that perhaps no Cezux would be left to save.

The sudden urgency drove me from the stables, horse in tow, and made me take a good look at the lives lost, at the men and women and children who'd been torn apart and distributed across the dirt-road crossing through the square. Bile rose in my throat, but I swallowed it, steeling my spine and my heart. This was only the beginning, and I couldn't afford to cringe at it. They had been my people, my responsibility, and I'd failed them. I'd failed them before when I'd been used by Cyrill as a symbol for the blessing of his rule. And I couldn't fail them again.

You're not enough. You'll never be enough.

I silenced the voice, grabbing the reins tighter and swinging myself into the saddle.

Tristan had ridden up to my side and was staring at the horizon where haze and clouds were brewing. Rare rain at the end of Cezuxian summer this far south in the realm.

Rogue skipped from his spot at the center of the square to my side, making the horse prance a few steps back. I soothed her with gentle strokes of my hand through her mane, but she was now scenting the blood, the wind turning, and threw her head up and down.

It was time.

Rogue lifted a hand in a parting gesture at both Tristan and me. But he didn't wish us luck or tell us what else to do. Tristan was an experienced Mage, and I had at least some power at my disposal so I wouldn't be smothered by the Crow the moment it laid eyes on me—at least, that was my hope.

The air rippled, and Rogue was gone.

And Tristan and I had somewhere to be.

"It would be easier if one of us could do what he does," Tristan pointed out, the dark expression lighter now that the fairy king he despised so much was gone.

"Site-hop?" I didn't remind him that it was the way I'd first used my Mage Stone. I'd tried it again but to no avail. Besides, even if I knew how, it wouldn't have helped me much with visiting Clio and Tori in their hide-out. Rogue had never shared its location on a map, and I didn't know if going by visuals was enough to find my way through the blurring world the way Rogue did. "Have you heard of Mages who can do it?"

We made our way through the village, new horror striking me at every turn we took. So many lives. Too many.

"Zelia has never mentioned it, and I've never read about it in books. Perhaps, there are spells that could make it work, but I never learned about them." His hand wandered to his artifact.

"Does it feel different?"

He gave me a questioning gaze. If nothing else, our conversation distracted me from the nausea that threatened to coil my stomach into a useless knot. I needed to keep a clear head even when everything surrounding us made me want to fall to my knees and weep.

Not yet—I'd do that later. I'd weep for each and every life lost in this village.

"Using the artifact instead of the Mage Stone," I specified.

Tristan loosed a breath as we crossed between the final few houses, entering the open road. "It's surprisingly easy," he said, gaze tracking the sky the way Rogue had.

Only a few clouds scattered across the azure horizon, a bird here and there. But no larger creature flying ahead.

For a moment, I wondered how we'd find the Crow, how we'd identify it if it could turn into a common black bird. But Tristan continued, "I was expecting for it to be different—feel different from the Mage Stone. But it oddly feels so similar that there are moments I forget it's not the same. Then I touch it, and it has the wrong shape, the wrong size"— I couldn't help but be thrown back into that first discussion I'd had with Rogue about the size of my Mage Stone—"and I know that everything was real: the days at the fairy palace, the challenges, the loss of my powers."

"You never told me what happened to you in those few days." When he'd been caged in gold and put on display for the entire fairy court to laugh at, to spit at, if they so pleased.

The horrors of those days still haunted me in my nightmares, but Tristan—he hadn't spoken about what had happened to him.

He gave me an unreadable look, but this was Tristan. And, no matter how much had changed between us, some things wouldn't.

I gave him a small smile that was supposed to tell him that I was here—no matter how wrong he'd behaved, how he'd attempted to break his promise to help me with Cezux once he had his powers back. That he could speak to me.

He shook his head.

We rode on in silence, nudging the horses into a trot so we'd not lose the Crow—not that we'd found it yet. But we were on the right track. I could practically feel it. In my bones, in my veins. In any part of me that had ever sensed magic. There was a trail of it winding from the village, heading southwest, thin and near-unnoticeable. But something had changed in my body. Perhaps it was the time I'd spent in the presence of the most powerful fairy of Askarea; perhaps it was the magic I'd channeled myself that now allowed me to pick up on that minuscule thread in the world and follow it.

By the time the sun had climbed over its pinnacle, the next village had come within reach. Calling it a village might have been too much. A small cluster of stone houses and wooden barns sitting between small fields of palm trees. Farmers of heart of palm. And they were running and screaming as we crossed into their settlement a short while later.

Panic was commanding their words, their actions, as they picked up pitchforks and swords, bracing themselves for an attack. A woman with curled black hair and rich brown skin shrank a few inches as my gaze landed on her. Shrank, then fell to her knees.

"Saint Sanja!" she shouted, letting her sword plop into the dirt as she got to her knees.

The woman first, then the rest of them, some bracing themselves on their makeshift weapons as they gazed up at us—at me—with wonder and that faith I didn't deserve.

"It's her. It's Saint Sanja."

Beside me, Tristan's hand tightened around the pendant of his necklace. I let my own fingers trace my Mage Stone on my wrist, the string long enough to let it slide into the palm of the hand it was attached to if so needed.

With the other hand, I grabbed the reins more tightly, nudging the mare a few reluctant steps forward as I scanned the area for any sign of bloodshed before I allowed her to halt. When I found none, I cleared my throat.

They were all gazing up at me—even Tristan was looking to me for how I would handle the situation.

A part of me wondered what Rogue would have thought had he seen this assembly, if he'd have laughed, called me Saint Sanja to tease me. I shut that part down.

"We are looking for someone," I said instead of giving them the blessing they probably expected. "Did anyone pass through this village recently?" The way they'd all been running around armed at our arrival let me guess there had— and it hadn't been a good experience.

The woman who'd recognized me lifted her head. "A man passed through an hour ago." Her gaze slid to Tristan, who sat stiffly on his horse.

I could have sworn his magic sputtered to life under the scrutiny.

"Is anyone hurt?" It was the only thing I could think of to say without giving away what I knew, what I'd seen in the village before. These people had been lucky the Crow had chosen to continue on its path rather than wreak havoc.

"Barker has a mean cut on his arm," one of the men said from the back of the tiny crowd. Twenty people perhaps. "He's in the house." The man pointed at the wall behind him with his thumb.

"The stranger was gone so fast that we didn't have a chance to take a good look at him. Barker is the only one who came close to him."

"What was he looking for? Does anyone know?" Tristan asked.

The woman shook her head, black curls sliding over her shoulders. "He was gone in a blink. All that's left are a couple of feathers."

"It's magic," someone hissed. "That man was a Mage sent from Askarea to look for weaknesses."

I shuddered at the prejudice, the assumption. These people kneeled before their saint, their queen. But would they do the same if they knew I was a Mage? Or would they pick up their weapons and attack?

Months among Mages and fairies had taught me to fear them, yes, but it had taught me even more that there were some who didn't aim to set fire to the human realm. Especially not the Mages, who'd given their lives in thousands to seal the border between Askarea and the rest of Eherea—the border that had become an unreliable protection.

"Where is this Barker? I'd like to speak with him."

The man in the back got to his feet, beckoning me toward the house. "If you'll allow, Saint Sanja... He's resting. But I'm sure I can wake him for you. The wound is deep, and he's lost a lot of blood. Healers are hard to come by in this part of Cezux."

Tristan gave me a warning look. *Don't trust them.*

I slid off my horse, handing him the reins and holding out my hand for Tristan's bag.

He shook his head. One of the women gasped at the obvious sign of defiance.

"Hand me my utensils," I said to Tristan, forcing all my court-trained authority into my voice. "I have healed plenty of wounds in Jezuin as you know. I might be able to heal the wounded man."

Silently, I willed him to understand that this was our chance to learn something about the Crow and potentially save a life. At least spare the man the pain.

Pressing his lips into a thin line, Tristan obeyed.

"I'll be back soon." A dismissal and an order to stay behind while I did my work.

From the way a muscle flickered in his jaw, I could tell he didn't like it one bit.

But I slung the bag over my shoulder, following the man toward the house.

"Rise," I said to all of them as I passed through. "Right now, I'm simply a healer."

Dark eyes rose to mine as I passed by an elderly man who inclined his head. A woman stood just as I stepped around her.

"If you don't mind, Saint Sanja," she said, her hands clasping before her stomach. "I'm his sister. I'd like to come with you to look after him."

"Is he alone now?" I prompted.

She bobbed her head, worry creasing her young forehead. "We were all outside to make sure we'd be prepared should the stranger return."

"He won't return," I said quietly. A promise I made myself. "Come, then." I motioned for her to follow me while the others were still getting to their feet, and with a backward glance at Tristan, I slipped through the narrow door into the humble farmhouse.

FORTY-TWO

A man, no older than twenty-five, lay sprawled on a cot under the open window, sweaty face turned toward the incoming breeze. One of his arms hung loosely at his side, wrapped in strips of linen. Blood had seeped through so much that it was running down his elbow and, from there, dripped to the dusty floor.

"Barker," the woman said, rushing past the older man and me to her brother's side. "Barker, I've brought help."

Barker groaned in pain as he slowly turned his head. "I'm fine," he claimed. And I almost laughed.

"You're not fine, Barker," I said as I squatted beside the cot, examining the linen bindings. A poor attempt to stop the blood flow. I'd seen enough cut wounds to know that, if they kept it bound like this, what it would do was block the blood flow to the lower arm and he'd lose that too. If he survived at all.

With careful hands, I touched his fingers. "Can you feel this?"

His gaze slid to me, and recognition crossed his exhausted features. "By the Guardians." He almost knocked me over as he tried to get to his feet, swayed, and sank back to the cot.

"Lie down," I instructed. "I'll need to remove the bindings." To his sister, I said, "Get me some clean linen and some hot water." And to the man who'd led me here, "Do you believe in the Guardians?"

He gave me a brief nod.

"Then pray for your friend."

I loosed the linens around his biceps, expecting to find the deep cut of a blade ... and had to suppress a gasp when I found three jagged slices, deep to the bone.

This was the work of talons.

"He came out of nowhere. I was lucky to have my sword on me when he attacked. You never know these days with King Cyrill's men coming to take apart your house to look for more coins we don't have."

I shuddered at the cruelty my people had been subjected to, that I hadn't yet found a way to shield them from. But I would. The Crow was the first step. Then Cyrill himself. With or without Tristan's help.

I picked up a piece of linen from the stack the sister brought me and dipped it in hot water before I pushed it on two of the wounds. Barker winced but put on a brave face.

I gestured at the linens. "Take one and cover the other cut." The woman obeyed, her hands nimble and careful.

"I thought you were someplace safe and hidden for the time being," she eventually said. "Word spread through the entire kingdom that the queen was with child and would return after birth—a measure to protect the crown heir."

She wasn't wrong. Yet—there was no round belly speaking of my supposed pregnancy.

"I lost the child." At least, I'd partly stick to the plan in case it would otherwise interfere with the bargain Rogue had made with Cyrill.

The woman's eyes lowered. "I... Apologies, Your Majesty."

I shook my head at her. "There is nothing to apologize for."

And there was no time to talk about what had happened to me, what hadn't. I needed to heal the man with one of the potions Zelia had packed for us and be back on my way. "Did the man use magic on you?" I asked Barker, who was observing our hands on his arm with wary eyes.

"He certainly had magic. His face wasn't human. It wasn't fairy either. The beak of a bird, eyes so black they had no white. And talons—" His voice was so weak...

"Instead of fingers," I finished for him. I'd seen those in the Seeing Forest. But if this village was like the rest of Cezux, knowledge about Crow Fairies would have long faded. "Did he say anything to you?" For if he had—

"He didn't speak. Just attacked and"—he gasped in pain as I slid the linen up to stop the flow of blood—"I got him with the flat of my blade on the side of his neck. A lucky blow, and unlucky because it would have sliced off his head had it been the sharp edge."

Lucky indeed to have landed a blow on a Crow at all.

So at least the Crow wasn't hunting down information. That was something.

Barker coughed. "Are you going to heal me, Saint Sanja?"

"I'm going to try." I reached into my bag with my free hand, pulled out one of the larger flasks that contained Leeneae extract, and said to the man, "Open this for me."

Barker watched his friend uncork it and hand it back to me. "What is that?" His voice broke on his labored breath.

He wouldn't make it through the night if he didn't get more than a bandage. And judging by the look the sister and the friend shared, they knew it too.

"A tincture—similar to what I used to make at the sick house in Jezuin." They'd heard about that here, knew that I'd helped many people there. But I understood the fear in his eyes as I poured some into the bowl of water and dipped in a fresh strip of linen. He'd just observed a magical creature, been injured by it. The thought of trusting a stranger—

But I wasn't a stranger. Not to them. I was their queen and their saint. So I swallowed my own fear. I was running out of time, and so was Barker. His face had already paled, his voice weaker and breaths shallow.

"This is to clean the wound," I informed them as I exchanged the blood-soaked linen on his arm for the one with Leeneae extract—with my magic added. It would heal him. Not immediately, but it would stop the blood flow and initiate the healing.

Barker's sister pulled back her hand, making space for me to spread the cloth across all three cuts.

"Mighty Guardians," I murmured, fully aware of their attention on every tiny movement I made. I couldn't risk using my Mage Stone. It would flicker and glow and expose me. But with the potion containing my magic for healing ... as their saint, I could work a miracle. "Bestow your blessing upon this brave man who has fought to defend himself and his village. May he be rewarded for his duty to the ones he cares for."

The words flowed even when I didn't believe a single one of them. What was important was that they believed it. And as I spoke, the crimson stains slowed on the linen, and Barker's breathing turned more even.

When I was done, I slid the cloth aside, picked up a fresh one, and dipped it in the Leeneae-infused water before I wiped off the smear of blood around the injury on Barker's arm. The wounds were already closing, subtle changes that I only noticed because I'd taken a good look at them before Barker's sister had returned with the linens and bowl. And even when I'd examined them through flowing blood, I could see the difference.

"Saint Sanja—" I heard the tears in the sister's voice before I turned to see them streaming down her cheeks. "I've heard about what you did for the man at the assembly in Jezuin. But seeing it with my own eyes."

Barker mumbled his thanks, as did the friend.

I merely inclined my head. "Pray to the Guardians that they'll bring peace over Cezux."

Whether they understood the warning in my words, I didn't wait to check. I merely bent back over the wound, binding it with fresh linens, and picked up the dirty ones, stuffing them into the bowl so the Leeneae water wouldn't be usable for anyone else. No matter how much I'd have wanted to provide them with a flask of the essence just to give them something to make their everyday lives easier, I couldn't afford to be found out. This had to be a miracle and nothing else. Magic would earn the distrust of my people, and that would lead to more misery. Especially if Cyrill heard about it.

I was almost done when a bone-shuddering scream ripped through the open window, making my hands slip on the bindings.

Barker jerked upright, tearing his injured arm from my grasp. His sister leaped out of the way as he grabbed for the sword on the windowsill, unstable on his feet but determined to bolt for the door. His friend caught him before he could topple over.

"It's him," Barker coughed before he was pushed back onto the cot.

"You can't fight. You can barely stand," his friend hissed.

Barker didn't fight him but grasped his sword harder. "He's returned."

I didn't think as I slung the bag over my shoulder and rushed for the door. "Stay in here."

A long-stretched squeal hung suspended mid-air until it broke, cut off by a thud and more screams. Shouts of panic wove into stilled air.

I had my hand on the doorknob when an arm slammed into me from the side, blocking my path. "You can't go out there, Your Majesty," the man said. "It's too dangerous."

But I had to. I needed to get out there so I could fight and stand a chance where none of them would. Panic writhing to break free in my chest, I inhaled a steadying breath. "What's your name?"

"Randall." The man bowed clumsily. A farmer who would stand against the Crow Fairy with nothing more than a pitchfork, a sword he'd never learned to properly use.

"Listen to me, Randall." I didn't wait for him to indicate if he would before I stormed on. "You just witnessed how I saved your friend. You have seen what I'm capable of, who watches over me and guides me." I wasn't proud enough to steal from Cyrill's book. Not when the lives of those villagers depended on it. And a Crow was on the loose just behind that shabby door. The man's eyes widened as I pushed down his arm with an insistent finger. "I am your queen, and I will walk out that door. And you will stay in here to watch over your friend and his sister. Understood?"

Randall bobbed his head, his tense posture slackening. Behind me, Barker and his sister were whispering, but I was already out the door, my attention on the group of men and women surrounding Tristan and the two horses, their gazes fixed on the sky where a large shadow was circling, a harbinger of pain and death.

"Get inside," I shouted at the villagers. "All of you. Seek shelter."

None of them moved, petrified by fear or duty, I couldn't tell.

"That's a command from your queen," Tristan barked.

Some of them had the good sense to move while others remained planted by the horses.

As I rushed across the road, I shielded my eyes to get a better glance at what it was up there—what stage of transformation the Crow was in.

"Get on the horse." Tristan threw the reins at me the second I was within reach. "We're faster up here."

He was right. So I climbed into the saddle, telling the woman with the curls who'd recognized me to run for her life. She didn't move.

It was only when I'd swung myself into the saddle that I spotted the source of that earlier scream: Halfway to the beginning of the palm fields, a twisted, broken body was impaled on top of the angled roof of a well. Blood dribbled from where the spike atop the roof had pierced through his flesh and bones, following the carved, wooden roof tiles all the way to the edge where it dripped into the clear water of the well.

"He has another one up there," Tristan said as he noticed where I was looking. "But she stopped screaming a while ago, so she must have either fainted or—"

Died. I didn't finish his sentence aloud, shudders raking through my body as I tried to think of a way to bring down the Crow Fairy.

One good shot at him, and I'd be able to weaken him at least. Even when my magic wasn't the same as in Askarea, he was also not as powerful as in the fairylands. All I needed to do was rally whatever magic was accessible in these lands and take aim—and forget that those people around us would be witnesses of who I was. *What* I was.

"Can you feel it?" Tristan asked, jerking his chin at my wrist where I'd slid the crystal into my palm.

The slow pulse against my skin wasn't reassuring the way I'd hoped but, like a weak war drum, giving the beat to the rest of my living moments.

I nodded. "You?" If he could draw enough magic from his artifact, perhaps I wouldn't need to use the Mage Stone. I wouldn't be exposed as a Mage. And Tristan... With his artifact, he could get away and start a new life somewhere, be happy...

Not without his magic, he wouldn't be happy. And that was strongest in Askarea where no Ultimate Sacrifice restrained the effects and where he'd have access to creatures who could recharge his Mage Stone replacement whenever he ran out of magic.

One of the three remaining villagers said over his shoulder, "After it dropped Griss, he took Salvia and took to the skies. But he hasn't done anything but fly in those circles overhead."

The obvious terror in his voice made my hands shake.

"Is it a Mage?" The third one asked.

"A Crow Fairy," I said, and for some reason, it felt like a betrayal. Even when it was a Crow Fairy and nothing like Rogue and Clio and Tori, mentioning a fairy in this brutal situation made me feel like I'd painted all of them in the worst possible way.

Murmured prayers to the Guardians were all the response I got.

"What do we do?" I asked Tristan. "We can't simply wait for him to drop her and pick up the next."

"We also can't just attack. He's half a mile above."

Tristan drew the blade at his hip. A plain short sword I'd never seen him wear before today.

My hand slid to my knife, grasping the hilt.

"He'll come down to get the next victim." Tristan turned in his saddle to follow the path of the Crow above.

"So you think we shouldn't try to save her?" The woman, Griss, who was hanging limply in the Crow's grasp. His talons.

Tristan's response was swallowed up by the caw rumbling across the village, making my bones shudder.

It had come for Cezux, for the throne—for *me*. So there was only one thing that could stop him.

With a nudge of my heels, I stirred my horse around the villagers. If we wanted to save them, we'd need to lead the danger away from them. Away from Jezuin. That would be our only hope to avoid more collateral damage.

I've become rather tired of collateral damage, Rogue had once said to me. I could feel that in my very bones as I glanced behind me where the three villagers were still standing, eyes directed toward the sky, their poor weapons less than toothpicks against the magical terror circling above.

Tristan had picked up on my idea, following me to the edge of the village.

"Hide!" I shouted at them—an order. It was all I could do before I kicked my mare into a gallop that took us north.

We'd passed a patch of meager forest a mile back. Some laurels, carob trees and pines, and a few palms. It would be enough to disappear and force the Crow to the ground if it wanted to get to us.

Unsurprisingly, the Crow's trajectory changed to follow ours, large, spread wings like a streak of black against the sky. But it didn't attack. Like an observer, it kept circling, biding its time. And I thought this was similar to the one in the Seeing Forest, who'd silently approached through the treetops until it was too late for me to run.

Faster—we needed to be faster. Tristan's horse had fully caught up with mine, and I could see his tight features from the corner of my eye while my focus remained on the road ahead, on the occasional flap of wings above.

Catching Tristan's eye, I gestured at the small forest. If we managed to hide there...

Tristan nodded, already a step ahead. Of course, he was. With his years and years of experience with fairies, he was better equipped to survive this. How many Crows had he seen? Had he ever fought one? I didn't dare ask. Not when the Crow above could probably hear every single word.

My heart was pounding in my throat when the green of the patch of trees appeared ahead. Just a little farther and we'd no longer be exposed, easily trackable. Then I'd summon my magic. With the damper on it in the human lands, every blow needed to count.

The Crow loosed another caw—one of protest—as it realized where we were headed. It dove from the sky, a dark arrow of menace, circling right above us once before it disappeared between the trees ahead, taking our advantage for itself.

Shit—

Where a moment ago I'd been dying to enter the shelter of mixed greenery, now everything inside me recoiled from the thought.

"Keep going," Tristan urged, his horse pushing past my mare as we flew toward the trees. "We can't lose it."

And he was right. As long as we had an idea where it was, it couldn't creep up on us. So the closer we got before it fully disappeared in the shadows, the better. I kicked my horse's flanks, ignoring how my shaking hands barely clung to the reins and knife.

The trees swallowed us up, enveloping us in shade and cool air, and—

There, right ahead, a body lay on the ground where the Crow had discarded it.

I debated stopping, helping, but Tristan hissed over the short distance, "She's dead."

I spotted her unseeing eyes a moment later, the sight instilling such coldness in me that I almost didn't notice in time how Tristan pulled his horse to a halt, my mare locking her legs and sliding a few feet until it nearly hit a tree to avoid tumbling into Tristan.

I clung to the mare's neck, my knife slipping from my grasp, and cursed Eroth and the Guardians when, from the treetops ahead, a whispering, hissing voice slithered through the forest.

"I'd been wondering how long it would take you to find me."

FORTY-THREE

If I thought my heart was racing before, now it kicked up the speed until it was nothing more than a thrumming in my ears.

Tristan had composed himself, fingers already locked around the tooth dangling from his neck. He'd sheathed his sword to free his other hand, which he now directed at where the voice had come from. His lips moved, but I couldn't hear his spell before light erupted from his palm, singeing the leaves from the branches.

My horse bucked, and I couldn't stop a scream as I was thrown against the tree trunk, ribs scraping along the bark. Fighting for breath, I made a mental note to thank Clio for the leathers later; without them, my skin might have been ripped off.

"You all right?" Tristan leaned over, eyes still on the spot in the trees.

Scrambling to my feet, I muttered some noncommittal response.

My horse had bolted, my side was throbbing, and from the hole in the leafy crowns, a pair of black eyes were staring down at me.

A glacial chuckle filled the air even when the Crow didn't have lips to grin.

Debating my next steps, I sorted through my knowledge of Crows: they hunted for brides once a year. The one in the forest hadn't cared it wasn't Ret Relah when it had come after me, so perhaps this one wouldn't either. My magic had, indeed, had an effect on it, even if only a small one.

Perhaps it liked to talk as much as the one in the forest; that would buy us some time to figure out a weakness.

I braced myself, hand uselessly reaching for the lost knife that was no longer at my hip.

"What do you want in my kingdom?" I asked, my fingers wrapping around my Mage Stone once more. Because, this time, there were no prying eyes to witness what Tristan and I were, no souls who could carry the news into the world so they might reach Cyrill.

"*Ahhh...*" The Crow's sigh raked through me like talons, and I had to brace my hand on the tree trunk to keep my knees from buckling. "The freedom of flying through the world, it is like nothing I've felt in hundreds of years."

Hundreds of years since the Ultimate Sacrifice.

"Perhaps it's good your kind can't roam Eherea the way you please," I provoked, just to feel out the Crow's temper. The one in the forest had been patient, cruel, playing with its prey.

"Perhaps it is. But my kind has been locked up in a tiny forest since the War. Spreading my wings over the heat of these lands is something I hadn't dreamed of ever being able to do again."

Civilized. When he spoke like that, he sounded almost civilized. But the beat of wings sounded, and he leaped from the branch, landing with powerful, black-clothed legs a good distance away. His all-black eyes were on Tristan. "Have you brought your mate to hunt me, Sanja Zetareh Lazar?"

Tristan flashed his teeth at the Crow but didn't deny anything. Perhaps to shield me from an attempt to be taken as a bride. He'd done it before in Aceleau—

My Mage Stone pulsed to life, stronger than in the village, and a subtle glow emanated from my closed fist.

I tucked it behind my back.

"I have brought myself to hunt you," I corrected, drawing upon the magic, calling it forward until warmth filled my arms, my chest, my entire body. It wasn't the same as in the Seeing Forest, but it was there. Just a little longer, and I'd be ready.

Light flashed from Tristan's palm once more as he attacked, the flicker easily crossing the distance to the Crow, catching on the feathers going from his arms and singeing them.

The Crow hissed at him, smugness hushed as the flames winked out along destroyed feathers. "Well, *he* seems to think that he's here to rid the world of me."

"I *am* here to rid the world of you," Tristan said, shooting another beam of light, which caught on the Crow's cheek, leaving a streak of angry red flesh where it bounced off.

Tristan smirked at the Crow, who'd turned his full attention on the Mage.

Perhaps Tristan was right; perhaps we should get rid of it fast, attack blindly. But something told me that the blows didn't take as much from the Crow as they took from Tristan; and that we needed to pace ourselves, trick the Crow, or we'd be doomed.

I'd just finished that thought when the Crow swung his arm in front of him in a wide gesture from his chest to his side, opening his fist as if releasing some dark power.

The air moved and twirled in its wake, spiraling toward Tristan and hitting him hard enough to tackle him off the horse ... which whinnied and bolted.

"Tristan!" My scream was cut off by the Crow's laugh, but I didn't stop as I darted for the Mage, who was rolling to his side, curling his arm in pain.

"Is it broken?"

Tristan shook his head, taking the hand I held out for him, and let me help him up.

"What a sweet little scene," the Crow taunted. "The fairy king informed me of the lengths you were willing to go to save your Mage. The one who claimed you'd been taken that day in Aceleau."

Oh—

Things started clicking into place. "You're not just any Crow, are you?"

"There is no such thing as just *any Crow*, Sanja," he hissed while Tristan tried to step in front of me. I didn't let him. "There are only so many Crows, and each of us is death."

The carnage from the village earlier sped through my mind—bodies ripped apart, walls sprayed with blood, houses destroyed.

"I don't particularly care for death."

The Crow laughed and lifted a hand to repeat the gesture that had knocked Tristan off his horse.

"*Yetheruh*," I said as I released the magic pooling in my palm.

It met the Crow's blow in a deafening crash that scattered in shards of lightning and mist.

Both Tristan and the Crow stared at me—one with wonder, one with fury.

"You've been busy, haven't you, Sanja? Learning the craft of human magic."

"While you've been busy trying to take my kingdom," I countered. "Trust me, I don't like what you've been up to either."

With a sideways glance, I tried to catch Tristan's eye. We needed to coordinate our attacks to combine our strengths. I could already feel how taxing the use of magic in these lands was. Where it had flowed like water in the fairylands, here it was like pudding, slow and reluctant.

But also denser. If we managed to pool enough to hit full force, we might stand a chance.

Tristan saw it too. He gave a subtle nod before he turned to the Crow. "So, tell me, what is so interesting about Cezux that you decided to take a tour?"

I could have sworn the cunning in his voice wasn't an act.

The Crow angled his head at Tristan, beak melting into human features, and I couldn't help but marvel at the handsome face he revealed. "It's a vast land of mountains and deserts and access to the sea. The green looks greener within the barrenness of the soil. The rivers are turquoise like the jewelry we put on our brides. It tastes like life and blood and fear."

I realized that he meant each of those words, that there lay a fascination for my kingdom in each sentence and that it was a compliment as much as it was a hit in the gut.

"The fairy king has promised us open borders, a reach beyond the limits of Askarea. And here I am to claim it."

"Even if staying in these lands will take your magic and your life, bit by bit?" I prompted, pushing for him to reveal more, to make a mistake ... while in my body, magic flowed like barely melted sugar. Too slow.

Tristan's hand lay around his artifact, white-knuckled and shaking. His eyes were on the Crow, measuring, trying to read him as hard as I was.

"The fairy king has also died, and his son has taken his place," I pointed out.

"And his son has been an even better partner in trade," the Crow amended.

Something in my chest quivered.

"He has taken you in his gracious care so Lord Cyrill can spin his tale of your sainthood, Sanja," he said, and when I couldn't hide the surprise on my face, "We've been well

informed about the ongoing procedures in Jezuin, Sanja."
Whether he omitted my title to insult me or because he
forgot, I didn't care. I didn't correct him either, using his
brief pause to focus on that slow-flowing magic of mine so
I'd silence him forever later. "About your supposed resurrection, your healing gifts, the heir that will never see the
light of day—" His gaze drifted to my belly, where nothing
but taut muscle stretched under the leathers, and quirked
a heavy brow. "So many tales have been spun around you,
Sanja. Which one is true?"

"I don't care what tales people tell about me." Truth. Except for that of my magic. It could cost me my throne even
if I managed to get Cyrill off it.

Tristan gave me a look that told me he guessed what I
was thinking. He inched closer, the motion not escaping the
Crow's attention. But he imperceptibly lowered his chin to
his chest where a subtle glow was leaking from his fingers
once more. He was ready.

Come on, I called the magic from the Mage Stone, luring
it with everything I had. If this didn't work—

I couldn't think about what would happen then.

"The late King of Askarea was a bastard," I said to the
Crow, "and the new one isn't any better." Lie. My heart twisted as I tried to hold on to that first image of Recienne the
Second. Of the prince who'd lingered by his father's throne,
taunting me, letting him torture me. I could almost hear his
words in my head.

If that's what you still choose to believe, Sanja.
Everything will be easier when you hate me again.

"He is ready to take from his minions what is needed to break the borders wide open, Sanja."

Everything inside me stilled as things clicked into place.

The borders. Not to the Seeing Forest but the borders to the human territories. Starting with Cezux, the way the late fairy king had hoped to achieve.

But Rogue had a weapon no one else had. A weapon he'd teased and flirted with and made forget what the cost would eventually be. A weapon he'd forged and honed with his words, with his little touches, until I'd become willing to fight for him.

Because he couldn't fight for himself. Just the way he hadn't been able to fight for himself when his father had been alive.

They'd only have replaced him.

His father. The Crows would have replaced his father. Would have replaced Rogue had he tried to act against them. They had even sent someone to keep an eye on the palace.

And now he had me—a last attempt at saving his realm.

All the other Mages had disappeared, what few had been left, killed by the rogue Crows or gone into hiding. And Tristan... He hated Rogue the way his parents had hated the royal fairy family. And Rogue would have never helped him had it not been for me.

"He's ready to bleed you out to make a tear in the borders and let the magic flow freely again. You and, perhaps, your mate here."

I debated informing him that Tristan wasn't my mate. But that would give him only one more reason to attack.

And considering what I'd learned about Crow brides, I might have preferred spilling my blood over the borders.

"He sent you here, to me, Sanja. An offering to honor our bargain."

Everything inside me went cold. All except for that tiny spot that was now throbbing; throbbing the way it had when I'd first felt pity for Rogue, then friendship, then something more.

I had to bite my tongue to keep myself from screaming that he'd never do that. That perhaps his father would have happily done so to extend his reach of power over the lands. It might have been the old king's plan all along, to use all four of us to open the borders with our blood, but when I'd made a bargain with him... His thirst for revenge had taken over everything, and he'd sacrificed three Mages in order to get his hands on the one he really wanted. His key to Cezux and his key to leave the fairylands and build his own kingdom where mine should have been.

If it had a kernel of truth, I'd never know. What I knew was that Rogue wasn't his father. He might have been arrogant, but he was also kind. If he became a monster, it was to protect Clio and Tori and everything he loved. The fairies who didn't have a voice of their own, the peace he so dearly hoped for.

He'd never make me a pawn and leave me to my fate to appease the Crows.

I exhaled a slow breath, forcing my attention on the magic flowing through me, collecting in my palm until it felt full to bursting.

Tristan's hand wrapped around mine where I held the Mage Stone and squeezed.

His power flashed from him in a bright glimmer, slower and weaker than before, but it hit the Crow in the chest, and I released mine, a moment later, aiming for the same spot where skin was sizzling, and shouted, "*Yetheruh!*"

The Crow screamed with fury as he staggered back, his face shaping into that beaked one from before, and his arms fluttered as they turned into massive wings. Talons ripped through his boots as he lifted off the ground, aiming for Tristan. I didn't think when I leaped in his path, hand out and magic still streaming from it. The Crow hissed and cawed, face now that of a bird entirely, but he didn't slow, and his talons hit my leather, grasped them—grasped me, and lifted me off the ground.

Tristan's sword was a slap of silver against the patches of sunlight. It stuck the Crow's leg right above where it was digging into my already injured side. I thrashed in its grip, panic now a living beast inside me, possessing every muscle, every vein, every bone.

Tristan shouted my name. Light flashed. A talon pierced my side, the pain drowning out everything else.

But my hand remained fast around the Mage Stone, my powers near drained but still flickering in the crystal like a promise.

My other arm was twisted and tucked behind my back where I couldn't move it an inch.

If I could wriggle into position to release some of it and get the Crow to open his talons, I might not break my neck with the fall.

The talon pierced further into my flesh.

With a gasp, I pulled what strength I had left and released my magic, hoping that it would do something to help me get out.

The talons remained locked in place. Tristan's scream tore through the building haze in my mind.

The air whipped around my face—and then we were flying, flying, flying.

FORTY-FOUR

I couldn't tell how much time passed as I was carried across my kingdom, the heat of late summer on the ground replaced by the cool, thin air high up in the sky. Gusts of wind assaulted my eyes when I tried to open them, making them water and squeeze shut. The pain in my side became a dull throb slowly spreading through my whole body until my limbs went numb from the pressure on my spine, and I started panicking, wondering if I'd ever be able to move them again. Eventually, exhaustion swept me into darkness, and I should have been grateful for the short reprieve.

But a tug in my chest shook me awake, and my eyes fluttered open again to the slicing heat of summer, the light near blinding as I squinted, and a groan slipped from my throat.

I could feel my legs and arms all right, but my chest had turned into an agonizing cage—not my chest but the talons around it, pinning me to the grassy ground.

"Time to wake up, Sanja," the Crow hissed.

Fingers fumbling for the Mage Stone at my wrist, I tried to push him off.

All I got was a laugh. "You didn't truly think that you'd stand a chance against me, did you?"

His talons were like massive bands of iron as he stood over me.

"Let me go." My voice was too weak for the shrewd demand I'd attempted to make.

"I will let you go once your blood has spilled into this soil and reverted what your ancestors have worked so hard to achieve."

The borderlands. We were in the borderlands. I managed to force my eyes open wider to find nothing but flat, grassy land when I turned my head to the side.

A spark of magic ran through me. Perhaps enough to push against those talons—at least, my hand wasn't trapped this time, and I could direct the channeled magic. If only I could manage a deep enough breath to brace myself for rolling away once he recoiled.

"Are you thinking about making a run for it?" He crouched, those massive talons pressing me down. "Don't bother. You're alone here. Your mate is still in that sorry excuse for a forest, probably cursing the day he ever met you."

My stomach roiled, and I couldn't stop myself this time. "He isn't my mate. I don't have a mate." At least, Tristan was safe now, even when it would take him weeks to return to the Hollow Mountains. If he returned at all. Perhaps he was smarter than that and would lie low for a while. I wouldn't blame him. And if he'd been injured... Then the village was within reach, and he'd find help there after what he'd done to protect them from the Crow.

Delight glinted in the Crow's eyes as he bent over me, bracing a feathered hand beside my shoulder. "That ... is very unfortunate," he huffed, and the hiss in his voice turned into a purr. "For the Mage, of course. As for me..." He studied me with predatory focus. "I'm debating letting you live in order to take you as my bride. Perhaps at Ret Relah. It would be quite welcome to not have to hunt for once."

I shuddered. But as he leaned closer, I was grateful because my magic would hit from up close, and that would assure the maximum impact.

Just a little longer. The gooey feel of my magic traveled through me until it gathered in my palm. A small amount but enough to try.

"*Yethe—*"

His hand covered my mouth, cutting off the word. My focus slipped, as did my magic, and I fought for air as he slid his palm higher to cover my nose as well.

Focus, Sanja. Use your body. Your strength. What was left of it. But I followed that voice in my head, my memories of having learned self-defense and being capable of freeing myself.

Every breath was too small to fill my lungs, and the pain in my side didn't help when I thrashed in the Crow's grasp.

If Tristan was here, he'd know what to do. Or Rogue—

He couldn't be here, or there'd be consequences.

I was on my own.

The Crow laughed. And I saw red—

I was in the borderlands where Cezux met Askarea. Magic should be accessible here. Even if it were mere scraps.

My fingers grasped the Mage Stone harder, and I stopped trying to wriggle out from under his hand, instead, biting his fingers with all my force.

The Crow cursed, pulling back his hand long enough for me to gulp down a deep breath, and air flooded my lungs, bringing back my focus.

"Help!" It was worth a try. If any fairy was nearby, at least, they'd try to save me to get me for themselves. I was still a human in the fairylands after all. I could negotiate with them, make a bargain. Anything—*anything* was better than this.

Magic cut through me like a slash of fire, and my stomach turned at the tug when the Crow lifted his talons a few inches, giving me space to move.

I locked my jaw as I rolled over, ignoring the screaming pain. If these were the borderlands ... we must have flown for at least a day and a half.

But the magic in my stone resonated, ready to strike, so we had to be.

I struck, unable to wait for what the Crow would do. Struck and scrambled to my hands and knees as he ripped back his talons with a screamed curse. They nearly didn't carry me, too weak from either the wound in my side or using too much of my strength on channeling magic.

It didn't matter. What mattered was that I got out of there—alive, preferably.

A chuckle carried across the open meadow, making my heart stop.

"Well, well... If this isn't my little human on the run," Rogue said in that melodious voice that made me feel like I had bathed in luxurious oils. But his words—

Panic grasped me where the talons had eased off. He couldn't be here. He couldn't—

In reflex, my head whipped toward him, toward the king dressed in fine velvet and silk adorned with golden embroidery. No sign of the bandit, of the flicker of fear that I'd noted before he'd vanished in the Cezuxian village. "I've been wondering where you'd gone." He marched up to me, bending over me while his body formed a shield between the surprised Crow and me.

He didn't even glance over his shoulder to see what the Crow was up to, either not fearing it or not wanting to show that fear.

A whisper of wind brushed my aching neck, climbing to my ear. "I thought we agreed, nothing stupid."

I was too shocked to grimace at him. But the amusement in his eyes was gone in a moment. "Play along, Sanja. Make me your villain. It's the only way."

Everything will be easier when you hate me again.

But I couldn't hate him anymore.

Gritting my teeth, I braced myself for whatever game he was playing that I was to be a part of and hoped that he knew what he was doing.

He straightened, turning on his heels and strolling toward the Crow who'd gone silent a few feet away. "Thanks for bringing her back. That saves me a trip to the human lands. Inconvenient little things, humans, wouldn't you agree?"

His words were like poison, but I shut out their meaning. I'd seen too much of the male who would give anything to protect his family and his people to not see this mask for what it was.

The Crow hissed, "I didn't bring her back for you, King Recienne. I brought her back for myself."

I could have sworn Rogue's shoulders tightened enough to break a bar of steel. But his voice remained unfazed. "For yourself? What are you going to do with her? Make her a bride? Haven't you heard? She's already married to the King of Cezux. Otherwise, I might have indulged in the allure of her human beauty myself," he amended, and the heat that crept through me wasn't for show.

"You're disgusting," I spat.

Rogue's dark breeze caressed my throat. "Oh ... am I now?" And the liquid gold of his eyes as he whirled on me wasn't for show either. But they iced over, and he waved a hand at me before turning back to the Crow who was studying him with displeasure.

"So what exactly do you need her for?" Rogue drawled, planting himself closer to me, even when he gave me a view of his back again.

I grunted as I tried to sit up, my magic barely responding in the crystal. But I wasn't done yet. Rogue couldn't kill the

Crow. It would break the bargain and demand more than his own life. But with him here, with a little air to breathe, even when, every time I inhaled, my chest filled with searing flames, I might be able to rid the world of one more Crow.

"Save your strength, Sanja," he ordered over his shoulder before turning back to the Crow. There was nothing kind about him now.

The Crow laughed. "I'm surprised you'd ask," he answered Rogue's question. His features became slightly more human as he cocked his head at me, how I was panting through the pain, trying to gather my thoughts, my strength.

Save your strength... Rogue had been serious about it. He knew I'd need my strength before the end.

"What this looks like to me," Rogue purred, and his tone was like ice against my mind, "is that you've been trying to use my little human here for more than just to weaken the borders—which I am all enthusiastic for, by the way. But if you are trying to lay a finger, a talon, or as much as a feather on *my* human, there is no bargain I'm not willing to break." A threat. A challenge. A dare.

The ice pierced right into my chest, into that well of fire that was my agony, easing the edge. And making space for the fear that came with the full display of the ire of the fairy king.

"Dear Sanja has been put in *my* care for the next few months, so unless *you* are trying to go around the bargain and take her for yourself to bypass *my* claim ... to the Cezux-ian throne," he amended smoothly before the Crow could use the pause to object, "I will not honor my side of our bargain. And I will destroy you."

So my instincts hadn't failed me. He hadn't made me a pawn, a vessel, a tribute.

I shuddered, managing to stand on my own two shaky legs. Rogue was distracting the Crow as much as he was threatening him. It wasn't an empty threat, I realized with horror; he would destroy the Crow. And if he did, the ancient magic of fairy bargains would come into effect.

So he couldn't fight.

It was I who needed to do it.

The Crow's wings flared as he tracked my every move, but he didn't speak, probably waiting for me to make a mistake, for Rogue to make one so he could bleed me out or take me back to the Seeing Forest.

Willing him to stay still, I inched closer to Rogue, Mage Stone grasped tightly in my fingers, and readied myself.

The Crow lifted his feathered arm, measuring the distance between us, and readied to push out his power—began to release it.

A snarl ripped from Rogue's lips, feral and wild, and the Crow's magic scattered on a gust of air. The monster I'd feared for so many months would hurt me—who was now defending me.

"We're going home," he said without looking at me. "No matter how much you're trying to return to the human lands, Sanja. Your place is in Askarea—at least until Ret Relah." He hadn't released the Crow from his focus while speaking to me. But he took a powerful step toward him now, the air turning near solid around him as he loosened the grasp on his power. "And *you* will return to your forest and stay there until the

Queen of Cezux has been returned to her lands. Anything we do sooner will put the bargain in jeopardy, and neither of us wants that. So be a smart Crow, and play along."

Because the cost would be too high on either side. And Rogue had already lost too much.

My Mage Stone pulsed in my palm, a response to Rogue's words, of what he'd shared with me over the past months—to the prospects of lingering in this place for a moment longer with a murderous Crow.

"What if I don't want to wait?" the Crow hissed, inching sideways until Rogue's shoulder was the only thing blocking him—and a healthy distance that would do nothing to stop a magical attack. From either side.

The Crow pounced—not at me but at Rogue, talons out and magic flickering. Rogue stumbled back, not lifting a finger to defend himself.

Out of caution perhaps. Or because he was brewing up a storm in that brilliant mind of his. The magic bounced off Rogue's shield in a spray of silver and gold.

At least a shield. But he wouldn't attack and risk the bargain.

A lick of his power ran over my arm, down to the palm holding my Mage Stone. A silent invitation to attack in his stead while the Crow was busy.

So I did. Throwing everything I had into the crystal, I ignored my throbbing chest and drew the magic from the stone, letting it thrum and resonate in my hand before I whispered, "*Yetheruh.*"

Light exploded from my palm, clear and bright, forging into a beam and rushing for the Crow's heart. He'd barely pulled his gaze from Rogue when the magic hit him, right in the chest the way the silver lance in the Seeing Forest had speared the other fairy. Hit and pierced.

Panting, I pushed myself to hold on, to defy the exhaustion following the initial rush, as I drove the beam deeper and deeper.

The Crow's widened eyes flickered, cawed scream dying on his lips as they shifted from a beak to a human mouth, and he sank to his knees then toppled to the side.

For a moment, I was entranced by the handsomeness of his features, now that his last breath had stripped the monster away.

Rogue's shout of warning echoed through me like a thunderclap in a cave.

Then I fell.

Fell into darkness, into soft grass, into a pair of arms too slender to be those of the fairy king.

Rallying the last of my strength, I dove out of the ocean of black waters gushing over me.

And found a familiar pair of black eyes peering down at me with wicked delight.

"I was prepared for a lot, Recienne." The voice wove through me in a thousand painful threads. "But I wasn't prepared for your weakness."

I knew that voice, had listened to it purr to Rogue at his own dining table. Had heard it whisper and murmur to the fairy king. Had heard it proposition Tristan.

My spine arched in the deadly embrace of Moyen Shae Wellows. And my hands grasped thin air as I fought for something—anything to hold on to.

FORTY-FIVE

"Sanja!"

I could have sworn the earth shook beneath me with Rogue's power as Lady Wellows placed me in the grass, her hands near gentle as they slid along my shoulders, my arms—had it not been for the invisible pins and needles that were her power, following every touch.

"You're making a mistake, Moyen." Rogue's voice was midnight and bright, searing sunlight all at once. Glacial wrath and ember-hot passion.

Lady Wellows laughed, a velvet melody, and I might have screamed at the top of my lungs when she tightened the hold of her magic around my body, pushing those needles deeper, or I could have been mute, gasping for air.

"No, you are the one who made a mistake, Recienne." She stroked a light finger along my cheek, skin burning under the scalding heat. Guardians ... the pain... "Don't think I haven't been observing your little games, Recienne—your lies."

My eyes... My eyes wouldn't stay open more than in slits, but it was enough to find her beautiful face above me, her viperous smile as she surveyed Rogue a few feet away, his face torn with conflict, hands shaking.

I groaned, and his gaze snapped to mine, solid gold splintered.

But he said nothing, face hard and unreadable, save for those eyes.

"I know you want to end this, Recienne. I've seen the way you look at her, the way you scent her when she enters the room. I *know*."

"You don't *know* anything," he growled, voice so guttural it might have come from the ground beneath us.

Do something, I begged in my mind. *Get us out of here.*

Lady Wellows's fingers stilled on my throat, the needles collecting on that one point where my voice might have formed. Breath strained past the pain as it rasped in and out of me.

The late king's torture master, I remembered. And as she grinned down at me, I wondered if Tristan had gone through something similar during those days at the fairy palace. It would explain his silence.

"Let's see if you're willing to speak when I break her apart." Her magic flashed over my skin like a branding iron, and this time, I screamed.

An icy breeze whispered against the streaks of fire in my cheeks, along my arms where the leather might as well have been grated from my skin by Lady Wellows's torture. But Rogue didn't look at me when I tried to catch his gaze again.

He'd turned into a statue of frozen rage.

My spine groaned under the pressure of magic as it snaked around my neck.

"What are you willing to give for her freedom, Recienne?" she purred. "Are you willing to give yours? Are you willing to yield to the Crow King and hand your kingdom to him on a silver platter? You can make a new bargain to save her." Her smile turned serpentine. "All you need to do is lay down your claim to the throne, Recienne. Hand it over to the Crows. And I'll leave her alone right now."

"No—" I gritted out, the word nearly lost in my panting breaths.

Her magic tightened around my throat.

"Don't do it," I croaked at Rogue, my voice collected by the dark breeze he commanded so it may be kept from her ears. "Think of what you've got to lose."

"I know exactly what I've got to lose," he said, voice trembling.

He was debating it; by the Guardians, he was debating her bargain.

But she wasn't a Crow. His interference might have no effect on the bargain whatsoever. I was about to voice as much when the air left my lungs as Lady Wellows pushed down on my windpipe, and not even a whisper remained.

His power exploded from him in a swirl of ice and night, fire and stars, engulfing the meadow, the skies above. Lady

Wellows screamed a moment before the pressure on my throat ceased.

I shielded my eyes where the blinding light of the sun wove into his power—was part of his power. As it stormed and raged in searing waves. But his magic didn't touch me, weaving past like daggers and spears.

Streaks of red fire sliced through the darkness, attacking the source of that power.

I caught a glimpse of Lady Wellows, hands spread to her sides as she sent her fire flying after Rogue. A gust of power coiled around her neck, bringing her hands to her throat to free herself.

I was about to draw a breath of relief when a knife scraped against my throat. A hand flapped over my mouth, smothering my scream. Feathers tickled my nose and cheek as the Crow leaned over me.

I'd killed him. By the Guardians, at least, I'd thought I had. But he was very much alive, smirking as he bent lower, hissing into my ear, "Time to break the borders, Sanja."

There was nothing left in me to rally, no strength to throw him off, my muscles already quivering from the strain of the fight before. My fingers fastened around my Mage Stone anyway, clinging to it, to the faint pulse reminding of a fading heartbeat. In the background Rogue and Lady Wellows's battle raged, magic pitted against magic—but the flames were already dimming, and Lady Wellows' power was losing against the near infinite one that was Rogue's.

With a tug on my magic, I sent a prayer to the Guardians—and was about to release what was left of it to fend off the Crow.

The knife found its path through my leathers with ease, lodging between my ribs. My body jerked, chest constricting, and the power that had been raging around us, concealing the Crow's attack, stilled, fractured like a snake recoiling. Rogue's eyes found mine over the distance.

"*Yetheruh*," I coughed into the Crow's palm.

Blood dripped from the Crow's lips as he slumped to the ground, his last breath rasping out of him.

The Mage Stone cracked between my fingers.

PRONUNCIATION GUIDE

CHARACTER NAMES

Astorian: Us-Toh-ree-an

Cadenca Bretegne Whithee: Ka-den-sah Bre-tehnj (like French Bretagne with 'e' instead of 'a') Whith-ee

Clio: Clee-oh

Cliophera Clarette Tarie Amaryll Saphalea de Pauvre: Clee-oh-phee-rah Clah-rett Tah-rie Ah-mah-ryll Sah-PHAH-lee-ah deh POH-vreh

Cyrill Tenikos: Cee-ryll Teh-Nee-kos

Dimar: Dee-mahr

Erju: Air-juh

Gerome: Geh-Roh-Mee

Leahnie: Lay-UH-nee

Naar: Nahr

Moyen Shae Wellows: Moh-yen Shae Wel-lows

Recienne Oilvier Gustine Univér Emestradassus de Pauvre: Reh-Syen Ol-liv-yeh Gü-Stin Oo-Nee-Vehr Eh-Mehs-trah-Dahs-sus deh POH-vreh

Sanja Zetareh Lazar: Suhn-Jah ZEH-tuh-rech Lah-ZAHR

Tori: Toh-ree

Tristan Bale: Tris-tan Bale
Zelia: Zee-lee-ah

WORLD

Aceleau: Ah-Seh-Loh
Ansoli: Un-soh-lee
Askarea: Us-KAH-reh-ah
Brolli: Brol-ly
Cezux: Dje-Zush
Cliffs of Ansoli: Cliffs of Un-soh-lee
Dunai: Doo-NAY
Eherea: Ee-HEE-ree-ah
Eroth: Eh-roth
Fort Perenis: Fort Peh-reh-niss
Horn of Eroth: Horn of Eh-roth
Jezuin: Jeh-Zoo-in ("J" as in "jelly")
Leeneae: Lee-nee-ae
Meer: Meer
Plithian Plains: Pli-thee-un Plains
Ret Relah: Reht Reh-luh
Tavras: TUH-vrahs

ACKNOWLEDGEMENTS

The Hour Mage drove me to the edge and back. So many of you ahve gone this path wiht me, and I am grateful for each and everyone of you!

Thank you to Barbara, who never fails to remind me that I need to get those words down to actually finish a book.

Dawn, you know I couldn't live without your keen eyes on my books before they see the light of day.

Belle, if I counted every grammar-tear you've dried... Thank you for always having an answer.

Sarah, you are like a sister to me... plus you write awesome books. You know that!

To Mette, for endless hours of philosophizing about the industry—and then kicking my butt so I go back to writing.

Kath... I don't know where to start. You're the first to see my work, and there's a reason why. Your wealth of experience awes me as does your amazing feedback and your endless optimism. The Quarter Mage series wouldn't be the same without you.

My incredible inner circle: Thank you for dedicating your time and giving such incredible feedback while artfully ignoring the mess of grammar, typos, and so much more that my first drafts are. You are amazing and I appreciate all of you!

My Royal Guard, for loving my books and your incredible support with promoting them. You make me feel like royalty!

Rhys, I love your map! It is exactly how I imagine Eherea. Thank you for working with me on bringing the vision for this new universe to life.

To Melody, Gabriel, Anthony, Jon, Travis, Cat, Emily, James, Diana, Ronnie, Ryan, Kenny, Briana, and Heather for giving me an idea what the future holds for The Quarter Mage series.

To the countless supporters of The Quarter Mage series, for your dedication and enthusiasm for my work!

Last but not least, to my family, my husband Mark and our son Rafael, for the continuous support for my writing adventures, the understanding for the late hours I work and my occasional mental absence when I have a plot epiphany.

I love you all! Thank you!

CAN'T GET ENOUGH OF ANGELINA'S WORLDS?

SCAN THIS CODE TO FIND MORE BOOKS BY ANGELINA J. STEFFORT:

About the Author

"Chocolate fanatic, milk-foam enthusiast and huge friend of the southern sting-ray. Writing is an unexpected career-path for me."

Angelina J. Steffort is an Austrian novelist, best known for her Wings Trilogy, a young adult paranormal romance series about the impossible love between a girl and an angel. The bestselling Wings Trilogy has been ranked among calibers such as the Twilight Saga by Stephenie Meyer, The Mortal Instruments by Cassandra Clare, and Lauren Kate's Fallen, and has been top listed among angel books for teens by bloggers and readers. Her young adult fantasy series Shattered Kingdom is already being compared to Sarah J. Maas's Throne of Glass series by readers and fans.

Angelina has multiple educational backgrounds including engineering, business, music, and acting, and lives in Vienna, Austria with her husband and her son.

Find Angelina on social media as @ajsteffort.

Scan this code to subscribe to Angelina's newsletter:

Made in the USA
Monee, IL
10 November 2023

46222614R00351